When the Sun Fades

First Edition

ISBN Paperback : 979-8-9988316-0-7

LCCN: 2025923337

Cover design by Melody Kepler

Interior design and formatting by Melody Kepler

Published by Kepler Production Studios

https://keplerpstudios.com

Editing: Anna Bowman

"KPS" and the Kepler Production Studios logo are trademarks of Kepler Production Studios, LLC.

TABLE OF CONTENTS

TABLE OF CONTENTS

Rachel,
This is book two of your paranormal romance. I
hope you love reading it as much as I loved writing
it for you..

Anna,
Thank you for your continued encouragement to
keep going. Your friendship means the world to me.

Trent,
Your impact is inexpressible. Maybe some day I
can reciprocate.

Cassia - Prologue

Holli pulls the jacket over my shoulders and tucks my hair beneath it.

"Why are we going in the middle of the night?"

"It's a new kind of game."

"Like hide and seek? Will Momma and Pappa find me?"

"It works like hide and seek. You will hide, and for a while your parents will seek. But you must do everything you can to not be found."

"What about breakfast?"

"I've packed your breakfast. Cass, baby, listen to me, please. You must never be found."

"Never?"

Holli kneels down, her hands trembling as she adjusts my collar. The moonlight streaming through my bedroom window catches the tears in her eyes.

"Never," she whispers, pulling me close. She smells like fresh bread and peppermint, just like every morning when she makes breakfast. "You're going to be brave for me, aren't you, Cass?"

I nod, though my stomach feels funny, like the time I fell from the apple tree. "What about you? Can't you hide with me?"

Holli's breath catches. She pulls back, cupping my face in her warm hands, though her fingers are colder than usual. A bandage is wrapped tightly around her wrist.

"I have to stay," she says, voice quieter than before, "to make sure they look in all the wrong places."

She reaches into her pocket and pulls out a silver locket—

the one she always wears.

"This was my grandmother's. It will keep you safe."

"But—"

A floorboard creaks somewhere in the mansion. Holli stiffens, her eyes darting to the door. She quickly slips the locket around my neck and tucks it beneath my shirt.

The creak comes again, slower this time—like someone dragging their feet.

"Remember what we learned about the stars?" she whispers urgently, guiding me toward the hidden door behind my bookshelf. "Follow the North Star, just like in your astronomy books. Mr. Parker will be waiting at the old chapel."

I clutch my small backpack, filled with the breakfast she packed and my favorite stuffed bat. "I don't want to go alone."

"You're never alone," Holli says, pressing a kiss to my forehead. "Every star in the sky is watching over you."

The bookshelf groans softly as it swings open. Cold air rushes in, carrying the scent of wet earth and fallen leaves. My feet feel heavy, like they're stuck in the mud by the garden pond.

A crash echoes from down the hall—breaking glass. Not like something dropped, but thrown.

Then another sound. A high, breathy laugh. It sounds like Mama pretending when she plays tea party, only this time the smile is on the *inside* of her voice.

Holli flinches and gives me a gentle push toward the darkness.

"But what if I forget the stars?" My voice trembles. Last week, I mixed up Orion's Belt with the Big Dipper, and Holli had to help me find them again.

"Count three stars to the right of the Big Dipper's handle," she whispers, just like she's done every night we stargazed from my window. "That's your North Star. It will never lead you wrong." Her voice catches. "Just like I would never lead you wrong, Cass."

Another crash, closer now. And voices—but Mama's is still wrong.

"Holliii," she sings, light and lilting. "Where have you hidden our little dove? You know she hates being late."

The air grows thicker and Holli's shoulders tighten as if she's holding her breath. Her face goes white as she presses something else into my hands—a piece of paper, folded small.

"Don't read it until you're safe. Promise me."

"I promise." The paper crinkles in my grip.

"When you reach the chapel, knock three times, then twice more. Mr. Parker will—"

She stops, head snapping toward my bedroom door when the handle jiggles once, slowly. Then stills.

"Go. Now."

"I love you," I whisper, because that's what we always say before hiding.

"I love you too, my brave girl." Holli's voice breaks. "Now run. Run and don't look back."

The hidden door closes behind me, leaving only darkness and the smell of damp stone. I clutch my backpack closer, feeling the hard shape of the locket through my shirt.

Somewhere above, I hear Papa's voice joining Mama's. The way they hum together makes my skin prickly.

I run.

The passageway air is cold on my wet cheeks as I count my steps like Holli taught me. Twenty steps forward. Turn right at the fork. Thirty more to the garden exit.

Don't look back. Never look back.

Behind me, muffled by stone and distance, I hear Holli's voice one last time—calm and clear, like when she reads me bedtime stories.

Then a scream. Something breaks. And a sound like someone drinking too fast.

Then silence.

Interlude 1: The Fall of the Old World

They say the end of the war was not marked by peace, but by silence.

Entire cities—emptied overnight. Settlements abandoned, their fires still smoldering, meals left unfinished on wooden tables. Those who remained behind were never seen again.

At first, the stories were dismissed as exaggerations. Raiders, perhaps. Plagues. Accidents.

Then the patterns began to emerge. The towns closest to Noctis activity were the first to go. Then the villages farther out. And finally, the fortified cities.

Nowhere was safe.

The first true famine was not of food… but of people.

Entire towns were emptied without a trace. Until the wind shifted and the stench told the truth. Bone piles with teeth marks. Rib cages displayed in spirals. Children's shoes still tied beside blood-slick thresholds.

Skulls were stacked in windows like warnings. Teeth left in bowls beside broken doors. Blood crusted over paintings that hadn't finished drying.

In one fortress city, they found bodies drained and strung upside down from balconies like trophies. In another, the people had eaten glass to avoid living through it altogether.

Elsewhere, whole neighborhoods burned themselves alive—gasoline poured down stairwells, prayers whispered as the match was lit—just to escape the knock at the door.

Governments collapsed under the weight of fear. Military

forces fractured, unable to fight a war where the enemy no longer played by the rules. Those in power made choices. While some abandoned their posts, others sought new alliances. Few held their ground, believing victory was still possible.

They were the first to disappear.

What happened next is unclear. The records from that time are fragmented—contradictory. Some claim a deal was struck, a quiet arrangement between the survivors and the Noctis. Others say the Noctis simply took what they needed and left the scraps behind.

Whatever the truth may be, one thing is certain.

The world did not end in fire or war.

It ended in surrender.

"No one remembers the moment they stopped fighting. Only that one morning, they woke up and realized they had already lost."

They called it survival.

But the children born into this new world had no say in what that survival cost.

1 - Cassia

Rule one of compound training: never show fear. Rule two: if you're going to break rule one, do it where no one can see.

Which is why I'm in the east wing's abandoned storage room, hands shaking as I wrap my bloodied knuckles. The floor's stained with old spills—ink or blood, hard to tell in the darkness. Even the shadows here feel abandoned. The training dummy lies in pieces around me, stuffing scattered like snow—third one this week. The room smells of copper and dust, and somewhere above, rain drums against ancient windows. It reminds me of the dream—darkness, the cold echo of footsteps, wetness that clung to dead air like breath on glass.

"Control your emotions," Warden Keller always says, like feelings are something you can lock away in a box. But control isn't what got me here. Survival did. And survival isn't always pretty. It means learning how to live in a world that already gave up.

The locket at my neck feels heavier than usual today. Nine years since Holli pressed it into my hands, since she told me to run and never look back. Nine years of foster homes and fighting and finally finding my way here, to this compound of lost children and broken things. Like some orphan shelter built on the bones of the old world. No one says that part out loud, but we all feel it.

My fist connects with the wall before I realize I'm moving. Pain shoots through my already split knuckles, but I welcome it. Pain means I'm still here. Still fighting.

"What did that wall ever do to you?"

I spin, blade already drawn from my boot. Felix stands in the doorway, hands raised in mock surrender. His easy smile doesn't match the concern in his eyes.

"Practicing," I mutter, sheathing the knife. He's the closest thing to a friend I have here, but that's not saying much.

"Right. Because we don't have enough actual practice dummies." He kicks through the stuffing at his feet. "Though I guess we have one less now."

"If you're here to lecture me—"

"Actually, I'm here to warn you. Warden's doing room inspections. Might want to clean this up before she finds her supply room redecorated."

I survey the damage—torn canvas, splintered wood, walls scarred with my rage. "Help me?"

His smile softens. "Always. But Cass?" He catches my arm as I pass. "Whatever's eating at ya... you know you can tell me, right?"

I think of the nightmare that drove me here from my bed tonight—screaming, smoke thick in my throat, and a figure that never comes into focus, pressing just under the surface like it's waiting to get out. I think of the letter that arrived yesterday, claiming to know where my family is. Of all the other letters that led nowhere.

"I'm fine," I say, pulling away. "Just restless."

He doesn't believe me, I can see it in his face. But he helps me clean anyway, and doesn't ask about the tears I quickly wipe away when I find my stuffed bat among the wreckage. Some questions are better left unasked.

By the time we finish, morning light streams through grimy windows. Other trainees will be heading to pre-breakfast training warm up sessions, trading stories about their latest bruises and victories. Playing at being warriors while real monsters stalk the world outside. We train for rules, but out there, the rules don't matter. Out there, the monsters make their own.

"Coming?" Felix asks from the doorway.

I touch the locket, feeling its familiar weight. "In a minute."

When his footsteps fade, I retrieve the crumpled letter from my pocket. The handwriting is elegant, precise—like all the others. But this one feels different. This one names a place, a city far to the north. Now it begs the question on who sent it and how they even found me.

Maybe it's another dead end, or another trap. Maybe it's bait strung from the same hands that left towns in piles of bones. But as I stare at my bloodied knuckles, at the cleanup from the destruction one nightmare caused, I know I can't stay here much longer. Something has to change.

The compound bells ring, signaling the start of another day. Another round of training, of pretending I belong here. Of preparing for a fight I'm not sure I understand completely because we only know what we're told, and that's as simple as, 'going outside at night means death.'

I tuck the letter away and head for the courtyard. Rule one: never show fear. Rule two: if you're going to break rule one, do it where no one can see.

Rule three? Sometimes the biggest battles aren't the ones we fight with our fists.

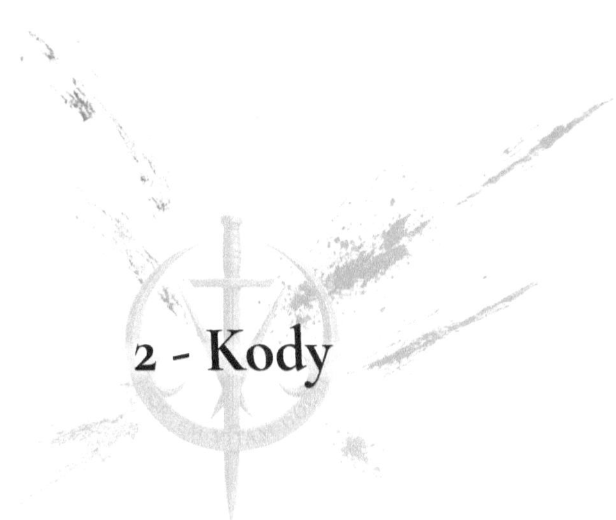

2 - Kody

The guild hall's ancient stone walls trap the morning's chill, making Kody's recently healed ribs ache. Around the scarred oak table, other hunters study a map marked with recent Noctis activity. Too much activity. The kind that reminds Kody of old Turig warpaths he's studied—precise, calculated, predictable. But the Noctis aren't predictable. They are strategic, yes, but in ways no one could anticipate. And that makes them worse.

Elena slams another report onto the growing pile. "Four more missing from the textile district." Her hunter's mark, an incomplete circle with a blade and a crescent moon on each side, stands stark against her dark skin. "Bodies are getting harder to find."

"Because they're not leaving bodies anymore." Marcus traces the pattern of disappearances, his hands steady despite the scars that wind up his arms. "They're collecting."

Kody studies the map, mentally overlaying it with older hunting patterns. These attacks don't match anything he's seen in his nine years of tracking. "They're organized. Moving with purpose."

"Organized Noctis," Marcus spits. "Just what we need."

"Not just any Noctis," Elena corrects, fingers tracing her raised hunter's mark. "We've seen Vita Noctis—well-fed, reasoning, but still cruel. And whispers of worse: the Umbrals… Elders—ancient ones who've fed for centuries. Some say they no longer need blood. Just fear."

"Some say they're as close to immortal as it gets. The

longer they live, the less they resemble what they once were." Marcus mutters, voice grim.

Elena exhales sharply. "We've been chasing whispers for months. And now, whole villages vanish overnight. No bodies, no signs of struggle. It's like they're plucking people from existence."

"Who's leading them?" Kody frowns. "Tenebris?" The word leaves a chill on his tongue.

Elena hesitates. "That's the thing. No one's seen him—the Tenebris. Just stories. Some say he can turn anyone with a single touch, like he doesn't need to follow the usual rules on transformation."

A beat passes and no one moves. It's the kind of silence that feels like prey holding its breath. Kody swears the air gets heavier, like the walls themselves recoil from the name. The Tenebris wasn't just a story. Not when Elena won't look anyone in the eye. Not when veterans stop breathing.

"Like Durham?" Chen's question carries weight. Everyone remembers Durham—the night they lost six hunters to a coordinated ambush.

"No." Kody moves another marker. "Durham's slaughter was about territory. This is different. They're searching for something."

"Or someone." Elena's eyes meet his across the table. They both remember the last time Noctis hunted with purpose.

"And how would you know that?" Richus sneers from his corner. The newer hunter never misses a chance to challenge Kody's methods. "Some of us actually kill Noctis instead of studying them."

"Some of us live long enough to learn from our kills." Elena's sharp tone cuts through the tension. She'd trained Kody herself, back when he was just another angry kid with a blade and a death wish birthed from revenge.

Chen clears his throat. "Which is exactly why Kody's taking investigative point on this."

"Sir—" Kody straightens, protest ready. They're down three hunters already this month. Tracking patterns is useful, but they need everyone in the field.

"The decision's made." Chen's tone brooks no argument.

"Track them. Find their origin. We need to know what we're dealing with."

"With all due respect," Kody keeps his voice carefully neutral, "we know what we're dealing with. They're Noctis. They need to be eliminated, not studied."

"Like you eliminated that nest in Solomon's Quarter?" Richus again. "Oh wait, three of them escaped while you were taking notes."

"Three escaped because your team triggered the alarm too early." Kody's patience frays. "If you'd followed the plan—"

"Enough." Chen's palm meets the table with a crack. "This isn't about past missions. This is about preventing another Durham. Another Solomon's Quarter." His eyes find Kody's. "You track better than anyone since Sarah. That's why you're handling this."

The name hits like a personal attack. Sarah. His first partner. His first failure.

"Three days," Chen continues. "Find out what they're after. Then we'll plan a strike."

Kody nods, already cataloging what he'll need. Silver blades, something for the fire of course—newer hunters rely on the standard methods, draining and beheading. But he's seen too many bloodless Noctis regenerate. Better to do them in completely, then burn what's left. Guild rules exist for a reason.

"One more thing." Chen's voice stops him at the door. "After you report back... I need you to visit the training compound."

"Recruiting? Now?" The words come sharper than intended. "I should be focusing on this threat, not babysitting trainees."

"We need more hunters." Chen's expression softens slightly. "Good ones. Ones who can think, not just kill."

"Like Sarah could?" The words slip out before he can stop them.

"Sarah was special." Chen studies him. "But she wasn't the only one who saw hunting as more than just execution. You used to understand that."

Kody's hands clench at his sides. "That was before I watched thinking get her killed."

"No." Chen's voice carries decades of experience.

"Thinking kept her alive longer than most. It's what keeps you alive now." He slides a folder across the table. "Three days. Then you visit the compound. Consider it a chance to prevent more Durhams... and more Sarahs."

The argument dies in Kody's throat. Chen fights dirty, using Sarah's memory like that. But he's not wrong. They need more hunters. Smart ones.

Richus mutters something about "wasted resources," but Elena's glare silences him. She catches Kody's arm as he turns to leave.

"Watch yourself out there," she says quietly. "Organized Noctis means organized intel. They might know more about us than we do about them."

Kody nods, the weight of quiet understanding hanging between them. They both remember Durham, and he only has three days to unravel this mess.

After that... well, maybe the compound won't be a complete waste of time.

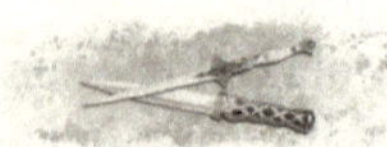

THE NIGHT AIR carries the cloying scent of rot as Kody stalks his quarry through hollow streets. The marketplace is a grave—booths sagging with time, bones scattered like discarded currency, ash still clinging to stone in places where fire met flesh. Whatever happened here was swift. Long over, but the scent riding the wind says the monsters came back.

Movement flickers to his left—too fast for a human. He spins, blade already singing through the air as the first Noctis lunges. Steel cleaves through flesh with a wet, snapping sound. Bone gives under pressure like overripe fruit.

Two more emerge from the shadows, moving with the ease that marks them as old—experienced.

Umbrals? Interesting.

"The hunter tracks well," one hisses, circling right while its companion shifts left. "Perhaps too well."

Kody adjusts his stance, cataloging exits, angles, terrain. "Just doing my job. Though you're making it easier than usual."

"Turig?" the left one whispers, almost hopeful.

"Movement style matches."

"And the scent…" says a third one still lingering in the shadows, watching instead of joining the circle. Its voice is low, curious.

"Only one way to know," the rightmost snarls, and lunges.

Kody spots the shift in weight half a second early and ducks. His blade shears through muscle and tendon. The Noctis shrieks as it stumbles back, half-limping.

The second one strikes immediately. Kody rolls, blade slashing upward—not enough to kill, but enough to spray blood across fractured stone.

"You don't know what you are," the injured one growls, clutching its ruined leg. "You don't even smell right."

"Come closer," Kody snaps, rising fast. "Find out why."

The wounded one lunges recklessly, and Kody catches it full in the chest, driving silver laced steel through bone. It collapses with a hiss.

The second dives at him, sloppier and overconfident, managing a rake across his shoulder before he spins, blade arcing. The Noctis staggers, choking, and drops. Dead—for now.

The third never moves. It stands at the edge of the broken stalls, half-shadowed. Watching. Smiling. "The Mistress grows impatient," it murmurs. "The search continues south…"

Kody raises his blade. "What search?"

"She will find what was taken," it says. "The blood calls to be a bound one."

Before he can move, the Noctis vanishes. Not running, not leaping, just gone, leaving only words hanging in the rot-soaked air.

HE BEHEADS THEM methodically, sets the bodies alight, and watches muscle curl and collapse—bones blacken in the flames. The scent of burnt sinew and cooked death clings to his coat, crawling under his skin. He'll carry it for days like he always does. But it's not the smoke that lingers in his thoughts.

The blood calls to be a bound one.

He doesn't know what it means. And that, more than anything, makes his skin crawl.

BACK AT THE guild hall, his report draws troubled looks.

"Zurich," Chen says, rolling the word like poison. "That territory's been unstable since the purge."

"There's more." Kody runs a hand through his hair, still damp from the humid night. "They mentioned a Mistress. Someone directing their movements. And a Turig."

Chen's eyes meet Marcus's before locking back on Kody, all color draining from his face. "Turigs died off ages ago. The strain was too unstable—they couldn't control their hunger."

"Unless some survived." Elena's fingers trace her hunter's mark. "Hidden… waiting."

Kody says nothing. But his chest tightens, like a fist closing around a memory half-remembered and half-dreaded. He'd seen old war remnants—bones splintered, faces torn off. But what clawed at the back of his mind wasn't a memory from a film. It felt... personal.

"Coordinated Noctis." Marcus spits the words. "We don't need this shit."

"Which is exactly why we need more hunters." Chen's eyes find Kody's again. "The compound awaits."

Walking down the hallway with bag in hand, Kody stops in place when he hears the whispers he shouldn't hear.

A younger hunter scoffs, shaking his head. "You think Noctis are bad? I heard the Turigs were worse."

"At least Noctis can be reasoned with." The other mutters, adjusting his gear. "Turigs? They didn't stop. Didn't think. Just tore through anything in their way. They weren't soldiers—they were weapons."

Kody's breath stills for a fraction of a second. A sharp prickle runs down his spine—an unexpected, unwelcome sting.

He exhales through his nose, rolling his shoulders to shake it off, but something about the words sits wrong.

He shouldn't care, but it feels like an insult and he doesn't know why.

He chalks it up to ego. Or maybe ghosts. But deep down,

a cold stirring coils in his gut—ancient, buried, and hungering for release.

The voices fade as Kody forces himself forward, focusing on the mission ahead. It doesn't matter. And it's better that it doesn't.

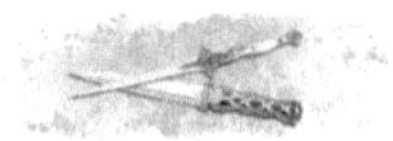

THE TRAINING COMPOUND rises from morning mist like a fortress—which, Kody supposes, it is in its own way. Warden Keller meets him in a sparse office that smells of moss and old paper.

Movement in the training yard draws his attention as they tour the facilities. Copper hair catches the morning light like fresh-spilled blood as one of the trainees takes down an opponent twice her size. Her technique is raw but effective, each move powered by intuition deeper than mere survival instinct.

She fights like Sarah did. Like someone who's learned the hard way that size doesn't matter—that speed and leverage can overcome brute force. But it's more than that. There's a grace to her movements that speaks of natural talent, and a quiet ache in her gaze that scrapes against the place inside him where grief never fully healed.

"That one's different," Keller says, following his gaze. "Found her way here on her own. No record of where she came from."

Kody watches her help her opponent up, noting how others give her space despite her small frame. The morning sun hits the tendrils of breath curling in the air, and for a moment he's reminded of everything he's tried to forget about why hunters need to think before they strike.

She turns suddenly, as if sensing his scrutiny. Their eyes meet across the yard, and a weight settles behind his ribs— recognition, maybe, or warning. She holds his gaze a beat too long before turning away, leaving him with the unsettling sense that he's just glimpsed a truth not meant for him.

"She'll be trouble," he says, more to himself than Keller.

The warden chuckles. "Aren't they all?"

But Kody's attention keeps drifting back to her despite his best efforts. The way she moves, the way she holds herself—

as if her blood carries the echo of those who ran, and the grief of those who never outran what chased them.

He forces his focus back to the other candidates. He has a job to do, after all. No time for distractions. Even if they do have eyes that burn like stars before dawn.

3 - Cassia

B lood sprays across my skin as Felix's nose cracks beneath my fist. He stumbles back, eyes wide—not from pain, but disbelief— as his hand flies to his face.

"Cass, it's a practice round!"

My breath comes hard, sharp as the red haze begins to fade. No torn bodies at my feet, no white nightgown soaked and dripping blood. Just Felix, bleeding and blinking, and our fellow trainees staring in stunned silence.

"Sorry," I mutter, my fists clenching to hide the tremor in my hands.

The nightmare is starting to bleed into daylight again.

Felix pinches the bridge of his nose and jams a wad of cotton into one nostril. "What's got into you today?"

"I'm fine." The words feel hollow and practiced in my mouth. My breath ghosts in the cold air, thin and shaky.

"You sure? There was a fire in your eyes I've never seen before. And the dummy this morning—"

"That's what I said." I yank my sweater off over my head, static dragging strands of wavy copper hair out of place.

I retreat to the edge of the sparring circle and drop onto the cold bench. It leeches warmth from my spine— goosebumps rising even as sweat clings to my skin.

Felix hesitates, then follows. "You wanna talk about it?"

I side glance at him, but a movement across the yard draws my eye. I nod toward the stranger.

Anything to shift the focus.

"What's up with mystery robes over there?"

Felix leans, squinting. "Oh. New instructor, I think. Some

bigwig the Guild's brought in to evaluate us."

I study the man—hair pulled back into a short low ponytail. As if sensing me, his gaze lifts and locks on mine. My insides still. Not in fear. Not quite.

"Hellloo? Cassia." Felix waves a hand in front of my face, snapping the thread.

"It's Cass," I say automatically, voice low.

"Yeah, I know. Are you ready for breakfast?" He asks.

"Not really hungry."

"Well, I'll eat yours then," He snorts. "I'm going to need it after nearly bleeding to death from your fist."

"Don't be so dramatic." I manage a faint smirk as he stands.

Grabbing my sweater, I pass through the open arch from the courtyard into the dining room, sparing one last glance toward the robed figure.

He's still watching me.

4 - Cassia

Janice stands behind the warming trays, hip cocked and grits spoon brandished like a weapon. "Get here on time and you won't have to eat the stuff intended for the pigs," she says as Felix grimaces at the burnt toast on his tray.

He flashes her his usual charming smile. "Oh, come on, Jan. We know there aren't pigs round here. That'd be a treat."

I glance back toward the instructors' table, where the black-robed man sits just behind Warden Keller, his face partially obscured. "Is he a new instructor?"

Janice raises a bushy grey brow at me as though I should already know the answer. "I'm not at liberty to discuss Mr. Akers' business here. Besides, you're likely to find out shortly after breakfast anyway." She plops a bowl of grits onto my tray with a routine matter of fact like authority.

"Akers..." The name tugs at my core as I follow Felix to an empty table.

"You probably read it somewhere." Felix shovels grits into his mouth, hunched over his tray like someone might steal it.

My upper lip curls. "Don't make yourself sick by eating too fast."

He points to my bowl with his tarnished spoon. "You better not make yourself sick by not eating at all. If he is an instructor and wants to test us later, you'll want your strength."

With a sigh, I lean against my arm, elbow propped on the table. The smell of half-fermented fruit makes my stomach turn as I dump it into the grits. After a good stir, I force down a spoonful.

"God be good and make me sick to my stomach so I can

skip today." Felix takes the last bite of his burnt, soggy toast.

My fingers find the locket chain at my neck, a nervous habit. "You'd rather be in the infirmary than training?"

"Wouldn't you?"

"Seriously?" I raise an eyebrow, tucking the locket back under my shirt when I catch Felix watching.

He shrugs, looking around the dining hall. "Do I look like I'm kidding?"

"The more training we get, the sooner we can get out of this hell hole."

Shaking his head, he licks his spoon clean and stares at my barely touched bowl. "You've honestly not been on your own for very long, have you?"

"That's none of your business, thank you very much."

"I started living on the streets when I was seven."

"So?"

"So, after ten years of it, it's kind of nice to have a guaranteed mattress and meal waiting for you every day."

"It's not like I've been spoiled or anything."

"I didn't say that. But living on the street and fending for yourself is different than jumping from foster home to foster home."

"No, I'm sure it's quite different." An image of one of my foster fathers grabbing for the punishment paddle flashes through my mind. My hand tightens around the spoon. "But foster homes aren't all gems and roses either."

"Attention." Warden Keller's voice cuts across the dining hall. "Sleep Hall C, report to the courtyard after breakfast."

Felix raises his eyebrows at me. "That's us. What do you think—"

But I'm watching Mr. Akers rise from the instructors' table, his black robes flowing like a drop of ink in still water. He moves with an unnatural precision as he exits through the side door. This time when his eyes find mine across the hall, I don't look away. Something about that gaze makes my hair stand on edge. I've seen monsters before, but they don't usually wear robes.

"Earth to Cassia," Felix waves his hand in front of my face. "Should we head out?"

I push my half-eaten breakfast away. "Yeah. Let's see if this guy can teach us anything real."

As Felix and I cross the courtyard, morning chatter crackles around us—complaints about drills, whispers of bruises and rivalries, the usual noise.

But near the weapon racks, a knot of younger trainees speaks in hushed tones, their eyes flicking around for danger like prey near water.

"I swear it's true. My uncle saw him once," one whispers.

"No one sees Vesper and lives," another hisses.

I slow my steps. Not because I don't know the name, everyone does, but because I want to hear what comes next.

"Then how does anyone know he's real?" One asks. "Could just be a scare tactic to keep us in line."

"He's real," a girl murmurs. "Just not always in the way you think. Sometimes he's there before the killing starts. Sometimes after. But always close."

I arch a brow and mutter to Felix, "Vesper myths again?"

He grins. "Trainee folklore. Can't beat it."

Still, I drift closer. Not because I believe them, but because some stories have teeth.

"A Noctis," one boy says, lowering his voice, "but older and smarter. Which is worse."

"He's not just some ancient bloodsucker," another argues. "They say he was made to kill."

"Could be a Turig instead." the wiry one says. "It would explain the way he moves."

The word Turig tugs at a colder part of my memory. I tilt my head, joining the conversation. "Thought they were wiped out."

"They were," the youngest girl says, eyes wide. "Or they were supposed to be."

"Turigs didn't just kill," the wiry boy adds. "They erased. Entire squads gone without a scream. Too precise and too fast. Like they didn't even enjoy it. Just… completed a task."

"They weren't soldiers," another murmurs. "They were weapons so deadly they even destroyed themselves."

"Vesper's different," the wiry one insists. "He watches. Waits. Doesn't just rip people apart. He learns."

I glance at them, eyebrow raised. "And that makes him better?"

"No," the girl whispers. "That makes him worse."

Another one of the girls—no older than thirteen—leans in, eyes dark with fear. "It's not a story. They say he doesn't kill like the others. He watches while he waits. Some think he's searching for something." The way she says it sounds like a warning, not a rumor.

"Or someone," another boy adds, barely audible.

Felix bumps my arm. "I don't know, Cassia. Sounds like he might be your type."

I scoff and shove him back, but the words stay with me.

"He watches. He waits."

I shake it off and roll my shoulders, focusing on the drills ahead.

Ghost stories. Nothing more.

5 - Cassia

A seasonal chill cuts through the sunlight, sending a shiver down my spine as I scan the compound's high fence.

Winter has stripped the courtyard bare. Our feet crunch over frozen mud as we search for our instructor. At the far end looms the stone wall, its dangling ropes stirring memories of my first test here—proving I could scale it. Barren bushes arch around the circular space, broken only by gates and pathways. A narrow strip of crystallized grass provides scant clearance from the frost-covered shrubs.

My breath clouds the air before me.

"Beliefs." The word echoes against the walls that separate us from the outside world, stopping us in our tracks.

"We're addicted to them. To the emotions of our past— seeing our beliefs as truths instead of ideas we can change." Heads turn in unison, searching for the voice. "Most people want something outside of them to change how they feel on the inside. Waiting for something to happen to permit themselves to be who they want to be."

Movement draws my attention to the dining hall we just left. Akers approaches, hands clasped behind his back, shoulder-length black hair framing his face. "Habits have presented each of you with specific beliefs, which are now holding you back from reaching your full potential." His pressed black pants appear untouched by the elements, rolled sleeves revealing intricate monochrome ink across his arms. His gaze finds mine. "I'm here to change that." He halts.

I hold his stare, studying each subtle movement as he quirks an eyebrow before shifting his attention to the others who've turned to face him.

"You are likely wondering who I am and why I am here. I believe I just covered the latter. To answer the first, my name is Kody Akers. You will address me as Mr. Akers, Mr. A., Or I will also accept Sir Akers of The Court De La Blanc."

Snickers ripple through the group. He smiles, eyes finding mine again as he points behind me. "You. Step forward." Stephen moves past me, his short brown hair defying gravity in every direction.

"It's funny?"

Fighting another laugh, Stephen shakes his head. "No, Mr. Akers."

"Why not?"

"I don't know, sir."

Akers sighs, circling Stephen with measured steps. "Thank you for volunteering to be first. I need a demonstration of the skills you already have. Please," He gestures to the rope wall. "Get to the other side of the wall."

Stephen blinks. "That's it?"

"That's it."

"Alright. Easy." Stephen grabs a rope and hoists himself up, only to slip back down. A second attempt gets him nearly to the top before he slides halfway and drops to the ground. "Sir. It's too cold, the rope is covered in ice and my hands are going numb."

"So, you are unable to complete this task?"

Stephen hesitates, glancing at the group. "Well, no. But we need to wait for the rope to thaw out."

"Very well. Would anyone else like to try?"

The following silence sends my heart racing and my stomach performs acrobatics until I step forward, if only to make it stop.

"Ah, another volunteer." His smile returns. "Thank you, Miss..."

"Cassia." I pass him, feeling his eyes track my movement.

"Yeah, good luck with that," Stephen mutters as he passes me and rejoins the group.

I roll my eyes and rub my hands together, stopping five feet from the wall. Bouncing in place, I shake out my hands and warm them against my arms, mapping the rope's best grip points. Then I sprint. At the wall's base, I leap for the edge rope, kicking off the stone and pulling my legs up. One swing carries me over the bushes and around the river stone wall to land in sunshine on the far side.

My chest heaves as I lean against the icy rock, every hair standing on end. The world goes quiet when I close my eyes, soaking in sunlight filtering through the iron gate that separates us from whatever lies beyond.

My name cuts through the reverie, snapping me back.

I flip the rope back over the wall's edge, climb partway up, and walk my feet around the side before dropping back into shadow.

"So, it seems the morning conditions don't prevent someone from reaching the other side," Mr. Akers says.

I rejoin the group, folding my arms. "Show off," Stephen whispers.

"Miss Cassia's success is exactly what was intended to prove in this exercise. Though, I expected to go through more of you before someone was able to accomplish it." Mr. Akers locks eyes with me again, offering a slight corner smile that makes me drop my gaze.

Around me, the others shuffle awkwardly. Mr. Akers doesn't say anything right away, just watches us like we're pieces on a board he's still arranging. I glance down, pretending to study the frost creeping along the flagstones, trying to ignore the strange weight of his approval. The silence stretches, waiting for what comes next.

6 - Cassia

Frost glitters on bare branches as the last student rounds the wall.

"We started off with seeing limitations due to something outside our control. We wanted to wait for the right conditions in order to achieve something."

"Mr. Akers," Trisha raises her hand, "Is it sometimes necessary to wait for conditions to line up, though? For example, if someone were wanting to be involved with another person, but that person wasn't ready yet or there's something getting in the way, like age or a different relationship, or enlisting in the war, it would be necessary to wait, wouldn't it?"

"If you're waiting for perfect conditions, move on. Anything worth having takes action, not complacency."

A frown crosses Trisha's face. Something in Akers' glance catches my attention—a look hinting his advice extends beyond romance. Something about waiting. About the right moment to act.

My fingers brush the crumpled letter about my family in my pocket. Waiting—always waiting

"Any more questions?" he asks.

"Yeah," I lift my hand from folded arms. "How long are you training here?"

Akers laughs, deep and genuine. "Tired of me already?"

"More like when will we have enough skill to leave?"

"Are you eager to leave, Cassia?"

"A little bit, yep."

"Grand plans outside these walls?"

"I'll be eighteen soon. I'm meant to locate my family after I'm done here."

His eyes narrow. "Nearly eighteen... I fear, if selected, my training would take a great deal longer than that."

"Selected for what?"

"Advancement."

I sigh. "That doesn't really answer the question. Do you have a pamphlet I can take with me, or something?"

A smile plays at his lips. "The things I teach can't simply be picked up from a pamphlet."

"So what are you here to teach us then?"

The other students focus on him now. "Utilizing every sense you have to survive. Some of you may know this already, but it's a dangerous world out there. And, sorry to break it to you, kid, but there aren't a lot of people around to protect us anymore."

"You're talking about beyond the border, aren't you?"

"Border lines on a map don't make the land any safer. See me after the lesson."

When the others filter inside to warmth, I stay behind—rubbing my hands together as I approach Akers. "You wanted to talk?"

"Ah, yes, Cassia. You're eager to leave. Why?"

"With all due respect, that's not really any of your business."

"On the contrary, it may be exactly my business." He rolls up his sleeve, revealing the hunters guild symbol branded into his skin.

My breath catches. "You... are a hunter?"

He shakes his head, lowering his sleeve. "A tracker. Which is why I'm here training kids"—he rolls his eyes—"how to use a different type of self defense and out of the box thinking. We're in need of recruits."

"Recruits for what, exactly?"

"You were right earlier about what's going on beyond the border. Our region of the country is much safer than most places out there. But a new pod has moved in. We're keeping an eye on them and the threat of growing outnumbered is real. Within a few years, give or take. And that's if we're lucky and they keep with their current pace."

"So, Noctis."

He nods, hands sliding into pockets. "I've told you mine, care to share yours?"

"I need to find my family." I check over both shoulders for eavesdroppers. "I was sent away as a kid. Moved through foster homes every half year. All I've ever had is this,"—I touch the worn paper tucked in my coat—"a note from the last night. It doesn't say to come back… not exactly. Just that the truth would find me when I was ready… and not to stop looking."

His brow creases. "Looking for what, exactly?"

"Answers. Forgiveness, maybe ? Or more." My voice softens. "It hinted that I'm connected to something bigger. That if I survived long enough, I might be able to fix what went wrong with the world."

"Fix…" he trails off, then breathes the words like a morning fog. "The cure."

"For the Noctis virus…"

"That's a heavy thread to pull, Cassia."

"My name is Cassia Bailey."

That stops him cold. His face blanches like he's seen a ghost. "Bailey—" he whispers. "As in Bailey Courle Estates? *The* Calvin Bailey?"

I press a finger to my lips. "You think I want everyone knowing I'm related to the man who broke the world?"

He exhales a slow, astonished laugh. "Oh, Cassia. The world was already breaking. He just gave it a name to bleed under. But yeah… I can see why you keep it quiet."

"Under the Hunters' Guild oath, you're bound to secrecy if I request it."

He nods solemnly. "I am."

"Then keep it."

"As you wish, Miss Cassia." His grin is softer now, edged with sparkle like admiration.

"I need more in-depth training. Not drills. Not wooden dummies. Real training. I want to know how to kill Noctis." I meet his gaze, unflinching. "Will you help me?"

His grin widens into a sharp smile, the kind that dares you to follow through. "So long as you stick around."

7 - Kody

The communications array takes up half the table, all brass dials and copper wiring that wouldn't look out of place in a museum. Crystalline components catch lamplight, their faceted surfaces throwing fractured patterns across the walls. The whole setup hums with a frequency just below hearing— more feeling than sound.

Kody adjusts the frequency modulator, its gears catching with precise clicks. Everything about the system is deliberate, engineered to be undetectable by Noctis senses.

Static crackles through the ancient speaker. He fine-tunes the tertiary crystal, watching it pulse with a soft blue glow as it aligns. The guild had adapted these after the war, when they learned Noctis could intercept modern transmissions if they could sense which frequency the broadcasts were on.

"Compound Base, come in." His voice carries the formal tone these old systems demand. "Hunter Akers, ID 847, reporting."

More static, then a voice breaks through: "Verified. Proceed with candidate assessment."

He spreads the files before him, each containing the last weeks worth of observation notes. The radio's warmth fills the room with the scent of heated brass and mineral oil.

"First candidate: Felix Marshall." Kody leans into the microphone, its metal cold pressing against his lips. "Shows aptitude for stealth work. Quick study. Adaptable in combat scenarios."

The crystal pulses as the response comes: "Note previous concerns about aggressive tendencies."

"Acknowledged." Kody remembers Felix's eyes during weapons training—hunger barely masked by enthusiasm. "Candidate requires careful monitoring."

He adjusts the frequency again, compensating for atmospheric interference. Outside, dawn paints the sky the color of old bruises.

"Second candidate." His hand hovers over Cassia's file. "Cassia." No surname—that detail stays off official channels. "Natural combat instinct. Fights like..." *Like Sarah did. Like someone who's learned the hard way that you never quit.* "Shows remarkable tactical awareness."

The crystal flares brighter, its glow reflecting off polished brass. "Assessment of risk factors?"

Kody studies his notes, choosing words carefully. There's too much he can't put in official reports—her family connection, the way she moves like hunting is in her blood.

"Candidate displays strong survival instinct." *True, if understated.* "Recommend immediate placement in advanced training program."

Static fills the pause that follows. When the response comes, it carries weight: "Approved for accelerated recruitment. Proceed with extraction protocol."

The array's hum changes pitch slightly, crystals dimming as the connection weakens. Kody reaches for the master frequency control, but stops at the next transmission:

"Be advised: increased Noctis activity reported in your sector. Exercise extreme caution with civilian transport."

His hand tightens on the dial. *They're getting bolder, then. Or desperate.*

"Acknowledged," he says, but his mind is already racing ahead. If they're hunting actively, the compound might not be safe enough. But leaving potential recruits untrained could be worse. "Increase in activity threat to future recruits. Permission to prolong training."

After a few moments of silence the response comes through. "Permission granted. Extraction protocol for candidate Cassia revised to sequence C."

"Sequence C extraction, confirmed. Transport

requirement… approximately three weeks. Will confirm on next transmission."

"Acknowledged."

The crystals fade to darkness as he powers down the array. In the sudden quiet, the words echo back: "Exercise extreme caution."

If only he knew whether the warning was meant more for the recruits, or for himself.

8 - Cassia

Moonlight catches the edge of my blade, turning steel to glimmering, light silver as I work through the sequence again. The training yard feels different after dark—more honest somehow. Ancient stone walls loom against a star-scattered sky, their shadows painting the packed earth in shades of midnight. The autumn air carries hints of wood smoke from the kitchen chimneys, mixing with the ever-present scent of leather and metal oil that permeates the compound. Fallen leaves skitter across the yard, their rustling almost musical in the stillness.

"Your left side's still dropping." Felix's voice drifts from the shadows, making me smile despite myself. He emerges from behind a training dummy, moving with the light step that makes him one of our better stealth fighters. Well, when he's not tripping over his own feet trying to impress the senior girls.

"Shouldn't you be in bed?" I continue the sequence, adjusting my guard as my breath clouds in the chill air.

"Shouldn't you?" He drops onto a nearby bench, producing an apple from his pocket. "Besides, someone has to make sure you don't train yourself to death. Though, death by training would be pretty impressive. Very dramatic title to take. Just your style."

"Says the guy who tried to backflip off the dining hall roof."

"That was one time! *And* I stuck the landing." He smirks with pride.

"After bouncing off the rain barrel."

The smirk turns to a chuckle. "Nothing gets past you, does it?"

The familiar rhythm of blade against air fills the comfortable silence between us. Torchlight from the main building catches the metal studs in his training vest as he watches, occasionally calling out corrections, but mostly just keeping me company. He never asks why I train so late, never pushes about why I can't sleep. He just shows up, night after night, making sure I'm not alone.

Felix tosses a training knife between his hands, the movement fluid and absentminded. "You ever think maybe this isn't the only way, Cass? That there might be another way out besides fighting 'till we die?" His voice is light, but the undertone in the way he says it makes my stomach twist.

I glance at him. "You got an escape plan I don't know about?"

He laughs, but it sounds forced. "Nah. Just saying, people have options. Some of us just don't know it yet."

"Can unknown options really be considered options?" I ask.

"Remember today's evaluation?" He tosses me the half-eaten apple, grinning when I catch it behind my back. "When you took down those senior trainees?"

"They got sloppy." I take a bite, the fruit sharp and sweet against the night's bitter chill. "Too confident."

"They got destroyed." His grin flashes in the darkness. "Did you see Jensen's face when you flipped him? Never seen Keller actually smile before. Think that's why Akers was watching you so closely?"

"He watches everyone. That's his job." I wipe apple juice from my chin with my sleeve.

"Not like that." Felix's voice takes on a teasing lilt. "Maybe our illustrious hunter has a thing for redheads. Or maybe he just likes watching people throw his star pupils around like sacks of flour."

"Maybe he just recognizes recruitment potential." The words come out with unintentional defensiveness.

"Right. Potential." But there's a shift in his expression, there and gone before I can read it. The wind picks up, sending leaves dancing between us. "Speaking of potential, I found something interesting in the east wing."

"Felix..."

"Come on." He's already moving, his footsteps silent on the frost-touched ground. "Better equipment, more space. They only keep it restricted because they save it for the elite trainees."

"Which we're not."

"Yet." He glances back, moonlight catching his profile. "Unless you're planning to stick around long enough to make rank? Could be fun—you, me, bossing around the new recruits."

"Daydreaming about living the dream, huh?" *But it's a fair point. We both know I'm leaving as soon as I'm eighteen.*

"You know it." He winks. "Now come on before I have to carry you. And we both know how that ended last time."

"You dropped me in the fountain!"

"I was aiming for the grass!"

The restricted training room is impressive—polished floors, advanced equipment, walls lined with specialized weapons. Moonlight streams through high windows, painting silver pools on dark wood. The space smells of polish and old leather, with an underlying metallic tang that speaks of countless practice bouts. Our boots echo slightly despite our careful steps.

"Better than our usual spot, right?" Felix runs his hand along a rack of training blades. "Jensen would kill to know about this place."

"Pretty sure that's why it's restricted."

"Details, details." He selects two practice swords, testing their weight. "First one to yield buys breakfast?"

"We don't buy breakfast."

"Then I guess we'll have to fight forever." He tosses me a blade, the metal singing as it cuts through air.

We spar until we're both breathless, our movements flowing like a dance we've practiced a thousand times. The moonlight turns everything surreal—Felix's blade flashing silver, shadows moving like liquid across the floor. My boots find purchase on the smooth wood, muscle memory taking over as we trade strikes.

"Not bad," he pants, parrying my thrust. "For someone who claims they're leaving soon."

"Maybe I'll start a fighting school." I spin past his guard. "Teach people how to properly fall into fountains."

"That was one time!" His laugh echoes off the high ceiling. "And you pushed me!"

"Did not!"

"Did too!"

Later, sprawled on the cool floor, when our laughter fades to comfortable silence, the night feels older somehow, heavier. Moonlight paints patterns through the windows, and somewhere an owl calls.

"I used to do this with my dad," Felix says suddenly, his voice different than I've ever heard it. "Train at night, I mean. He worked late shifts at the factory, but he'd always make time when he got home. Said the stars made better company than people anyway."

I turn to look at him, surprised by the admission. The moonlight catches the tension in his jaw.

"How old were you? When they—"

"Seven." His voice carries an edge now, sharp as unsheathed steel. "They found his work jacket by the river. Mom's too. Everyone said accident, but..." He shrugs, the movement too casual. "That was the last time I trained at night. Until you started sneaking out."

Words feel inadequate, so I just reach over and squeeze his hand. His fingers are cold despite our exercise. He squeezes back.

"Footsteps," I whisper, hearing the distinct rhythm of Keller's walk in the corridor—that slight drag on her left foot from an old injury. We scramble up, slipping through shadows toward the door.

"Wait—" Felix pulls me back as lamplight spills under the doorway. We press against the wall, barely breathing, until Keller's steps fade. The warmth of Felix's hand lingers on my wrist even after we start moving again.

We make it back to our bunks just before final check, our boots muddy but our spirits light. The dormitory smell of wool blankets and wood smoke sinks in, with the undertones of training that seem to permeate everything here.

"Worth it, right?" Felix whispers across the darkness.

"Go to sleep."

"Admit it—I'm a genius."

"You're something, alright."

His quiet laugh follows me into dreams. It's only later I realize neither of us yielded during our match. But that's Felix—always finding ways to make me smile, even on the darkest nights.

9 - Cassia

Morning mist clings to the training yard, turning everything ghost like. Sweat drips down my back despite the autumn chill as I move through the sequence again. Kody circles, his boots silent on the frost-touched ground.

I shift, aiming a strike at his ribs, but he's already moving—faster than he should be able to. His arm snaps up, deflecting my blow with barely a glance.

"Again," he says.

Frustration prickles beneath my skin. "How do you always know where I'm going before I even move?"

Kody smirks, but it doesn't reach his eyes. "Years of training."

Except... it's more than that. The way he anticipates, the way his balance never falters—it's almost unnatural. He doesn't just react; he predicts. Like he can feel the shift of my weight before I've even decided to move.

"Your weight's too far forward," he says, hands finding my shoulders. "You'll throw yourself off balance."

From his perch on the fence, Felix grins. The rising sun catches his breath in the cold air as he waggles his eyebrows suggestively. I narrow my eyes at him, which only makes his grin wider. Frost sparkles on the wooden rails around him, making the whole scene surreal somehow.

"Focus," Kody's voice carries that edge of authority that makes even Felix sit straighter. "A Noctis won't give you time to reset."

We work through the movements until my muscles burn, leather creaking with each strike. The yard gradually fills with the sounds of other trainees starting their day—boots on stone, practice blades singing through air. Every time Kody's hand guides my form, adjusting stance or position, Felix's expressions grow more ridiculous. But, I manage to keep my face neutral… barely.

When Kody finally calls break for lunch, the sun has burned away most of the morning dew. Felix hops down from his perch, landing with exaggerated precision. "Quite the hands-on lesson today," he says as we head toward the dining hall, fallen leaves crunching under our boots.

"It's called training."

"Is that what we're calling it?" He ducks my half-hearted swipe, spinning away with a laugh. "I'm just saying, he doesn't correct my form that much."

"Maybe because you don't need as much correction."

"Or, maybe, because I'm not his type." Felix's eyes sparkle with mischief in the midday sun. "Too tall. Not enough red hair."

Heat creeps up my neck. "It's professional interest."

"Professional, sure." He holds the dining hall door for me with an exaggerated bow. "Very professional."

Inside,the smells of lunch wrap around us like a blanket. Kody catches my eye from across the room, offering a slight nod. I return it automatically, trying to ignore how the dining hall's warmth suddenly feels more intense.

"See?" Felix whispers with a raised brow, far too pleased with himself. "Professional."

"Shut up and eat yo~~ ~~~~~."

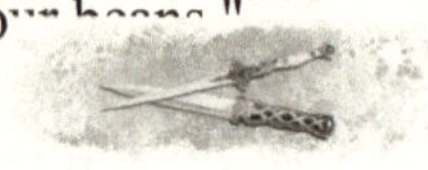

AFTER MOST OTHERS have gone to bed, we claim our usual spot on the roof. The slate tiles still hold some warmth from the day, despite the night's growing chill. Felix produces an apple from his pocket—his usual trophy from a kitchen raid. Stars glimmer overhead, autumn's bite carrying winter's promise in the wind.

"You ever wonder what it would be like?" I ask, the

question slipping out before I can stop it. "Having a normal life?"

Felix takes a thoughtful bite, the apple's crisp sound sharp in the night air. "Define normal."

"You know. Family. Friends. Connections that don't involve hunting monsters."

"You have friends." He bumps my shoulder. "You got me."

"For now." The words come out listless.

Felix goes quiet, studying me in that way he has when he's actually being serious. The moonlight catches the scar on his chin—a souvenir from one of our less successful training sessions. "What's really bothering you?" He asks.

I stare at the stars, remembering other nights like this as a child, before everything changed. "Everyone leaves eventually. Or gets taken. Like your parents. Like mine." My fingers find the locket at my neck, its metal cold against my skin. "Maybe it's better to just... not get attached."

"That's the dumbest thing you've ever said." But his voice is gentle. "And you once tried to convince me a training dummy was haunted."

"It moved on its own!"

"It fell over because you kicked it."

I laugh despite myself, which I suspect was his goal. He hands me the apple, our fingers brushing in the darkness.

"Look," he says, voice carrying an unusual weight. "I can't promise I'll never leave. But I can promise I'll always try to come back." He grins, but something in his expression seems forced. "Someone has to keep you from becoming a complete hermit."

I throw the apple at him. He catches it, laughing, but the sound fades quickly.

"Not that it matters," he adds, suddenly intent on studying the fruit. "I won't be advancing this time anyway."

"What? Why?"

He shrugs, but I catch the tension in his shoulders. "Overheard some things. Put pieces together." His eyes find mine in the darkness. "They're watching you, you know. All that extra training..."

"It won't matter if they pick me. I'm leaving as soon as I turn eighteen, remember?"

"That's stupid." The words come sharp, surprising us both.

"Stay. Train. Get better. It'll make finding your family easier." He cleans off the rest of the and tosses the apple core into the darkness. "We could even go together, once we're both ready. I'll help you."

"I have to be ready enough now." My hands clench in my lap. "I'm tired of waiting."

Felix is quiet for a long moment, the kind of silence that means he's actually thinking instead of just planning his next joke. "You know what I'm tired of?" he finally says. "Watching you push yourself so hard you can barely stand some days. Acting like you have to do everything alone."

"I don't—"

"You do." He turns to face me fully, moonlight catching the concern in his eyes. "Even when people want to help. Even when they care about you."

The cut in his voice makes me look away. "Felix..."

"I know, I know." He flops back against the roof tiles, arms spread wide. "The great Cassia works alone. Too busy for mere mortals like the rest of us."

"That's not—"

"Unless they're tall, brooding hunter types with mysterious pasts."

And just like that, the tension breaks. Felix grins up at the stars, clearly pleased with himself. "Besides," he adds, voice lightening, "at this rate, I'll be the one chasing your shadow while you run off saving the world with your tall, brooding mystery man."

This time I actually push him. He catches himself before sliding off the roof, laughter echoing across the compound.

"I hate you," I mutter.

"Nah, you don't."

He's right. I don't.

10 - Cassia

The moon hangs low over the training yard, casting long shadows across frost-touched stone. My blade cuts through the night air, each movement accompanied by the soft creak of leather and my steady breathing.

The compound feels different at this hour, more honest somehow, without the clash of practice weapons and shouted instructions filling the space. A thin steam rises from the ground, curling around my ankles like ghostly fingers.

"Your guard's dropping."

I spin, blade ready, heart suddenly pounding. Kody emerges from the shadows near the equipment shed, moving with a smoothness that makes even experienced hunters look clumsy in comparison. The moonlight catches his features, turning him almost statuesque against the darkness.

"Couldn't sleep?" he asks, though it doesn't really feel like a question. My palms grow damp on the leather grip of my blade.

"Just getting some extra practice in." I lower my weapon but don't sheath it. The night air carries the scent of approaching winter, making my skin prickle—though maybe that's from his proximity.

"Alone?" He circles slowly, assessing my stance with a hunter's eye. "That's not like you at this hour."

"Felix is..." I hesitate. Actually, I don't know where Felix is tonight. He's been more quiet lately. "Busy, I guess."

Kody nods like this explains everything. "Show me what you're working on."

I move through the sequence again, blade singing through the darkness. He stays silent as he watches, occasionally adjusting my form with each tiny misstep. Each correction is precise, professional, but something about the night makes every touch feel like fire through my clothes. My heart refuses to steady, and I tell myself it's just from exertion.

"You have natural instincts for this," he says finally. "The way you move, how you read opponents. You could be an exceptional hunter."

"I'm not staying." The words come automatically, a reflex built from countless similar conversations with Keller.

"Because of your family."

It's not a question, but I answer anyway. "I have to find them."

"And you think you'll have better chances alone?" His voice carries no judgment, just curiosity. "Without resources, without backup?"

"I think..." I lower my blade, searching for words. "I think I've spent enough time waiting. Training. Preparing. At some point, I have to actually do *something*."

Kody watches me carefully. "Doing *something* without knowing exactly what you're walking into is how you get killed."

I shake my head. "I know what I'm up against."

He exhales. "You think you do. But this isn't just any Noctis activity increase. Something's changed. We've seen fresh transformations—too many and too fast. Whoever's behind this has a motive."

The night chill suddenly sharpens. Kody moves closer, close enough to smell leather and sandalwood on his skin, and see the tension in his jaw.

"The world out there..." He stops, choosing words carefully. "It's not like our training scenarios. Noctis don't fight fair. They don't give second chances."

"I know that."

"Do you?" His eyes find mine in the darkness. "Or do you just think you know?"

Heat rises in my cheeks. "I'm not some naive recruit who thinks—"

"No." He cuts me off, but gently. "You're someone with exceptional potential who's ready to throw it away because she's *tired of waiting*."

The words cut, sinking in deep. "That's not fair."

"Neither is dying because you rushed into something you weren't ready for."

"Felix said the same thing. That I should stay, train more.. ."

Kody looks away, pulling a blade from his belt and pressing his thumb at the tip. "Felix is smart. Has potential." His voice carries a weight I can't place. "But his recklessness.. . it makes him dangerous. To himself and others."

"But he's one of the best. How is he not getting pulled for integration?"

"Word travels fast." His expression shifts as he resheaths the blade. "He's not ready. Too focused on glory, not enough on survival. Teamwork."

"And you think I'm different?"

"I think you have something you're fighting for beyond recognition." His eyes lock onto mine again. "But that won't matter if you get yourself killed."

We stand in tense silence, close enough that I can feel the heat radiating off him despite the night's chill. My pulse thunders in my ears. Part of me wants to argue, to defend my choices. But another part remembers the fight that put me on my back last week during training—remembers how easily I let distraction slip my guard.

"One more month," he says finally. "Give me that long to teach you what you really need to know. Then, if you still want to leave..." He shrugs, all too casual. "I won't stop you."

I should say no, should stick to my plan. Instead, I find myself nodding, trying to ignore how his proximity makes my skin feel too tight.

"Good." He steps back, cold distance returning like an invisible wall between us. "Now, from the beginning. And this time, keep your guard up."

The moon climbs higher as we work, my blade cutting silver arcs through darkness. When my heart won't steady, and my hands shake slightly when he corrects my form—well, that's just from exertion.

At least, that's what I tell myself.

II - Kody

Dawn paints the compound walls gold as Kody stands before Warden Keller's desk. Reports spread between them—training evaluations, advancement recommendations, and one file that keeps drawing his attention. Cassia's file. Outside, fog clings to the training yard, turning the early risers forms ghost like as they begin their exercises.

"She's not ready to leave." The words sound as hollow as they feel.

Keller studies him over steepled fingers, morning light catching the silver in her hair. Somewhere in the compound, a bell signals breakfast. "The extraction protocol was approved a month ago," Keller says quietly.

Kody nods. "I thought if I could convince her to stay longer, bring her in officially, she might change her mind about leaving."

"In your own evaluation, you note her exceptional progress. Her natural combat instinct," Keller replies. "She's progressed significantly, and already given you more time than she intended."

He was never meant to stay, either. Recruiting efforts rotated through compounds for a few weeks at a time—train, assess, move on. But Cassia had made that harder than it should've been.

"You know natural instinct isn't enough." Kody's fingers brush the edge of Cassia's file, the paper rough against his calluses. "She's still reckless, still—"

"Still determined to find her family." Keller's voice carries no judgment. A trainee's shouts echo from the yard, followed by the distinct sound of someone hitting dirt. "Like someone else I once knew." Her implicative eyes meet his.

Before Kody can respond, a knock interrupts them. A young messenger, Marcus's son, barely old enough to train, enters with a sealed document. "From the guild, sir. Marked urgent."

The report is brief—a missing person in the northern territories. He's about to set it aside when a detail catches his eye. The missing woman had received an invitation to a private gathering. The description of the seal tugs at his memory—a symbol he's seen before, buried in old records tied to the region where the Baileys were last seen.

"I'll need to arrange transport," he says, tucking the report under his arm.

"What about your recruit?" Keller asks.

"Give me until tonight to convince her to stay longer." The words taste like desperation. "Then, I can be back within three days."

But the depth in Keller's expression suggests she knows better.

The communications array's brass dials catch afternoon light through dusty windows. Kody adjusts the frequency crystal, watching it pulse with soft blue light as he transmits his travel plans to the guild. The familiar heated mineral oil fumes settle in the air.

A scuffed boot crosses the threshold behind him. "So it's true then?"

He turns to find Felix in the doorway, shadows under his eyes suggesting sleepless nights. The setting sun casts his face in sharp lines, turning his usually boyish features harder, older.

"What's true?"

"I'm not advancing." Felix's voice carries a new edge. His fingers tap against the doorframe—a nervous habit he hasn't quite trained out. "After everything. All the training. All the work. I thought this time might be different."

"You're not ready."

Felix's laugh is short and bitter. "Not ready?" His gaze sharpens. "I'm better than half the senior class. Better than—"

"Being better isn't enough." Kody powers down the array, the hum fading to silence. Cold air seeps through the windows, carrying the scent of snow. "You're reckless. You take unnecessary risks. That gets people killed."

"Like you never take risks?" Felix steps forward, eyes catching more shadow than before. "I've seen how you fight. How you bend the rules."

"I know the limits."

"Do you?" Felix's voice drops. "Because it sure looks like you're willing to gamble with other people's futures, not just your own."

Kody exhales, jaw tight. "You're not advancing. Maybe next time."

"I spent my last year banking on 'next time,' and here I am hearing it again."

"Work on your control. Learn to function as part of a team. You can hold your own, but having a partner changes every dynamic. They need to know their trust in you isn't misplaced."

Felix huffs a bitter breath, shaking his head. "And now I get another lecture? Like the ones you've been giving her?"

"Watch yourself."

Felix snorts. "I'm just saying—must be nice. Getting her to stay an extra month. Making her think she needs more training—needs you. All while you're packing your bags to leave."

"A new case came in this morning," Kody says, jaw tightening. "This is the job, kid."

Felix laughs, low and humorless. "Maybe. But from where I'm standing? Looks like Cassia gets special treatment—extra time, one-on-one training, a sponsor who just happens to be shaping her whole future."

Kody's eyes narrow. "That's not what this is."

"No? Then—"

"I'm recruiting for the hunters guild."

"Does *she* know that?"

"It's not a secret."

"But did you *tell* her?"

"I don't need to."

"She'll take it personally. Like she's just another trainee not worth staying for. And you're another person walking away."

"You don't know what you're talking about."

"Don't I?" Felix crosses his arms, but his voice tightens.

"I've seen how she looks at you. How she listens to you. You push her harder than anyone else—and she still thinks she's not enough. And now you're just leaving without a word?"

Kody moves away from the array, his voice low but firm. "Watch your tone."

Felix stiffens, a flicker of regret flashing behind his irritation.

"You don't get to question my integrity just because you're not where you wanted to be." Kody's voice sharpens. "And if you want to serve with the guild someday, start acting like it. Learn when to speak, and when to shut your mouth."

Felix crosses his arms again, but the fire has dimmed. "Figures Keller wouldn't have a problem with you leaving in the middle of a training block. Some people get to make their own rules."

"I'm not a student. I don't run by compound rules."

Felix tilts his head, studying him. "No? Then tell me— does she know?"

Kody stiffens. "...Who?"

Felix's lips curl slightly, almost amused. "Don't." The single word is quiet, weighted. "You know who. Does Cassia know her precious instructor is abandoning her? Just like everyone else she lets herself rely on?"

Kody doesn't answer. He can't.

Felix lets the silence stretch, jaw tight, then exhales sharply. "Right," he mutters.

Kody steps in fast, voice low and razor-sharp. "You don't mutter at a superior. You shut your mouth and take the correction." He takes a step closer. "And not that I owe you any disclosure—but you were close to getting pulled for advancement. Keep this shit up, and I'll make sure your file's buried so deep it won't see daylight again."

The reprimand lands hard. Felix flinches, shoulders going rigid. "Understood." He straightens, brushing off invisible dust. "Sorry, sir. Won't happen again, sir."

Kody doesn't reply. Just watches him go, the words burrowing under his skin like splinters. From the training yard comes the familiar sound of blade against wood—Cassia, working through forms in the dying light.

Tomorrow, everything changes.

She'll leave soon. He'll already be gone, chasing a case he didn't ask for.

He should tell her. About the seal, the timing, what it might mean—particularly in regard to her family. He should ask her to come with him.

But if he does, it stops being a guild case and starts being a choice of personal investment. She's not ready for that, not yet. Not with the kind of danger he knows he's walking into.

He wasn't meant to stay this long. He came to assess and train—not to get involved. And certainly not to care. But Cassia… she changed things. And that carries an uncertainty he doesn't know how to haul. Now he's taking on this case, because somewhere along the way, it did become personal. And the only thing worse than dragging her directly into danger, is not having the answers she needs before he does.

The sun sinks behind the compound walls, bruising the sky in muted violets and greys. He still has preparations to finish before nightfall.

Maybe it's better this way. Cleaner… safer.

But as darkness claims the training yard and Cassia's practice finally quiets, he wonders if clean breaks ever really heal.

12 - Cassia

Two days left. One month of extra training—already more time than I ever planned to stay. But now, with only forty-eight hours remaining, my doubts scream louder than ever.

The cold stones bite into my back. Again.

I shove against him, expecting only slight resistance—but it's like pressing against a wall. Solid. Unmovable. My boots scrape against the ground, but he doesn't budge.

Kody frowns at my struggling. With a sigh, he steps back, rolling his shoulders like the effort was nothing.

I exhale sharply, shaking out my arms. "How are you not even tired?"

He gives me a flat look. "Because you're not coming at me hard enough."

"That's not—" I cut myself off, staring at him. He's barely even winded. Meanwhile, my arms drag like lead.

He grabs my wrist, flipping me effortlessly back into position. "Less talking. More fighting."

I grit my teeth, irritation flaring. My muscles ache, my reflexes are sluggish compared to his, but I force myself to focus. He's relentless—every mistake met with immediate correction, every misstep exploited.

Fine. If he wants me to fight, I'll fight.

I track the way his weight shifts, how his grip tightens a fraction of a second before he moves. For the first time, I see his attack coming. My body shifts left, muscle memory transforming defense into counterattack. Days of relentless training have rewritten the way I move.

I block his attack, and he whips around, catching my foot

with his.

"Why the hell do you keep dropping your guard?" Kody growls, his hand gripping my forearm to keep me from diving face first into the dirt.

"For defense!" I grip his wrist.

"If that's why, then defense gets you killed," he snarls. "You shouldn't ease back at all until we're no longer close enough for me to hit you again. A Noctis won't tire. Won't hesitate. The moment you drop into pure defense, you're as good as dead."

"Easy for you to say," I mutter. "You never get tired."

Kody snorts. "Everyone gets tired."

"Really? Because we've been at this for an hour, and I'm pretty sure I'm the only one dying."

He scoffs. "You're just out of shape."

I roll my shoulders, wincing at the ache. "Maybe. But you don't even look fazed."

I expect him to brush it off, but a flicker of unease crosses his face—like I've hit a nerve he didn't expect to have. His stance shifts—small, nearly imperceptible—but suddenly, he's not just watching me. He's studying me.

"Pain is temporary," he says after a moment. "You learn to work through it."

That's not an answer.

I narrow my eyes. "Mr. A—"

"Come on." He gestures for me to attack. "Go again."

I step forward, shifting my weight, but instead of charging, I feint left. He doesn't take the bait. He's fast— quicker than I expect. His eyes are locked on me, calculating. I aim a low strike, but he sidesteps with a speed that forces me to adjust mid-move.

"You're not thinking far enough ahead," he says, voice sharp, taunting. His next movement is a blur, and I barely manage to block the jab he lands to my ribs.

I stagger back, forcing myself to breathe through the sting. He's relentless, barely giving me a moment to recover before he's on me again. My arms ache, my feet slip on loose gravel as I pivot, trying to find an opening.

"Focus," he urges. "You won't get anywhere if you keep rushing."

I grit my teeth, frustration mounting. *This isn't a fight—it's a lesson in control. But he's not going to make it easy. Not for me.*

"You're improving," he says, eyes tracking my movements. "But you're still too defensive. You drop your guard the moment pressure hits."

"That's what defense is," I counter, circling him cautiously. "Creating distance when you're overwhelmed."

"Not with a Noctis." In an instant, he closes the gap, pinning me against the stone wall. My back hits hard enough to knock the breath from my lungs. "You need to position with an upper hand."

"Well, you never step back long enough for that to happen."

"We're in battle to the death, sweetheart, not dealing solitaire at some fucking tea party." His breath is hot against my frost-chilled face, each word a tactical lesson. "If you're cornered by one of them, you have seconds. Maybe less."

A shadow flickers through his expression—his eyes darkening as he pushes away. For a moment, his gaze sharpens, not just focused but feral—a glimpse of the hunter beneath the surface, the part of him that doesn't belong to the guild or its rules.

Then he moves faster than anyone I've seen— demonstrating with inhuman speed, pinning me again with his face at my neck. "Dead. Once they get this close, it's over. Your scent gives you away before you even see them coming."

I try to shove him off, but he's locked in place, too sturdy. My breath is sharp, uneven. "So? What do I do?"

His voice is low. "Pray you never cross paths with the Tenebris. He doesn't need to bite to turn you—just a touch, some say."

My grip tightens on my belt without thinking, knuckles white. The chill in the night air is sharper now, pressing against sweat-damp skin. A sound in the dark, just the wind, makes my shoulders flinch before I catch myself.

"What does that mean?"

Kody steps back, gaze unreadable. "It means there are monsters even hunters fear."

"Then, how do I—"

"Mask your scent. Crushed vervain mixed with pine tar. But more importantly—" He lunges again, just as fast as before.

This time, I'm ready. I drop and roll, coming up with a handful of dirt that I throw at his face. He blocks, but I'm already moving, putting the wall at my back.

"Better," he says, wiping his eyes. "Either overpower them or use the environment."

"Like with a knife?" I wipe blood from my lip, the pain more progress than injury. "One you wouldn't let me have?"

He chuckles. "A knife is fine—unless it's all you know how to use. One blade won't do it, anyway. You need to drain them, or take the head. Or both. Then burn what's left. Anything less and they'll regenerate."

I force a breath. "I don't get it. I should've landed at least one clean hit by now."

"You just need practice."

"We've been practic—"

"Stop telegraphing. They smell fear, anticipation. Use it. Make them think you're afraid, then strike."

He holds my gaze and I shift to break the tension, but the air stays taut.

"Our deal is up in two days. I'll be leaving after that." I bite the inside of my cheek. "I need to be ready."

"I know." His voice softens. "I spoke with Keller. You can stay longer, if you want."

I scoff, kicking a pebble across the courtyard. "Staying longer than necessary isn't an option."

"Then we have two days of after-hours practice to get you as close to ready as we can."

The night air sharpens against my skin as I shoulder my gear and turn away. "Thanks, Mr. A. I'll see you tomorrow."

"Good night, Cassia."

"Good night."

13 - Cassia

I grip Kody's wrist with new confidence, pulling him down as my knee drives upward. The connection is precise—technique over raw strength. His breath rushes out as I catch his shoulder, forcing him to the ground with a control I couldn't have managed days ago.

"That's what I've been waiting for," he says, tapping my calf for release. "You packed a lot of improvement into just a few days."

I offer my hand. "So, you think I'm ready?"

He takes it, brushing pebbles from his arm. "Slow down, turbo. 'That's what I've been waiting for' isn't the same as 'you're ready.'"

"I have to be ready." Guilt twinges as I notice blood on his forearm. "I leave tomorrow."

"I arranged transport," he says. "They'll be here at dawn."

My chest tightens. "You assumed I'd still go?"

"I hoped you'd change your mind. Maybe pursue training with the guild. But I knew better than to bet on it."

I blink, heat flooding my throat. "Why would you do that? Especially if I'm not joining…"

The edge of sarcasm fades from his eyes as they hold steady. "Because the path back to your family isn't just a journey. It's a gauntlet. And you need to stay alive."

"Obviously. Who doesn't know they need to stay alive?"

He chuckles, brushing it off. "Never mind. Just be ready."

I stare at him, reluctance pinning me in place. "I… don't know what to say."

He shrugs. "Then don't say anything. Consider it a

birthday gift." He chuckles. "Welcome to adulthood."

I step forward anyway, before I can think, arms wrapping around his neck. My throat tightens. "Thank you. I guess."

He hesitates before returning the embrace, chin brushing my shoulder, arms careful. His chuckle hums through me. "Well, 'thank you' is the appropriate response. So you're welcome."

"I suppose... goodbye then, Mr. A."

"More likely a 'see you when I see you.'"

I manage a smile. "Expecting to see me again?"

"Given my job and your surname? I'd be surprised if we didn't cross paths. Just stay alive long enough for me to actually say a real goodbye. Because you won't be getting one before you leave."

My stomach flutters. "Alright then. Deal. You can say goodbye next time."

"Deal."

His hand extends, I shake it, and that's all it takes to solidify the quiet bond sharper than spoken words.

14 - Cassia

I tighten the straps on my pack, pressing down on the top to make sure it's as compact as possible. It's not much—just the essentials. A change of clothes, some supplies, the letter, and the locket still warm from my skin. The dormitory is nearly silent except for the slow, steady breaths of the other trainees lost in sleep.

A cold draft seeps in from the cracked window, carrying the scent of damp stone and the distant burn of firewood from the kitchens.

It's strange. After years of never staying in one place for long, I should be used to leaving. But this time feels different, heavier.

Light, careful footsteps fall behind me. I know who it is before he speaks.

"You really going through with this?" Felix's voice is quiet, careful not to wake the others.

I stay focused on my pack. "Yeah."

He exhales slowly, like he's been holding something in. "Figured you'd at least pretend to have second thoughts."

I zip the pack closed and sling it over my shoulder, finally facing him. He's leaning in the doorway, arms crossed, his usual smirk absent. Shadows cling to his face in the dim light, his expression unreadable.

"I've been waiting for this for a long time, Felix. I can't stay here."

A flicker passes through his eyes, tension… maybe regret, but I can't quite name it. "Right. Because you have to find your family."

"Yeah."

He studies me like he's chasing an answer I'm not offering, jaw tight. "And after that?"

I frown. "What do you mean?"

Felix lets out a quiet, humorless laugh. "Come on, Cass. Say you find them. Say they're alive. What happens then? You think they're just going to welcome you back, give you all the answers you've been looking for?"

The edge in his voice makes me bristle. "That's what I need to find out."

He tilts his head, gaze narrowing. "You sure it's really about them? Or is it about *him*?"

It takes me a second to realize who he means, and my stomach twists. "What are you implying?"

Felix shrugs. "You and Mr. A. All those extra lessons. Staying late. Getting special treatment." His voice stays light, but the bitterness beneath it is impossible to miss.

I roll my eyes. "It's not like that."

"Yeah? You sure about that?" He pushes off the doorframe, stepping closer. "Because the way I see it, he's got you thinking you're not ready. That you *need* him."

I shake my head. "Mr. A just wants to make sure I don't get myself killed."

Felix's jaw tightens. "He's not the only one."

The weight in his voice gives me pause. It isn't just concern—there's a darker undercurrent threading through it.

I sigh, shifting my pack higher on my shoulder. "You'll be fine here without me."

"Obviously," he mutters, though the bitterness in his tone lingers like a bruise.

I don't know what makes me do it, but I step forward and pull him into a hug. He stiffens like he wasn't expecting it, like he doesn't know what to do with it. For half a second, his arms hover at his sides before he exhales and returns it—just a little too tight, like he doesn't want to let go.

I pull away first and his hands linger on my arms for a fraction too long before he lets go.

"Take care of yourself," I say.

Felix holds my gaze, eyes darker than usual. "You too." His expression flickers—guarded and intense. Not quite anger, and more like regret wrapped in restraint. As if he's caught between saying too much and not enough. Then the mask slides back into place, a crooked smirk hiding the shift.

"Try not to let Mr. Perfect's training get you killed."

I roll my eyes, but the tightness in my chest won't budge. I turn to go, needing space to breathe, but his voice stops me.

"Hey, Cass?" I pause and glance back.

He's still watching me, posture loose but eyes sharp. "Don't be so sure this is the only path." His voice is quieter now—measured, deliberate. "There's always another way."

A warning? An offer? I can't tell.

I frown. "What's that supposed to mean?"

His gaze lingers on mine a second too long before he exhales, almost like he's disappointed. "Forget it."

But as I step into the hallway, I swear I hear him whisper under his breath. Too soft to catch, too pointed to ignore.

The chill that follows me down the corridor has nothing to do with the cold and everything to do with what I saw in his eyes. It settles beneath my skin and stays.

15 - Cassia

The tavern's oil lamp casts my shadow long across the rain-slicked cobblestones.

Six months alone since leaving the compound—three more chasing dead ends. But this lead feels different.

Moisture clings to the air, thick and cold, and the lamplight blurs at the edges.

I still hear the innkeeper's voice: "A man and woman passed through last spring. Paid in old coins—Bailey estate sigil."

Movement flickers at the edge of my vision. A figure slips through the mist, too smooth and deliberate for a drunk or casual traveler. My hand goes to my knife, training kicking in.

Then I catch the scent—expensive cologne over metal. Sharp. Wrong.

"Still quick with that knife, I see." The voice is unmistakable. A lazy laugh in the fog. "Though your form's sloppier than ever, Cass."

"Felix?"

He steps out of the mist with that same crooked grin, the guild's silver insignia glinting on his fresh leather armor. But he moves differently now—more confident and somehow more dangerous.

"What are you doing here?" I ask.

"Working a case." He spreads his arms, the hunter's burn mark still scabbing on his forearm. "No hug for an old friend?"

I hesitate, then step into his embrace, letting the familiar warmth cut through the cold. His arms feel stronger than I remember—anchoring.

"You've changed," I say as he lifts me clean off the ground.

"Guild training will do that." He sets me down with an easy grin, though something unreadable lingers in his eyes. "You look... tired."

I huff. "Thanks a lot."

He doesn't laugh this time. "You're running yourself ragged with this search, aren't you?"

I don't answer. Because he's not wrong. And for the first time in months, I don't have to pretend I'm fine.

A gust of wind tugs at my coat and I nod toward the door. "Come on. Tell me what you're really doing here."

We claim a corner table in the tavern, the worn wood bearing decades of knife marks and spilled drinks. Felix orders ale with the confidence of someone used to frequenting such places now. He tells me about his guild missions— tracking Noctis movements along the border, investigating disappearances, learning patterns.

"It's different out here," he says, gesturing with his mug. A serving girl hurries past, giving our weapons a wide berth. "Not like the compound's controlled scenarios. Real stakes. Real victories."

His enthusiasm is infectious, but his stories have an edge—his fights too stylized, his victories too clean. When he demonstrates a new combat technique, he nearly upends our table.

"Careful!" I steady my drink, ale sloshing over the rim. "Maybe save the showboating for outside?"

"You sound like my trainer, Rolf. Real hard ass." But his eyes glitter in the tavern's dim light. "Speaking of which, I'm actually working a missing persons case in the region. Three disappearances in the past month, all following the same pattern."

My pulse quickens. "What pattern?"

"That's the interesting part." He leans forward, voice dropping. "The timing, the locations… they line up with some of the old files. Witness accounts and incident logs surrounding your family's disappearance. It's like the same story is happening all over again."

The air leaves my lungs too fast. "What kind of reports?"

"Guild records. Stuff that didn't make the official logs. Back channel testimonies, a few redacted memos. Some of them mention the Baileys by name." He traces the rim of his mug, suddenly solemn. "Let me help you look into it. Two sets of eyes are better than one."

I stare into my ale, trying to steady the storm building in my chest. This was always mine to carry, to chase alone. Felix never asked questions about it before, never tried to insert himself. But now he's looking at me like we were always meant to do this together.

"Why do you want to help?"

His voice is soft. "Because I remember how many nights you spent training when everyone else slept. You weren't just driven—you were haunted… maybe you still are."

I don't answer right away. My fingers tighten around the handle of my mug.

"Come on, Cass," he says. "We were a good team back then. Let's try again."

I nod. Because saying no feels harder than I expected.

His grin lights up his whole face. "First thing tomorrow then?"

"Why wait?" I drop coins on the table. "Where did your latest victim disappear?"

16 - Cassia

The next week finds us combing through the city's underbelly. The eastern quarter sprawls like a maze of narrow alleys and crumbling tenements. Laundry lines crisscross overhead, creating a patchwork of shadows that Felix seems too eager to charge through.

He tackles a suspect through a produce stall, sending crates of vegetables skidding across the slick cobblestones. The man lands hard—head slamming against the stone with a sickening thud. Blood pools quickly, bright against the wet ground.

"Got him!" Felix grins, his eyes bright and wild as he rises, brushing dirt from his shoulder. His knuckles are already bloody.

I move to check the man's pulse, but he's unconscious. "What happened to being careful?"

"Got the job done, didn't it?" Felix tosses a coin at the vendor without looking. "Intel said he had ties to estate coin circulation."

He crouches and slaps the man awake, fingers digging into the suspect's collar. "Wake up. We're not done."

The man stirs, groaning, but when Felix leans close, voice low and cold, I catch only pieces: "Names. Routes. Who else has the coin."

The suspect flinches from him. His body starts to tremble, then goes limp again, eyes rolling back as he slumps to the ground, unconscious, or worse, before a single answer leaves his lips—blood mixing with rain where his head struck stone.

I step in. "Felix. He's out."

Felix releases the man with a sound that's somewhere between a grunt and a curse. "He passed out before I even got started."

His disappointment unsettles me.

We walk the length of the alley in silence, the smell of blood still sharp in my nose. Felix flexes his hand, wiping dried red flakes off with a stained cloth, seemingly unphased.

"We need to cover more ground," I say finally, voice lower than before.

Felix slows his steps. "Thought we made a good team."

"We do," I hedge, not meeting his eyes. "But if we split up, we can track more leads faster."

He watches me for a beat too long, the silence stretching. "You sure you're not just trying to get rid of me?"

My stomach knots. I don't have an answer for that, so I lead with the truth. "This is your case. I don't want to get in your way."

He scoffs, but the sound lacks conviction. "Right. Because working with you has been such a burden."

I glance up. There's tension behind his smirk now—a sharpness I don't remember being there before.

"I'll take the eastern quarter," I say, adjusting the strap across my shoulder. "You head west."

Felix nods, but doesn't move right away. As I turn to go, his hand finds my shoulder—not for balance or attention. Just a touch, too still to be casual.

"Be careful out there, Cass," he says. The nickname landing heavier than usual. "The streets get meaner after dark."

"I know," I say quietly, forcing a smile that mirrors the hollowness that I feel.

He holds my gaze like he wants to say more—needs to— but the words never come. Then he turns, disappearing into the dark fog without another look.

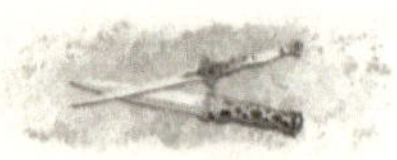

THE NIGHT CHILL is colder without him.

I circle back to the tavern, hoping to pick up the trail we lost in the market. The tavern door groans as I step back inside and the warmth hits me like a wave—suffocating.

The crowd has thinned. Only the true regulars remain

now—men with haunted eyes, women clutching worn charms, a couple hunched near the hearth as if the darkness outside might reach in.

A man at the bar hasn't stopped muttering since I arrived, voice too low to be talking to anyone but himself. His hands tremble around his drink. "Whole village, I tell you. Turned. Not killed—turned. Every last one of them turned." His voice rasps like a frayed rope. "That's what makes the Tenebris different—worse. That's why Vesper is worse."

The name lands like a cold slap. The barkeep hisses, eyes darting to the shadows. "Hush. We don't speak that name here."

"Why not?" the man barks. "He's already taken everything." His voice is high and thin, wobbling on the edge of hysteria. "My Clara warned the guild. Said he collects bloodlines, not bodies." The man's hand shakes violently as he lifts his drink. He spills most of it. "Said he doesn't feed— he takes. Makes people forget who they were before he even touched them. And when he does touch…"He trails off. The silence that follows is unnerving.

"Enough!" The barkeep slams a bottle down with a solid clunk on the countertop. "You want to bring him here? They say he can smell when people speak his name."

Another patron mutters nearby: "Not even a Noctis. Not really."

I turn toward the voice. An older woman clutches a talisman, worn smooth with prayer, between knotted fingers. Her eyes flick to mine.

"What do you mean?" I ask.

The woman doesn't meet my gaze. "Those like Vesper, like Tenebris, don't just feed. They erase. People disappear, and no one remembers them after. Their names vanish from ledgers, homes standing empty like they were never lived in."

My throat tightens. "That's just a story."

She snorts. "Aren't they all? Some say Vesper was the first. The last true Noctis. Older than the war. Older than the bloodlines and the hierarchy of Noctis status."

I hover near the bar, pretending to study the drink menu. The barkeep moves away, but not before making a sharp, protective sigil with his fingers. One I've only seen in books used against old magic and when prayer isn't enough. It's not superstition, it's fear—bone-deep and quiet.

A chill skims up my spine. I've heard the name Vesper before, always in fragments, always hushed. But now... it circles with this new threat of Tenebris like a curse, dark and heavy.

Clara. Bloodlines. Erasure.

My gut twists.

This isn't just another missing persons case we're working.

I want to ask more, but I feel eyes. Heavy. Watching.

Time to go.

17 - Cassia

The rain hasn't stopped for three days. It drips from the tavern's eaves in a slow, merciless rhythm—like a clock bleeding time. I check our meeting spot again: the corner table at The Hollow Bell, still empty. Just like yesterday. Just like the day before.

Felix's half-finished case notes sit in my pack, the margins filled with his messy scrawl about missing persons and estate coins. Useless fragments.

"Still no sign of your friend?" the barkeep asks. Her sympathy has curdled into pity as she sets down a mug I didn't order. "On the house."

I leave it untouched.

The eastern quarter feels different in this endless rain. Dirt and oil gather at the gutters, turning puddles viscous and dark. The cobblestones shine slick with runoff and streaks of black-red seeping toward the drains—fluid too thick to be just rainwater.

I retrace his last route again, more out of ritual now than hope. Past the market where he tackled that suspect, through the alley where we fought off a pair of drunk thieves—one of the few nights we'd actually laughed. Up to the old guild safehouse he found on a whim and never stopped checking.

The door is ajar.

It wasn't yesterday.

My blade is in hand before I realize I've drawn it. Inside, the air is damp and stagnant. Rain seeps through broken windows, forming warped puddles across the rotting floorboards. Papers litter the room like fallen leaves, some still fluttering where the breeze cuts through.

Someone left in a hurry... Or was taken.

Felix's guild insignia glints dully beneath an overturned chair. No blood, no major struggle, just... silence. As if the space had been scrubbed of him entirely.

His journal lies open on a table with water-stained pages still drying.

*Bailey estate connection confirmed—not just coins. Records show regular payments to local authorities. Arrangements? *Check warehouse district.**

Below that, a messier line, hastily crossed out:

Tell Cass? Might be better to handle alone. Possible promotion if solo discovery.

A white-hot sting blooms behind my eyes. Not fear. Fury.

Promotion? He left me in the middle of our search... to hoard glory?

I can't breathe. The betrayal hits harder than anything in training ever did.

Behind me, a floorboard creaks.

The fine hairs on my arms lift. Something unseen coils in the shadows—a presence. Heavy... Watching.

Then it moves.

Fast. Too fast.

The Noctis flows from the dark like smoke given muscle, its limbs too long and fluid—its grin glinting with too many teeth. My blade swings up on instinct, but it dances sideways, circling. Laughing.

The sound is wet. Wrong. It echoes in ways that twist the space.

I swing again, wild and stupid. I know better—but the fear is louder than logic.

It knocks my weapon aside like a toy, pounces, and slams me through a rotting table. Wood splinters against my back as I hit the floor, breath gone. It's toying with me—watching how I flinch. Testing.

My other blade finds its shoulder. Luck, not skill. It barely reacts as it steps back into the shadow.

"The Mistress will be pleased," it hisses, licking blood from one long, curled claw. "A Bailey, hand-delivered."

Its voice sounds like it's being whispered in two places at once. Inside my ear, and behind my spine.

I run. Not proud, nor brave. But I remember one lesson: Sometimes survival means knowing when to retreat.

BACK IN THE crumbling shed I've been squatting in all week, I slam the door shut behind me, fingers trembling. The walls leak and the floor creaks. My breath fogs in the cold air, but the chill clinging to my spine goes deeper than temperature.

I pull Felix's scattered notes from my pack again, spreading them over a crate I've been using as a desk. A note I hadn't seen before sticks to the bottom.

Antique music box. Green with porcelain flowers. Estate markings. Unique lock. Shopkeeper says only family blood may open it.

A second note, tucked behind, falls into my lap. Not in the same handwriting as before. A smear of blood, dry, but unmistakable, marks the page's edge. But not from the fight…

Sorry, Cass. This mission of yours… it's bigger than both of us. And I need to focus on my future. – F

My vision blurs. I read it again. And a third time.
After everything… he left.
Not captured. Not killed. Just gone.
For a promotion? Recognition?

I crumple the note in my fist, fingernails biting my palm. I trusted him. Let him get close. I almost thought—I don't know what I thought… Maybe that the boy I remembered wouldn't change.
Stupid.

Dawn bleeds in through the warped roof. I press my hand to my chest, feeling the throb of panic somewhere beneath my ribs. The Noctis knew my name, my family. They know who I am.

I'm not ready. Not strong enough yet.

But the music box… Blood may open it. The words catch in my chest like a breath I can't release. It's connected—has to be. That strange lullaby I only remember in pieces, the way the lock etched itself into my memory the moment I read about it.

I buy a ticket south with the last of my coin. I'll train harder, smarter. Town by town, fight by fight. I'll learn what I have to—because I can't afford to fail again.

Felix made his choice.

Now I make mine.

My hand drifts to the knife on my hip—the one he gave me at the compound gate.

By nightfall, I'll sell it. Some ghosts don't deserve to be carried any longer.

18 - Kody

The archives' silence presses against Kody's ears as he traces the faded ink of another document. Three days of searching yielded more questions than answers, each discovery making his chest tighter with the weight of each new discovery.

"Found anything interesting?"

He looks up to find Marcus, the guild's senior archivist, watching him from between the stacks. The old man's eyes hold the knowing look of someone who's seen too much.

"Just more dead ends." Kody pushes aside another stack of papers. "Though I did find this." He holds up a document marked with the regional governor's seal. "Notice of a 'selection ceremony.' Any idea what that means?"

Marcus's expression tightens. "Ah. The gleaning records."

"The what?"

"Not all regions handle their Noctis problems the same way." Marcus pulls out a chair, its joints creaking as he sits. "Some fight. Some run. This region... found another solution."

Kody's fingers tense on the paper. "What kind of solution?"

"The kind that keeps the peace." Marcus's voice drops. "But at a price."

The archivist reaches across the table and pulls out a leather-bound ledger from beneath the other documents. Its spine is cracked, pages yellow with age. "These are the old feeding records. Before they started redacting them."

Kody's stomach turns as he reads. Numbers. Dates. Names of "volunteers." And beside each entry, a designation:

Sustained Source.

Blood type.

Feeding schedule.

Recovery periods.

Some entries span months, others years.

"They're not just killing them?" he whispers.

Marcus shakes his head, weathered hands spreading more documents across the table. "No. They're keeping them. Like livestock."

As Kody flips another page, a scrawl of ink catches his eye. A name, separate from the others.

Tenebris.

No lineage. No origin. Just fragmented accounts spanning centuries.

Beware the Tenebris. He does not serve. He does not rule. He only remains.

Kody traces a line of text, bile rising in his throat. "Some of these dates... they span decades."

One of the documents isn't like the others. The ink is uneven, the handwriting rushed. A personal account, buried beneath the statistics.

Recovered Testimony, Case #4172 (Year 96 A.W.)

"They called it a 'voluntary selection,' but we never volunteered. They fed from us with soft words and sharper teeth. Then let us recover—if we were lucky. If not, they found another use for us."

"The worst part wasn't the pain—it was the way they looked at us after. Like cattle. Like meat."

"I stopped looking at the stars. I stopped counting the days. When you are nothing but a body waiting to be drained, time ceases to matter."

"I remember her. The girl before me. She stopped speaking after the second year. She stopped moving by the third. By the fourth, she was gone. They replaced her within the week."

Kody's hands clench the paper, anger rising in his chest.

"The arrangements evolved after the war." Marcus's voice carries the weight of forbidden knowledge. "Some regions found it more... efficient to maintain a stable food source."

"And the ones who don't survive?"

"Become case files. Like the ones you're investigating." Marcus studies him with eyes that have seen too much. "But you're not here about feeding records, are you?"

Kody hesitates but finally breathes. "Do you know much about the Turig strain?"

The question hangs in the air like smoke. Marcus's eyes narrow, fingers stilling on the papers. "Died out around the same time as the war." He pauses. "Officially, at least."

"Officially?"

"Records are scarce. But it's said the Turig strain was different. More volatile." Marcus glances at the door before continuing. "Their soulless drive... exposure to the strain... it changed things. Changed people. Even when they didn't mean to."

"Changed how?"

"Some say they could turn almost anyone. That their blood carried something older, more potent." Marcus closes the ledger with deliberate care. "But those are just stories now, aren't they?"

The question carries weight Kody chooses to ignore. "And the ones who survived? The stories about them?"

"Careful, boy." Marcus's voice drops lower. "Some questions are better left unasked. Especially about that strain."

Thunder rolls outside, and for a moment, Kody swears he sees fear in the old man's eyes.

BLOOD QUOTAS. TERRITORIAL arrangements. Protected feeding grounds. And now gleanings and Turigs. Hours spent poring over reports in his safehouse, and still the pattern grows more disturbing. Crouched in the shadows now, Kody reviews it all in his mind, connecting pieces while he waits.

This morning's report weighs heaviest—another redhead taken from the western quarter. Not a criminal, not a tribute, just someone in the wrong place when the quota wasn't met.

Like the others, no body found. Unlike the others, this one fought back. Left traces.

Elena's words from the last guild meeting echo as he settles deeper into his hiding spot: "They're not just feeding. They're collecting."

Three years of tracking disappearances, and the pattern spans out in his memory like the map on his safehouse wall. Red markers spiraling outward from Zurich—missing persons. Black markers showing confirmed Noctis kills— mostly in districts that failed to meet their quotas. The blue ones... those are the ones that keep him awake at night. The ones who vanished completely.

Movement ahead snaps him from his thoughts. Right on schedule.

The shadows peel back as the Noctis emerges—its movement smooth, boneless, like a thing that had to relearn walking in a human skin, unaware it's being tracked. Three nights Kody's followed this one, watching it meet with others, exchange information. Tonight feels different though. There's an urgency to its movements.

He follows at a distance, using the techniques that have kept him alive these past years. Vervain oil masks his scent. Soft-soled boots silence his steps.

He trails it through tight alley bends, the smell of wet stone and rot lingering heavily. Then, voices.

"...the Bailey girl."

The words slide through the darkness like a knife. Kody freezes mid-step, blade hovering at his belt.

"The Mistress grows impatient," the first voice adds— rasping, eager.

A second, deeper voice answers, more composed.

"She's proven difficult to track. The guild trained her well. But word travels—she's been asking the wrong questions in the wrong places."

Kody's heart kicks against his ribs.

Cassia...

"Her scent was traced to the southern territories."

The first one lets out a dry chuckle. "Mistress believes she's searching for her family."

"The parents?"

"Still under the arrangement. Loyal. Bound. But the girl…" A pause. A cruel grin in the voice. "She may be more valuable than they were. The Mistress wants her alive."

Kody's jaw tightens.

"As a tribute?"

"As a bound one. The Mistress wants her for herself."

The silence that follows is too heavy.

"And if she resists?"

The voice that responds now is colder. "She'll learn the cost. We've made examples before. The quota ensures we never run out of reminders."

A murmur ripples between them—low, reverent.

"The Mistress feeds. The Mistress binds. She will not be denied."

Kody's hand clenches around the hilt, blood rushing in his ears. But then the tone shifts—unease threading through the dark like smoke.

"We need to keep a lower profile. The Umbrals are getting nervous."

"They're weak. New to the way of life. But—"

The second voice lowers. "The Tenebris stirs."

Even from a distance, the name shifts the air. A pressure, a presence.

"Fairy tales," the first mutters, though his voice is tight. "The Elders use him to frighten the Umbrals and tributes."

"You say that, but tell it to the ones who vanished. The ones who thought the dark was empty—until it wasn't."

A hush, then—

"And Vesper?"

That name lands heavier than the rest. Kody flinches.

"Not yet. But once he hears it's a Bailey…" A knowing pause. "He'll come."

The two Noctis nod to one another, initiating their meeting's end, and move apart. One slinks down the alley. The other veers south.

Kody doesn't hesitate and follows the one heading south—that's the one. Cassia's name rings too clearly now. They don't want her dead. They want her claimed. And worse, they think they already have a right to her blood.

He's moving before thought can catch up—silent, fast, hunting. His training tells him to report back, to alert the guild. But this isn't just about duty anymore. It's personal.

Let the one whispering stories of Tenebris vanish into the dark. Let the guild sort out that shadow.

Cassia is being hunted. Just like Sarah was. Only this time, he won't be too late.

19 - Cassia

The rain hammers against my hood, the familiar companion after countless nights like this drowning out even my own thoughts. A chill crawls down the back of my neck, refusing to leave. Through the tavern's grime-streaked window, lamplight bleeds across the slick cobblestones—faint warmth behind glass, indifferent to the cold world outside.

Three years now chasing whispers about the Baileys has taught me to recognize a pattern—where there's drink, there are loose tongues, and right now… I need both.

I slip inside, shrugging off the rain while scanning the room. The tavern's layout mirrors a dozen others I've haunted since leaving the compound—worn wooden tables scattered across uneven floorboards, a bar built more for function than beauty, and the usual mix of locals and travelers hunched over their drinks. My training kicks in automatically now: identifying exits, noting potential threats, searching for faces that might mean trouble.

Mr. A would be proud if he could see how his lessons have become instinct.

Finding an empty corner table, I settle in where I can watch the room while keeping my back to the wall. The position gives me a clear view of two men whose voices rise above the general hum of conversation.

"You're bloomin' crazy!" The taller one slams his tankard down, sloshing dark ale onto the already sticky table. "There's no way that's true."

"You think I'm lying? I ain't got no reasons to lie!"

A waitress approaches my table, her automatic smile

doing little to hide her exhaustion. She balances a plate in one hand while her hip cocks out, glancing over her shoulder at the arguing men. "Ignore them. They're in here every few days talking about old fables." The plate lands in front of me with a dull thud.

"Old fables?" I keep my voice casual, the way I've learned over years of gathering information. Sometimes the smallest comments yield the biggest leads.

She rolls her eyes, clearly used to curiosity about the local drunks. "Just some dumb legend about one of the elite group selling a trinket to a pawn shop. They say it belonged to the family of the man who created the Noctis." She shakes her head. "But I'm doubtful. All of that happened at the military base a few days' trip from here. Why would something that valuable end up in a local pawn shop?"

My heart quickens, but I've had too many false leads to let excitement fully settle in. Instead, I offer a small smile. "Seems unlikely."

"Mhmm." The waitress studies me longer than necessary, her head tilting slightly. "You look familiar somehow. Something about your eyes..." She shakes her head. "Never mind. Just tired, I suppose." But I notice how her gaze lingers, the same way people used to look at my father in the old photos—like they're seeing something they can't quite place, something important.

"Enjoy your meal." As she walks away, I study my plate—a meat pie with a breaded crust, brown gravy staining the edges where steam escapes through a cross-shaped vent. The sight reminds me of compound meals, though this looks more appetizing than anything Janice ever served us. Three years of actually fending for myself has given me a new appreciation for even mediocre cooking.

By the time I'm halfway through my meal, my mind has wandered, conversations around me fading to background noise. My attention snaps back when the tavern's normal hum shifts.

The tavern door groans open, and the man who steps through seems to drain the warmth from the air around him. Cloaked in black, face shadowed beneath a hood, he moves with a predator's certainty—the kind that makes instincts tighten and blood run colder.

Three years ago, I might have dismissed him as just

another traveler. Now, I know better.

The man approaches the bar where the two locals I'd been watching sit. His movements are smooth and precise.

He says something to the men that I can't hear, but their reaction is immediate. They burst into laughter, throwing insults with drunken bravado.

"What do you think you are, some kind of hero, dressed like that?" the larger one sneers.

"Better be careful, people might think you're a time traveler from the past!" His companion slaps the bar, pleased with his own wit.

I look back to my plate, trying to appear disinterested. But when I lift my fork, a chill races down my spine, raising goosebumps across my skin. The conversation at the bar has shifted.

The drunken laughter falters like a record skipping.

"No one said a damn word about the Baileys!" one of them snaps, too fast and loud.

The name clings to the air, silencing half the tavern. Even the barkeep's rhythm slows, like the walls themselves started listening.

My head snaps up and the tavern seems to contract around me—smoke-blackened beams hanging lower, amber lanterns casting longer shadows. The regulars at their carved tables grow quieter, while the barkeep's mechanical polishing slows to a watchful stillness.

"That stuff's all just nonsense anyway," the other man mutters, voice pitched too high.

The stranger grabs both men by their collars in one fluid motion, pulling them close. Whatever he whispers makes the blood drain from their faces. He shoves them backward, they stumble, nearly falling, and he turns away. The moment his back is to them, their fear transforms to nervous laughter, a show of bravado that doesn't reach their eyes.

I finish my meal quickly, watching as the stranger exits and the men drain their drinks with shaking hands. Something about their reaction, about the name "Bailey" being thrown around—I need to know more.

When they finally leave, I follow at a distance. The alley is dimly lit, just bright enough to navigate without tripping—though the drunker of the two still manages to stumble through puddles from the earlier storm. I move silently behind them, years of tracking making my footsteps light even on wet cobblestones.

"Ahh, shit, I forgot my ring at the bar," the larger man groans, patting his pockets. His ruddy cheeks gleam with sweat despite the cool night. "Margie'll kill me if I lose it again."

His companion—wiry, with a distinctive limp and shock of graying red hair—leans closer, something sharp and calculating in his eyes that makes me think he's the more dangerous of the pair.

I step from the shadows then, letting my boots splash loudly enough to announce my presence.

The tall one spins, loses his balance, and crashes into a stack of crates. His friend's laughter booms through the narrow alley. "You're scared of a girl!"

"He should be scared," I say, drawing my knife in one smooth motion. The blade catches what little light filters into the alley. "I need to know where that pawn shop is located."

"Y-you what?" The shorter one's laughter dies, a stutter replacing his confidence. "It's just a s-story."

"Maybe. Or maybe it's exactly what I'm looking for." I flick the knife into view—clean, cold, hungry-looking. "Last chance," I say, stepping into the half-light. "Point me to the shop, or I start carving answers."

"The damned box would be worthless! It's cursed." The fallen man scrambles backward, words slurring through a lisp. "Nothing of value at all!"

"I'll decide what has value to me." Another step forward, the knife catching the moonlight. "Where is the shop?"

"F-Farr Street!" The short one stammers, all pretense of bravery gone.

I pocket the blade with practiced ease. "That wasn't so hard, was it? Thank you, boys."

I leave them shaking in the alley, puddles rippling with their breath. The start of another rainstorm masks their curses as I disappear into shadow, the map to Farr Street burning itself into my thoughts.

Doesn't matter if it's cursed. It could open the gates of hell itself.
If it can tell me what happened to them… I'll step off the edge and let the darkness swallow me whole.

20 - Cassia

I stand before the pawn shop's weathered facade, rainwater dripping from my hood as I study the darkened windows. Something about the place feels wrong. The streetlamp's glow dies a foot from the door, as if the building devours light—even the shadows here feel heavier, deliberate.

The door handle turns under my grip, and my stomach tightens. Three years of searching, and I've learned that anything coming too easily usually means trouble. Still, I slip inside, careful to ease the door closed without a sound.

The shop's silence presses against my ears. Moonlight filters through the grimy windows, catching on brass and silver, creating patterns of light and shadow that seem to shift when I'm not looking directly at them.

Behind the glass counter, tarnished jewelry gleams like rotting teeth in a corpse's grin, glinting with mockery rather than value. The air is thick with dust, anticipation, and a prickle of fear.

Taking a tentative step forward, I scan the shelves packed with relics of the old world. A porcelain doll with a cracked face stares at me accusingly. Next to it, a tarnished pocket watch ticks arhythmically, marking time in uneven beats. Behind the counter, metal bars guard cabinet shelves built into the wall, their shadows striping the floor like prison bars.

The floorboard creaks behind me.

I freeze, my heart suddenly loud in my ears. No light had changed, no shadow had moved to warn me. My fingers find the knife at my belt as I strain to listen past the blood rushing in my ears. Nothing—just the watch's broken timing and my own careful breathing.

Slowly, I ease into the shadows, turning to face the sound's source. The hallway at the far end of the room gapes like an open mouth, leading to what looks like a bathroom and storage room. Drawing my knife, I approach the storage room door. The blade trembles slightly as I use it to push the door wider, positioning myself to peer through the widening crack.

Darkness floods out, broken only by weak reflections off metal surfaces. A prickle of instinct crawls up my spine—not from the cold, but the primal certainty that something in the dark is breathing with me. Closing my eyes, I wait for them to adjust to the darkness, listening to rats scurrying in the corners—or, what I hope are rats.

Finding a candlestick, I light it with hands steadier than I feel, using my body to shield most of the light. The flame throws more shadows than illumination, making the stacked boxes seem to lean inward, creating corners where anything could hide.

That's when I see it—the music box, perched on the highest shelf like it's waiting for me. The candlelight glints softly off the box's green surface, its finish worn but carefully preserved. Porcelain cassia flowers drape over the corners—delicate, hand-formed petals still intact despite age. It doesn't feel cursed or powerful. Just... personal. Like something meant to be held by someone who would know how to open it. It pulls at me, even as every instinct screams that this box sitting here in front of me is too perfect… too easy.

But I can't stop myself from standing on my tiptoes to reach for it. My fingers brush the cool surface, and a shiver of anticipation runs down my spine. Setting it beside the candle, I study the intricate design—white porcelain decorated with green leaves, bronze accents at the corners matching the tarnished latch.

As I reach for the latch, the air changes. The candle flame wavers, though there's no draft. The hair on my arms stands up, and my stomach drops as though I've missed a step in the dark. Without conscious thought, my body moves, spinning as I draw my knife and throw it in one fluid motion.

A tall hooded figure dodges my strike. In the split second my eyes track the knife stuck in the wall, he closes the distance. His hand clamps down—cold, clawed, inhuman—and bone grinds in my wrist as he wrenches it behind me. His breath hits my skin like the first wind of winter through a graveyard.

I test his hold, sliding my hips to the side, pushing upward and slipping underneath until we're face to face. My free hand finds another knife at my belt, but he anticipates the move, stepping back just as I sweep. In the same moment, my foot slides out and I hit the floor hard, gasping for air.

Pristine boots approach, and I barely get my leg up to defend. He deflects the kick, using my momentum to roll me aside. I complete the rotation, plant my palms, and push up to sprint for the door. Yanking my knife from the wall, I stumble around the corner and duck behind a display of antique metal trinkets.

I hold my breath, anticipating footsteps.

The box—I left it behind.

Peering around the corner, I watch him stalk through the room. I take three breaths to steady myself, then ram my shoulder into the display.

The tower crashes into him, buying precious seconds. I dash back to grab the box from the counter and secure it in my hip pouch.

He's not after the box—he's after me. But why?

I slip behind the open door, pressing into shadows as he enters. One step forward, knife ready—

He whirls and catches my wrist, twisting until the blade clatters to the floor. His forearm slams me back, pinning my shoulder to the wall as he goose-necks my arm. In one savage motion, he drives my own blade through the meat of my shoulder—muscle tearing from bone with a wet, wrenching rip. The pain isn't sharp—it's a white-hot, blinding roar behind my eyes. Hot blood spills down my arm, soaking into my sleeve in warm pulses. I bite down hard, trapping the scream in my throat.

"What do you want?" I growl.

Without a word, the figure leans closer and rubs their nose along my neck, inhaling so deeply I can hear it.

I stifle a gag and bring my knee up to gain some distance between us. My hope falls when it is ineffective and I'm pinned down harder. There's a tingle on my thigh where he prevented me from my maneuver. My eyes adjust to the dark as I stare at the line of light shining on his face from the crack in the door. Silver eyes hold a cold lifeless feel against his pale skin. His lips part and his teeth catch his lower lip, pulling it in slightly while he breathes in deeply.

My heart jumps as his lips part in a predatory smile. In the dim light, I catch glimpses of elongated canines, deadly sharp and unmistakably inhuman. They're not the crude fangs from old stories—these are elegant, translucent daggers, barely visible until they catch the light just so.

So this is what haunts the alleys. What the survivors won't speak of. The myth in flesh. And it has my blood on its breath. Three years in this god forsaken city and I haven't seen one until now?

"Who are you?" I ask, not expecting an answer. Uncertain if he can even speak.

"The more intriguing question would be why your smell is so intoxicating in comparison to others nearby." His voice comes out in a smooth, sickening, hiss like fashion. "What's your name, girl?"

"My name?"

"Are you hard of hearing?"

"What's it matter to you of my name or my hearing?"

"I don't enjoy games, almost as much as I don't enjoy displeasing my master."

"Your master? So you're someone else's bitch. That explains your lack of ability to kill me."

"You reek of promise," he hisses, tongue flicking at the air. "Like you were grown for her altar. The name, girl. Give it to me so I can carve it into my memory."

I jerk against his hold, biting back a cry as my wound flares. Gathering what little saliva I have left, I spit in his face.

His lips part in a smile, sending a shiver down my spine. "Though, nearly alive is still alive." He presses his body against mine and moves his head to the side of mine. "Maybe by the time we get back you'll enjoy the whole process." He presses closer, breath ghosting my neck. My heart races. My eyes darting around for anything that could help me. "That's it. The adrenaline is delightful. But don't worry, it won't be enough for you to join us."

I brace for the bite with eyes wide and every muscle locked, when another dark figure crashes into the Noctis from behind with a force that sends both of them sprawling. The monster releases me with a growl, its claws slashing my skin open as it's yanked away.

I crumple, sliding down the wall, smeared blood leaving a slick trail above me. My shoulder screams, the blade still buried in my flesh sending blood soaking through the fabric of my jacket. My sleeve clings to my arm and everything I touch stains red. The world tilts and blurs as shock claws at the edges of my vision, trying to pull me under.

Through the haze, I watch them fight—the figure and the Noctis locked in savage combat, moving faster than anything human. Blows land with brutality, bone and muscle breaking beneath inhuman force. I hear the crack of ribs, the crunch of impact against stone.

Then a hollow thud.

The Noctis's severed head rolls across the floor like a grotesque offering. Its silver eyes stare blankly into the dark, no longer seeing. The body slumps a moment later, twitching before going still.

The figure that killed it turns toward me.

Panic takes over and I force myself upright, gasping through clenched teeth. My legs tremble beneath me, blood leaking freely from my shoulder, streaking wherever I touch to steady myself. Each breath is fire. Each heartbeat a hammer in my ears. I stagger toward the exit, one hand clutching the wound, the other dragging my weight.

Survival instinct flares the moment I hear movement closing in behind me.

In a final, desperate maneuver, I whirl on the dark figure rounding the corner from the storage room. My vision doubles and my body lurches. I throw a punch that doesn't connect, but I manage to drive my knee upward into his gut. He barely reacts.

I reach for the nearest object, something cold and heavy, and smash it against his head. He flinches but recovers fast, grabbing my arms in a vice grip.

We struggle, bodies crashing into shelves and displays, sending trinkets flying. I slip, my boot catching on broken wood, and we crash together through the glass jewelry counter. The impact steals the breath from my lungs as glass explodes around us—shards slicing into my side, my hands, and my already shredded shoulder. The pain blinds me, tearing through already raw nerves.

But I don't stop. I can't. I have to survive.

Fingers slick with blood, I grab a jagged shard, ignoring the sting as it carves deep into my palm. I drive it through a gap in his leather armor, slicing skin. He hisses and twists, but I use my knee to pin him, pressing the shard to his throat.

"Why are you following me?" I snarl, the words trembling with exhaustion, pain… fury. I try to sound dangerous, but I'm broken—drenched in blood and barely conscious.

Then in one effortless motion, he flips our positions, hands gripping my thigh and shoulder, pinning me down in the wreckage. Glass grinds beneath us. My blood paints his gloves. The world narrows to the sting of glass and the roar of my pulse in my ears.

Shards dig into my back, into my shoulders, into the raw, open wound pulsing like fire down my arm. I can't move. I can barely breathe.

His weight pins me down, breath hot against my throat. I twist, instinct taking over, but my limbs won't respond the way they should. Every nerve screams.

I claw for anything—leverage, a weapon, a way out. My fingers close around glass, my palm slicing open further, but still, I fight.

"You need more practice, Cassia."

The voice doesn't belong in this hell. Low, steady, impossible. It cuts through the static like a light in darkness. Calm, measured… familiar.

My heart stutters violently and I blink once—twice. The blur sharpens just enough to catch the shape of his jaw, the slope of his cheek, the furrowed brow I memorized long before I ever admitted I had.

And then his eyes—guilt, exhaustion, but beneath it all, burning with fierce resolve. A fire that doesn't flicker or waver.

Mr. Akers.

The name lands in my chest like a punch. For a second, the pain fades beneath the flood of recognition. I'm still bleeding. Still on my back in a pile of glass. But the chaos recedes. Just enough. My breath trembles through my teeth.

He's real. And he's here—the person I'd trusted to teach me how to survive, now dragging me out of the fire by force.

21 - Cassia

"**M**r. A?" The words claw out of my throat, dry and cracking, almost drowned by the blood thudding in my ears. My vision tunnels. Every breath tastes like copper and rust.

I don't know if he's real or if my brain, starved of oxygen and reeling from pain, has conjured a ghost.

The room warps around the edges—then a memory from my first year alone punches through, unbidden and sharp.

The scent of blood. The feel of broken wood beneath me.

The man's coat had been too fine for the tavern, his voice too polished when he said he had information about my parents. The paper he slid across the table reeked of setup, but I still reached for it. When I said the Bailey name, his smile dropped—replaced by a hunger I'd only ever seen in Noctis eyes.

I fought dirty. Not with form or strategy, but the flailing desperation of someone who knew no one was coming to help. I remember the blow to my jaw, the crunch of bone against bone. The table saved me more than technique, tripping him when I twisted away. Kody's voice rang in my memory afterward: "Simple beats flashy. Survive first. Ask questions later."

I did survive. And every fight after that carved the basics into muscle memory until they became second nature. Instinct.

I blink—and it's now again.

Kody is standing over me. Real. Solid… And I'm

bleeding all over him. I can't tell if the universe is laughing or showing mercy.

"So formal." His voice anchors me. That same steady tone I remember—lower now, edged with exhaustion and a cocky smirk. "It's Kody, when I'm not training."

He steps in close, shadow blotting out the last remnants of light. His fingers press against the inside of my elbow, checking for a pulse, or strength, or whatever proves I'm not halfway gone yet. My arm jerks at the touch, a flinch I can't stop.

Blood coats my hands, sticky and hot from the shard I'd gripped too tightly. It trails down my arm, soaking my sleeve. My shoulder throbs with each heartbeat—deep, gnawing pulses that feel like the bone itself is echoing the damage. My shirt clings to my ribs, heavy with wetness.

"What the hell are you doing here?" I rasp, the words scraping their way out like glass on stone.

He doesn't answer right away. Just studies the shadows, peeling me off the floor like I weigh nothing. His movements are all control and readiness—like he's braced for another fight.

"Let's get you patched up." he says finally.

"I'm fine." The lie collapses along with my leg. The adrenaline drains all at once, and the pain floods in—bright and blinding.

He catches me easily, an arm around my back, pulling me in like a shield from the broken world. "You're not," he mutters, jaw tight. "And unless you want me carrying your half-dead ass out of here, you need to move. I still have a head to collect."

I try to laugh, but it comes out wet. Something trickles down my throat—thick and metallic. Blood or bile.

The smell of leather, steel, and vervain oil clings to him like smoke. My shoulder pulses like it's being hollowed out from the inside. My thigh lights up, fire racing to my hip. Every inch of me hurts. Every surface I touch turns red. I even leave a streak across his jacket.

"Still dramatic," I manage, the words barely more than breath—teeth clenching against the pain. I sag against him, vision blurring, ribs grinding with every breath, and every muscle trembling with effort I don't have left.

By the time the pain recedes enough to think clearly, we're somewhere quiet. Safe—presumably.

The library's floor-to-ceiling shelves rise like dark sentinels around me, filled with spines I can't focus on. My leg stretches stiffly across worn black leather, every movement pulling at torn muscle. The air smells of mint and eucalyptus—sharp, clean, and purposeful. Masking scents, hiding blood. The rest of it is dust, paper, and ink soaked too deep into parchment to ever leave.

Like that night in the archives... when fear clung thicker than dust.

"The Bailey estate?" The archive librarians wire-rimmed glasses caught lamplight. "Sealed since the incident."

She never looked me in the eye. Just turned and walked away.

But her fear stayed.

Even now, it lingers—settling into the corners of this room like smoke.

Now, nearly two years later, I finally understand what she was afraid of.

A hiss escapes through clenched teeth as Kody tightens a wrap around my freshly stitched thigh.

I'd nearly forgotten the injury there—shock and the ripping in my shoulder eclipsed everything else. But now, even after the salve, the pain resurfaces under the bandage pressure like a serrated blade raking through bruised muscle.

"Sorry."

"I'm fine." I eye the needle he prepares for my shoulder, tension tightening my spine. The shoulder stitching worries me more than I'll admit. It's not the needle... It's the sensation I know will come with every tug of thread

"Mhmm... Clearly."

I try not to stare at the thread as he lines it up. Try not to notice the way the needle gleams in the low candlelight. "You're really going in with those glasses still on?"

"They help." He threads the needle with ease, throwing me a look over the double magnifying glasses that makes me feel like his student again. Like I was still the girl who finished last on drills, and always caught his eye anyway.

"You look like a dissecting owl."

His mouth twitches, but he doesn't rise to it. "Ready?"

I nod and he settles his palm against my good shoulder, forearm braced lightly across my chest—not enough to pin, just enough to steady.

I don't realize I've tensed until I feel the tremble in my own breath.

"You'll want to be lying down for this," he says, motioning to the couch cushions beneath me. I ease down under his direction, spine dragging against worn leather. He leans forward to retrieve a small glass container, twists off the lid, and scoops out a pale green gel. "Sorry," he says again.

"For wha—" The pain lances through me, sharp and immediate, when he presses it into my exposed muscle. My head snaps back, vision whitening at the edges—and just like that, I'm not here anymore.

I'm back in the north. Nine months after leaving the compound. My first real Noctis encounter.

I'd been following a half-buried lead in the northern territories—cheap lodging, sketchy inn, patrons too quiet.

I missed the signs Kody warned us about—the too-sweet scent over rotting air, the way people refused eye contact.

Until the innkeeper smiled and his pupils reflected the lantern light like a cat's.

The fight was fast and feral.

Every drilled lesson about controlling fear vanished in the blur of his strength.

"Such sweet panic," he whispered, lunging.

But Kody's voice cut through the chaos—not real, just remembered. "Don't hold your breath. Control what you can control."

Inhale four. Hold four. Exhale four.

My hands stilled enough to find my knife and when the Noctis charged, I remembered the final lesson: Noctis get cocky.

My blade met his throat. Not enough to kill, but enough to escape.

I jolt as the needle pierces skin. Heat flares across my

shoulder when the thread tugs through me. I grit my teeth, the burn white-hot, seeping down my back like spilled fire, all of it pooling at the base of my skull.

"I should've listened better… during your wound-care lectures."

Kody pauses mid-stitch. "You survived. That's what matters." Then, quieter: "Though I'm glad you remembered something I taught you."

"More than you know," I whisper, eyes fixed on the ceiling.

His fingers return, and the next sting cuts through the quiet again.

"Did you find your folks?" he asks without looking up.

"No." My palms grow clammy against the couch. "I've been looking for three years."

"Three? Feels like a decade. You sure you're not pushing thirty by now?"

"Try again," I mutter, ribs flaring with the effort of laughing.

He smirks. "Well, I was ancient then—twenty-four."

"Twenty-seven now. Practically decrepit—"A gasp cuts me off as the needle digs deeper.

"Sorry."

"Just finish." I clench my jaw and breathe through the sharp tug of skin and sinew being drawn closed. The room narrows to his breathing and the burning track of the thread.

He works in silence until the last suture is in place.

"So," he says, cleaning tools, "you never found them. That why you were at the antique shop?" He doesn't look at me when he says it. Just cleans, calmly, like we're not still knee-deep in my blood.

I nod slowly. "It was the only lead that didn't scream scam. I had to try."

"In the middle of the night?"

"I hoped fewer people would be watching."

"Did you find what you were looking for?"

I blink, exhaling slowly. "I hope so... Otherwise this sewing me up bullshit is for nothing."

A low hum answers me—noncommittal. He dabs the last of the blood from my shoulder, fingers firm but not rough.

"Mr. A—" I stop myself. "...Kody. Why were you there?"

He doesn't answer right away. Just busies himself with the

tools, hands moving slower now. "Tracking that Noctis. Got lucky he was distracted with you." His hands move to pack the remaining tools. The candlelight flickers across the lenses of his glasses. "Usually I'm the one needing stitches."

I stare up at the ceiling. My pulse's frantic tempo starting to fade. "Thank you."

He pauses. Just for a second. "I should've taken him out sooner." He avoids my eyes. "Didn't expect him to get to you before I did. Thought I had more time."

"You like to play patient when lives aren't at stake?"

"I study their habits," he says, tone clipped. "Quirks. Weak spots. It's how I stay alive." He doesn't look at me when he says it. "Doesn't always work." The chill in his voice lands colder than the salve.

"Noctis are nasty things," he says, voice gone quiet. "Best to lie low. Let the wound seal." He sets the last tool aside— careful, precise. The soft clink of metal on metal echoes louder than it should. A pause. Then, almost gently, "You're good to go, kiddo."

"Don't call me that. I'm almost twenty-two."

He chuckles, removing the glasses. "Didn't mean it like that."

I try to sit up, but my arms tremble under the effort—body protesting every movement. Pain flares sharp and immediate through my shoulder. I grit my teeth and breathe through it, but the whimper in my throat betrays me. Before I can fall, his arm is there. Steady. Solid.

He doesn't say anything—just eases me back, bracing with one hand as the other steadies my uninjured side. His palm is warm through the bandages. Controlled and clinical, but not cold.

"I've got it," I mutter, embarrassed.

He doesn't let go. "Save it," he says. "You're running on blood loss and bad luck."

I exhale, not quite a laugh. Not quite anything.

He watches me a moment longer, then scoots closer and lifts a candle, peering at my stitches. "Hold this." His eyes squint behind the glow as he reaches for another bottle.

"You always patch up ghosts from your past in the middle of stakeouts?"

He doesn't answer. Just unscrews the dark glass jar and dips his finger into a gel-like salve—thicker, more iridescent than the other one.

"Little sting." He reaches for my shoulder.

I brace, but this one soothes more than it burns.

His eyes lock with mine as he works the salve into my skin, touch gentler than I expect.

It lingers a breath too long, and my pulse jumps.

He doesn't speak, but his fingers still for half a second—like he noticed, and the moment hit harder than expected. Then he clears his throat and keeps working.

I watch him with his intent eyes. "When did you realize it was me in the shop? Not just the owner?"

"When you pinned me with your knee. Shard to the throat. Your signature move." His smile is crooked and playful, as if recalling the memory.

"You made it effective as the only way to take you down during training," I mutter, heat crawling up my neck as I bite the inside of my lip. I glance toward the shelves again, their shapes softening into shadow behind the candlelight. "Kody... what do you know about my family?"

"Basic lineage. Why?"

"At the tavern... some men were talking about Calvin. Called him a fable. Said he created the Noctis."

His eyes narrow. "Cassia... history like that doesn't stay clean. He led the supersoldier project—but whether or not he meant for this?" He shakes his head. "There's no one left to say."

I stare at my fingertips, pushing back the quick on my thumbs. "Maybe I shouldn't keep looking."

"Why?"

"I've followed whispers and half-lies for years. Letters written in elegant script, always unsigned. Always showing up right when I was ready to quit. It's like someone's watching—but never showing themselves."

He takes my hand, softer now, thumb gliding a salve over fresh cuts. His gaze drops to my shoulder one last time.

"Don't let drunk bar talk sway you. That's not doubt, Cassia. That's fear talking."

I stare at him, throat thick, eyes fixed on his fingers running over my skin.

"I've felt so damn lost. But every time I'm ready to give up, something pulls me forward again."

"Then maybe you're not supposed to give up."

His thumb stills and I look up—eyes holding mine. A shiver runs up my arm.

"You'd hate to discover you were wrong—that they were waiting all along."

"You're right."

His words linger, but my focus drifts to the weight pressing against my hip. The box. I hadn't meant to reach for it—but somehow, my fingers are already loosening the knot.

I draw it out slowly, its surface still warm from being pressed against me. Porcelain flowers gleam faintly in the candlelight.

A folded slip of paper peeks between the seams. The same heavy cream stock. The same elegant hand—identical to the letters that have haunted me for three years. Each one arriving in time to pull me back from quitting.

The first letter found me in a rotting barn outside a nameless town. I'd curled up between hay bales, half-starved and dreaming of warmth, when a creak by the door pulled me half-awake.

By the time I scrambled up, the boy was gone.

The envelope was cream-colored, weighted like luxury. No return address. No demand for coin.

Just a single line in looping script: Your parents' legacy awaits. Proceed with open eyes.

I was young enough then to rush toward every lead. Young enough to trust. Until the night I met a "messenger" who knew too much about bloodlines and asked too many questions about traits I might have inherited. If not for my training—

Kody's voice pulls me back. "That what you picked up?"

I nod, fingers curled around the wood.

"Have you opened it?"

"No. I was about to... then the Noctis attacked. Said something about... lineage. His master..." I shiver. "Wanting me alive."

Kody's eyes haven't left the box. "Cassia... you need to leave the city."

I stare at him. "Excuse me?"

"Tonight changes everything. Word will spread. Fast.

You're not just a Bailey anymore—you're a visible one. And if that box is what I think it is..." He trails off, gaze narrowing like a blade honing to a point. "People will come for you. You need space to recover and train. To be ready."

I blink, heart stumbling. "Now you want me to run?"

"I'm telling you to prepare." He straightens and begins pacing behind the couch—controlled, but coiled. A man not just anticipating a storm, but bracing for it.

I let the box settle on my lap and stare at it. "You think this changes me?"

"That box—it *is* from your family. And it's said to contain the original strain of the virus... or its cure."

I stare at the lid, as if it might open on its own. "Why would anyone hide something that powerful in plain sight?"

"Because no one believes it exists. And anyone who does would kill for it."

I lift my eyes. "I'm not leaving until I find my family."

His expression darkens. "You're not ready for what's coming."

My jaw tightens. "What then? Give it to you? The guild?" I shove it toward him, harder than I mean to.

He doesn't flinch, just looks at it. Then at me. "No. It's your birthright. But I know somewhere you can lay low. We'll train you up."

"So, my grand legacy comes down to this?" I exhale. "Hide and wait? Hope no one finds me?"

"Until you're strong enough to fight back," he says quietly. "Word of a Bailey in the city won't stay quiet long."

My breath catches. The couch creaks beneath me. "And if I don't go?"

His voice is low, certain. "You won't make it through the week."

I hesitate, gnawing the inside of my cheek.

He kneels beside me—not looming, but grounded and places a hand on my good shoulder—light, but anchoring. "You don't have to trust me. Just trust that staying here makes you a target."

I search his face. "Why are you trying to help me?"

He doesn't look away this time. Doesn't pretend not to hear. "Because you finding that box... now?" His eyes flick to the lid, then back to mine. "Is the first time I've ever believed the old stories might be more than stories.

22 - Cassia

It took a lot of convincing, but eventually Kody got me to leave the city and hide out in his secret, crumbling estate in the country. It wasn't even his words that did it—it was a raw, compelling urgency in his eyes. Like he knew something I didn't. Like… maybe this was my last safe move.

I sit in the back of the carriage, rocking with each dip in the road, trying not to focus on the pain. The interior is lined with deep violet velvet, tufted in gold-threaded diamonds—luxury untouched by the world outside. The cushions, black suede, still hold the faint trace of mint and eucalyptus—Kody's careful preparations evident even here. But the scent calms nothing.

Outside, the countryside blurs past, and I miss all of it. My eyes are locked on the box in my lap, fingers tracing the delicate porcelain inlay on its lid.

"Nervous?" Kody's voice breaks the silence like a pebble in still water.

"There's not really anything to be nervous about." I glance up, offer a half-smile, trying not to notice how the morning light sharpens the amber in his eyes. "I am a little scared, though."

"Yeah?" The question barely rises above a whisper, but it carries more care than I know how to hold.

"I don't want to get complacent and abandon hope of finding them. Again." The words scrape out, bitter and hollow.

"I'm not gonna let that happen." His voice is low, firm. The kind of certainty that should irritate me—but doesn't. It settles in my chest like a promise I'm afraid to trust.

"Everyone I've ever known has bailed after a short time." I meet his gaze head-on. "Why would someone who barely knows me do any different?"

The carriage rocks, but he holds still—his eyes fixed on mine, intense enough to steal breath. He leans forward, elbows resting on his knees, until I can see the faint scar slicing just above his brow. "I can be sure of my own intentions. Even when you don't believe them to be pure."

I look away, back to the window, and sit with his statement.

Outside, the road ends at a towering iron gate, bars snarled with rose vines, thorns glinting in the pale light. Beyond it, mist hangs heavy, swallowing detail, but a dark outline looms through the haze—broad, waiting. A monument lost to ruin.

Kody opens the door. "We're on foot from here," he says, stepping down and offering his hand.

Pain lances up my leg as I follow him out, gritting my teeth against it.

The roadside grass is tall and brittle underfoot. The air is colder here, sharper—tinged with petrichor, rot, and something faintly metallic. The forest around us presses in, ancient trees groaning in the breeze like old sentinels. There's no birdsong, just wind, breath, and the distant creak of old wood.

I limp forward, refusing to favor the injury, and press my hands to the gate's bars. The metal bites into my palms, cold and rough. The road beyond curls downward, half-swallowed by brambles and wild overgrowth. Trees lean close over the path, their branches knotted like grasping hands. Nature has clawed its way back with purpose, as if trying to smother whatever waits ahead.

"Breathtaking, isn't it?" Kody's voice is quiet, almost reverent, but there's an unsaid tension in it.

"Yeah," I say, eyes still on the towers of the mansion.

He swings the suitcases up. "Door's this way. Hinges on this old bastard don't even work. Which is why we're hoofing it."

I glance back at the carriage, a thread of unease tightening through me. "Is the driver part of your guild?"

"He's loyal." His jaw ticks once, shifting a toothpick from one side to the other. "That's what counts."

I nod and fall into step beside him as we follow the outer wall. Every step drives a dull throb up my leg, sharp enough to jolt my shoulder wound until fire lances down my arm. The cold air bites at the raw edges under my coat, but I keep my face steady, forcing my stride even—though each breath grates like gravel in my chest.

Kody slows just enough to glance sideways. The look is brief, unreadable, but it burns hotter than the pain. I fix my eyes on the grass brushing my knees, willing him not to press, not to see the depth of my struggle.

The walk drags—thorns snagging at our coats, morning air raw against my skin. By the time he stops, sweat runs cold down my spine despite the chill. He pulls a heavy ring of keys from his coat, flipping through until he finds a brass one, and fits it into a small inset door carved into the stone wall. The lock groans with a harsh metallic screech that splits the quiet.

We both flinch.

Kody forces it open, waits for me to slip inside, and locks it again behind us.

Then we're standing face to face with the manor.

The estate rises from the treeline like something out of a half-remembered nightmare—sharp-spired and sorrow-worn, its silhouette jagged against the winter-dulled sky. Vines crawl across the upper towers, threading through fractured stone and weathered railings, and the far wings bear the worst of time's weight—collapsed roofs, shattered windows, blackened walls stained by decades of rain.

But the central structure still stands, solemn and whole— its great doors shut tight as if still guarding whatever legacy it once held. Its windows are dark, but intact. The slate roof weathered, but unbroken. A faint trail cuts through the overgrowth toward a smaller entrance tucked beneath a heavy archway, half-hidden by ivy and fog.

Kody steps beside me, silent. His shoulder brushes mine, just barely, but it's enough to anchor me when the weight of it all threatens to crush my breath.

"This is the place?" I murmur.

He nods once. "What's left of it."

And what's left… is still hauntingly beautiful. The stone is pale and veined like bone, the balcony above us held aloft by carved gargoyles whose faces have blurred with erosion. There's a wildness to it, like the forest has tried to reclaim the place and failed. It feels forgotten. Guarded… sacred.

"Stone this thick holds heat better than it looks. There's a cellar for wood. A hearth in every room that still stands. We'll need to seal the worst of the drafts, but it's solid." A pause. "Safer than anywhere else you'll find this far north."

A gust cuts through the trees, and I pull my coat tighter. I glance at him, and find his gaze already on me. His expression is unreadable—steady and familiar in a way that makes my chest ache.

I look away first.

There's something about this place, the way the wild tries to reclaim it and fails, that makes it feel like it shouldn't exist anymore. But it does. Still standing… waiting for resurrection or collapse.

My hand grazes the stone arch beside the doorway. It's cold and damp, but it anchors me.

"I don't know why," I murmur, "but it feels like once I step inside…" I trail off, uncertain.

I won't want to leave…

I huff a breath. Not quite a laugh, but close.

Kody doesn't press. He doesn't say anything at all.

I look up. His eyes catch the pale light, unreadable—but steady.

And when his hand brushes my elbow, just a touch, steady and grounding, I don't pull away. Then the truth settles sharp in my chest: I already belong here. To this fight… To him.

I already don't.

23 - Cassia

My chest heaves as I press against the cold stone wall, the chill seeping through my shirt and anchoring me in place. Every nerve is stretched thin, tuned to the smallest echo. Footfall breaks the silence—Kody's measured stride, steady and deliberate. Too deliberate, like he wants me to know he's coming.

I count the steps under my breath, lips barely moving, trying to quiet the thud of my pulse. When his shadow slides past the cracked door into the dark kitchen storage room, I force my body to move.

But I'm too slow.

He moves like smoke. No warning, no sound—spinning in a blur that catches my wrist mid-strike. A sharp twist, and pain flares through my arm as he traps it behind my back. I pitch forward with a cry, barely catching the scent of worn leather and sandalwood before my ribs smack the hard floor, knocking the air from my lungs.

"You're still too loud and too slow." He stands over me, voice dripping with quiet authority. He releases me, and I curl to my side, coughing for air, eyes watering. "I could hear your breathing echo off the walls," he adds, crouching beside me. "It gave you away."

"I kept the count you taught me," I grit out, clutching my ribs. The stone beneath me smells of old mildew and dust, sharp against my nose. "How else am I supposed to do it— hold my damn breath?"

He offers a hand. I hesitate, then take it, trying to ignore how the contact shoots straight to my spine like a live wire.

He pulls me to my feet and spins me around with a precision that feels almost inhuman. His palm presses against my stomach, firm but not unkind, and everything in me goes taut as the world narrows to that single point.

"Stop using your lungs," he murmurs against my ear, his breath warm where the cold still clings. "Breathe from here instead. Fill your belly. Deep. Slow. Quiet." Each word lands like a beat against my skin. "It keeps your heart rate down. Makes you harder to track."

I swallow hard, my pulse thudding traitorously in my neck. "It's been two weeks... When do you think I'll get full use of my leg back? Feels like that's half the problem."

"It is." He leans in to examine my shoulder, so close I can see the rough line of stubble across his jaw—sharpened by the dim light, like a shadow carved into his skin. His face is unreadable in the dark, but I can feel the heat of his breath, steady and calm. "That... and your shoulder."

"Shall we go again?" I ask, eyes fixed anywhere but his mouth.

"No."

"No?" The word catches in my throat.

"You need rest. You overdid it on that last go." He gently presses at the joint. Pain flares, blood welling beneath his touch. "You tore open."

"Damn it." I hiss through my teeth. "Again?"

"I told you not to push so hard. You don't listen." He stands, wiping his fingers on a cloth. "That one's on me too, though. I let you train before you were ready. Slowed your recovery." When he steps away, the absence of his touch is abrupt—a cold rush in the space he leaves behind. "Come on."

I fall in behind him, limping down the dim corridor, the ache in my leg pulsing in time with my pride.

The conservatory greets us with late-afternoon light slanting through the glass walls, casting long shadows across the worn wooden floor. Dust floats in golden ribbons. Outside, birds flirt with the wind, rustling the berry trees—their limbs tapping gently against the glass like fingers asking to be let in.

"Sit," he commands, disappearing behind the shelves to fetch the medical kit.

I ease onto the old leather sofa, worn at the seams, and

glance out the window. Beyond the glass, the world feels distant. Cold. Quiet.

"You know... if you have other obligations back in the city, I get it," I say, voice low. "You don't have to stay here to babysit me."

A dry chuckle filters through the air. "It's not like that."

"Then what is it like?"

"I left things in order before we came. Snow'll block the pass soon. Wouldn't be able to get back if I left now."

"So we're stuck?"

"It hasn't snowed yet," he says, returning with the kit. "But I planned to stay. I didn't want to risk leaving and not being able to come back."

"I can make it through a winter without you," I mutter, softer than I mean to. "I made it through my whole life before you. And three years after... so far."

But when he's close, the loneliness I've worn like armor doesn't feel so necessary. And that quiet where I used to feel nothing starts to feel like warmth instead. And that's dangerous.

He pauses, crouched in front of me, and the look he gives is too gentle for how hollow I feel. "I know. But I promised to help you defend yourself so you can find your family."

"So?"

"So I follow through." He presses gauze against my shoulder. I flinch, hissing through clenched teeth.

"Sorry," I murmur.

"It's alright." His fingers are steady. "You've had no one but yourself to depend on. I understand. But that doesn't mean you have to keep pushing people away."

"I'm not pushing. I just... don't want to be a burden."

"Burden requires obligation." His voice lowers. "I'm here by choice."

That stops me. Leaves me empty of argument.

"You okay?" he asks, right before the needle slips in.

I nod stiffly, jaw locked. "Yeah. Just... not used to others' kindness."

"Vulnerability isn't weakness, Cassia."

I look down at my hands, thumbs pressing hard against each other. "I don't think of it as weakness. Just... dangerous. It's gotten people I care about hurt."

His hand covers mine—warm, steady... real. "You're

safe."

My eyes drift to his lips.

Does he feel it, too? This fragile, crackling tension? Or is it all in my head?

He returns to stitching without comment, and my chest aches with the space between us.

"I feel safe," I say, quieter now. "Probably the safest I've ever felt."

He smiles—small, but it shifts the quiet weight he always carries. "Then I'll take that as progress."

"You're the only person I've told about this stuff."

"Do you remember your parents much?" he asks, standing to return the kit. "Before they sent you off? What were you—eleven?"

"Eight." I rest my chin on my good shoulder, watching him vanish through the conservatory doorway.

He's silent for a beat. Then: "Did that box have any answers for you?"

The porcelain box comes rushing back to mind, its secrets still locked tight.

"I… forgot all about it."

"Forgot? Nearly lose your life and you didn't even try?"

"So much happened so fast." I bite the inside of my cheek, ashamed of the real reason. Fear.

"Shock does that." He reappears, hands in his pockets as he examines my tells. "Might be something quiet you can do tonight. Keep from tearing anything else." He holds out a hand and I take it—letting go too fast after I stand. "In privacy or not, if you want."

"I'll get it," I say, easing into the ache in my legs.

Outside, the wind howls low through the trees, and a sharp scrape, maybe a branch,drags across the glass. It sends a warning chill up my spine as I limp into the dim hallway—the weight of the day pressing into each step.

24 - Cassia

The box sits on the table between us, green-stained wood inlaid with delicate porcelain cassia flowers—familiar, fragile things blooming in unnatural stillness.

My fingers tremble above the lid.

Could the rumors be true?

A cure for the Noctis virus—or a pure form of it?

And why would my family entrust this to me?

Are they even alive?

With shaking hands, I lift the lid.

Black velvet lines the interior, and the scent of cedar rises, warm and sweet like a memory preserved long ago. A roll of paper bound with twine rests beside a small brass key.

I glance at Kody. "A recipe related to Noctis, maybe?" I ask.

"The guild could be wrong. It might not be Noctis related at all." His gentle smile steadies the nerves threading through my chest.

The paper unfurls beneath my fingers:

Dearest Cassia,

If you're reading this, then the time has come for the truth to begin unfolding.

This box holds what remains of your birthright—a fragment of the Bailey legacy that must not fall into the wrong hands. What's inside is not just for you. It's a thread to something larger. Something buried.

Our family line is more than a name. It's a key—one many

would seek to turn for their own gain. You, Cassia, are part of that key.

We regret the years apart. What tore us from you was not a choice made lightly. The world has changed, and with it, so have we. But the path forward requires strength, clarity, and above all—willingness.

If you follow where this key leads, you will find us. But be warned: the journey may reveal truths you aren't ready for. Not everything is what it seems. Not everything you remember is the full story.

Where wisteria and cedar grow side by side,
With orange blooms and lemon trees,
A princess tower stands tall with pride,
Its secrets carried on the breeze.
Below, in chambers dark and cold,
Where ancient fires once burned bold,
A container waits for key of gold.

Find it, Cassia. Follow the thread. What awaits may test your heart, your history, even your sense of self. But it is yours to face.

Live boldly. Love if you can. And above all—do not fear the fire.

With all our love—
Mom & Dad

The words blur as tears well up and I blink hard, trying to force them back. My throat constricts around all the things I want to say, all the questions I've carried for years.

Without thinking, I reach into my pocket and pull out the worn scrap of paper I've kept in my since I was eight. The note I always believed came from Holli—slipped into my hand as she sent me away.

I flatten it beside the letter.

"May I?" Kody asks softly.

I nod, sliding both toward him.

He studies them under the flickering candlelight. "The handwriting looks almost identical," he says after a moment. "Same curl on the lowercase g. Same ink pressing harder on the downstrokes."

I stare down at the old note. There's no name at the

bottom. Just the words: *You are loved. Be strong. Stay hidden until the time is right.*

No "Mom and Dad." Just the message. For years, I thought it was from Holli. Now… I'm not sure what to think.

The key bites into my palm as I clench it, using the pain to keep myself from crying.

I can't break.

Not here.

…While he's watching.

Not when I'm too weak to stop the part of me that wants to lean into him instead of away.

"You okay?" Kody's voice is soft, threatening to crack the walls I'm desperately trying to hold together.

I nod quickly, not trusting my voice. The key grows slick in my sweating palm as I fight to steady my breath.

"They didn't... send me away to protect me," I whisper. The words feel foreign on my tongue. "At least, not like I thought. It almost sounds like they're... waiting—calling me back." I hesitate, throat tight. "But other parts... feels like a goodbye. Like they knew I'd find this and still chose not to come." My voice cracks on the last word, and I press my lips together, hating how exposed it makes me feel.

"Hey." Kody's hand covers mine—solid, steady. "People don't leave keys and cryptic notes unless they give a damn. However backward that looks."

A bitter laugh slips free. I pull my hand away, wiping my eyes under the pretense of tucking my hair back. "Maybe." I place the key on the table with a soft click, forcing steadiness into my shaking fingers. "It says the estate is gone—but this key still leads somewhere. But I don't know what they mean by 'birthright.'"

His brow furrows. "Gone? That can't be right. I was checking through old property records a few months back. Bailey holdings were still active."

"Maybe someone's using their name," I mutter. "Easier to steal a life than build one. Especially if no one's around to prove you wrong." My fist slams against the table, the wood thudding under my knuckles.

Kody doesn't flinch. "Hell of a theory." His eyes narrow, his jaw working. "You could be right."

"I should've waited. Should've opened that damn box

with a shot of whiskey."

Kody arches an eyebrow. "Not exactly the healthiest strategy."

"Health be damned if it makes the ache tolerable."

He doesn't argue. Just stands and crosses to a wooden cabinet. Glass clinks. When he comes back, he sets a bottle and two tumblers on the table with a soft thud.

"If you're going to spiral, might as well have company."

I nod, voice quieter now. "Thanks." Heat creeps up my neck as I slide the letter and key back into the box and close the lid. "I don't really feel like being alone."

25 - Cassia

Candlelight dances across amber liquid as Kody moves quietly around the room, lighting more candles. I curl into the worn leather sofa, cradling my whiskey against my chest. The coffee table's tree rings seem to paint stories from a world before ours shattered.

"What do you think your life would've looked like if the Noctis never existed?" I watch him settle into the opposite end of the sofa, his posture relaxed yet controlled. He drains his glass smoothly, immediately pouring another before leaning back, one arm draped casually along the back of the sofa.

"Different… Better. Less complicated, at the very least."

I swirl the amber liquid thoughtfully. "The note said to find happiness… love. Do you think either still exists in a world like this?"

He eyes me from across the space between us, thoughtful and quiet. "Humans always find ways to love. It's what keeps us alive. What makes us human."

"Maybe." I sip slowly, the heat sliding down my throat. "Have you… ever been in love?"

He chuckles softly, a sound edged with a weight I can't decipher. "Me?"

"What's funny?"

"Love is just a strange thing."

"Strange how?"

He pauses, turning the glass slowly between his fingers. "Sometimes it happens without you noticing. Other times it hits you like a storm."

"So... you *have* been in love?"

His eyes flick up to meet mine. "You haven't?"

Warmth floods my cheeks and I press my glass against my skin, seeking coolness. "Honestly? I don't think I'd even know if I had."

His mouth quirks in amusement. "What about that kid always shadowing you at the compound? Phillip or something?"

"Felix?"

"Yeah, him." Kody refills his glass, eyes glinting warmly in the candlelight. "You two weren't ever—"

I interrupt him with a scoff, eyes rolling. "If you consider being followed around by a hungry puppy love, then sure."

"No feelings at all, then?"

My pulse quickens as I meet his gaze, watching him swirl his whiskey. I tug anxiously at my sweater cuff. "None. I moved around so much as a kid, I never had the luxury to stop long enough for something real. Love always felt... impractical."

"Perfect word for it." His voice is quiet, almost wistful. "When you spend your life training fighters and hunting Noctis, making room for love sounds like a bad joke."

"So... this impractical joke… You never answered my question."

He hesitates, eyes distant, expression unreadable. "Maybe once or twice."

"Did you tell her?"

He laughs once, a quiet scoff, and shakes his head. "No."

"Why not? She probably would've wanted to know."

"Probably." He exhales slowly, staring at his glass. "But professionalism was always the priority—even when the person in question made it damn hard."

I arch a teasing eyebrow, warmth rising in my chest. "Made it hard, huh? You have a thing for difficult women?"

He smirks, eyes lifting slowly to mine. "I have a thing for women who keep life interesting. Though interesting in this world tends to mean complicated."

My chest tightens, his meaning not quite clear—but close enough to spark a thrill of uncertainty. "So… is sharing whiskey alone with your trainee considered professional?"

His gaze sharpens, smile turning dangerous. "Hardly."

"So you make it a habit of breaking professionalism

now?" I ask, emboldened by whiskey settling in and the candlelight softening everything.

His smirk deepens, eyes intense. "I'd say our situation is… unique. Wouldn't you agree?"

My eyes linger on him—taking in how the shadows soften his usually severe features, the broad sweep of his shoulders under the dark fabric of his shirt. My mind drifts, whiskey-warm and hazy, imagining what it'd be like to feel that warmth pressed against my skin.

"You haven't brought anyone else up here before, have you?" I ask softly, trying and failing to sound indifferent—like the answer doesn't matter more than it should.

"Never had reason to, 'til now."

My heart pounds, my pulse fluttering with intoxicated anticipation. Our legs are stretched out toward each other, feet almost touching in the middle of the couch. Without thinking, my toes brush lightly against his ankle, and an electric charge dances along my skin.

"Kody, I—" My voice falters, words vanishing before I can grasp them. I want to thank him, to acknowledge how much he's done, but my tongue is suddenly clumsy and useless.

He seems to guess anyway, a gentle half-smile curving his mouth. "Don't mention it."

Warmth spreads through me, fueled by drink and the quiet, elusive energy pulsing between us. Our feet remain close, the faint pressure of my toes still lingering at his ankle, waiting for him to respond. His eyes hold mine, unreadable yet warm in the low light, and after a heartbeat, his foot shifts gently against mine—an answer to a question neither of us voiced aloud.

Silence thickens around us, charged and fragile as glass. I set my empty cup down carefully, afraid the slightest sound might break whatever we've just created. Slowly, I draw my knees toward my chest, inching closer without fully realizing it. A few strands of hair slip forward, brushing my cheek, shimmering softly in the flickering light.

Kody leans forward, his gaze locked intently on mine. My breath catches as his fingers lightly skim my forehead, tucking the loose hair behind my ear. His touch lingers, warm and careful, and I search his face desperately for confirmation— proof that this feeling, this crackling tension, isn't just in my head.

"Cass…" His voice is soft, barely audible, heavy with restraint.

"Yeah?" I whisper, memorizing every detail—his warm touch, the flicker across his skin, the electricity hanging between us.

"We should get you to bed."

Disappointment knots my throat. I close my eyes briefly, and exhale, frustration simmering beneath my skin.

"That's not fair," he mutters.

My breath catches. "What isn't?"

"You—" He sighs quietly, jaw tightening as if he's holding back words he can't let out. "You're not allowed to look at me like that."

"Like what?" My voice comes out softer than intended, edged with hope and confusion.

He rises abruptly, breaking the delicate connection. "Come on," he says gruffly, extending a hand. "You need rest."

"I feel fine."

"I know." He holds my gaze, expression guarded but eyes heated, his offered hand steady. "Just… humor me."

Reluctantly, I place my palm in his, grimacing at the ache in my leg as I stand—flaring a sharp reminder of injuries still healing.

"See?" He steadies me gently, his hand lingering at the small of my back as I shift my weight. "A few more days of rest, then we'll assess your progress before we head out."

"Head out?" My heart sinks at the thought of leaving behind this fragile intimacy we've just started building.

"You want to find your family, don't you?"

"Yeah," I murmur. "But… I don't even know where to start looking." I bite back the words I truly want to say—the ones admitting I'd rather stay here, discovering how it feels to be held by him.

"I have some ideas." His voice is reassuringly confident, warm against the shadows of doubt creeping into my chest. "But we'll need to move soon, before the snow hits."

I lean into him slightly as we move toward my room, savoring the quiet strength of his presence, the warmth radiating through his palm against my back. By the time we reach the doorway, a sense of weariness settles heavily over me, mingling with frustration and longing.

Sitting on the edge of the bed, I stare at the floor, emotionally drained and physically exhausted. My mind spins with everything—every impulse I've carefully tucked away beneath layers of caution.

"You alright?" Kody pauses, his hands slipping into his pockets. His eyes search mine, expression guarded but hopeful, as if he expects, or perhaps fears, I might ask him for something more.

"Just tired," I say softly, unable to voice the yearning tightening my throat.

"Right." He hesitates, lingering just a moment longer before turning toward the door.

"Kody—"

He looks back, eyes dark and unreadable. "Yeah?"

"Thank you." My voice steadies, earnest rather than timid. "For everything—for choosing to stick this out with me."

His expression softens, tension melting into warmth. He nods slowly, the slightest smile touching his lips. "My pleasure."

The door closes quietly behind him, and I collapse back onto the bed, heart racing wildly in my chest. I stare at the ceiling, replaying the hushed timbre of his voice—*You're not allowed to look at me like that.* My skin remembers every faint touch, every fleeting glance, every careful hesitation.

Sleep feels impossible when all I can think of is the quiet, dangerous truth that lingers unspoken between us—a secret I'm terrified to forget by moving forward.

26 - Cassia

Morning light spills across the training room floor in golden rivers. I move through the forms Kody taught me, each motion deliberate despite my protesting shoulder. Pain is information, I remind myself, pushing through another sequence.

"Your stance is still off."

I turn to find him watching from the doorway, arms crossed. Sunlight catches in his dark hair, gilding the edges in gold. My heart skips—a reaction I immediately try to suppress, remembering his lessons about controlling my pulse.

On impulse, I toss my training dagger at him—just to see what he does.

His hand snaps out, catching it by the hilt before it can so much as graze him. No hesitation, no flinch—just pure instinct.

I blink. "You knew I was going to throw that."

Kody spins the dagger between his fingers and shrugs. "No. Just reflexes."

I narrow my eyes. "That was too fast."

"Your stance shifted. It was obvious."

Cassia frowns. "No one else notices those shifts."

"Then maybe they aren't paying attention," he says smoothly, but his eyes flick away—just for a moment.

I bite the inside of my cheek, assessing the avoidance. But before I can press him, he tosses the dagger back. "Try that in a real fight, and you'll be dead before you blink."

I huff out a breath, rolling the dagger between my fingers.

"Not if I see it coming first."

His lips twitch, like he wants to argue, but instead, his gaze flickers to my stance. Assessing. Calculating.

"The shoulder's still tender," I admit, rolling it experimentally.

"Because you're pushing it even though you should rest." He crosses the room, feet silent on ancient wood. "But you can use it." His hand settles at my waist, the heat of his palm burning through my shirt as he adjusts my position. "Pain can be a weapon if you know how to wield it."

His breath stirs the hair by my ear. I force my attention to the lesson, not the solid warmth of him behind me. "Show me." My voice remains steady, a small victory.

"A Noctis's first instinct is to find weakness." His chest presses against my back as he guides me through the movement. "When they come at you from the right," his hand slides up my arm, leaving electricity in its wake, "they'll expect you to favor your injury. Use that expectation."

I let him move me through the sequence, memorizing how each position can turn an opponent's assumptions into openings. His familiar scent wraps around me, making concentration increasingly difficult.

"Like this?" I twist, using my injured shoulder as a pivot point, feeling the pull of healing muscle.

"Better." His approval warms me more than it should. "But keep your guard up here." Fingers brush my neck, lingering just above my pulse. "Noctis always go for the throat. They can sense blood flow from yards away."

I was already aware of how close he was—the warmth, the pressure, the hum beneath my skin. But when I turn to face him, the air shifts. His eyes catch mine, and suddenly it's not just proximity—it's vulnerability. "Even through clothing?"

"Fabric doesn't mask life." His hand stays at my neck, thumb brushing the rapid beat beneath my skin. "They smell fear. Anticipation…" His voice lowers, rougher now. "Desire."

"Is that the reason for controlled breathing?" I meet his gaze, the look he gives me edged with heat and warning.

His smile is quiet but sharp. "Among other reasons." His thumb drags slowly across my pulse before he steps away, leaving heat in its absence. "Go again. Remember, their arrogance is your advantage. Let them walk straight into it."

I swallow hard, struggling to find my breath as he steps away. My skin still burns where his hand rested.

"Right. Again."

I plant my feet and try to focus, but his voice, his nearness—it all curls inside me like a match just waiting to be struck.

We train until sweat darkens my shirt and my muscles quiver with exertion. Each time he corrects my form, his touch lingers longer, his eyes hold mine deeper. I notice how he positions himself between me and the door—a protective instinct I'm not sure he's even aware of.

"You're getting stronger," he says, watching me flow through a particularly complex sequence. His tone carries quiet pride—but also judgement. "But you're still telegraphing here."

He steps in close and his hand finds my ribs—fingers firm as they guide my weight. "A Noctis will read this shift before you strike."

The heat of his touch seeps through fabric, and I hold perfectly still—afraid even a breath might break the charged stillness.

I clear my throat, trying to focus on his words instead of the press of his fingers. "How do I hide it?"

"Misdirection," he murmurs, stepping into my space with a slow, fluid shift. His body aligns with mine, one hand guiding my wrist while the other finds my waist, firm but careful. He stops with his lips close enough that I feel his breath at my neck. "Make them focus on what you want them to see... while you prepare the real strike."

My breath catches. "Like now?"

He stills behind me, the shift barely perceptible—but I feel it. His voice, when it comes, is low and rough at the edges. "Exactly like now."

When he finally steps back, the space between us chills. I exhale slowly, the moment still burning beneath my skin.

He tosses me a towel, dragging a hand through his hair. "That's enough for today. You're doing well with learning to use everything as an advantage."

"I have a good teacher." I wipe my face, eyes following the ritualistic way he gathers the training weapons—like it's the only thing keeping his hands busy.

"Kody—"

He looks up, expression unreadable.

"Thank you," I say softly. "For not treating me like I'm broken."

His hands still. "You're not broken, Cass." His gaze finds mine, and the weight in it steals my breath. "You're becoming exactly what you need to be."

He turns away—but not fast enough to hide the flicker I catch in his eyes. Pride… but also something else—something that makes my pulse spike in a way no Noctis would miss.

I press a hand to my shoulder, feeling the scar beneath the fabric. The pain's no longer sharp—just a hum, a memory. Not weakness, a mark I carry forward.

Everything's shifting. The way I move. The way I think. The way I feel when he looks at me like *that*.

Whatever's waiting out there… I'm starting to believe I can handle it. Because I'm not who I was when this started. Not anymore.

27 - Cassia

A cold droplet slides down my palm, tracing an icy path toward the tip of my pinky.

Blood...

My breath echoes harshly, the sound distorted as though passing through deep water, stretching out time into a nightmare I can't escape. An invisible grip crushes my chest, tightening with every frantic heartbeat. Slowly, numbly, sensation returns to my legs, pulling my gaze downward.

So much blood…

A dark, spreading pool seeps out from beneath my feet, dripping steadily from the soaked hem of my nightgown. Shadows press inward, swallowing the room inch by inch. From the darkness emerges a familiar shoe, a shape I recognize instantly yet desperately wish I didn't. My eyes climb upward slowly, unwillingly, taking in the grim details of a face I dread to see.

A suffocating ache claws viciously upward through my chest, crawling into my throat, strangling any sound that tries to escape. I open my mouth to scream, but silence chokes me, leaving me mute and desperate. Tears scorch my eyes, blurring my vision, threatening to spill as horror grips me tighter.

No… not him. You can't have him…

My breath shudders, caught painfully behind the rising wall of panic. Another flicker of movement across the room tears my attention away, dragging my eyes toward a small, motionless figure draped in white atop the bed. The scream trapped inside me rises again, pressing violently against my voice, aching to break free.

No… oh God, please, no…

"Holli!" The name rips from my throat as I lurch upright, breath ragged. My shirt clings to me, soaked in sweat. I rub my face, trying to shake the dream, but the blood's still there—just out of reach under my skin.

Why does this nightmare keep finding me?

It's been three restless nights since the couch—marked by whiskey and the moment Kody looked at me like he saw something he wasn't allowed to.

Each night since, I've woken gasping, heart thundering from dreams I can't outrun.

Lightning splits the sky, casting my too-large room in stark relief, throwing shadows into corners that seem to breathe. Sweat trickles down my temple, my mouth sticky with thirst. My leg aches dully as I push myself from bed—a steady reminder of slow healing since the injury and not listening to my mentor to take it easy.

The kitchen is dark, silent except for the storm and the rhythmic creak of the makeshift faucet pump filling my glass. I stare at the steady flow of water, lost in thought until another flash yanks me back. The dream feels familiar somehow, but I can't place it—almost like a memory trying to surface...

Holli's face flashes in my mind—followed by the ghosts of everything I've lost. The memory won't let go, clinging like the storm outside. Sleep feels like a lie, so I slip toward the conservatory, chasing calm I don't expect to find.

Thunder rattles the windows as I settle onto the leather sofa, wrapping myself in a blanket stolen from my bed. Lightning illuminates rows of books in sharp bursts, their spines creating strange patterns of shadow and light.

"Can't sleep?" Kody stands in the doorway, two steaming mugs in hand. The scent of herbs and honey drifts toward me as candlelight plays across his jaw. His hair is mussed from sleep, eyes still adjusting to wakefulness.

He must have heard my scream and waited until I calmed down... maybe he thought tea would help more than words.

"The storm reminds me of the night Holli sent me away." I accept a mug, letting its warmth ground me. "Though I guess that's not the only thing keeping me awake."

He claims the opposite end of the sofa, stretching his legs. His knee brushes mine before he shifts, both hands cradling his drink. "Want to talk about it?"

I sip the tea—chamomile with a sharper herb beneath. "Have you ever found something you were looking for…" I watch lightning fracture the sky, "and wished you hadn't?"

His fingers tighten around his mug. "Once. A truth I wasn't ready for."

I study him in the dim light. "What did you do?"

His eyes find mine, shadows flickering behind them. "I learned that ignorance isn't always bliss. But knowledge isn't always freedom either."

I huff a quiet laugh, bumping his leg lightly. "That's cryptic."

A slow smirk tugs at his lips. "Occupational hazard. You spend enough time hunting, you learn some truths are better discovered slowly… sometimes not at all."

"Is that why you became a hunter? To find truth?"

Lightning casts his face in stark relief. For a moment, he looks older, weighted by memories he doesn't voice.

"I had a sister," he says finally, voice quiet, staring at his drink. "Younger… disappeared during a Noctis raid when I was sixteen."

The air between us shifts and I sit straighter. "Did you ever find her?"

"No." He sets his mug down, fingers tracing the rim. "But I found others. Some alive. Some..." He exhales sharply. "That's when I learned there are worse things than not knowing."

An ache spreads through my chest at the tightness in his voice. I move closer until my blanket brushes his arm. "Is that why you're helping me? Because of your sister?"

"At first." His gaze locks onto mine, unreadable. The space between us shrinks, tension coiling tight. "Now... now it's more complicated."

My pulse quickens as I take in the color of his eyes.

The storm rages outside, but I barely hear it over the sound of my own heartbeat. The warmth of the library, the blend of chamomile and Kody's presence, the weight of his gaze—it drowns everything else out.

"Kody…" My voice barely carries over the rain.

His eyes flick to my lips, lingering, before his jaw tightens with restraint and he pushes off the sofa. "You should try to get some sleep." His voice is steady, controlled, but tension coils in his shoulders as he gathers the mugs. "We've got a lot of ground to cover tomorrow."

At the doorway, he hesitates, thunder filling the silence. "Cass?"

"Yeah?"

He looks back, a brief yearning passing over his face before it's hidden with neutrality. His voice softens. "Whatever we find at the estate... just remember you're not alone anymore."

The words settle over me like a second blanket, warmer than the one I'm wrapped in.

I stay there long after he's gone, my skin still tingling from his closeness, pulse thrumming with possibilities.

Sleep comes easier after that, despite the storm.

28 - Cassia

Kody folds the paper neatly, sliding it into his jacket pocket. His jaw ticks, just barely, and that's the only sign something's shifted.

We've been on the road for three days now, putting miles behind us in quiet stretches broken only by training drills and the occasional shared meal. I should be used to his silences by now, but this one feels different.

"You studied the maps more than I did," I say, shifting my weight. My thumbs hook under the straps of my backpack, bracing for direction.

"Had enough time between training sessions." His voice is even, but he doesn't quite meet my eyes. Instead, he steps past me toward the tavern, head tilted as he studies the weathered sign above the door. The paint is cracked and peeling, the old war slogans half-faded by time and rain.

He lingers longer than I'd expect. "Hungry?" he asks over his shoulder, voice neutral in a way that makes me study him more closely.

I hesitate. "We could grab something quick. Depends how long the next leg is."

He nods, but doesn't answer, already moving toward the door.

I follow, watching the way his shoulders shift—like he's bracing for something. Not danger, exactly. More like discomfort. Anticipation.

A gust of cool air follows us inside. The tavern glows with amber light from kerosene lamps mounted on rough wooden pillars. The scent of old smoke and damp timber clings to everything. Faint traces of old wartime slogans linger on the walls, painted directly onto the wood in flaking black script. Victory Through Strength stretches across a ceiling beam near the hearth, the letters cracked and faded with age—a ghost of propaganda from a war no one living remembers.

Kody heads straight for the bar. He doesn't glance around the room. Doesn't check the exits. Just… walks. Like he knows exactly who he's going to find.

The woman behind the bar looks up, her eyes lighting with familiarity. Chocolate-brown hair twisted into a messy bun—a slow smile spreads across her face.

"Kody Akers." Her hip cocks to one side as she flashes him a knowing smile. "Didn't expect to see you back this soon."

"Just couldn't stay away, Evie." He leans casually on the bar, forearms braced against the worn wood like he's done it a hundred times.

Color rises to her cheeks. "What can I do for you?"

His shoulders stiffen the moment I step up beside him. "My cousin and I are on a bit of a quest."

Cousin.

The word slices cleaner than any blade. I hold my expression steady, biting back the sting it leaves behind.

So that's what I am now. A cover story, easy to discard.

Evie's stance softens, her smile turning playful. "Oh, Kody, you always make work sound like some kind of storybook."

He grins, easy and practiced. "It is an adventure. Just hoping it leads to a happy ending."

"And who's gone missing?" she asks, her tone dipping into mock-concern.

"My parents," I say flatly, the words landing harder than I intend.

Kody steps in smoothly, before the moment can fracture further. "We're looking for an old church with a bell tower. My maps are out of date."

Evie tilts her head, sympathy curling at the corners of her mouth—but it doesn't quite reach her eyes. "Your parents wouldn't be living in that run-down garden, love."

"It's not a home," I bite out. "It's the next clue."

She flutters her lashes at him like I'm not even there.

I tighten my grip on the edge of the bar, nails digging into the wood. Just enough pressure to keep from saying something I'll regret.

Kody doesn't respond right away, but I catch the flicker of a glance—quick, sidelong, like he knows I'm bristling and wants to handle it. His voice shifts, a shade cooler. "Cass, I'll manage from here."

The conversation hums on, but I can't stand the way she keeps leaning in, like I'm not even standing beside him. My lungs start to tighten and I turn away under the pretense of scanning the tavern, letting my eyes drift to the grime-slick windows just to keep from glaring at her.

Outside, the street is just as scarred—blackened stone, a toppled statue near the corner, its base choked in scorch marks. Ghosts of another war, still lingering like smoke.

Cousin.

The word scrapes against my ribs, raw and splintered.

What, I'm not even worth claiming? Every look, every touch during training—was I just imagining it?

"Cass." His voice pulls me back.

Kody holds up a folded slip of paper. "Ready?"

Evie trails one finger along the bar. "Make time for a longer visit next time, Kody."

I shove past him without waiting for his reply, the air outside hitting colder than I remember from only five minutes ago.

"Right. West," he says behind me, like nothing's wrong.

"Great." I start walking fast, letting my pace speak for me.

"Cass!"

"Like I said, I'm in a hurry."

"*This* is west." His voice holds a flicker of amusement as he gestures the opposite direction.

I don't answer. Can't. If I open my mouth, I might scream. Or say something I can't take back. I just grit my teeth and pivot, following him in silence.

We walk side by side, the distance between us wider than it's felt in weeks. Every step lands louder than it should, every breath harder to control. I try to shake the tavern from my thoughts, but it lingers—her voice, his smile, that word.

Cousin. A convenient lie.

That's all I am. A way to avoid questions. A shield.

Maybe I was imagining it.

The heat behind my eyes builds, but I blink it back.

No way in hell I'm giving him the satisfaction of seeing me crack.

Kody walks a step ahead, scanning the rooftops like he's just focused on the mission. Good. Let him be the professional. I'll be the idiot trying not to choke on disappointment.

"You okay?" His voice breaks the silence as he falls back into step with me.

"Yup."

"Nervous?"

"Nope."

"We're walking fast. Is your leg—"

"Yes, Kody. God." My frustration slips out unintentionally. "What's with the interrogation?"

"You're not acting like yourself."

I bark a laugh. "Just trying to make sure you have time for that longer visit."

His laugh is low, amused. *Infuriating.* "Jealous?"

"No!" Too fast. Too loud. The word snaps out of me like a reflex I can't pull back.

"There it is." He points ahead, mercifully shifting focus just as the top of the bell tower rises into view above a curtain of ancient trees.

I don't know if he's talking about the tower or the way I just betrayed myself. But either way, I say nothing and keep walking.

The botanical gardens sprawl before us, a skeleton of pre-war grandeur overtaken by time. Crumbling stone benches bear the faded etchings of long-dead leaders, many faces defaced or scorched away. The wrought-iron gates, warped and blackened by fire, still cling to a rusted crest—a symbol of a world that no longer exists.

I pull out the riddle, forcing my focus to the page instead of the way Kody stands beside me, too close yet not close enough.

"Wisteria and cedar…" The words catch on my breath.

The paper crinkles under my grip as my fingers brush a faint smudge—his fingerprint. A mark from before the tavern. Before cousin.

I want to burn that word out of my memory. Instead, I

press it deeper into the back of my throat and pretend it doesn't taste like blood.

"It's isolated enough." His voice is low, professional. Like we're just any hunter and trainee. "Good place to start."

The gates groan as we push through. What was once magnificent now lies in elegant decay. Wisteria vines, thick as rope, coil around cedar trunks, strangling them in slow silence. Shadows stretch unnaturally across cracked walkways, and the air carries a faint, bitter trace of old smoke—like whatever burned here didn't happen long ago.

I pause, breathing it in. Not the war. Something more recent.

I stumble on a slab of broken stone, the edge biting at my boot. His hand catches my elbow before I can fall.

A spark flares at the contact—unwelcome and undeniable.

"Careful." His fingers linger, just long enough to remind me how much I hate that I notice.

"I'm fine." I shake him off, too aware of how my body leans toward him, even now, when I'm supposed to be furious.

"Just, watch your step," Kody says, stepping over a half-collapsed statue. "Looks like the place's been abandoned for a couple decades, maybe since the fire."

I nod, but my focus drifts—drawn not to Kody's words, but to the world crumbling around us. The scent of citrus rides beneath the heavier reek of rot. Fallen oranges and lemons litter the fractured path, their skins soft with decay, their brightness dulled by time. Each step squelches beneath my boots, treacherous and wet. Or maybe it's just me—unsteady, distracted, too aware of Kody moving behind me.

"The tower should be just ahead." His voice is too calm—like this is a routine stop, not a graveyard of clues about my parents. "Through that archway."

I push forward, forcing past overgrown vines. He tenses behind me when I slip out of his reach, but I don't slow. I need space to think. To breathe.

The tower looms ahead, rising through the trees like a memory refusing to die. Its stone base is weather-streaked but solid, ivy clawing up its sides. A tarnished plaque rests near the foundation, its inscription mostly worn away by time and rain—another forgotten monument left to fade.

I draw the folded riddle from my pocket and run a thumb

along its edge. "This has to be it." My voice barely carries over the wind. "The wisteria, the cedar, the tower... It all matches."

"Cassia." His voice cuts through the air, calm and familiar, meant to steady me. But all I can hear is Evie's invitation and the knot it left in my chest tightens.

"What?" It's sharper than I wanted, but I don't take it back.

He steps past me, deliberate in his distance, like he knows I'm too close to snapping. His fingers trace the weathered curve of a carved stone. "The design. Look at it."

I force myself to follow his motion. The pattern is crisp, the edges too fresh. This isn't a relic—it's a replica. A pit opens in my stomach.

Wrong century, wrong place... false hope. Again.

"There's no sign of recent activity," he murmurs, crouching beside the base of the tower. His tone shifts— composed. He brushes aside leaves, studying the overgrowth with experienced observation. "The vines are overgrown... probably haven't been touched in decades."

"This isn't the place." The words splinter as they leave me. I sink to my knees, stone biting through fabric, the cold seeping in as a wave of hollow frustration crashes through me.

Three years searching. And still nothing but echoes and dust.

"Cassia." His voice is low but clear. More command than comfort as his hand lands on my shoulder, firm and unflinching. The space between us disappears, and all I want is to collapse into him. "You need to breathe."

"I can't keep doing this." The words quake from my chest. "Every time I think I'm close..."

He shifts beside me, pulling a folded page from his jacket, creased and weathered.

"Look at me, Cass." There's weight in it, not softness— the kind of voice that stops a free-fall.

I do. His eyes are calm and grounded, unreadable except for the concern threading through them. It lands harder than I expect—makes me want to shove it away. I don't want his comfort. Don't need it... except maybe I do. And that terrifies me.

"We're not out of leads yet," he says, unfolding the paper. "There are three more locations that match the description.

One's only a few days north."

I stare at the page. "Why didn't you tell me earlier?"

"I didn't want to overwhelm you." His voice stays even. "But I should've told you. These things... they rarely lead somewhere on the first try."

I swipe at my eyes, furious at the burn in them. "How do we get there?"

"I'll arrange transport. We'll leave at first light."

A branch snaps to our left. Kody's hand drops to his weapon in one fluid motion. My breath catches—not from fear, but from the comfort of knowing he's there. Always watching and ready.

But it's not just the dead end that weighs on me now. It's him.

The way he only reaches for me when I'm breaking. The way he always lets go too soon.

The scent of citrus and rot clings to the garden as we move through what's left of it—fruit soft underfoot, wisteria heavy overhead. The sun slips behind the horizon, turning the stone paths to shadow.

Neither of us mentions how his hand stays at my back, guiding me over broken stones. Or how quickly he withdraws it once we reach the street.

DAWN FINDS US in the courtyard, fog clinging low to the stones. Kody speaks in hushed tones with the coach driver while I linger near the gate, the brittle morning air threading through my sleeves. I study the list of possible locations, fingers brushing over the ink. His handwriting is precise, methodical—like everything else about him. Every angle measured. Every word considered.

Except maybe the way he touched my shoulder in the garden, unguarded and real. The kind of touch that lingers longer than logic allows.

"Ready?" He appears at my side, taking my travel bag before I can protest. His fingers brush mine, but the contact is fleeting and his eyes meet mine.

"That eager to get back to Evie?" I don't know why I say it. Maybe I want to hurt him a little. Maybe I just want to see if he'll react.

A flicker crosses his expression—hurt, maybe, or regret— but the driver calls out before he can answer. And just like that, the moment folds in on itself and is gone, piled up with all the other things we're refusing to air out.

The coach's interior is plush purple velvet with gold-trimmed curtains tied back to reveal a view of the still-waking street—a luxury that seems at odds with our mission. I slide into the seat across from him, hands curled in my lap.

As the wheels creak into motion and the inn falls away behind us, I catch Kody watching me in the reflection of the window—eyes shadowed and unreadable. But when I turn to meet them, he's already looking away, as if he always was.

29 - Cassia

Trees blur past the coach window in a streak of green and gray. I keep my eyes forward, resisting the pull to glance sideways—to look at him. Four days of silence weighted with too many almosts. His sudden coldness has settled into me like a bruise, tender and slow to fade.

"Shouldn't be long now." His voice breaks the silence, carefully neutral.

I nod, fingers finding the metal chain at my neck. I trace its familiar curve without thinking, eyes tracking the scattered houses beginning to break through the trees.

"Are you sure I'm ready for this?" The words slip out before I can stop them. After the disappointment at the garden, I'm not sure what I'm really asking. Ready to fight? Ready to know? Ready to hope again?

Kody clasps his hands in his lap, gaze forward. "Even with your leg, you've made progress. Fieldwork will teach you more now than waiting for a perfect recovery."

I bite the inside of my cheek. "You think it won't come?"

He hesitates—just long enough for the silence to press between us. "I'm not a physician," he says at last, voice low. "But… from what I've seen, some pain might linger. For a while, at least."

"Oh." I nod, eyes dropping to my lap. Outside, the light shifts—trees casting long, splintered shadows as the coach rolls on.

Finally, the coach rolls to a halt. Kody steps out first, then pauses, offering his hand in a motion so practiced it could be muscle memory. Hunter to trainee. Nothing more. I ignore it, and the ache that rises with it, using the doorframe to lower myself down instead.

The driver passes me my pack. I sling it over one shoulder, tug my hair free from the strap, and glance around.

Colorful buildings flank the narrow street, window boxes overflowing with blooms that spill petals onto the stone walk. White numbers and faded block letters mark each painted facade, uniform but cheerful. The floral scent is rich in the air, softening the edge I hadn't realized I was still carrying.

"Beautiful, right?" Kody adjusts the strap across his chest.

"Yeah. It's almost like the destruction of the Noctis hasn't even touched this place." When I look over, he's watching me. I think of Evie. Of "cousin." And four grueling days of quiet withdrawal. But I don't look away. Instead, I unfold the note from my pocket, focusing on its creases instead of his expression. "Where are we, exactly?"

"A city called Enna," he says.

"And this will help find my family?"

"The note mentions wisteria and cedar growing together, citrus trees, and a royal tower open to commoners." His voice shifts—measured, informative. Detached. Like we're back to titles and roles.

"You got all that from a poem?"

"Deductive research." He gestures for me to follow. "The cathedral here once maintained a garden. Religious leaders used it to house the broken—help them heal before rejoining the world."

He walks ahead, careful to keep a few steps between us. Always that space now.

"There's no way it's that simple."

"Probably not," he admits. "But it's a place to start."

"Then why not just drive straight there?"

He glances back with a hint of his old smile, the one that makes my heart skip. "No road."

We round the corner, and I stop short. A tower rises from the cliff above us, its silhouette cut sharp against the sky. Winding switchbacks snake through dense trees to reach it, the incline steep and unforgiving. My gaze tracks the path down to a weather-stained stone archway and its rusted iron gate.

"You can't be serious."

"Why not?" he quirks a teasing brow.

"Kody, that's a climb."

He only shrugs, hands slipping into his pockets, the very image of casual indifference. "Perfect time to stop babying that leg."

And just like that, he starts toward the gate—controlled, measured, unreadable.

I gape for a moment before hurrying to catch up. "Babying it? I am not—"

"If you say so." He glances back with the ghost of a grin, but his tone stays light, cautious. "If you can't make it, I'll either carry you or go alone. But I'll need the key."

He trails his hand along the arch as he passes under, like it helps him avoid looking at me.

"Fat chance," I mutter, following.

"What was that?"

"Nothing." I flash him a too-sweet smile, pulse jumping at the flicker of recognition in his backward glance. Almost like old times. Before everything got complicated.

The switchbacks prove gentler than they looked from below, the path surprisingly intact despite two centuries of erosion and growth. We walk in relative silence, the only notable sound being the wind moving through the trees. A breeze lifts my hair—and when I glance sideways, I catch Kody watching.

He looks away too quickly.

For a breath, I glimpse something raw beneath the calm exterior, a flicker of the man beneath the role. But the moment vanishes as he steps forward to help me over a fallen branch. His touch is careful. Neutral.

"Thanks, cousin," I mutter under my breath.

His hand stills on my elbow. "Cassia—"

But I've already pulled away, heart hammering in thought of everything I want to scream at him.

We walk in silence for a while longer, our footfall rustling the overgrowth. At some point, Kody moves ahead, letting the distance stretch.

Maybe he thinks I need space. Maybe he just doesn't know what to say.

Pain flares through my leg, each step sending a dull throb

up to my hip. I slow without meaning to, cursing the injury, the heat, and him. The ache only sharpens the tension knotting in my chest.

Up ahead, a large tree stretches over the path, casting a pool of much-needed shade.

"Hey," I call between heavy breaths. "Gonna rest under that tree." I motion ahead, and he stops, turning back.

"Let me help—"

"No." It comes out sharp, carrying the weight of days I haven't unpacked. "Just need water. Normal out-of-shape human stuff."

He watches me the whole way up, gaze steady, unreadable. When I reach him, we walk together again in silence—thick and tight.

Then, soft: "Why won't you let me help you, Cassia?"

I flinch at my name. "Can you not call me that?" I try to keep it casual, but my voice catches. "Cassia feels... distant. Like you're keeping space between us. And I don't think I can take any more distance right now."

He doesn't answer right away, just watches me for a beat—long enough that I wonder if I've said too much. Then he looks away, brushing a hand over the back of his neck.

"You don't like your name?"

The shift throws me. I blink, grateful and stung all at once. "It's fine, I guess." I dig through my pack for water, the silence between us stretching. He's still nearby, but not close. Never too close.

"Better than Kody."

"What? No, Kody suits you." The words leave too easily. I hate that they're true. I also hate how easily I can hear Evie saying it.

He rolls his eyes as we reach the shade, dropping onto a patch of moss, and stretches his legs. "My parents probably thought they were being clever with the spelling."

"At least they didn't name you after a flower."

"Ever smelled golden waterfall flowers?"

I press my lips together, trying not to laugh. "What?"

"Golden waterfall?" His eyes glint with mischief. "That's what they're called. They look like—"

"So I'm named after a plant that resembles peeing?"

His bark of laughter echoes off the trees. "I wasn't going to say it."

"But you were thinking it." I nudge his boot with mine, grinning despite the ache in my leg.

The air shifts again—lighter now, easier. Still stretched between us is the space he's carefully maintained since the tavern, but for the first time in days, it doesn't feel so wide.

"You're impossible." Kody shakes his head, a real smile tugging at his mouth as he leans back against the tree.

I gape at him. "Rude!"

"In a good way!"

"Whatever." I dig a packet of dried fruit from my bag and flop down beside him, shifting just enough so our arms don't quite touch. I glance out at the city below. It sprawls like a map of untouched possibilities—clean lines, blooming terraces, the soft glint of glass undisturbed by ash or ruin. For a moment, it doesn't feel like a world shaped by Noctis hands. For a moment, it feels almost... Like that I imagine normal would be like.

"We should move. Getting dark." He stands, brushing moss and dirt from his pants, eyes scanning the thinning trees ahead.

I haul myself up, biting back the ache in my leg.

"You good?" he offers his hand.

"Yeah." I don't take it. "Race you to the top."

I take the lead, but the air shifts the higher we climb— subtle, like a sound just outside hearing. The breeze dies, the birds go quiet, and shadows stretch longer than they should.

It's probably nothing. But my body doesn't believe me. Something's wrong. Not between us. Between us is its own quiet mess, but ahead, up there, something is waiting.

30 - Cassia

The cathedral looms above us, carved from weathered limestone and shadow. Time has left its mark—cracks spidering across the stone. A cross recessed into the wall stretches its wings outward, more relic than symbol now. The tower rises to our right, set apart from the main cathedral but connected by a narrow, covered walkway. A second entrance. Separate. Secluded.

"Tower?" I nod toward it, trying to keep my voice level—professional… detached. Like the climb hadn't stripped my nerves bare. Like I wasn't too scared to let hope in—because hope, after this long, feels more dangerous than disappointment.

Kody studies it, hands deep in his coat pockets. "Worth checking out."

As we approach, the air shifts—cooler, quieter. My boots crunch over gravel and weeds, and the courtyard opens before us, wild and overgrown. Rusted shell casings glint beneath dead leaves. A bent pole juts from a patch of thornbush, its base ringed with snapped grommets and a few stubborn threads—barely enough to hint at the flag that once flew there.

Etched into the outer stone wall, nearly swallowed by creeping lichen, a weatherworn mural depicts a Turig soldier looming over cowering civilians. The lines are crude now, softened by time and rain, but the fear in the faces remains. Faded words ghost across the bottom, barely legible:

THE ENEMY WALKS AMONG US. REPORT ANY SIGNS.

A few paces away, another warning lingers—newer, but

still worn by decades of neglect. This one was painted, not carved. The red letters bleed slightly at the edges, as if time couldn't quite erase the message:

BLOOD IS CONTROL — NOCTIS CANNOT BE TRUSTED.

It hums with a different kind of dread—less about history, more about what still waits in the dark.

I draw a slow breath, chest tight.

Something about this place feels… not abandoned. Just waiting.

"I don't see any wisteria. Or cedar," I murmur, scanning the cracked courtyard.

"Citrus, there." Kody nods toward a cluster of trees beyond the building, voice deliberately even. "And just because something's gone now doesn't mean it wasn't here at one point."

A chill coils down my spine. "Still… it doesn't feel right. Why would they send me to a church?"

"Used to be common." He keeps his eyes on the path ahead. "Religious sanctuaries held important relics—kept them hidden. Before the Noctis started burning them out."

I hug my arms around myself. The building looks long deserted. "It's definitely abandoned now."

We stop at the door. Kody tries the handle, then steps back and drives his shoulder against it. The heavy wood groans but doesn't move.

"Maybe a window?" I offer, uncertain.

He gives me a sidelong look, one brow lifted. Then, with a sharp exhale, he plants his boot against the frame.

"Come."

Crack.

"On."

Thud.

"You."

Snap.

"Piece."

Crack.

"Of."

CRUNCH.

The jamb gives way with a splintering sound, and the door lurches open into darkness.

He adjusts his jacket, not quite smirking. "See? Easy."

Then he gestures me forward—his voice dipping into familiar cadence, equal parts dry command and careful watchfulness. "After you."

The words pull taut in my chest. Muscle memory. Training. Trust.

I step inside.

Dust carpets the stone floor like ashfall, muffling our steps. A narrow hallway stretches to the left, swallowed by shadows. To the right, a crumbling staircase coils upward, its edges worn smooth by time and use. A door at the far end of the hall bears a small, shattered window, its glass crusted with grime.

I lean forward, squinting around the base of the stairs—and freeze at the soft crack beneath my boot.

I lift my foot.

Bone. Pale and brittle, snapped clean through. A quiet chill worms down my spine.

Kody doesn't comment, just surveys the hall with a wary sweep of his eyes. We move deeper. The air smells of rot and mildew, thick with the metallic ghost of old blood.

To our left, makeshift barricades lean against the wall—splintered furniture, rusted sheet metal, crates stacked in haste. I step around one and catch sight of a field manual stuffed inside, its pages browned and fused together with something dark. Blood, maybe. A faded military insignia peeks out from the spine.

Further on, a propaganda placard juts from the rubble, corners curling and edges stained. This one's newer than the others we've seen—painted, not printed. A Noctis figure towers over a fallen soldier, its face sunken with hollows for eyes. The words beneath it scream:

THEY LOOK LIKE US. BUT THEY ARE NOT US.

I stare too long.

"Gonna frame it, or keep moving?" Kody's voice floats back with artificial levity—the same too-casual tone he's adopted since the tavern.

"This place is creepy," I mutter.

"Been empty a long time."

"Doesn't feel like my parents ever left anything here." I cough, trying to clear the thickness in my throat. "Smells like death and dust."

"I can check the place myself if it's too much." His tone is neutral, but I hear the jab beneath it.

"Fat chance." I step forward, brushing past him before he can pretend he didn't mean it that way.

"Then let's go." He starts up the stairs, shoulders tight, eyes scanning. All purpose and distance.

I follow him up, one hand trailing the cold, rough stone. Each step pulls a throb from my leg, but I press on. The stairwell coils tighter, shadows clinging to every curve. But then—light.

Soft at first. Then growing.

It spills brighter with each step, blooming like dawn through the gloom. By the time I reach the landing, I have to squint.

A stained-glass window towers before me, awash in hues of rose and gold. A dove arcs through the center, wings spread wide over a world divided—one half lush with wildflowers, the other cracked and scorched. The light bleeds through the glass, casting fractured color across the worn wooden floor.

Something about the image tugs at the edge of memory. Not quite recognition. More like déjà vu.

Kody waits at the end of the hall, arms crossed loosely, his frame silhouetted against another door.

"Locked?" I ask.

"Waiting for you."

"Why?"

His eyes meet mine, steady and unguarded. "Because this part's yours, Cass."

The way he says it—low, sure, familiar—sends a flicker through my chest I thought I'd buried. Like for a second, we're back in the quiet spaces of training, before silence sharpened and distance calcified between us.

"Right," I breathe, gathering myself. "I'm ready."

The door groans open, stirring dust into shafts of dying sunlight. What remains of a picture window stretches across the far wall, its jagged frame catching the last blush of day. Pink-tinged clouds float above the city, soft and surreal, turning every shattered edge of glass to gold.

For a moment, I forget why we came.

"It's…"

"Yeah." Kody's voice is quiet behind me. "Beautiful."

A floorboard creaks, shattering the hush. He's already

moving, methodical and focused—checking drawers, scanning corners.

Right. The key.

I turn toward the armoire and ease it open.

A scent wafts out—sweet and powdery, laced with something darker underneath. Dust. Dried flowers. A note of fruit, maybe. It clings to the air like memory.

And suddenly I'm small again.

The room is whole. Bright. Safe. The weight of the present blurs under the rush of something half-remembered.

Cold floor beneath my bare feet as I race from wall to wall, showing off for my mother. Her laugh rings bright, her braid slipping over one shoulder as she claps for me.

Then the door opens.

Father enters. The air shifts. His anger fills the space like smoke. I dart to Mother, clutching her skirt as she lifts me onto the bed, her hands soft against my cheeks.

"Stay here, dove. Just until I return."

When she comes back, it's with our traveling case. Crashes echo from the kitchen below. Her dress tangles in my fists as I cling to her.

"Hush now, Cassia. My little dove," she whispers, crouching to meet my eyes. "We must play a very quiet game. Do you want to play?"

I nod, though my lower lip trembles. Her grip tightens on my shoulders.

"It's a hiding game. Only come out when Daddy or I find you." She leads me to the closet, pulls aside the false wall, and settles me on a small wooden stool. Her kiss lands soft on my forehead. Her hands cup my face. "Stay very still. Very quiet."

Fear clenches my throat. Last time we played this game, we walked for days, hungry and cold. My vision blurs with tears I don't want her to see.

"Remember, baby," she whispers. "Not a sound. Try not to cry. It'll be over soon."

A sharp creak draws me back. The scent—sweet and powdery, like jasmine clinging to old fabric—still clings to my nose, tethering me to both past and present. But it's the sound that truly breaks the memory: the soft drag of something across the floorboards behind me.

I blink, staring at the closet door across the room, pulse loud in my ears. My feet won't move.

"Kody…" My whisper comes out thin and frayed.

He straightens from where he's crouched, letting a dusty blanket on the edge of the bed fall. "What is it?"

"It's behind that door. It has to be."

"The closet?" He frowns slightly. "Already checked. Empty."

I manage a step. Then another. The floor feels colder now. Each breath shallow till my hand reaches the handle.

Kody rises behind me, his presence a steady warmth at my back. "See?" he says, nodding toward the open space inside. "Empty."

I stare at the rear wall. At the seam that doesn't belong. My hand lifts on instinct. "It's not," I murmur. My fingers brush the edge of the false panel—

Glass shatters below.

Kody's movement is immediate, the scrape of blades drawn sharp in the thick silence.

"Noctis," he says, voice low, eyes already scanning. "Close the door. Don't come out until I tell you."

Then he's gone.

The door closes between us, and suddenly I'm six again—alone in the dark, wrapped in shadows and silence. My breath sticks in my throat as the closet yawns around me like it did back then. Like it's waiting to swallow me whole.

A crash echoes up the stairwell.

I flinch violently, heart slamming against my ribs. My hands fumble at the door, pulling it shut with trembling fingers. Dust stings my nose, mixing with the sharp tang of fear.

Below, the sounds of fighting explode—flesh against stone, metal against bone. Real and far too close.

I press my hands over my ears, but it's no use. I still hear my father's voice—shouting. My mother's scream: "Eli, no!"

A sob claws up my throat. My chest seizes.

It's happening again.

I'm trapped. Again.

I'm not that child anymore.

Not helpless and hiding.

My fingers curl into fists.

This time, I fight.

I wrench the door open, my dagger already in hand. The hallway is empty, the light strange, and pink, and wrong. Another crash downstairs. Pain surges through my leg as I run anyway, faster than I should, faster than fear can stop me.

Kody's voice rises—sharp, desperate. I can't make out the words, but the tone says enough.

He needs me. And I won't let him down.

At the bottom of the steps, I peer around the corner. The hallway opens into what was once a kitchen—now a ruin of shattered tile and broken chairs. Kody's pinned face-first against the wall, arm twisted unnaturally high behind him, blood smearing down the cracked plaster.

My blood spikes hot. "Hey!"

The Noctis turns, smile peeling across his too-sharp features. "You didn't mention she was a redhead," he sneers, tightening his grip.

"Kody!" I lunge forward. "Let him—"

"Cassia, stay back!" His voice cracks under the strain. "I told you—"

"I'm not a child anymore." My blade is already in my hand, knuckles white. But I never see the second one coming.

A hand like splintered bone clamps down on my injured shoulder, sending molten agony ripping through the half-healed wound. I scream, buckling as pain blinds me.

He leans in, breath hot at my ear. "Such sweet blood," the Noctis purrs. "The mistress will know instantly if this is a bloodline. One taste to confirm..."

His fingers clench tighter—nails like daggers digging into the torn flesh. My legs give out and I sink to my knees with a strangled gasp—the cold stone biting through my pants.

He twists his grip, and a fresh wave of white-hot pain arcs down my side. It steals the air from my lungs.

I twist, a raw sound tearing from my throat. My blade slashes upward but he jerks away just in time, laughing—a thin, rattling noise that slithers down my spine. My blood stains his fingers as he brings his hand to his lips, and licks one.

That sound again, low and primal, grinds from my throat, and suddenly I'm moving. Fast and reckless. I barrel through the doorway after him, blade slicing at air. He darts down the stoop stairs, his taunting laughter bouncing off the stone walls.

Rage explodes in my chest and the world narrows to the rhythm of my breath, the wet pound of my feet, and the weight of the knife in my hand. My scream rises from somewhere ancient—wordless and wild.

Strong hands clamp onto me from behind. Another Noctis. *Kody—where is Kody?*

"Such a pretty thing, isn't she, Roger?" the first one murmurs, stepping from the doorway shadows.

I kick out wildly, feet slipping on the stone, but the one behind me—Roger—locks his arms around my torso like iron bands, lifting me off the ground with effortless strength.

"You're right, Vlad," Roger breathes against my hair, inhaling slow and deliberate. "She smells like promise. Like prophecy."

I twist violently in his grip, and my knife slips from my hand, clattering uselessly to the ground.

Then he shifts—one arm still around my waist while the other rakes across my shoulder wound. His nails sink into the torn flesh and twist. A scream tears out of me, raw and broken, as agony blazes through my shoulder.

My knees collapse, but Roger doesn't let go. I dangle, legs kicking uselessly while he hauls me upright again, spine crushed against his chest like a rag doll.

But I don't stay limp. I slam my elbow back into his ribs. The impact stings my arm, and he grunts—but his grip tightens. My breath chokes in my throat as he locks both arms again around my torso and wrenches me upright, spine to his chest.

I twist, buck, snarl, and scratch. My fingers claw at any part of him I can reach. At last, I get one hand free and drive my knuckles into his throat.

He laughs—a low, guttural sound that vibrates through my spine.

"You've got fire," he growls, dragging me tighter against him. "The mistress will appreciate that. She always did like her prey unruly."

"Fuck you," I spit, thrashing harder.

Vlad steps in now, his eyes gleaming like polished obsidian encased in ice. He presses two claws into my shoulder wound, and they come away slick and shining red.

"Did you really think you could hide from her?" His voice is all ice and silk. "From us?"

He drags a bloodied finger across my jaw, slow and deliberate, like a lover marking what's his.

"Your blood sings," he murmurs. "It calls to her. And gods, sweetness… we're listening." His smile is all blade and hunger. "Rest assured—she'll peel you open just to see what makes it so divine."

My stomach twists.

I jerk my arm downward, finally finding the hilt of my second dagger, pinned awkwardly between our bodies until now. In one desperate motion, I flip it and drive it backward into Roger's side.

He hisses, the sound serpentine and wrong. His grip slackens just enough for me to twist free.

"You'll regret that," Roger snarls, swiping for me—but I duck low, staggering away, blood hot and slick down my arm.

Vlad circles, calm and slow, like a predator enjoying the chase. "I was going to be gentle," he muses. "Just a taste to confirm your lineage." His gaze drags to my bleeding shoulder. "But now... you've made it personal."

He advances.

There's a glint in his eyes—those deep obsidian pools ringed in burning blue—that freezes my limbs. Not hunger. Not anger. Exhilaration.

I hesitate. Fatal mistake.

Roger lunges and grabs me again, arms cinching like chains. I thrash, biting back a scream as he crushes my wounded shoulder.

"Hold her," Vlad commands, voice low with anticipation. He closes in and fists a hand in my hair, wrenching my head back until the bones in my neck strain.

His breath ghosts over my face, cold and sharp.

"The mistress prefers her prizes unmarked," he murmurs, almost to himself. "But she'll forgive a little bruising. Especially from this bloodline." His nostrils flare. "Your scent—gods, it sings."

My mind races. I strain to hear anything from inside—Kody's voice, a shout, a footstep. Anything.

Nothing.

Only Vlad.

"We don't need your permission," he whispers. "We were always going to take you."

He bares his teeth.

I spit in his face.

Vlad recoils, wiping his cheek with the back of his sleeve. The disgust in his expression curdles into something colder. "Such a waste. What do you think, Roger? Quick death here, or let the mistress confirm she is a Bailey?"

He's bluffing. Or trying to rattle me.

Roger's laughter is low and liquid, like bones grinding under water. "Mistress would prefer this one intact. You know how she is about the bloodline. Ever since Eden slipped away…"

Eden. Eden Bailey?

The name cracks through my thoughts like lightning, but there's no time to chase it—no time for anything but staying alive.

"True," Vlad murmurs, dragging a finger along the line of blood soaking my shoulder. "But she's already injured. And the mistress does hate damaged goods."

"Then minimize further harm," Roger says, his grip tightening like a chain around my ribs. "One taste to confirm the bloodline. The other wounds? Already there when we arrived."

A cold surge of panic rises—but Kody's voice cuts through it, a memory pressed into muscle: *Breathe. Don't give them what they want. Make them underestimate you.*

I let my body go still. Let them think I'm fading. A limp body draws less caution. My pulse thunders in my ears, but I fixate on it—anchor myself to the rhythm of survival. It buys me a second. Maybe two.

Vlad steps closer again, brushing my hair aside with a slow reverence that turns my stomach. His hand cups the back of my skull, fingers splayed through my scalp like a lover. The other clamps my shoulder, thumb dragging across torn skin until it comes away red.

He lifts it to his lips… inhales deeply, but doesn't taste. "The scent can be tainted," he murmurs, more to himself. "Dust, sweat, iron—too many variables. But a bite…" His gaze cuts to mine. "A bite is honest. Tells the truth."

Terror chokes me, my body stiffening as his cold breath ghosts down my throat. A whimper escapes—betrayal from my own lips.

Behind me, Roger shudders like he's savoring it. "I can smell the fear on her. It's thick… like honey mixed with blood." His nose presses against my hair, and he breathes it in with a disgusting groan. "Gods, I'd bottle it if I could."

"Indeed," Vlad purrs. "One taste. Then we take her somewhere... quieter." His lips graze my throat. Then he jerks.

A wet choking sound, a sharp hiss—and hot liquid sprays across my already blood-slick shoulder.

There's no bite. No pain. Only the thud of a body hitting stone.

"Vlad?" Roger's arms tense, then loosen.

Another thud. Then nothing.

I drop to my knees, shaking as Roger's footsteps scramble backward into the shadows. Vlad lies motionless, with Kody's dagger buried deep in his temple. Blood spreads in a dark halo beneath his head.

A hand clamps down on my shoulder and I jerk instinctively—elbow slamming backward in a desperate strike.

A grunt. Then—"Could've done that to them earlier and saved us both some trouble."

That voice. Relief floods me so fast it steals my breath. *Kody.*

I spin and throw myself into him. All the cold distance, all the unspoken bitterness over "cousin" and Evie—gone. Burned away by the raw terror of what almost happened.

His arms close around me like they've been aching to. Fierce and grounding. He holds me like he's afraid I'll vanish.

"I thought I'd lost you," I whisper. The words catch, nearly breaking. "When I heard—"

"I'm sorry." His voice is hoarse, breath ragged against my temple. "I should've been faster. Should've known there'd be more." His fingers slide into my hair, cradling the back of my head. Not just reassurance, but need. I cling tighter, and only then do I realize how badly he's bleeding. A gash above his brow. Blood staining his shirt at the ribs. He must've fought the other Noctis alone. Was overpowered. Only now breaking through.

I bury my face in his chest, breath catching on the mix of old leather and sweat, and the faintest trace of smoke and iron. The scent of violence. Of survival.

And under it, that familiar warmth from our training days. But it's not the same now. The way he holds me has changed. No caution. No boundaries. Like nearly losing each other shattered the walls we built between us.

I lean back just enough to see his face. There's blood across his cheek. Dirt smudged under his eyes. But those eyes—they're dark with more than concern. There's heat there. A hunger I don't dare name.

A branch snaps in the dark and we break apart instantly, both reaching for our weapons. The moment vanishes— tucked away like so many others we've never spoken of.

"The key," I say, forcing steadiness into my voice. "It's upstairs. Behind the panel."

He nods, slipping back into hunter mode. But as we move, his hand brushes the small of my back—light, lingering.

Not for guidance. Not to steady me. Just to feel me there.

31 - Cassia

Kody insisted he didn't need patching up after sewing me back together. The process feels routine. Salve, stitch, try not to get sucked in by the intensity in his eyes as he works. Then, everything goes back to normal.

We stare at the box on the table. After everything we've been through to reach it—the climb, the memories, the blood—it feels too plain. Just an old metal case, scuffed at the corners and latched shut like it's guarding something sacred.

Kody exhales. "Not much to look at compared to the last one."

"Maybe it's just another dead end." My voice comes out flat. "I'm not sure I can do another trail of riddles."

"We'll figure it out." His hand finds mine, the gesture simple but deliberate. Solid. After tonight, the weight of it settles different.

I hold on, even as my throat tightens. "I think they're dead, Kody. My parents."

He doesn't speak right away.

"That memory in the tower…" I force the words out. "The fighting—it sounded like tonight. Screaming. Crashing. And then she told me to hide. What if they didn't make it out?"

"They made it out. You did."

"Holli sent me away... I was eight."

"Holli lived at the church with you?"

"...No. A much bigger house. The estate was huge. Surrounded by lots of land and a tall stone fence around it." I gnaw at my lower lip.

"See? They made it out. You were a kid, hiding in a closet." His voice is steady, but softer now. "Everything feels bigger and louder when you're that small. Could've been anything. A drunk neighbor. Some raid. The Baileys weren't exactly... beloved."

I nod slowly, but the ache doesn't ease. "We were always moving. Always looking over our shoulders."

"Which means they got out. Maybe they kept running."

"But I remember not running. Right before I saw them last." My voice is barely a whisper.

The silence that follows is thick and waiting, like the air before a storm.

"I remember always being hungry and cold." I look up at him. "Until we found the chapel. It felt like a sanctuary. But that night, after the fighting..." I shake my head. "We left. A few years later, Holli sent me away from the estate."

Kody pulls me close, and I let myself melt into the warmth of him. "Maybe they thought you'd be safer without them," he murmurs. His hand moves gently against my back, not quite soothing the ache his words stir. "Safer than growing up hunted."

I sigh into his chest. "Maybe. But they never came for me. Not once."

His breath hitches, just barely. "Maybe they couldn't."

I nod, but the ache lingers. "I was angry for a long time. I think... I still am."

He doesn't try to fix it. Just holds me tighter, like that's enough.

I lift my head. "Thank you. For what you did today."

His mouth curves—not a smirk, not a grin. Just the ghost of a smile. "You have a habit of surviving. I just helped a little."

The tension shifts—softer now, more fragile. I watch the way the light plays in his eyes, how his gaze drops briefly to my lips before flicking back up. My breath catches.

He brushes a strand of hair from my cheek, fingers lingering. "You don't have to open it now."

I swallow, throat tight. "No. I want to."

I turn to the box. It's unassuming in the low light—gray with age, brass at the lock. When I slide in the key, it turns with a clean click, followed by soft, chiming tones that stir something deep in my chest.

A soft smile tugs at my lips as the melody plays—familiar in a way I can't explain. I close my eyes, letting the sound settle through me, quiet and sure, like the warmth of a voice I hadn't realized I missed.

"You recognize it?" Kody's voice is quiet, almost reverent.

I nod, throat tight, and lift the lid. The scent of old paper and cedar drifts up, stirring more memories I'm not ready to face. The contents shimmer through tears I refuse to let fall.

One by one, I lay them on the table:

—A roll of paper, bound in twine.

—A silver key, gleaming unlike the tarnished one we used to open the box.

—Two sheathed daggers, slim and deadly, drawing Kody forward with interest.

—A frosted glass bottle, ridged and cool beneath my fingers, its gold cap glinting above the faintly raised letters: EB.

—A leather-bound notebook, its deep brown cover stamped with initials that make my breath catch: CB.

My hands tremble as I untie the twine. Kody's palm settles lightly on my shoulder—solid, warm, grounding. After everything, the Noctis, the memory, the fear, his touch steadies more than just my hands.

I smooth the letter open against the table, bracing myself for whatever truth waits inside:

Dearest Cassia,

If you're reading this, then you've found the chapel—and remembered where to look. Good. You always were clever. We're proud of you. So proud.

Kody's thumb strokes my shoulder as I keep reading, throat tight.

By now, you've likely encountered the ones who hunt our bloodline. We had hoped—perhaps foolishly—that you could live free of it. But fate rarely grants such mercy to Baileys. If you're reading this second letter, it means we are no longer together. We pray you made it far enough, long enough, to grow strong.

We can't offer you all the answers here. Maybe we never had them to begin with. But we wanted to leave behind pieces of our story, and of ourselves, in case we were separated too soon.

Inside this box are heirlooms we couldn't risk keeping at the estate—sacred to our family, and now to you.

The perfume was made by your great-great-great-grandfather, Calvin, for Eden—the only scent she ever wore. The formula is in his journal, along with other secrets our family has guarded for generations.

The blades were forged by Benjamin Hale, Calvin's closest friend and a master smith during the Turig War. He crafted them specifically for Calvin and Eden, designing each to match their fighting styles. More than weapons, they were symbols of protection, loyalty, and the bond they shared. You'll find Ben's name throughout the journal—he was family in all the ways that mattered. If these blades have lasted this long, it's because he built them to endure, just like us.

And the journal... This is the most important. Within its pages lies more than family history. Some believe it holds the key to a cure—others, a weapon to use against the Noctis. We don't yet know which. That's for you to discover. But guard it fiercely. In the wrong hands, it could change everything.

You've already come so far, Cassia. We wish we could be there to guide you the rest of the way—but if not, know that we love you beyond words.

We always will.
—Mom & Dad

P.S.

If you ever receive a message signed only with a V, trust it. We never saw his face, never learned his name. But his guidance kept us alive longer than we had any right to be. If he's still out there, follow his signs.

I look up from the letter, mind spinning with questions. Beside me, Kody has gone still—not the alert stillness of a hunter, but something heavier. His gaze stays fixed on the journal, jaw tight, shoulders locked like he's holding back words he doesn't trust himself to say.

He doesn't speak. But an intensity just beneath the surface of his silence makes my stomach knot.

Not fear.

Purpose.

32 - Cassia

Kody hasn't moved. That hunter-stillness, the kind that masks adrenaline and calculation, clings to him. But now I see it for what it is—not just focus. Alarm.

"What's wrong?"

His answer comes slow, measured. "A cure... If that's real, every Noctis house would kill to possess it. And we're walking it straight to your family's doorstep."

The weight of that settles like stone in my gut. "You think doing this was a mistake?"

"I think," he says, voice lower now, "we won't get another warning. What happened tonight? That was just the beginning."

The perfume bottle is cool in my palm. I twist the gold cap, and a bloom of scent unfurls into the air—jasmine and black currant, undercut by something wilder. Older. Like forest smoke and sun-warmed stone.

Kody watches me closely. Not just the bottle—me. Every blink, every breath. His eyes cataloging threat, yes—but also searching for something else.

I set the bottle down gently, my attention drawn next to the matched blades. The first knife slides partway from its sheath, revealing CB stamped into the steel of the blade. In the lamplight, the metal gleams—elegant, deadly, and ancient. It feels like it remembers.

"Calvin's," I whisper, fingers grazing the second blade. It's slimmer, more refined, but no less lethal. "And Eden's."

"Perfect weight distribution," Kody murmurs. His tone is professional, but there's a reverence in his eyes. "These weren't ceremonial. They were meant to be used."

The journal comes last.

The leather is unusually warm beneath my fingers as I untie the worn straps. The first page crackles with age, revealing a single line—an address. But it's the photograph taped just beneath it that steals my breath.

A blonde man with sharp green eyes has his arms wrapped around a redhead whose ocean-blue gaze matches my own. They're both smiling like the world is still whole.

"This must be them." My voice is barely a whisper as I turn the photo toward Kody.

His smile softens. "You look just like her."

"Yeah… I guess I kind of do." I flip through the pages, faster than I can process them—anything to distract from how close Kody is leaning, how the warmth of him mixes with the ancient perfume still lingering in the air. Jasmine, smoke, dust... Him.

A loose photograph slips free, fluttering to the table like a leaf.

The man in uniform stands proud despite the easy slope of his shoulders. There's a knowing in his smile—sharp, steady, full of life. HALE, the name patch reads. G.F. NAVY with the Global Forces symbol on a pocket patch.

"Benjamin?" The name feels too small for the weight in his gaze. Eyes like carved glass, catching every angle of light. The kind of eyes that don't let you forget them.

"The one who forged the knives…" Kody murmurs.

I turn back to the journal, fingers trembling slightly as I flip to the page where writing seems to bleed from the past.

The journal's words catch me off guard: "Benji almost died today—" My breath trembles as I read.

"I got a call—barely a call, more like a breathless warning from someone on the squad. Said he was being brought in and it didn't look good. I just… ran.

I got to the hospital just as they were wheeling him in.

There was so much blood. Thick, dark… wrong. It was black as ink.

I shouted his name, but he didn't open his eyes. His skin was gray. His mouth... I think he tried to speak. I think he saw me.

They wouldn't let me through. Closed the doors. Locked me out.

"Critical care," they said. "Family only." But I'm all he has—"

I close the journal gently, pressing the pages together. "I can't... not right now."

Kody doesn't press. His hand lands on my shoulder— steady, calloused. Not soft, just solid enough to stop the shaking in my hands from spreading to the rest of me.

I stare at the letter, jaw clenched. "They left me perfume, weapons, cryptic warnings, and a journal that talks about a cure like it's some myth—and they couldn't write a single line about what happened to them?" My voice climbs before I can stop it.

My fingers tighten around the paper until it crumples in my grip. "It's not fair." The words scrape raw against my throat. "They had time to pack a box, to write all this... and not one damn sentence telling me why they disappeared. Where they went. If they even tried to find me."

Kody stays silent, letting the silence hold it.

I exhale slowly and smooth the wrinkled letter. My fingers tremble as I flip back to the first page of the journal. "This address... it's the only lead we have."

Kody leans in, scanning the page. "Zurich," he murmurs. "Could be a contact. Could be a dead end."

"Doesn't matter," I say. "We're going."

"It's a pretty long trek North."

"That makes sense, though, right? If they were trying to keep me safe... putting that much distance between us."

"It would," he says quietly. He straightens, but his hand doesn't move far from mine. "We'll need to stop at the guild base first."

My heart shorts. "Is that... a problem?"

"No," he says after a beat. "Just means we'll need more time. The old maps—archived ones—will be better than anything modern. And we'll need supplies."

"We?" I ask, the word catching in my throat. After everything—Evie, 'cousin,' the walls he's built—it's hard to trust it.

He arches a brow. "Unless you'd rather go alone?"

"No!" It flies out too fast. I catch myself, bite down on the rush of emotion. "I just mean... you've done what you promised. You don't have to keep going."

"And if it leads to nothing?" His eyes lock on mine. "That promise isn't fulfilled until you find your family." He moves to the window, moonlight tracing the sharp lines of his profile. "We'll stop at the hideout on the way back. One night. Real sleep."

"Don't do it for me. I can keep moving."

He turns, arms folding slowly. "You sure?"

I nod, gently tucking the items back inside the box. "Yes."

But as I stand, the weight of it all crashes down—like my bones have remembered what they've been holding up.

"We won't leave till morning. I still need to secure transport." His voice softens—less command, more concern. "Rest. Please."

I eye the narrow bed in the corner. My body protests even the hesitation. "Fine," I murmur. "I'll try." I slide the box beneath the frame, into the dark.

"I'll be back soon." Kody pulls the curtain closed, softening the room's edges. At the door, he pauses. "Just need to send a message. Lock in our transport."

Our.

It settles something in me I didn't know was unsettled. For now, I'm not alone.

33 - Cassia

The carriage jolts over another rut in the road, and I stifle a yawn against my palm. Outside the window, shadows stretch long over the frost-bitten countryside. The sun hasn't risen yet—early travel was part of the plan, but I didn't expect to feel it in my bones this quickly.

"You didn't sleep like I suggested." Kody's voice is quiet, edged with a note of reproach, but softer than usual.

"Neither did you." I glance at him, catching the dark smudges beneath his eyes. "How are you even functioning?"

"Training," he says simply.

A snort escapes me. "Right. Because training teaches you how to survive on zero sleep."

"You'd be surprised what the body can handle."

There's a flat distance in his tone that makes me think he's not just talking about sleep deprivation.

I yawn again, this one hitting deeper. My eyelids dragging down like they're weighted.

"Here," he says.

"What?"

He gestures for me to come closer. "Come here."

I hesitate. The space between us had felt sharp these past few days—tight with things unsaid. But right now, exhaustion speaks louder than pride. I scoot toward him, watching as he lifts the seat cushion and pulls out a small, well-worn U-shaped pillow.

"I'm fine," I start to protest, even as the velvet catches the weak light, soft and strangely inviting.

"I know." His fingers brush my elbow—gentle, steady.

"Just humor me."

I give in, letting him guide me down against his shoulder. "Just for a minute," I murmur.

Sleep finds me before I can question what it means to feel safe here, in the warmth of his presence, on the edge of everything still unknown.

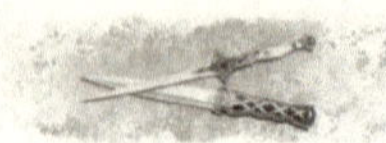

I wake to warmth and darkness. At some point, I've shifted—my head now resting against his thigh, his arm draped loosely across my side. Above me, his chin has dropped to his chest, eyes closed, his features slack with a rare kind of stillness.

I shift slightly. My hand brushes his forearm, and he stiffens. When he starts to pull away, I curl my fingers around his wrist, pressing it gently back into place.

"Don't," I murmur.

A breath passes before his hand lifts—not to pull away, but to rest lightly against my shoulder. No stroking, no pressure, just contact.

"Morning," he says, his voice gravel-thick with sleep.

"It's pitch black."

"Few hours till dawn."

"I slept that long?"

"You needed it."

I sit up slowly, careful not to tip the balance of warmth and quiet. The motion makes my head spin—whether from sleep or the sudden loss of contact, I'm not sure.

"Here." He leans forward, grabbing a water canteen and a food container from the travel pack. The clink of metal in the dark feels louder than it should.

I drink too fast and cough, wiping my mouth on the back of my hand as laughter bubbles up between us.

"Forgotten how swallowing works?"

"Shut up." I swat at his arm without much force, hyper-aware of the way he doesn't move away. He nudges the food toward me, and I focus on tearing a piece of bread into tiny bits—more to keep my hands busy than because I'm actually hungry.

The bread melts on my tongue. I close my eyes and sigh.

"That good?"

"How can you tell?"

"The look on your face." His voice dips, rougher than before. "Seen it before."

Heat creeps into my cheeks. "Excuse me?"

"At the compound," he says, quiet. "When you nailed a new technique. Sometimes… when you were asleep."

I open one eye, aiming for playful. "You watch me sleep? Creepy."

He huffs a soft laugh. "You passed out on my lap for half the day. Not like I had much else to do."

"…Fair."

"No better view anyway."

I try not to smile. Fail. "That was terrible."

"Sorry. Was trying to be smooth." A pause. "Didn't really work."

"Don't be sorry."

Our eyes meet in the darkness, and suddenly the space between us crackles with a charge—like the breath between lightning and thunder.

His gaze flicks to my mouth, then away. "I've been worried about crossing lines."

"Like when?"

He shifts slightly, adding distance where none was asked for. "Whiskey's dangerous around beautiful women."

"Why's that?"

"You know why."

"Maybe I don't." I lean in, drawn to him like gravity pulling on the tide.

"Cass…" His voice catches—part warning, part prayer.

The carriage jolts over another rut and I fall forward, catching myself against his chest—my palm spread over the thunder of his heart. Time dilates, thick and silent.

His breath brushes my lips. "We should focus on finding your family." He leans his forehead to mine, eyes closed like the words cost him. "Everything else… after."

I let myself feel it—what *after* could mean. Then I press a kiss to his cheek, soft and lingering. "You're too good to be true."

He doesn't answer. He doesn't need to.

The rest of the journey passes in quiet, but something has changed between us. A door opened. Neither of us stepped through—but we're both standing on the threshold.

34 - Cassia

Three and a half days on the road, and every mile is haunted by that almost-kiss in the dark. Even Calvin's journal, with all its secrets and grief, can't distract me from stealing glances at Kody when I think he won't notice. I keep rereading that line about Eden's ocean eyes and quiet strength—how she could calm a room just by walking into it, how Calvin swore she was made of something softer than the rest of them. It's Calvin's handwriting, but I can't help hearing it in Kody's voice… or imagining him saying it about me.

When we finally reach Zurich, I'm grateful for the excuse to move, to put space between us before I do something reckless—something that might cross the very boundary he so carefully drew.

Night has already claimed the city. The sporadic glow of oil lamps casts soft halos between long shadows. A chill wind curls through the streets, carrying scents I now recognize from training: sweet rot, rusted iron. Blood and death. Noctis territory.

I rub my arms to erase the unease crawling over me.

Kody moves close, his presence both an anchor and anticipation, as he studies the map beneath a swaying streetlamp. The glow catches the tension in his jaw, the alert edge in his eyes. "Well. Zurich, finally. Should we find a place to get some real sleep?"

The word sleep is enough to pull a yawn from me. I cover it with the back of my hand. "Probably easier to get our bearings in daylight anyway."

"Not to mention safer," he says quietly, his voice weighted

and clipped. The tone makes me glance behind us, that familiar sense of being watched tightening around my ribs.

We find an inn at the edge of a stone-paved square, its white facade and iron-railed balconies a remnant of grander days. Inside, warmth and lamplight create an illusion of safety, though my skin still prickles with that sixth sense Kody has worked so hard to develop in me.

The blonde at the counter looks between us with practiced amusement as Kody arranges a room. "Only one left," she says, sliding a worn ledger across the desk. "The rest are occupied… or closed. Safety regulations." The way she says it makes the hair on my neck rise.

Kody glances over, clearly waiting for me to object. One brow lifts in question. "Well?"

"You're the strategist," I shrug, feigning nonchalance even as my cheeks warm. "I go where you go, remember?"

"Noted." He turns back to the woman. "We'll take it. Pillows and blankets, please."

Her smile curves slow and sly. "Of course." She slides the key across the counter, fingers lingering just a moment too long. "I'll have them sent up—though I doubt you'll need that many." Her gaze drops to where Kody's hand brushes mine as he takes the key. "Enjoy your night."

The bell above the door chimes as she disappears into the back, and I swear I hear a muffled laugh behind it.

I don't look at him.

He doesn't look at me.

"Did she just—?" I ask.

"Yep." He clears his throat. "Stairs?"

"Lead the way," I mutter, grabbing my pack with a little too much force. My shoulder twinges in protest, but it's still a welcome distraction.

The room is larger than I expect, dominated by a bed draped in white linens that suddenly seems far too intimate after the carriage. I set my bag down, trying to ignore how the single piece of furniture underscores everything we're not saying.

"Weird," I mutter, just to break the silence.

"What's weird?" Kody moves past me, his scent trailing behind him.

"It's so clean."

He chuckles, though the way his eyes scan the corners and glance toward the window tells me he's already noting exits, calculating angles. Always the hunter. "Most inns are. You've never stayed in one?"

Heat creeps up my neck. "No. I usually find barns, cellars, hollowed-out places with a door I can wedge shut."

A knock interrupts, saving me from further elaboration. Kody answers it, taking an armful of folded blankets with a murmured thanks.

While he lays them out on the floor, I cross to the window and push aside the heavy crimson drapes. "It's so quiet for a city this size."

"It's two in the morning," he says, smoothing one of the blankets, arranging them on the floor in what is clearly meant to be his bed. The gesture somehow makes my chest ache—both grateful for his respect and frustrated by it.

"You're really sleeping down there?"

He glances up. "What did you think the extra blankets were for?"

I fidget with the curtain cord. "I guess I thought the bed might not have them already…" My cheeks flush the moment the words leave my mouth.

"Seriously?" His grin grows, teasing but not cruel.

"Don't make fun!"

"I'm not." His expression softens. "There's running water too. You should wash up. Sleep."

I hesitate. The bathroom door feels a mile away.

"You don't have to," he adds, rubbing the back of his neck—a rare crack in his confidence. "But I know I'd like to feel human again after that trip."

"You go first—"

"Cass." The way he says my name makes my heart stop. "Go."

"Thanks." I slip past him into the bathroom, careful not to let our bodies brush.

The shower scalds away the chill of the road, the blood and dust of everything we've survived these past few days. A luxury I didn't know I needed. I stay under the spray longer than I should, watching the water swirl down the drain in muted spirals. As if it could carry the weight with it.

When I finally step out, I wrap myself in one of the towels—thick, soft, almost too gentle for the bruises underneath. Steam clings to the air as I wipe a clear patch on the fogged mirror. My reflection stares back—softer without the grime, but still worn around the edges. Not like a Bailey. Not like Eden. Even with her eyes staring back at me, I can't find her in this face.

I reach into my bag and pull out the perfume bottle. It catches the light like a relic. Cool and solid in my palm, heavier than it looks—as if it carries history in its weight. I uncap it slowly, holding my breath as the scent rises: jasmine, black currant… and a colder note beneath, sharp and metallic, like steel hidden in silk. A deterrent, Calvin had written. Designed to keep the Noctis away. Made for Eden. Meant, now, for me.

The glass presses into my fingers as I hesitate.

"I hope you knew what you were doing," I whisper to the empty room then press a drop to my collarbone and let the chill of it settle into my skin. When I open the door, my face is dry, my hands steady, but the weight in my chest has shifted— no lighter, just more tightly held.

When I emerge in my sleep shirt, the scent of warmed jasmine clinging to my skin, I find Kody stretched out on the bed. One arm tucked beneath his head, eyes closed, his features soft in the dim light.

He doesn't look like a hunter the Guild shaped. He looks real. Breakable.

I blow out the candle before I can second-guess myself, then pull back the covers and ease into the bed.

He stirs. "Sorry," he mumbles, already shifting to move. "I'll take the floor—"

My hand finds his chest, firm and warm beneath my palm. "Stay." It comes out in a breath.

He goes still, his heart beating fast beneath my hand. "Cass..."

"I know," I say. "But just tonight."

A pause. His breath catches, then lets go slow. He sinks back, muscles relaxing under my hand.

His arm curls around me, slower this time. Like he's aware of every point of contact. I settle against his side, my head over his heart. His body is solid heat, all sharp edges turned quiet by the dark.

Then I feel it—his breath against my temple, a tremor in the way he pulls me closer. His nose skims my hair, a slow inhale. "You smell..." His voice is rough. "Different."

"Perfume," I murmur. "From the box. It's supposed to ward off monsters."

A laugh, soft and aching. "Bit late for that."

I tilt my face up without thinking, our lips a breath apart.

His eyes find mine in the dark—searching, wrecked. "Cass..."

I don't move. Neither does he.

The air stretches between us, heavy and fragile. My heartbeat fills the silence.

And then—he leans in. Just barely.

His lips graze my forehead. Desire... denial. A line drawn in silence.

I close my eyes, breath shaking. He stays close, but says nothing more.

I let myself fall asleep like that—close enough to feel him, far enough to still wonder what it might be like to be kissed.

35 - Cassia

*B*lood *runs down my arms—sticky, clinging, filling the cracks between my fingers as I clutch the baby tighter. My breath comes ragged, shallow, and still the smell of it thickens—sweet, metallic, suffocating.*

The dog's whine fades somewhere distant. Brave and broken, but gone.

I can't stop shaking. I can't stop seeing her—smiling with my blood on her mouth. The shadows still carry her laughter, cruel and endless.

"Benji…" My voice trembles as I lift my head.

And he's there. Framed in the doorway, eyes wide, breath caught. For a heartbeat, hope flares. He came. He always does.

But even as I look at him, my chest caves with dread. Because I see it. The hunger burning in his eyes. The way his shoulders tighten as though fighting himself. He smells it. He wants it—wants me.

Still, my lips form the words. "Promise me…" I push the baby toward him with what little strength remains. My arms ache, shaking from blood loss. "…keep him safe."

He tries to soothe me. His hands on my back, his voice steady—"You'll be fine. I'll get you to the hospital." Lies we both know.

I shake my head. The truth claws its way out. "She bit me. I feel it—inside. I won't… I can't…" My throat breaks on the words. "Please, Benji. Don't let me become her."

His denial is desperate, his eyes bright with rage and sorrow. But I know him too well. He's always fought the darkness inside himself, and now he has to fight it for me.

"I trust you," I whisper, words dragging like lead.

His arms fold around me—strong, trembling—and for a moment I let myself believe in safety. In love. In the future we were never allowed to have.

Then his mouth is at my throat. A hot sting, a tearing ache. My body jerks, instinct screaming to fight, but my soul stills. Because this isn't betrayal. It's mercy.

The world blurs at the edges and my fingers find his, weak and trembling.

"Benji..." The name leaves my lips like it belongs to someone else, pulled from a throat that isn't mine. His arms crush me close, his mouth at my throat. Pain blooms, warmth pouring away. My grip falters as I whisper the last word I'll ever breathe—

His sob breaks against my ear, raw and shattering. My pulse stumbles, blood slipping from me in a slow tide I cannot stem. He holds me tighter, as if his strength could anchor the falling world.

Then the pressure eases. The noise softens like the tide waters pulling back. Cold seeps in at the edges—not cruel, but inevitable—and I let go, drifting into a quiet that feels almost like peace.

I jolt awake, choking for air. My chest heaves like I've surfaced from drowning. Sweat slicks my skin, pooling at the hollow of my throat, dampening the sheets. My nightshirt clings, plastered to me. My pulse hammers in my ears, and I don't realize I'm sobbing until salt stings my lips. My throat burns as if I had been screaming. My neck aches, hot, as though teeth pressed there, too sharp to dismiss as dream.

"Cass?" Kody's voice cuts through the haze. He's already moving toward the bed, concern sharp in his dark eyes. "Bad dream?"

I drag a trembling hand down my face, trying to steady my breath. "Not like the ones I've had before." The words scrape out ragged. "It felt like... it wasn't even me. I was dying, and—" The rest collapses in my throat.

His brow furrows, that hunter's wariness flickering behind his eyes. "Did you see anything? Hear anything useful?"

I shake my head faintly, fingers knotting in the blanket. "It was just a dream," I whisper, though the ache in my chest, the echo of someone else's grief, says otherwise.

It lingers, sharp and tender all at once. Not just fear, but something deeper—a love so fierce it burned even as it broke. I can still feel the arms that held me, the voice that refused to let go, the desperate weight of devotion pressed into a final breath.

The images fade, but the pull doesn't. It hums low under my skin, an ache without reason, a yearning that unsettles even as it refuses to let go.

I clutch the blanket tighter, shaken by how something so fleeting can leave a mark so deep.

His brow furrows, that hunter's wariness flickering behind his eyes. "Any information could be significant. Even dreams. Sometimes our minds catch details we don't realize." He straightens, tension tight across his shoulders. "All our leads point to Zurich, but it's a labyrinth. The archives will have property records. And locals... rumors have a way of surviving even when history gets erased."

"Breadcrumbs," I murmur, sliding to the edge of the bed. My legs wobble under me, unsteady. My chest still aches with the phantom of another death, another life, but the fear that once gripped me is gone. What lingers instead is sharper. Hungrier. "If my family really did settle here..."

"Then someone remembers." His gaze holds mine, steady and grim. "Rich families leave scars. Especially ones with unusual histories."

I square my shoulders, even as my hands still tremble. "Where do we start?"

"Archives first. Then taverns near whatever properties we find. People talk more freely over food." His eyes lock with mine. "But Cass, whatever we uncover—"

"I know." The words leave steadier than I feel, the echo of another woman's last breath still inside me. I meet his gaze without flinching. "I'm ready."

THE BUILDING STANDS resilient despite its age—wood and stone weathered by time, yet meticulously restored. No small feat after the war.

My fingers trail along dusty spines until I find the ledgers marked B. I pull one free and carry it to the long table where Kody sits surrounded by maps and folded land plots.

I flip it open. "Bac... Bah... Bai..." I murmur, thumbing through the pages.

My stomach sinks. "It's not here."

Kody looks up. "What do you mean?"

I slide the book toward him, tapping the spot. "Bailey should be right here. But there's nothing."

He frowns, scanning the column of names—then stops. His finger lands on the jagged edge of a torn-out page. "It was here. Someone removed it."

My pulse quickens. "Why would they do that?"

"Because they didn't want it found." He closes the book and stands. "Let's ask."

The archivist sits behind a polished desk, her silver bun wound tight as wire. She doesn't look up until Kody stops in front of her.

"Excuse me, ma'am," he says politely, laying the book open. "Do you happen to know what happened to the Bailey record? This page is missing."

The woman peers at the torn gap through narrow glasses, and for the briefest moment, her posture tightens—just enough to notice.

"Ah. Yes," she says smoothly. "Well, if it's not there, I'm afraid we no longer have it on file. You might try the estate census maps. Section IKH-49."

"Thank you," Kody says, voice easy. But the moment we're out of earshot, he mutters, "She flinched."

"What?" I look over my shoulder.

Kody's voice lowers as we move deeper into the stacks. "Did you catch the way she stiffened at the name?"

I blink, replaying the moment. "No... I didn't even notice."

He glances sideways at me, lips tugging into a knowing smile. "You really didn't, huh?"

"I guess... I'm still waking up."

He bumps my shoulder gently. "Slept too well, clearly."

I shoot him a look. "Whose fault is that?"

He turns to me, the look in his eyes enough to make my pulse skip. "I don't know... you're the one who asked me to stay."

I roll my eyes, but the heat in my cheeks betrays me.

"That was for survival. Don't get cocky."

"Too late." His smirk deepens. "Cocky's kind of my specialty."

I shoot him a look, half warning, half smile. "Careful. That ego's going to get you killed."

He grins, then abruptly straightens. "Ah. Here it is." Kody pulls a bundle of rolled maps and documents from the shelf.

We retreat to the desks, our footsteps too loud in the hush of the archive. I sit across from him as he unrolls the first page, his attention narrowing with focus. A prickle creeps along the back of my neck. I glance over my shoulder, empty space, but a single yellowed clipping now lies near the next table. I didn't hear it fall. There's no breeze.

I reach down and pick it up. "Did you drop—?"

Kody's already flipping through map corners. "I think this might be it. Do you know if there was another name before the Baileys took over?"

I don't answer. I'm staring at the headline printed in faded ink:

Incident at the Bailey Manor.

"It made the news," I whisper. "So whatever happened… it wasn't quiet."

I pass it to him, my fingers trembling slightly.

His gaze sharpens as he reads. "Shit," he mutters. "'Local philanthropists Eli and Jori Bailey vanish after mysterious fire claims east wing. Daughter's whereabouts unknown.'" He meets my eyes. "The date... it's right around when you were sent away."

"A fire?" I echo. "I don't remember a fire."

"Not just fire." He leans in, voice low. "'Witnesses report strange lights, unusual sounds in weeks prior. Local authorities cite accident, though staff interviews suggest otherwise.'" He touches the torn edge. "The rest is gone. But there's mention of 'nocturnal disturbances' and 'missing servants.'"

A silence stretches between us like a held breath.

"We were always moving," I murmur, trying to make sense of the shift. "Hideouts, aliases... Mom said we couldn't stay anywhere too long. Then suddenly... we weren't running anymore. We had staff. A mansion."

Kody folds the clipping carefully along its pre-creased lines. "That kind of shift doesn't happen unless they found something. Or someone found them."

A flicker of memory surfaces—burnt air, the acrid sting of smoke. "I do remember smoke... But I thought it was the kitchen. Holli was always burning toast."

"Holli?"

"My caretaker. She felt like... family. And she's the one who—" I stop, swallowing hard. "She's the one who sent me away that night. I thought because my parents told her to."

Kody scans another document. "The staff interviews mention a 'trusted employee' who vanished the same night. No body was found."

My breath catches. The walls close in. "She told me to follow the North Star. That Mr. Parker would be waiting at the chapel." I run a thumb over the torn newsprint. "But I panicked. I ran to the forest. Hid for days."

"Probably saved your life." His tone is tight. "Most of the staff reports end abruptly. The phrase 'relocated without notice' appears too often."

"You think they were silenced."

He nods once. "I think someone wanted to erase every trace of what happened that night. And they almost did."

I stare down at the clipping, heart hammering. "The lights. The sounds. The way we stopped running…" I meet his eyes. "It wasn't safety. It was a trap."

"And you got out before it closed," he says, standing. "But now we're back in its shadow."

He extends a hand—not just to help me stand, but to anchor me. Still, his grip lingers. Steady and steeling.

"There's a tavern near the old market," he says. "The kind where secrets live longer than people."

"And if they don't want to talk?"

His smirk is quick, but it doesn't reach his eyes. "Everyone talks to a pretty girl asking the right questions."

"And her dangerous-looking backup?"

"Exactly." But his gaze darkens, jaw tight. "If they don't talk... we find the ones who made them afraid to."

I glance one last time at the headline in my hand—
Incident at the Bailey Manor.

Flames. Shadows. Names crossed out and pages torn. Some truths don't want to stay buried. I take a steadying breath. "Lead the way."

36 - Cassia

Outside, the afternoon sun does little to warm the chill that's settled into my bones. The article burns in my memory as we navigate the narrow, crooked streets of Zurich, ancient buildings leaning inward as if listening.

"The tavern's just ahead." Kody's hand brushes the small of my back as he guides me around a corner. "The Silver Crown. Been here since before the war, according to the maps."

"How do you know they'll talk to us?"

"Places like this… regulars treat afternoon drinks like church confession." His gaze flicks over the street. "And the owner's name came up in the census records. His family's been here a long time."

I catch the subtle shift in his posture as he glances behind us.

"What is it?"

"Nothing." But his hand doesn't move. "Just making sure our digging hasn't drawn attention."

Ahead, a weathered wooden sign swings gently in the breeze, its paint faded but still legible: The Silver Crown. Unlike the other buildings, its windows gleam, brass door handles polished to a shine. Someone still takes pride in this place.

"Let me handle the questions at first," Kody says. "Owner's name is Henrik. His grandfather would've been pouring drinks the night of the fire."

"And you think he'll just hand over the truth?"

"Not directly. But if we—"

He breaks off, one arm pulling me closer as a group of men exit the tavern. They move quietly, smooth and predatory in a way that sets every hair on my neck upright. They pass without a glance, but the air behind them sours with a scent I now associate with death: syrupy-sweet rot.

"You still think this is a good idea?" I whisper.

He watches the men disappear into the shadows. "Now I think our chances are even better. Noctis don't linger unless there's something worth guarding."

"You think they're here because of the Baileys?"

"I think Henrik's about to become very interesting." His fingers brush mine, warm and grounding. "Ready?"

I squeeze once, then let go. "As I'll ever be."

The door closes gently behind us. Dim oil lamps cast flickering shadows across dark wooden beams, their glow barely reaching the corners of the room. The tavern stretches deeper than expected, tables scattered across uneven floorboards worn smooth by centuries of boots. A massive stone hearth dominates one wall, long cold.

That faint rot from outside lingers here—sharpened now by the tang of cooking meat and stale ale, like a feast laid out in a graveyard.

Patrons glance up at our entrance—too quick and too in sync to pass for casual curiosity. In the far corner, three men sit unnaturally still, glasses full and untouched.

"Welcome in," calls the man behind the bar, wiping his hands on a cloth that's seen better days. "What'll the day be for you? Casual lunch ale, romantic champagne?" He wriggles his eyebrows with exaggerated charm.

Kody approaches, and I follow close behind, fighting the chill crawling up my spine since we walked in. His posture shifts subtly—looser, like he's adapting to the room's strange undercurrent.

"Just travelers passing through," he says easily. "Looking for fresh water and a quick bite. Can you accommodate?"

"That we can. Menu's above the bar." The man gestures lazily. "Let me know when you're ready to order."

"We were hoping to try the Henrik special."

The cloth stills. "What did you say?"

"The Henrik special." Kody shifts his weight, letting his sleeve slide back just enough to reveal the hunter's guild brand on his forearm. "Close friend said it's a must."

The barkeep's smile sharpens, widening without softening. His shoulders stiffen even as he nods. "Well then. You and your lady take a seat. I'll get it out to you."

We claim a table near the back wall, Kody choosing the seat that gives him a full view of the exits. I watch him scan the room with a quiet efficiency I've come to rely on.

"That was weird," I murmur once we're seated.

"What was?"

"How fast he changed."

Kody's smile doesn't quite reach his eyes. "Sometimes all it takes is saying the right thing at the right time."

I study him, then lean forward slightly, the tavern warmth making it easier to pretend we're not here for dangerous reasons. "And how do you know what that is?"

He looks at me then—not just a glance, but a study. His eyes flick to my mouth before returning.

"Experience." A beat. "Want me to show you?"

My pulse skips. For a moment, the tavern disappears—the chill, the threat, the unreadable patrons. All I feel is the press of his words in the charged space between us.

A glass clinks too loudly at the bar. I blink, heart thudding, and glance away.

We're not alone. Not safe. Not here for this.

Kody doesn't push it. But he lifts his water glass, angling it slightly. "Watch how the light hits it. What do you see?"

I mimic him, eyes narrowing—and nearly drop my cup. Reflected in the glass, the men in the corner aren't just watching us. Their eyes shimmer when the light catches them. Too bright and too still.

"Lesson one," he murmurs. His free hand finds mine and brushes a kiss to my knuckles with a chuckle that's too smooth. "Sometimes what you don't see matters more than what you do."

My heart stutters. I should be focused on the lesson—but the intimate gesture, even if it's for show, derails every thought in my head.

"Do you think Henrik knows anything about the fire?" I manage, clearing my throat to mask the tightness.

Kody opens his mouth, but Henrik appears beside our table with the timing of a stage cue. He sets down our plates with slow precision. "Special of the day," he says aloud. Then, quieter: "Best eat while it's hot. Some folks around here… they get twitchy when others linger. Makes them eager to play sports."

My fork stills halfway to my mouth. "Sports?"

Henrik leans in to wipe the table—unnecessary, but methodical. "That article you were reading," he says, eyes flicking to me. "The fire? You might find more answers up at St. Michael's bell tower. Old district. It overlooks what's left of the Bailey grounds."

I lean forward. "Wait, the fire—?"

Kody's fingers close over mine, gently but firmly.

"Thank you," he says with careful calm. "We'll keep that in mind."

Henrik gives the smallest of nods. "Sun sets in three hours. Best be up there before then." He glances toward the corner table. "Not every place keeps the same rules after dark."

With that, he returns to the bar, leaving behind two fresh plates of food and a cold knot in my stomach.

Across the room, the three men lift their glasses—not to drink, but in silent toast. Their smiles don't reach their eyes.

"Kody…" My voice comes out thin.

"I see them." His thumb draws slow circles on my palm. "Eat. We head for the bell tower before the light fades."

We finish the meal in taut silence, counting the minutes until sunset—and the distance between answers and whatever waits in the dark.

37 - Cassia

"He said the bell tower was in the old district," I murmur, studying the city map under slanting afternoon light.

"Yes, it should be this way." Kody rolls the map and tucks it into his coat. "If we're lucky, we'll reach it with enough daylight left to get a general position on the estate. We can backtrack from landmarks after that."

The streets narrow the deeper we go. The scent of rot creeps in again, faint but insistent, and the buildings here lean toward each other like conspirators—their windows shuttered, faces blank. Strange symbols mark the stone and wood around us. Wards or warnings, I can't tell.

Locals hurry inside at our approach, doors clicking shut behind them like a trail of falling dominoes.

The iron gate creaks open with a shudder that seems too loud for the silence pressing in around us.

Kody pauses beneath the arch, eyes catching on a carved symbol embedded in the stone.

"Interesting," he murmurs.

I step closer. "What?"

"This symbol here…" He brushes away dust with a thumb.

It's circular—barbed and radiant like a sun twisted by violence. Sharp flares extend from a dark ring, and at its center, a jagged V shape overlaps it, piercing through the ring like fangs.

"I've seen this before," he mutters, voice low. "In the archives, when I was researching your family. But it wasn't associated with the Bailey name."

"You think it's connected to them somehow?"

He doesn't answer immediately. His eyes scan the rooftops, then the narrowing path ahead. "I think it's a lead. But we need to be careful."

Ahead, the bell tower rises above the fractured skyline— its steeple blackened, its bells long silent. A weathered stone path winds up toward the base… but partway along, a narrower trail splits off, curving into shadow.

Kody's jaw tightens. "The tower entrance is ahead. That side path might lead to the overlook Henrik mentioned."

I follow his gaze, feeling the weight of the decision before he even speaks again.

"I'll check the main tower," he says, reluctantly. "You take the overlook. But stay sharp. Shout if anything feels wrong."

I raise a brow. "What happened to never splitting up?"

"Everything here feels wrong." His expression softens— just a little. "But if we don't, we might miss the daylight ."

"I'll be quick." I manage a smirk for his sake, though the unease in my chest is hard to ignore.

He doesn't smile back, not really. "If I'm not back in ten minutes—"

"Then I come looking." I rest a hand on my knife hilt. "I've got your back."

His eyes linger on me for a beat longer than necessary, then he nods and heads up the main steps toward the bell tower.

I turn toward the path veiled in overgrown vines and shadow. As I round the corner alone, movement snaps at the edge of my vision. I spin, blade raised—

"Still quick with that knife, I see." The voice freezes me. "Though your form's different than I remember, Cass."

"Felix?" My voice barely carries as he steps from the shadows.

He grins wide, his features sharper now, almost sculpted, as if something peeled away the human beneath and left only precision. His skin is unnaturally smooth, stretched tight across cheekbones that once softened when he laughed. His eyes gleam with pale hunger, catching the light like glass.

I glance toward the bell tower—Kody's last direction. If he returns now…

Felix spreads his arms, grin deepening. "What, no hug for

your old friend?"

I should run. Scream. Anything.

Instead, my feet move forward, drawn by reflex. For a moment, the boy who once made me laugh through bruised ribs and grueling drills is still there. His arms close around me—cold, wrong—and yet the spin, the laugh, it feels like stepping into a memory already spoiled by decay.

"Look at you." He sets me down, appraising me like a collector might a forgotten relic. "Still diving headfirst into danger, I see."

"You're one to talk, stalking through shadows." I try to keep my voice even. But his grin is off. The way his pupils dilate, then retract. The way he watches my pulse in my neck. I glance toward the tower again.

His gaze follows. "Worried about your handler?" his lip curls at the word.

My spine stiffens. "Kody's not—"

"Relax," he says. "He's busy. I made sure of it." His smile tightens. "I wanted you to myself for a moment."

"What happened to you?" I whisper.

"The guild happened." His voice darkens. "Sent me into a trap. I was bleeding out in a cellar, wondering if they'd even bother to collect my tags." He steps closer, voice reverent now. "And then she found me. The Mistress."

He stands straighter, something proud and hungry curling in his shoulders. "She saw my potential. Never had to prove myself like the guild required. She saved me, revealed my true nature."

My stomach twists.

"She gave me strength. Purpose. I'm not hollow anymore, Cass. I'm awake. You've been shackled your whole life, told lies about what we are. But you don't have to be anymore."

"You're a Noctis," I breathe.

"She is more than Noctis," he says, eyes flaring. "And I am more than Felix now. She gave me clarity. And… she's curious about you." he tilts his head.

My breath stalls. "Why?"

"Because you're not like others. You belong with us."

"I'm nothing like you," I snap.

His voice turns low. "You could be. Strong. Untethered. And you'd never have to wonder what your little hunter truly thinks when he looks at you."

My pulse stutters. "Don't."

"Oh, Cass." He smiles like it's a joke only he gets. "You think he wants you? He wants what you represent. A mystery. A mission. A means to redemption. But the moment you become real—flawed... broken? He'll toss you aside. The guild always does."

I step back.

"You should've come with me years ago. You wanted to. I could feel it, even when you wouldn't say it outloud." His voice turns rough. "And I know you feel it now."

"Stop." The word is sharp. "Whatever we had—it wasn't that."

"You were mine," he says, like a claim. "You just didn't know it yet." He pauses, voice cooling. "But go on. Chase the Baileys. Your *family*. You think finding the truth will set you free? It won't. You're already bound to it. Your name, your blood, it's a chain. You just haven't felt the weight around you yet."

Footsteps echo behind me in the tower—Kody.

Felix's head tilts. "You should come now, before he drags you down with him. You think he'll die for you?" A laugh slips out. "He will die. *Because* of you. That's a promise."

"Leave." I force the word through clenched teeth. "Now."

He fades into the shadows like he was never there at all. "We'll talk again soon. The Mistress is very interested in family reunions."

"Cass?"

I turn. Kody stands at the path's end, gaze sharp, reading me as he approaches.

"Found a path," I lie. "It led nowhere."

He watches me too long. Then nods, brushing his hand against the small of my back, grounding me.

"Let's keep moving." he looks over his shoulder where Felix just disappeared. "We're not alone."

I don't look back. I don't need to. I can still feel Felix watching, waiting. Convinced I owe him for a promise I never made—and terrified he might be right. And apparently, Kody can sense him there, too.

38 - Cassia

The walk back through narrowing streets feels longer, heavier with unspoken weight. Kody's hand never leaves my back, steady and warm—but he's alert now. Every glance sharp. Every step measured.

The last sliver of daylight vanished while we walked. Now the sky is deep blue ink, the kind that makes shadows feel thicker than air.

"One more stop," Kody says, steering us toward the Hollow Bell—a tavern tucked beneath street level, half-submerged in old stone and older secrets. "Note in the tower said we could get info here." Fog curls against the crooked door. Its warped wooden sign groans in the wind like it's warning us off.

The moment we step inside, the warmth is wrong. The air wraps around us like a damp blanket—heavy with pipe smoke and a sickly-sweet floral musk. Too sweet. It clings to my throat. Gas lamps cast flickering halos across walls mounted with rusted weapons and hunting trophies with teeth that don't belong to any animal I know.

In the corner, a man mutters over a half-empty glass, hunched like his bones are trying to hide. "Tribute season," he says to no one. "Pretty ones first. Always the pale ones. Always…"

The bartender looks up—and stills, eyes locking on me. Not my face… my hair. Recognition flashes and disappears behind a well-rehearsed smile. "Evenin', travelers. Bit late to be out, isn't it? What can I get you?"

"Looking for local history," Kody says, stepping forward

like he owns the room. "The Bailey estate."

The drunk's voice sharpens. "They took my Gwenny. Right from her bed—left the window open. No footprints. No mess. Just gone."

The bartender places two glasses on the bar with too much care. "That abandoned mansion down Parlem street? Place has been dead a long time now. Just an old ruin with ghosts these days."

The drunk grinds out another laugh. "And the deals that keep it that way... they're still breathing."

Then I smell it—cloying and sweet, like lilies gone soft in the heat. It prickles behind my eyes. Thickens the air.

Behind us, three figures sit motionless in the far corner. I could've sworn their table was empty when we entered. They haven't touched their drinks. Haven't blinked. And they watch us, heads tilted just slightly—still and silent.

Kody doesn't turn—but I know him. He's already cataloged exits and every threat. "What deals?" he asks, tone light. Controlled.

The bartender's eyes dart to the far corner—then quickly away. "Just rumors. Stories locals like to scare each other with. Best not to repeat them. Or listen."

"Seems like people believe them," Kody says evenly, motioning to drunk at the end of the bar.

The bartender leans in just slightly, his voice barely audible. "You don't want to be here after dark. Not with her." A beat. "Finish your drinks. Leave quietly. If they think you're just passing through, they won't follow."

"You said Parlem—"

"I said nothing," the bartender says louder, eyes now on the corner table. "Just travelers, right? Nothing to ask. Nothing to say."

Another bark of drunk laughter as the man slams his cup down. "Doesn't matter what you say. Once they catch your scent, they follow. And they wait."

I feel it—the cold, creeping behind me like a breath down the back of my neck.

One of the men rises from his seat with a predator's stillness, movement smooth and unnatural, like muscle memory practiced too many times. His boots make no sound on the warped floorboards.

"Leaving already?" a woman's voice murmurs behind

me—velvet-lined and serrated.

A second man from the booth joins her, this one drifting in from the right.

"Such lovely color," she purrs, the words brushing against me like fingers on skin. "Like blood kissed by morning sun."

My head swims. I turn, and the edges of my vision pulse—warped glass, bending around their silhouettes. Four figures now block the exit after the last joins them, sharp-featured and hungry-eyed. Their bodies seem to sway with a rhythm I can't steady.

"The Mistress has a taste for rare things," a new voice cuts in, this one flatter, colder. "And it's her season."

Mistress. That name again.

My thoughts stagger. Kody's blade flashes from his belt like light cracking the dark, but smoke is already pouring from the vents above, curling thick and sweet.

"Cass," he barks. "Cover your mouth."

I try—but the scent is already in my head, dripping down my spine. Honeysuckle. Ash. Rot masked with perfume. My limbs go heavy, my thoughts tarred with warmth that isn't mine. The room sways like a sinking ship.

"They always resist at first," the woman hums. "But it passes."

Kody shoves me behind him and I stumble, knees buckling, fingers grasping air. His blade moves like firelight in slashes and sparks, but there are too many.

A table crashes to the floor. Glass explodes. A scream cuts through the smoke—raw, human.

"Feeding ground!" the bartender yells, but it sounds like it's coming from underwater. "They weren't supposed to take any tonight!"

My fingers close around my dagger. It feels wrong—like it doesn't belong to me. I lurch toward Kody, but he's a blur in the smoke, locked in with two of them.

Then—ice down my spine. Fingers twist into my hair. "The Mistress will be so pleased," the woman hisses beside my ear.

I try to stab, but my arm won't move. My body betrays me.

Kody hits her like a storm, and the next moment I'm soaked in heat—blood or sweat or both. Her shriek splits the air.

More shouting. Another crash. The wooden beams above groan.

His arms find me, lifting, dragging—I don't know. The stairs blur beneath my feet. I hear myself gasp but I can't feel my lungs.

"I've got you," he says again and again, like saying it can make it true. His voice trembles, raw at the edges.

The streets outside are empty, wind slicing down them like blades. Light flickers from windows above, but no one opens a door. I try to keep my eyes open and fail as the world smears.

"Sorry," I try to say, but the word never leaves my mouth. Only silence follows, pulling me under.

39 - Cassia

Consciousness returns in fragments. Stone walls arch overhead, their surfaces etched with old symbols—wards or warnings, maybe both. Dried herbs hang from exposed beams, their scent sharp with rosemary and bitterroot, mixing with the faint woodsmoke curling from a dying hearth. My head throbs, heavy and slow, thoughts dragging like they're wading through syrup.

"Welcome back." Kody's voice pulls me toward the present. He sits beside the narrow bed, one arm strapped tight to his ribs, tension carved deep into his features. A blooming bruise shadows his jaw. Behind him, weapon racks sag with age, their contents dulled and dust-covered. Training dummies slump in corners, still bearing the marks of long-abandoned drills.

"Where..." My voice rasps, mouth dry. Flashes of memory stab through—smoke, pressure, blood, those eyes.

"Old guild safehouse." He offers a tin cup, supporting me when I try to sit and falter. The water tastes like metal and earth. "Locals drove the hunters out years ago. Word is, they preferred dealing with the Noctis."

"Why didn't we stay here before?" I ask between slow sips. "Instead of the hotel?"

He huffs a humorless sound. "Hotels have mattresses that don't smell like mildew. And we weren't hiding then." His expression darkens. "Now we are."

The room resolves around me: a cot disguised with storage compartments, a cracked mirror angled toward the door, faded curtains hiding more than windows. Escape routes, kill zones—this place was built by people who expected to be hunted.

"Your ribs..." I glance at the torn fabric of his shirt. The bandages are tight.

"I've had worse." But the lie rides his shallow breath. "How's your head?"

"Like someone stuffed it with wet cotton." I rub my temples. "That smoke…"

"Dhatura," Kody mutters, the word like rust on his tongue. "Hunters used to burn it to draw Noctis out of hiding. It doesn't hurt them—just… changes the way they smell. Dogs trained on the altered scent can track them for miles." He exhales sharply, jaw tense. "Most people exposed to it just get a headache. Maybe nausea. But you—" His voice cuts off, then resumes lower. "You were affected differently."

A quiet dread settles in my chest. "Why?"

He looks at me then, the firelight sharpening the depth of his eyes, making his restraint visible in the way his fingers curl into his leg. "I think someone altered the compound. Changed it to make certain people… compliant. Willing."

I sit up too fast and immediately regret it. The nausea claws back up my throat. "So it wasn't meant to kill me."

"No." His gaze hardens—not at me, but at the memory. "It was meant to deliver you."

I press a palm to my forehead, recalling the whispered suggestions in the smoke—how easy it would have been to follow. To go with them.

"It didn't affect the Noctis?"

He shakes his head. "It's meant to affect them differently, so they moved through it like it was incense. But it turned you into a target. The moment you started swaying, they knew it had worked."

A cold shiver crawls down my spine. "Because of the red hair?"

Kody's expression shutters. "Not just that." He pauses, voice tightening. "There's a reason the Mistress fixates on certain traits. Could be genetic. Could be symbolic. Doesn't matter. What matters is, she wanted you compliant. Not dead."

His hands flex once, then still again. Controlled. Careful. "She knew you'd fight. So they found a way to take the fight out of you."

I reach across the small space between us, fingers brushing his wrist. He doesn't pull away, but his jaw ticks as if it physically hurts him to accept the comfort.

"You couldn't have known," I say softly. "You got me out. That's what matters."

"No." His voice is low, fierce—not aimed at me, but at the broken edges of his own judgment. "I should've known the signs. Should've seen the setup the moment we walked in. Henrik warned us, and I still walked you straight into it."

"Kody—"

"They almost had you." His voice cracks on the edges. "If I'd been slower by seconds—"

"But you weren't." I tighten my grip. "I'm here. Alive."

He looks at me like he's still not sure that's true. Like he's waiting for the guilt to ease and knowing it won't. But after a long breath, he lets the tension bleed out through his shoulders.

"What's all that?" I ask gently, nodding to his documents.

His eyes drop to the papers. When he answers, his voice is steady—but quieter, like he's trying to stay calm for my sake.

"Property registries. Maps. There's a name that keeps showing up near the Bailey estate. Not a person—just a symbol." He taps the edge of one worn page. "Same one we saw carved near the bell tower."

Realization creeps in like cold air under a door. "You remembered what it looked like?"

"The bartender was lying." He spreads out the documents, showing me property deeds and tax filings. "That estate's not abandoned. It's been continuously occupied. By the same family. For years."

My heart stutters. "My parents?"

He nods slowly. "The names match."

He hesitates, and that pause, that look in his eyes, says everything he's afraid to.

"Cass..." he starts.

But I'm already spiraling. "They've been here? All this time?" My voice breaks around the words. "While I was bouncing from one foster home to the next, sleeping with a knife under my pillow, they were—what? Hosting dinner parties?"

"Cassia—"

"Did they even look for me?" I push myself upright, legs

trembling beneath me. "Even once?"

The room spins, but I cling to the bedpost like it can steady the chaos inside me. "Or was it easier to forget? To let me disappear while they started over with their perfect little estate?"

"You don't know the whole story," Kody says, quiet but firm.

"No. I don't." The words rip out of me, bitter and raw. "Because they never came for me." I force the next part out before it can dissolve into something weaker. "Maybe Holli sent me away. Maybe it wasn't their choice. But after that? After I disappeared? They let me stay gone." My voice shakes. "They had years, Kody. Years to try. To search. To leave some kind of sign. And instead I got a locket and a line about following the stars—as if that was supposed to raise me."

The room spins and I sway, but Kody moves instantly, catching me around the waist despite the sharp inhale he can't quite hide. I brace my weight against him, and for a second, everything is heat and pressure and muscle. Safe.

"I was eight," I whisper, voice ragged. "I didn't know how to be alone."

"I know." His voice breaks with quiet fury—not at me, but at the people who made me feel this way.

"And now they're here. Just... living like nothing happened. Playing along, paying their taxes, pretending the world makes sense..." My throat knots around a half-laugh, half-sob. "I don't even know if I want to hug them or scream in their faces."

"Both are valid." His chin rests gently against the crown of my head. "But maybe save the screaming until we know the full story."

I laugh—a real one this time, small and shaky. "When did you become the reasonable one?"

"One of us has to be," he murmurs, but there's no smile in it.

He pulls back just enough to see my face. His hand lifts, rough and careful, brushing away tears I hadn't realized were there. His eyes search mine—not asking, not pushing, just... holding space.

"Cass," he says, voice low, thick. "Whatever we find tomorrow—whatever they did or didn't do... I'm not going anywhere. You got that?"

I nod, leaning into the warmth of his palm. "Okay."

We stay like that. Breathing the same air. The fire crackles softly behind him, casting shadows that dance across the old stone walls. My pulse pounds in my ears, too loud in the quiet. His hand lingers at my cheek, his thumb tracing the curve of my cheekbone, a touch so gentle it nearly undoes me.

"I'm sorry," I whisper, eyes lowering. "I know I keep… reading into things." I force a shaky breath. "It's probably all in my head."

A muscle ticks in his jaw. He hesitates, then quietly says, "We shouldn't."

"I know."

"I'm supposed to be the professional here."

I huff out something like a laugh, brittle around the edges. "You're terrible at it."

He smiles and presses his forehead to mine. Slow, careful. "It's not."

I search his eyes. "What's not?"

"All in your head."

My breath catches.

I don't move. I just feel—the weight of everything in his eyes, the way his fingers tremble ever so slightly. It doesn't feel like he's holding me because I'm fragile. It feels like he's steadying himself, too. Like if he lets go, I might fall apart again. And maybe I will.

Because for the first time in days, my head isn't spinning. The ache in my chest is still there, but his presence cuts through the noise. Solid, grounded, and real.

I tilt my chin. Just a little. And that's all it takes.

He closes the distance with aching slowness, like he's afraid the moment might shatter. His lips brush mine—tentative, feather-light. A question.

I answer with a breath. With the way my fingers curl into his shirt. With the way I kiss him back, soft and sure.

It isn't a wildfire. It's a spark we've been guarding for so long that finally lit. It burns slow. Deep and reverent.

When he pulls away, it's only an inch—but his hand lingers against my cheek like he's memorizing the shape of me.

"I've wanted to do that for longer than I should admit," he murmurs, voice raw.

"So why now?"

"Because you looked at me like you weren't afraid," he says. "And I finally believed it."

Silence settles again—warm this time, like the moment after a storm when the world is still dripping but clean.

He pulls away, and I catch his hand before he can retreat. "Kody..." I whisper.

His eyes close like the sound of his name hurts. "Don't."

"Stay."

"I can't." His voice is hoarse. "Not tonight."

I close my eyes. "Why?"

"Because tomorrow… we go to the estate. And things will change." His thumb brushes my cheek again. "Tomorrow first. After that… everything else."

He releases my hand like it hurts to let go and I sink back onto the cot—not because I'm retreating, but because I can. Because despite the dust, the cracked frame, and the paper-thin blanket, I feel safer than I've felt in years. Because I know he's still here, watching. Still with me.

"Rest," he says, handing me the blanket. "I'll be right here."

"Promise?"

"Wild Noctis couldn't drag me away."

I close my eyes, his kiss still warm on my lips.

Tomorrow I'll face whatever truths the estate holds.

But tonight, in this broken safehouse with this man who looks at me like I'm something precious and dangerous all at once, I let myself believe that whatever comes next, I'm strong enough to face it.

And the last thing I hear before sleep claims me is Kody's whispered words to himself: "Just please let me be wrong about this one."

40 - Cassia

I stare at my mud-crusted boots, heart drumming like it's bracing for a fight. Dust stirs with every shift of my weight on the worn sofa cushion, curling in the morning light like smoke.

I should be ready. Last night, I was ready. But the closer we get, the more wrong it feels—like stepping into a dream I already know how to wake from.

"Ready?" Kody steps out from the side room, a preserved food packet in hand. His hair is damp at the edges, like he tried to scrub away more than sleep. He looks… steady. Still. He offers a small smile, like maybe he's trying to meet me halfway.

"I'm… not sure." The words come quieter than I expect.

He sinks down beside me, the quiet weight of him grounding. "Second thoughts?" He offers the packet. Not pushing, just there.

I take it, our fingers brushing. "I've been wondering if… maybe they don't want me? Or worse—what if they do, and it's not enough?" My voice is barely above a whisper. "What if I built them up to be more than what they are? And they're just people who let me go and never looked back?"

He doesn't answer at first. Just lets the silence hold without cracking under it. His shoulder touches mine—solid, reassuring. "Then you'll deal with it. Like you've dealt with everything else."

I want to believe that. But my voice catches. "I've spent so long needing them to be more than they probably are."

He studies me for a long moment. "Sometimes it's not

about fear. It's about knowing that once you open that door... you can't close it again."

My thumb drags across the sealed edge of the food packet, eyes fixed on it like the answer might be hiding beneath the label. "You think I'm running?"

He's silent for a breath. When I glance up, he's staring at the window, scanning the tree line, jaw set. Like it's easier to face the woods than me. "I think you're smart," he says finally, voice low. "And gut feelings don't lie. If something in you is pulling back... maybe it knows something your head hasn't caught up to yet." A beat passes. Then, softer: "Sometimes waiting gives you space to figure out what actually matters."

My eyes linger on him. Still, he doesn't look over. "Like what?" I ask.

He lifts a shoulder in a shrug that almost passes for indifference. "Whatever's real."

My chest tightens. I work the edge of the packet, appetite long gone. "And if I decide I don't want to find them after all?"

He's still. Then, without fanfare, he slips his hand into mine—slow, sure. A choice, not a reflex.

"You've helped me get this far," I murmur, guilt twisting in my chest. "I dragged you crossed a continent chasing people I'm not even sure I want to face anymore."

"I wasn't dragged," he says, voice quieter now. "I came with you. Because I wanted to."

That stills me. "I thought... you'd be frustrated."

Kody shifts, his fingers trailing lightly against my palm— a slow, deliberate movement, like he's grounding himself in the contact. His gaze stays fixed on my hand. "I'd be lying if I said I didn't want answers too. There are a lot of questions surrounding your family. But I'd rather you be okay than to get them."

I blink, throat tight. The warmth of his touch echoes louder than his words. I don't move. Don't breathe. I don't want him to pull away any further.

"There's work in this region," he offers. "We could take some contracts. Stay close. Let things settle until... if you decide you're ready."

That pulls my gaze to him—sharp and sudden. He says it so easily, *if*. But I hear the truth in the pause. He's not convinced I should meet them. Maybe he knows something I don't. Maybe he's afraid of what I'll find. Or worse, who I'll become if I do.

"You… really think I could do this? Be a hunter?"

His smile is small but real. "I wouldn't waste my time on someone I didn't believe in."

The words settle deep. More than encouragement but shy of saying out loud how much I matter. They sit in the hollow of my chest like a seed waiting for light.

I lean into him, letting my temple rest against his shoulder. Not just gratitude, not just comfort. I just want to be here—beside him, where things feel solid.

"Thank you," I whisper.

His fingers slip between mine, steady and sure. He leans in, his chin resting gently against the top of my head.

"I'll contact the guild," he murmurs but he doesn't move—doesn't let go.

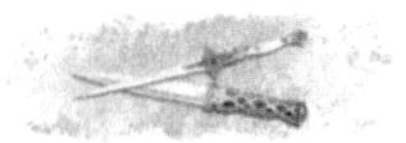

THE CARRIAGE JOLTS hard over another rut, the wheels groaning beneath us. Outside, mist coils low along the lake's edge, clinging to stone and tree like it's reluctant to let go.

"You're right. We need to avoid the towns between destinations," Kody says, map spread across his lap. His eyes track our route with mechanical focus. "We'll cut through Stafa, then walk the ridge into Rapperswil. Never let anyone outside the guild know where you're actually headed."

I nod, but my attention drifts to the trees. The forest thickens as we pass deeper into it, shadows twisting in unnatural ways. For a moment, I think I see movement—a shape too still, watching.

Felix?

My breath catches.

Kody notices—his hand instantly on his weapon. "What is it?"

I blink, but the shape is gone. "Nothing," I murmur, settling back. "Just… ghosts."

His expression shifts—jaw locking, eyes narrowing. "Those tend to follow us in this line of work."

"Do yours visit often?"

He doesn't respond right away. When he does, his voice is low. "Some nights more than others." His fingers curl slightly against the map. "Sarah used to say ghosts are just memories we're not ready to face."

I study his profile, sharp in the dusky light. "Is that why you push people away?" The question feels too bold once it's out, but I don't take it back.

His gaze lifts to meet mine. There's no anger in it—just a quiet kind of ruin. Weariness, sharp as shattered glass. "Maybe I'm just tired of watching the people I care about turn into memories."

"Isn't that what makes the memories worth it?" I ask gently. "That they mattered enough to haunt you?"

A faint breath escapes him—almost a laugh, but missing its shape. "Sarah said something similar once."

"Tell me about her?" My voice barely carries above the hum of the wheels.

He looks away, jaw tightening. But a moment later, his hand finds mine between us. "She was like you in some ways. Stubborn. Brave. Wouldn't take orders unless she already agreed with them." His thumb brushes the back of my hand in slow, absent circles. "She always saw angles I didn't. Saw people differently, too. Even the monsters." He pauses. "She thought every Noctis had a story. That if we could understand them, maybe we could stop the spread. Help people resist."

"And did she?"

His grip tightens. "She tried. Followed a rumor about a Noctis whose bite would turn anyone no matter the circumstances. Not like regular Noctis… She said it was a mutation, or maybe something ancient resurfacing. If she could study it, maybe she could stop it."

"What did she find?"

His knuckles pale as his hand curls into a fist. "Vesper." The name hangs in the air like poison. "She got too close. By the time I found her, there wasn't enough left to save." He turns back toward the window, eyes distant—but not detached. The kind of distance that holds grief too sharp to touch.

I stay quiet. But I don't let go of his hand.

"The locals don't speak his name anymore," he adds. "They pretend he's a ghost story. But I saw what he did. What he is."

"That's why you're so careful now," I say.

"No." His gaze snaps back to mine with fire behind it.

"That's why *you* have to be." He leans forward slightly, the intensity of his voice low but searing. "Some Noctis can't be understood, Cassia. You think you can read them, reach them, but all they do is read you back and twist what they find till you don't even recognize yourself."

I don't flinch. "Is that what you think happened to Sarah?"

He doesn't answer—doesn't have to.

THE ROAD TO Stafa winds along the lake's edge, darkness settling like a shroud. We haven't spoken since the ghost conversation, but Kody's hand remains linked with mine, anchoring me in the growing shadows.

When the carriage stops, reality snaps back into place. We're hunters now—or at least, a hunter and his trainee. As we gather our bags, Kody's fingers slip from mine, replaced by the quiet tension that means we're on mission again.

"Stay close," he murmurs, eyes scanning the tree line. "Two hours till full dark."

The weight of my blade at my hip is grounding as we walk. "How far to the safehouse?"

"Hour and a half if we keep pace. Longer if things get complicated." He consults a weathered map in the last of the light. "And they usually do."

A twig snaps and we both freeze. A deer bolts through the undergrowth—but Kody's hand stays near his weapon the rest of the way.

"Most safehouses used to be old homes, monasteries, or outposts—long before the war," he says eventually. "After the Noctis rose, the guild repurposed them. Quiet places. Defensible." A pause. "Good for learning the land."

The path narrows, forcing us to move single file. Kody leads, I cover our backs. The rhythm is instinct now—this choreography of survival we've built between us.

By the time we reach the safehouse, the moon has risen. The cottage is a squat stone shadow pressed into the hillside. Wards I recognize from training mark the lintel—weathered, but still holding.

"Home sweet home," Kody mutters, unlocking the door with a rusted key.

Inside, the air is stale but dry. Weapon racks line one wall.

A narrow bed sits beneath a shuttered window. A trunk marked with the guild's insignia rests nearby.

"I'll set up comms," he says, already moving. From his pack, he pulls a strange contraption—radio bones wired together with copper and crystal, humming faintly with latent power.

"Old tech?" I ask.

"Safer than new." He connects the array, hands steady. "Noctis can't track signals like this. Power grids made us targets. Anyone who understood how to run them didn't last long."

I crouch beside the trunk and ease it open. Inside: neatly labeled compartments. Food. Weapons. Medicine. A leather-bound inventory rests on top.

"So that's why newer tech disappeared?" I ask, flipping to the medical section.

"Electricity draws them. Using it was like lighting a beacon." He adjusts a dial. "Check for vervain and silverstock. We'll resupply tomorrow."

I begin counting, the familiarity of the task settling my nerves as static crackles from the comms.

"Rapperswil to base, come in. This is Hunter Akers requesting update."

A pause. Then: "Confirmed activity in your sector. Three disappearances last week. Witnesses report sound anomalies and biolight residue. Signs of organized feeding. Possible quota enforcement."

My hands still over a box of silver-tipped arrows. Blood quotas. The rumors weren't exaggerations.

"Location?" Kody asks.

"Textile district. Official report lists industrial accident. Survivors report elevated auditory distortion. Suggests selective targeting."

Kody's eyes meet mine. "We'll investigate."

As he copies the report, I close the trunk. "We're short on vervain and gauze."

He nods. "There's an herbalist in town. Assuming it hasn't been burned out." He spreads a map across the table. "Come look."

I step beside him, careful not to brush his arm as I lean over. Red markings fan across the city map.

"There's a pattern here," I murmur. "Almost circular."

"They're working inward." His voice is tight. "Testing wards. Probing response times. Could be a coordinated push."

A second report crackles through the radio.

"All active units: increased movement in neighboring sectors. Three teams out of contact. Unconfirmed reports of—" Static swallows the rest.

"Of what?" I whisper.

Kody's jaw tightens. "Whatever it is… it's spreading."

He begins sorting the documents, building a case file. I finish rolling out my bedroll on the floor.

"You don't have to sleep there," he says, nodding toward the bed.

"I'm not taking your watch post," I say. "Besides. The floor's familiar."

He huffs a breath—almost a smile—but turns away. "We'll start scouting tomorrow. You'll take lead."

My eyebrows lift. "A test?"

"A step," he says. "And a chance to prove this wasn't just about putting something else off."

The words hit deeper than I expect. The mission. The rhythm. The distance from everything I thought I needed. Finding my parents used to be the goal—but now it feels suspended. Not gone, just… waiting.

Maybe I don't need to chase what's behind me. Maybe what I need is here. Close. Tangible.

Him.

Outside, something howls—too far to be a threat. Inside, with Kody nearby and a mission ahead, I feel steady.

Even if tomorrow brings blood quotas, disappearances, and everything else this world can throw at us—I'm facing it with someone I trust.

And maybe, despite everything he won't say, he's starting to trust me too.

41 - Cassia

The herbalist peers at us, eyes sharp beneath a thicket of gray hair. His gaze flicks left, right, then back to us. "That particular herb's hard to come by these days," he mutters, leaning closer. "Not since your cousin's last visit."

Kody rubs his jaw, producing both payment and a tightly wrapped bundle. The man's eyes brighten instantly.

"That'll do nicely." He packages our herbs swiftly, movements efficient and tight. A potted plant joins the bundle. "Pleasure doing business.

"Cousin?" I ask as we turn away.

"Guild code," Kody murmurs. "Safer than advertising what we're really here for." His expression shifts, sharpening. "Don't look too fast. Three men, dark jackets, sunglasses. See them?"

I glance casually as we pass a row of fruit stalls. The men stand too still. Watching. Waiting.

"They're just… standing there," I murmur.

"They're stalking," he says. "Marking people. Looking for traits. That's not normal behavior for blood collectors."

"Can you tell who they're after?"

"Not yet. But—" He pauses, then: "Let's give them a distraction."

Before I can ask, he turns to an elderly vendor, raising his voice just enough. "The Bailey estate—anyone been through there lately?"

The woman's face goes bloodless. She leans in, her voice a whisper. "Best not ask questions like that." Her eyes dart to me—and widen. "And get that girl out of here."

"Now look around," Kody says under his breath. "Like you're scanning for someone."

I stretch up on my toes, pretending to search the crowd. Across the plaza, ice-cold eyes lock onto mine.

"Did they notice?"

"Yes," I say tightly.

"Good." His hand finds mine. "Walk. Window coming up on the left."

We weave through the stalls. I catch our reflection—three shadows following, closer now. My heart drums faster with each glimpse, each angle of mirrored glass.

"This isn't exactly ideal fighting ground," I whisper.

"Not planning to fight." His voice is taut. "Just needed them to switch targets."

"They have."

His grip tightens. "Now we run."

He pulls me into the crowd, then a side passage, and suddenly we're in a narrow alley. Cold stone presses against my spine. Kody cages me there, arms braced on either side of my head, breath harsh against my cheek.

The air vanishes. The roar of the market falls away. It's just him—heat, scent, proximity. His eyes scan the mouth of the alley, but when they flick to mine, they catch. Drop— linger at my mouth.

My breath hitches and I forget, for one sharp second, what we're running from.

A snarl echoes down the alley. Someone screams—close.

Kody jerks back from me, hands still brushing my arms as he glances toward the sound. "Medical supplies," he says, breath ragged. "Then we track—"

He stops. So do I.

The three men block the alley's exit now, faces wrong in the light—skin smooth, eyes still. No more pretense.

"Kody," I whisper.

"They're not here to talk." His hand finds his blade. "Run."

I draw mine and we bolt—cobbled streets flashing underfoot, walls closing in around us. Footsteps echo, not behind us but around, like they're corralling prey.

"We need to split up," I call, breath sharp in my throat.

He keeps running straight as I veer left into a narrow gap between buildings, shoulders scraping stone, Kody disappears down the corridor in a blur of motion, two follow him. One pivots after me.

Good.

I don't stop running until the passage ends at a slick stone wall. I whip around, blade up.

The Noctis steps through the shadows, movements liquid. His mouth curls in a jagged grin. "Brave little Bailey. But so, so stupid."

He lunges. I dodge, like in training, rolling low, slicing at his leg. My blade connects. He snarls and catches my wrist mid-swing, his other hand slamming into my ribs. Air leaves my lungs in a gasp.

"Feisty," he hisses. "The mistress will be pleased."

I claw at his arm, but he's fast—inhumanly so. He throws me back, spine cracking against the stone. Before I can rise, he's on me, nails digging into my shoulder hard enough to tear skin. I scream, pain white-hot.

He pins me with one hand around my throat, the other gripping my injured arm as he leans close. ""You think hiding will help?" His breath reeks of something rotten, too sweet.

I thrash, trying to drive my knee into his gut, but he slams me back against the wall again, rattling my teeth.

"The Mistress wants you broken. Begging. She'll make you—"

Then, an impact. A wet, tearing sound.

The Noctis jerks. His eyes widen in something like confusion. Kody's blade punches through his chest, blood blooming from the wound in a thick, dark rush.

He crumples forward, and Kody catches me before I hit the ground again.

"You okay?" he asks, voice low, dangerous.

I nod, gasping. "The others?"

His only answer is to step forward, pull the blade free with a sickening squelch, and decapitate the Noctis in a single motion.

"Reckless," he growls, wiping his weapon clean. "That was reckless."

"It worked."

He doesn't answer. Just looks at me. Then: "We need to go. More will come when they don't report in."

He pulls a canvas bag from his pack. "We take the heads."

42 - Cassia

The safehouse feels smaller now, the air thick with smoke and old stone and blood. Lamplight catches the copper flecks dried on my hands as Kody moves through the room with quiet purpose. The fire doesn't chase the chill from the walls—just stirs the shadows.

"We really need to stop meeting like this," I murmur, my voice dry as he rifles through the medical pack again.

He gives me a look, half exasperated, half tender, as he steps in closer. "You need stitches," he says, gently lifting my arm.

"I'll try to stop getting mauled."

One of his hands braces against the table beside my hip, the other hovering near my shoulder as he studies the damage. The heat of him is close—steadying and unbearable all at once. He wipes the blood away in careful strokes, and I flinch when the sting hits bone-deep.

"Sorry." His voice drops. "We got lucky today."

"You always say that."

He doesn't smile this time. "Sarah used to say luck didn't save lives—decisions did." His fingers ghost over the scrape along my collarbone, eyes tracing each bruise and cut like they're coordinates on a map he hates. "But the day she died... that wasn't just bad luck. It was misplaced trust."

The raw edge in his voice pulls my gaze upward. This close, I can see the scar above his brow, the tightness in his jaw. "What happened to her?"

He starts to answer—but stops. His hand falls away from my shoulder, retreating for more gauze. "She believed in second chances," he says. "Trusted the wrong one…" He shakes his head, focus shifting to the supplies. He doesn't finish.

I don't press.

The silence stretches between us until I break it. "It was dark when Holli sent me away," I say quietly. "She had me leave through the tunnel behind my wall. I remember how damp it was, the smell of mold and… something burning. But I didn't leave right away."

Kody looks up.

"I lingered too long at the end. I could see the house, and I thought maybe… maybe they'd come after me." I bite the inside of my cheek. "But they didn't. And I remember… I heard voices. My parents, I think. But they didn't sound right. They weren't scared or angry while calling for me. They were… calm."

He doesn't interrupt. Just listens.

"And the lights," I add, voice lower. "Not firelight. Not candles. Electric. I didn't realize it back then, but now…" I trail off, the cold from that night curling around my spine like a warning sign I missed too late.

Kody's jaw tightens.

"I told myself I imagined it. That I was just scared and confused." My fingers brush the edge of my locket I made into a pin on my vest, the metal cold against my skin. "I think I knew something was wrong. I just didn't want it to be real."

His hand brushes mine as he presses clean gauze to the gash across my shoulder. The touch is gentle. Wordless.

"I swore I'd never be afraid of shadows again," I whisper, not sure if I'm speaking to him or to myself.

Kody's eyes meet mine then—searching and steady. "You're not afraid," he says. "You hesitate when it matters. That's different."

Somehow it doesn't feel like a weakness when he says it. It feels like survival.

I don't look away. Neither does he. And for a heartbeat too long, the space between us holds.

"Cass…" The way he says my name makes my pulse trip. His forehead lowers to mine, his eyes closing as our breaths fall into sync. We're not speaking—but I can feel everything in the space between us. The weight of grief. The need for something solid.

His hand slides from my cheek to the side of my neck, thumb resting over the frantic beat of my pulse.

The lamplight flickers, casting his face in wavering gold. Outside, the wind rises—carrying a distant howl through the trees. Wolves, maybe, or worse. But in here… the danger feels distant—contained. His body leans closer, his warmth closing in around me, carrying the scent of leather, smoke, and wood.

I can barely think over the thrum beneath my skin. "I can't keep pretending this isn't happening," I whisper, my fingers curling into the fabric of his shirt.

His other hand curls tighter against the table, wood groaning beneath his grip. "Cass, I—" His breath grazes my lips—warm, unsteady. His thumb traces the edge of my mouth, slow and careful, as if he's memorizing the shape of me through touch.

His eyes dip to my lips, and he closes the distance with quiet certainty. His lips brush mine soft and hesitant—like he's still asking, still giving me a chance to pull away. But I don't. I can't.

My breath catches and I press closer without meaning to, my fingers curling into his shirt tighter, the kiss deepening for one suspended, aching moment.

And that's all it takes.

The shift in him is subtle but immediate. The tremble in his hands vanishes, replaced by a need sharpened at the edges. He kisses me again, deeper this time—like he's been holding this back for years and just realized he doesn't have to anymore.

He breaks the kiss only long enough to whisper, barely restrained: "Tell me to stop." His voice is low, hoarse, like it's dragging itself up from somewhere he's buried it for too long. "Because I won't be able to if you don't."

I shake my head, breath shallow. "Don't."

His mouth crashes into mine again—no longer hesitant, but hungry.

His hands find my waist, then slip beneath my shirt, mapping my skin like he's memorizing every inch. I pull him closer, feeling the press of him, the heat of his breath hitch when our bodies align in a way that leaves no room for misunderstanding.

We move together like we've done this before—not physically, but in every other way. In every near-miss. Every touch held too long. Every moment we turned away instead of leaning in.

He kisses down my jaw, to the hollow of my throat, and breathes against my skin, "I thought I lost you today."

The words crack something in me and I draw him closer, my hand tangled in the back of his shirt. "You didn't."

"I couldn't handle it."

"You don't have to." My voice is barely more than a whisper.

The tension between us coils tighter, breath and touch blurring as I reach for the fastenings at his belt—he doesn't stop me.

He lowers me to the cot with the same care he's used every time I've been hurt—but now there's hunger beneath it. Want. Awe. His hands shake again when he strips off his shirt, and I realize it's not restraint—it's reverence. And when he sinks down to kiss me again, skin against skin, breath mingling, everything else falls away—my parents, the mission, the weight of what waits outside these walls.

There's only this. Only him. Only the way he says my name against my mouth like I'm sacred.

When our bodies finally come together, it's not frantic— it's a slow, consuming burn. We don't fumble. Don't rush. Just feel. Every kiss deepens. Every breath shortens. And every touch says, I'm still here.

His name leaves my mouth like a plea. Mine breaks from his lips like an oath.

When we finally let go together, it's not fireworks. It's a riptide pulling us under—merciless and absolute.

And in the stillness after, tangled in his arms, his breath warm against my temple, a thought drifts through me like smoke—I let myself believe, for the first time, that I don't have to face what's coming alone.

43 - Cassia

By morning, the safehouse feels colder than it did last night—its walls too thin, its silence too loud. Outside, frost coats the clearing. Mist coils through the ancient pines, their branches tangled above us, filtering the early light into silvery shards.

"Two blades is ideal," Kody says, testing the edge of his knife. Dawn catches on the steel, bright and cold. "Makes the heads come off easier."

"I have the daggers my parents left." I draw them slowly, the initials CB and EB flashing in the pale light. They feel heavier now—sharper, more real. Like they've been waiting for this. "Might as well put them to use."

"Whatever weapon you choose, train with it until it's part of you." His voice carries the quiet edge of experience. "A Noctis won't give you time to think."

We don't speak of last night.

Not the way his mouth found mine with equal parts honor and hunger. Not the way our bodies found answers that words never could. There's no need.

I'm not anxious. Not overthinking. I'm just… steady. Certain.

The questions that used to knot in my chest—what we are, what it meant, if he felt it too—have gone still. Quiet. There's no fog in my head anymore. No noise between us.

And without that noise, it's easier to breathe. Easier to move. Easier to fight.

We're back in the clearing behind the safehouse, but

everything feels sharper now. After yesterday's ambush, he's rerunning me through training drills—moves I technically already know, but now they land differently. Now what it feels like to have a Noctis hand around my throat is fresh.

Kody demonstrates the first sequence. "They're faster than us. Stronger. You can't react—you have to anticipate." His blades flash, striking the air in calculated arcs. "Most will rush in, arrogant. Let them. Let them think they've got you—until you prove them wrong."

His movements are terrifyingly inhuman, each motion fluid and exact. When I mimic the sequence, the daggers feel balanced in my hands—familiar and right. Like extensions of myself.

He steps in to adjust my form, fingers gliding from my shoulder to my elbow, correcting my grip. His touch is precise, professional—but now I know what it feels like when he stops holding back. And that knowledge makes every brush of his skin louder.

"Intel comes first," he continues, voice professional despite the way his hands linger. "Learn their patterns. Their feeding grounds. Most won't leave their territory. Some hunt in pairs. Others, alone. The smart ones..." His grip tightens faintly on my arms. "The smart ones let you think you're in control. Until you're not."

"Like the ones at the market?"

"Those were stalkers—tracking, marking, collecting. Hunters kill outright." He guides me through another sequence, every motion deliberate. "You have to know what you're dealing with before you draw your blade. Some Noctis are cruel. Some are methodical. Some just... enjoy the chase."

The movements flow more easily now. Strike, pivot, slice. I can feel the rhythm settle in my muscles, as though it's been waiting. The blades don't feel borrowed anymore.

"Remarkable," Kody murmurs behind me. "You have a natural instinct for this. The way you move..." He steps closer, adjusting my follow-through. His chest brushes my back. "It's like you've been doing this your whole life."

His praise lands differently now. Not because I crave his approval, but because I trust it, and I trust him.

I laugh—short and winded. "Strange, considering I come from a long line of science nerds."

"Maybe it's in your blood more than you think." His

hands settle at my waist, repositioning me. "The Baileys weren't just scientists. They were—" He stops.

"Were what?"

Before he can answer, static bursts from the radio inside.

"Alert all hunters. Recent disappearance in sector four. Suspected connection to Vesper confirmed. Extreme caution advised. Repeat: connection to Vesper confirmed."

Kody goes rigid, his breath catching. The knife in his hand drops slightly, knuckles whitening around the hilt. He doesn't blink.

"Kody?"

I turn to face him, but his eyes aren't on me. They're staring through the trees—haunted, locked on a memory I can't reach. Not fear. Grief, sharpened into rage.

His voice is raw when he finally speaks. "Training's over."

He steps back, severing all contact.

"Time to go," he says, already moving toward the safehouse.

The way he shuts down—it's not rejection, but it's close. Like the version of him I had last night is already buried again.

I don't follow right away.

"Damn you, Vesper," I whisper—just loud enough for the trees to carry it.

The clearing feels colder now. But as I watch him disappear into the mist, the set of his shoulders, rigid and unshaken, plants a quiet resolve in me. If we can find Vesper, end this… maybe one of the ghosts clinging to Kody will finally let go.

My eyes drop to the daggers in my hands, the initials etched into the steel—CB. EB. My parents once used these. Faced their own monsters.

Kody's helped me survive this long.

Now it's my turn to help him.

44 - Kody

Kody watches Cassia as she stares out the carriage window, her features unreadable in the fading light. He hates how easily the name "Vesper" unraveled what they'd just begun to find between them. How her voice had gone tight when she said, "Back to Zurich." Then softer: "It was only a few days here."

"It's part of the job," he had told her. "Being able to leave fast." The words felt hollow. A rehearsed excuse. Every mile closer to Zurich drags behind his ribs like a blade. She said she wasn't ready to find them, her parents, but Zurich makes that choice impossible. And while he's not sure exactly what they're walking into, there's a weight pressing at the edges of his instincts. A pattern he hasn't fully pieced together.

They pass through a village as dusk settles in, the streets too quiet, doors marked with tarnished silver guild sigils. A woman hurries past, scarf tight around her throat despite the warmth, her eyes fixed on the ground.

Kody's hands tighten in his lap. It's starting here too—the patterns, the silence, the quotas Sarah warned him about.

Cassia breaks the silence without turning. "It's personal now, isn't it."

He blinks. Not a question, a statement. Her tone holds no judgment—just understanding.

He exhales slowly. "Always was."

She nods faintly, but doesn't speak.

"I don't just want to stop him," he admits after a beat. "I need to. Before he makes more ghosts I never finish chasing."

Cassia looks over then, and the way she studies him—it's

not pity. It's quieter. A recognition he hadn't let himself hope for.

He almost says more, confesses the weight he's been carrying since Sarah died. The guilt. The suspicion. The fear of dragging Cassia into a story that might end the same way.

But he doesn't.

THE ZURICH GUILD archives smell of dust and secrets—old stone and older parchment steeped into the very bones of the room. Shelves rise like battlements along the walls, lined with leather-bound volumes whose spines crackle softly when opened. Iron sconces flicker with gaslight, casting golden halos over worn hardwood tables and a sagging sofa pushed against the far wall. A low coffee table in front of it is buried in loose papers and hand-copied maps.

Kody takes the long table nearest the records alcove, spreading out census books and guild ledgers. Cassia claimed the coffee table earlier, intent on keeping their piles separate.

He loses himself in the rhythm of research: flip, scan, note. Anything to distract from the way her silence stretches longer than usual. Every so often they reach for the same document, an instinctive movement, and every time, her fingers jolt back like she's afraid touching him might mean she's not focused. Like the tension between them is a live wire they've both agreed not to touch.

The missing persons file confirms his worst suspicion— another redhead, same age range, same quiet vanishing. Just like Sarah. Just like...

He glances at Cassia, bent over a stack of witness statements, her copper hair catching firelight. His chest tightens. How many coincidences before it becomes a pattern?

They sift through hours of police reports, guild records, and backlogged census pages. Every case follows the same pattern: young woman, red hair, no signs of struggle. No witnesses, no remains—not even ash.

Night deepens around them, thick and heavy. The gaslamps hiss softly, their flames guttering low, throwing restless shadows across brittle parchment and half-traced bloodlines. The archive has settled into its late silence—pages whispering with every shift, the occasional creak of old timber overhead.

Cassia sits cross-legged on the stone floor, hunched forward at the coffee table, sleeves smudged with ink. Her posture is stubborn as ever, spine straight, jaw set like she can will herself to stay awake through sheer defiance. But her movements grow slower—the gap between page turns stretching. Her head dips once, snaps back up.

Then again. Slower this time. Until eventually, she folds, quietly and unconsciously, slumping forward onto the pages she'd been fighting to finish—copper hair spilling across the parchment like flame.

And that's when he finds it.

The document is brittle at the edges, yellowed with age. But the inked lines of the family tree remain sharp— meticulous in their record of generations: births, deaths, marriages. Kody's eyes follow the branches, fingers tracking lightly over names long forgotten.

Lucile Hawthorne.

The missing woman's name—he follows the thin line that stretches back to a familiar one. A Bailey cousin. Four generations back. Descended from Layla Grady.

His breath goes still.

He looks up from the document, gaze drawn to where Cassia has collapsed in sleep—curled against the edge of the coffee table, cheek pillowed against an unfinished page.

Kody rises slowly, the family tree still in hand. He crosses to where she worked, kneels beside the sprawl of papers she'd been combing through. Birth certificates, census maps, estate deeds—the kind of records easy to skim past when you're not looking for a pattern.

But now he knows what to look for.

Names repeat. Properties cycle between the same bloodlines. Deaths line up too neatly with disappearances. Every thread Cassia followed loops back, quietly, consistently…to the Baileys.

The deeper he digs, the colder it feels. This isn't coincidence, it never was.

He should wake her. Move her somewhere more comfortable. Instead, he watches—because a part of him still can't believe she's real. That she let him in. That she chose him, even if just for a night. And that makes everything more dangerous.

So, he commits to memory what he's tried for too long not to see. The curve of her cheek. The faint furrow between her brows, even in sleep. The way her fingers still clutch her pen, like she's ready to fight even in her dreams.

So different from Sarah. And yet, he feels just as powerless to protect her.

The documents blur. Exhaustion crashes over him in waves—thick, dull, and impossible to fight. He scrubs a hand over his face, then lets it drop.

Just a few minutes.

Just to rest my eyes. Clear my head.

He leans back against the sofa, gaze drifting toward the flicker of lamplight on parchment.

Then we can keep piecing it all together.

When he wakes, her warmth is curled against his side and Sarah's name is dying on his lips.

Sometime in the night, they drifted together. Cassia's head rests on his shoulder, her breath a soft whisper at his neck. His arm has wrapped around her instinctively, a protective coil he didn't realize he needed. Her fingers are tangled in the fabric of his shirt, anchoring herself to him even in sleep.

Dawn spills across the archive in gold and for one fragile moment, Kody lets himself imagine a world where this could be simple. Where the papers on the table don't mean what he knows they do. Where he doesn't have to choose between keeping her close... and keeping her safe.

Where the warmth she stirs in him doesn't come with guilt, or the weight of another failure.

Cassia stirs, murmuring something that might be his name as her fingers tighten in his shirt.

He should move. Should rebuild the boundaries they've both worked so hard to keep. Should remember Sarah's death and all the reasons he's not allowed to want this.

Instead, he presses a kiss to her hair. Soft. Lingering. A moment of quiet weakness he won't allow himself again.

Then, carefully, he untangles her grip, easing her back onto a blanket. He leaves her sleeping, and takes the family tree with him as he heads to make coffee.

They have a long day ahead. And he still hasn't figured

out how to tell her the truth—that her family ties to all of this somehow. That maybe the reason she fights like she was born to it… is because she was.

He just hopes he can protect her better than he protected Sarah.

The family tree on the table seems to mock him, its connections spreading like a web. Like fate. Like a trap waiting to spring—one that might take her from him before he ever figures out how to keep her.

45 - Cassia

"Thank you," Kody says to the shopkeeper, sliding a coin across the counter. Outside, the sun blazes overhead, relentless and blinding.

I gather my hair up and twist it into a knot, exposing the back of my neck to what little breeze stirs the dusty street. "I don't think we'll find a lead in this heat."

"You're right." His gaze lingers at my throat a beat too long before shifting away. "Let's grab lunch, then check out where Lucile Hawthorne disappeared. Might get us closer to their ground game."

The café we find is narrow, shaded—blessedly cool. We settle into a corner booth, its cushions cracked with age but softer than the stone benches outside. The food arrives—simple but filling. Beans, bread, and a few thin slices of cheese.

I tear off a piece and scoop it into the beans. "I still don't understand why they're breaking pattern. Going after specific people instead of feeding where it's easy."

"There's a correlation between the victims." His tone is too casual. Controlled.

"You said that before," I say, chewing, "but never explained."

"I don't have concrete proof yet." His jaw ticks.

"But you're sure."

"I know how they operate." He pushes his plate aside. "Noctis are predators. They don't change feeding behavior without reason. The quota system keeps the balance. These targeted attacks? They put everything at risk."

"Then tell me more about Lucile Hawthorne." I tear another piece of bread. "Why her?"

"Twenty-three. Lived alone. Textile mill shift worker." Kody's voice is neutral, but his fingers tap a slow rhythm against his cup. "No family nearby. No close ties. She disappeared walking home after sunset. No signs of struggle."

"Except it wasn't random."

"No." He meets my eyes. "Red hair. Solitary. Unconnected. Just like the others."

"Like me," I say quietly. "Like when they tried to gas me out."

His hand twitches, like he might reach across the table, but instead it folds into a fist. "We don't know that's why—"

"Don't lie to me, Kody."

His sigh is heavy. "Yeah," he admits. "You fit the pattern. Which is why we can't take chances."

Silence settles between us, heavier than the heat outside. I don't know if it's fear or fury curling in my chest—maybe both.

Finally, he rises, slinging his pack over his shoulder. "We should go."

The motion pulls his shirt tight across his back, muscles shifting beneath fabric, and my breath catches—just for a second. Not only because of the way he moves, but because I remember how it felt to trace those lines with my hands. Not imagined, not a maybe. Real.

I stand slowly, brushing crumbs from my fingers. "Where exactly was she taken?"

"East edge of town. A side street near the mill's back gate. We'll wait nearby." His voice lowers. "Look for clues, or maybe another abduction."

As we walk, Kody explains more about the quotas. "Each district has arrangements—designated feeding times, approved donors. Some use it as punishment for breaking local laws."

"How different can the systems be?"

His hand brushes my arm, guiding me around a deep puddle. "Southern regions rely on volunteer rotations—people trade blood for protection or supplies. Northern districts..." His jaw tightens. "They use prisoners. Or people they call prisoners."

"And here?"

"Mixed approach. Volunteers, criminals, and arrangements with powerful families." There's a flatness to his voice, like he's holding back. I glance at him, but he's already moving on. "It keeps the peace. Mostly."

"But what about the people they feed from?" I step closer to avoid a passing cart, catching his scent. "I never understood why more aren't turned."

"Remember when I was drilling you about controlling your breathing. Your fear?" His voice drops lower, intimate despite the subject. "Adrenaline changes your blood chemistry. When the Noctis enzyme isn't present, it acts like a catalyst. That's why some turn... and others don't."

"Enzyme?"

He nods. "Their saliva contains one. It suppresses the virus—keeps it from binding to blood. Think of it like a failsafe. But it's fragile. Hunger depletes it."

I glance at him. "So if they haven't fed..."

He nods. "The enzyme drops. If it gets too low, the virus is directly exposed to the blood. Latches on—specifically to the hormones."

"But even volunteers or prisoners—surely they're afraid?"

"It's not just fear," he says, voice quieter now. "Any heightened emotion changes the blood. Adrenaline, yes—but also dopamine. Serotonin. Oxytocin." He steps closer as a group passes, pulling me into a narrow alcove. His body brushes mine, heat bleeding through our clothes. "Joy, trust, desire—they all prime the body in ways the virus can sense and react to."

My breath catches. "You're saying... intimacy can trigger transformation."

"There's a reason emotional bonds are discouraged on the front lines," he murmurs. "The closer you get to someone, the more likely you are to be susceptible. Hunters. Noctis. Doesn't matter. Feel too much, and the failsafe slips."

A beat of silence. Then his fingers brush a strand of hair from my cheek, tucking it gently behind my ear. The touch is careful, reverent—but his eyes haven't left mine.

I offer a smile I'm not sure I mean to give. It's automatic. Ache and comfort, tangled together.

His throat bobs, and he draws back before the moment can deepen.

I steady myself. "Why don't they tell people this?"

"Because fear is useful. But empathy? Desire?" His jaw flexes. "They're dangerous. If people knew how close the line is—how easy it is to cross—some would avoid Noctis altogether like they already do… but others? They'd fall in love. Try to fix them. Try to save them."

"You think people would turn willingly."

"I know they would. Some already have. That's why anyone who talks about this gets eliminated. Quietly. You get labeled a heretic or security risk. At best, you disappear. At worst, they feed you to the ones you're trying to understand."

My chest tightens. "To stop the truth from spreading."

"To stop the lines from blurring." He exhales. "They built this system on fear. But truth breeds empathy. And empathy breaks control."

I nod slowly, the pieces starting to form a picture. "So keeping them fed really does prevent outbreaks."

"Exactly. That's why the quota system was created after the war. Before that, they were turning too many. Humanity couldn't keep up." His voice tightens. "Even Noctis started losing control out of desperation to preserve their food source."

I'm quiet for a moment, then ask, "You've seen the feeding centers?"

His expression darkens. "Once. Northern district." His hand flexes at his side. "Let's just say the solution there was worse than the disease."

We walk in silence for a while, the sound of our boots on cobblestones filling the space between us. Ahead, a woman ushers her children indoors, casting anxious looks at the lengthening shadows.

"The enzyme," I say at last, "is that why some Noctis are.. . different? Why some turn almost anyone they bite?"

Kody's step falters. He doesn't speak right away. "Some strains of the virus are stronger. Older. Mutated. The Turig strain was wiped out." His voice turns grave. "Some Noctis, like Tenebris, don't produce the enzyme at all."

"And… Vesper?"

The name lands hard. He grips my hand, tight enough that it almost hurts.

"You need to stay away from that thread." He looks at the sky. "We should keep moving," he says quietly. "Sun's getting low."

We walk on, shadows stretching across the ground. He doesn't let go of my hand.

"Who created the feeding districts?"

"They're more like treaties. Every region does it differently. Lines are drawn by city limits, mostly. Here, it's rotations—donors selected by the leadership. Keeps people alive, even if it doesn't keep them free."

"Supposedly," I murmur, catching the edge in his voice.

"Supposedly." His reply is quiet. Bitter. "Some districts are stricter than others. Some Noctis follow rules better than others. But overall, the system works—random attacks draw attention. Risk retaliation." Kody scans the street as we walk. "That's why these disappearances don't make sense. They're risking everything."

"Maybe they're desperate?"

"Noctis don't get desperate." His tone sharpens. "They get hungry, or they get orders."

"But what—"

His arm shoots out, catching mine. He yanks me into a narrow alley, one hand rising.

I exhale to speak, and his palm covers my mouth, firm but not cruel. His body presses into mine, shielding me against the cold stone.

Footsteps tap the cobblestones, too light to be human.

My breath catches. "This early?" I whisper against his hand.

He doesn't answer, doesn't need to. The air changes.

Two voices drift by the alley mouth.

"The Mistress grows tired of Vesper's interference," one hisses—his tone sharp, reptilian.

The second scoffs, lower and colder. "Then let her send Tenebris after him."

"You think Vesper isn't his creature?" the first snaps back. "No one survives Tenebris's bite—and yet Vesper walks free, unchallenged. Makes you wonder."

The other laughs under his breath, humorless. "Careful, that's what leads to throats being ripped out." A beat. Then, more quietly: "He's always been unpredictable. Shows up, disrupts the Mistress's work, vanishes again."

"He must not know about the girl," the deeper voice mutters. "If he did, he would've intervened already. Like he always does when it's Bailey blood."

"The Mistress is being careful this time. Quiet. She's waited years for this."

The first voice drops to a hush. "Once she has the girl—"

"The girl is protected," the second cuts in. "That hunter never leaves her side."

A pause. Then a dark laugh. "Hunters can be dealt with. Ask Vesper—he's left enough in pieces."

"Still…" The first voice is wary now. "If he finds out who she is—"

"It'll be war."

Their footsteps fade, swallowed by the dark.

Still, Kody doesn't move.

His arm remains braced beside my head, body a tense wall between me and the mouth of the alley. I can feel his heartbeat—calm, but strong, hammering beneath the surface.

My own pulse echoes his, throat tight as I try to process what we just heard. *Once she has the girl. He always interferes when it's Bailey blood.*

My blood.

My breath shakes out, barely audible. "They were talking about me."

Kody's jaw flexes, but he doesn't answer.

"They said war," I whisper, eyes lifting to his. "If Vesper finds out who I am…"

He lowers his head slightly, forehead almost brushing mine. His voice is low and strained. "Then the Mistress doesn't just want you. She's counting on Vesper not knowing you exist."

"And if he finds out?"

His gaze sharpens, dark and unblinking. "Then we're in the middle of a fight the rest of the world doesn't even know is coming."

I try to swallow, but my mouth is dry. "Kody… what the hell am I caught up in?"

"You're not caught up," he says, finally pulling back—just enough to search the street again. "You're at the center of it."

My knees nearly give. He steadies me without thinking, his hand gripping my arm, grounding me.

"I'm not letting them take you," he says quietly. "Not her. Not even Vesper. Ever." The words don't stumble from his lips in assurance. They seat into the depth of his eyes and the set of his jaw as a covenant.

His grip tightens for a breath before he lets go, casting one more glance at the alley's edge. "We need to move. Now. Quietly."

But as I follow him back into the empty streets, one truth pulses louder than my heartbeat.

Vesper doesn't know who I am.

But when he does...

There won't be anywhere left to hide.

46 - Kody

The Noctis claws miss Kody's throat by inches, slicing the air with a hiss of wind and rot. He drops low, rolling across frost-hardened earth as talons gouge deep furrows into the ground behind him. Stone trembles beneath the impact. The evasion buys him only seconds, but it's enough. He springs up, blade arcing in a brutal uppercut that parts leather and flesh in a wet, meaty rip. Blood spatters his cheek—dark, thick and oily.

Not deep enough. Not fatal.

They'd tracked the trail well past dusk, following scattered signs of a struggle—Lucile Hawthorne's abduction weeks old by now, but still etched into his routine. Noctis often returned to familiar ground. That pattern had led them here. To this ruin. To this ambush.

Somewhere behind him, Cassia's daggers ring against stone. He shouldn't be able to hear her from here—not over the pounding in his head—but he does. The tempo of her strikes, the controlled cadence of her breath. She's holding her own.

"The Mistress grows impatient," the Noctis hisses, circling. Its movements are sharp, serpentine. Too precise to have ever been human—every step calculated to herd him. "The arrangements must be maintained."

"What arrangements?" Kody shifts left, letting his blade dip like a novice. The Noctis takes the bait, predictably overeager, and lunges forward, claws extended. Classic overcommit. Kody pivots hard on his back foot, sidestepping the claws, and slashes his blade across its ribs. A satisfying slice, followed by the slap of dark blood spattering stone.

The Noctis chuckles, low and joyless. Already, the wound is sealing. "Ask the Baileys. They understand the importance of bloodlines."

A chill roots itself in Kody's gut. He shoves the implication away and narrows in on the fight.

The Noctis is young—turned by bite, not injection. His steps are too loud and eager. Not like the elders. Not like the tenebris. The footwork telegraphs each strike before it comes, but speed makes up for inexperience, and this one is fast.

Their blades meet in a staccato rhythm—strike, parry, slash. Metal clashes against claw, vibrating up Kody's arm. A headshot nearly lands, but the Noctis bends impossibly backward, spine cracking as it avoids death. The sound turns his stomach.

"She doesn't know, does she?" the Noctis taunts as he rights himself—vertebrae realigning with a hideous pop. "What her family really—"

Kody's blade finds its throat—slicing across mid-sentence. The spray is warm and metallic. The wound starts closing in seconds, but the words cling like oil.

Then Cassia's scream tears through the dark—high, pained, wrong.

Kody's world narrows. Her voice cleaves through the haze. Not again. Not this time.

"Vesper thinks he can interfere," the Noctis snarls, reading the shift. It strikes fast, claws raking the air inches from Kody's face. "But the Mistress has plans for—"

The name ignites him and all thought is gone. Replaced by clarity sharper than any blade.

He doesn't feel the cold, the weight of his body, or the ache in his lungs and the pain in his shoulder. But he can sense the movement of his target.

Kody drives his blade with brutal efficiency—joints, tendons, the delicate cartilage of the throat. Every strike calculated to disable, not just harm. A perfect predator.

The Noctis reels, snarling, leaking blood that hisses against stone.

Images flash—Sarah's torn body, Cassia's bloodied shoulder, the look she gave him when she let him in. He won't lose her.

Kody steps in for the kill—but he's too fast, too committed. His balance shifts forward, but lunges too far, rage dragging him off center. A claw slips under his arm guard, tearing through leather, into flesh. He feels the impact, but not the pain as warm blood trickles down his side.

"Kody!" Cassia's voice pierces through the storm raging in his head. Her daggers flash past his vision and into flesh as she barrels into the fight, a force of steel and fury.

She's everywhere at once—quick, controlled, vicious. She moves with deadly rhythm, not just trained but transformed. Beautiful and terrifying.

The Noctis dodges—but not fast enough. Her blade slices across its chest. Kody joins her, and for a moment, they move as one.

Cassia drives the Noctis back with feints and slashes—aiming high to expose the chest. Kody reads her rhythm, and matches it, cutting low. They don't speak, they don't need to. When it leaps to avoid his sweep, she's already midair—her blade raking across its face.

They drive it toward the wall and Cassia's dagger sinks into its shoulder, pinning it. It thrashes forward, forcing the blade deeper into itself to swipe at Kody.

He doesn't flinch. Doesn't hesitate and ducks before it moves. Body acting on instinct faster than thought. Not learned—instinct.

The Noctis pauses. Recognition flickering in its ruined face. "You move like us, hunter. But you're not one of—"

Kody's blade drives deep into the Noctis's chest mid-sentence—a brutal answer forged in steel. He yanks it free in one fluid motion and swings.

The head separates cleanly, the wet crunch of vertebrae snapping beneath the force. It hits the stone with a sickening thud. The body follows a beat later, collapsing in a boneless heap.

Stillness crashes in like a wave.

The world narrows around him—frosted stone, blood in the air, his own breath fogging as it catches in his chest. Time lurches out of sync. The memory of each movement replays behind his eyes, not as thought, but reflex—his body having moved with lethal precision he hadn't consciously summoned. His pulse hammers in his ears. Muscles locked. Legs planted. Blade still clutched in his hand.

He's standing, but it feels like waking from a trance. Then, a touch. Cassia's hands, bloody and shaking, find his face.

"Kody," she breathes, framing his cheeks, grounding him. "Look at me." Her touch burns through the numbness. Her eyes, wide, fierce, alive, and fixed on his.

He blinks. Her voice sounds far away, muffled as though it's underwater.

"Stay with me." she breathes. "Don't go wherever your mind's trying to take you."

Her warmth cuts through the static, her voice slowly pulling him back from the edge. He tries to look away, but can't. "I can't lose you," he says, and it's not just fear—it's truth bleeding out with his words.

"You won't," she whispers.

"You don't know that." His voice breaks. "Everyone I let in… ends up dead or worse." He doesn't speak Sarah's name. He doesn't need to. He sees it flicker in Cassia's eyes—she knows.

"I'm not everyone." Her thumbs trace his skin, grounding him. "And I'm not Sarah." She whispers.

His forehead lowers to hers. Breath to breath—their tether. "That's what scares me," he murmurs.

They stand there, suspended. Neither whole nor shattered. Just here. Together.

Cassia pulls back just slightly, eyes searching his.

He exhales, his grip tightening on the blade. "We gotta burn the bodies."

The words are practical, but the look she gives him is anything but distant. Her hand finds his again as they move. Not an accident. Not a shield. And he holds it like a lifeline.

They move in silence. Blood drips from the gash in his side, soaking into his shirt. He doesn't feel it—not fully. Pain flickers at the edges of his awareness, dulled and muted. His thoughts circle the way his body moved—faster, sharper, colder. Instinct—not training.

It was precision and something else. He's always been good. But this… this wasn't normal.

Cassia stacks the bodies. Kody strikes the flint.

As fire consumes flesh, the heat draws sweat to his brow, but he keeps his eyes on her. On her presence tethering him back to himself.

Tomorrow, he'll face what the Noctis said—what he felt shift in his bones during that fight and it hasn't settled.

Tomorrow he'll finally face what he suspects about her family.

But tonight… tonight, he'll let himself believe her promise not to leave.

47 - Cassia

Kody pours another drink, his movements sharp. The bottle clinks sharply against the rim of the glass, edged with frustration. The table between us is chaos—maps, scribbled witness statements, ink-stained reports marked with dates and names and blood-red circles. It's a mess. One that reeks of conclusions he won't say aloud.

I take a sip from my own glass, the whiskey burning less than it did an hour ago. "It seems this Mistress and Vesper have a personal feud," I say, watching the way he drains his glass like he's hoping it'll silence whatever he's thinking. "I thought Vesper wasn't even in this region."

"He's further south." Kody downs the contents of his glass like water, then refills. "Which means the politics go deeper than we thought."

"South…" I tilt my head, trying to recall. "Isn't that where—"

"Yeah." His jaw ticks. "That's where the rumors started. About a different kind of arrangement. Less violent. More... humane."

I swirl the liquid in my glass. "The quotas here feel like a patchwork of old systems and whatever those southern ones are."

His laugh is brittle. "Down there," he cuts in, "I refuse to believe he's behind any of those *humane* arrangements. Or that it's as clean as people want to think." His eyes flick to mine—dark, unsettled. "Rumors can be pretty lies. Or worse—truths twisted just enough to look safe."

The fire pops, sending shadows leaping across his face. He studies the drink like it holds answers he can't find anywhere else. "I told you before that every region made their own system after the war," he says. "Some more civilized than others. The Mistress runs this one like a regime—fear, quotas, arrangements with the right names and bloodlines."

He doesn't say mine. But I feel it in the silence that follows.

I hesitate. "But the south, Vesper's territory, is… different?"

"So they say. Fewer disappearances. More volunteers." His voice drips skepticism. "Could just be better cover. Or maybe people just stopped fighting."

He tips the glass again, but doesn't drink this time. "Whatever the case, don't let the prettier stories fool you. Vesper's a monster."

Something in his tone has changed. Not just anger—grief, maybe. Grief that lives too close to the surface.

"I was supposed to be a medic," he says after a moment, like it slips out without permission.

I blink. "What?"

"That's what I was studying for. Before everything." His mouth twists.

"What happened?" I ask, my voice softer now, more careful.

"My sister, Emilia," he says. "You know that part. I was sixteen when she was taken. Emmie was ten. She used to wear this ridiculous purple scarf everywhere." A pained smile paints his lips. "Thought it made her look grown up."

I watch the hard lines of his face falter. His voice doesn't crack, but it thins. Frays. "When she disappeared… it wasn't a choice anymore… Not really."

"You went after her," I say gently. "And put everything else aside. Gave everything up to find her."

He doesn't answer. Just lifts the glass and swallows.

"Do you miss her?"

The pain in his eyes is raw when they meet mine. "Every damn day."

The words settle between us as I study him, his profile lit by firelight—strong and sad and quiet in a way that makes me ache.

"I lied before…" he says.

I glance up at him, brow furrowing as my heart races. "About what?"

"When I said you and Sarah were alike." He leans back against the edge of the table, knuckles grazing the wood. His mouth quirks—tired, sad. "She was a little older than Emmie, but… there were moments. The way she talked. That sharp curiosity. Always trying to fix things." He glances at me. "She reminded me of her. And I couldn't save her either."

My heart aches, raw in my chest, but words won't come. So we sit in the quiet, the space between us heavy. The fire crackles low, its light fading to ember-glow and shadow. I draw a slow breath and trail my fingertip around the rim of my glass, over and over, like the motion might loosen the knot in my throat.

I have to go. I have to face my parents.

I've been thinking about it since Zurich. Since the alley. Since the moment I heard the Noctis say the Bailey line still calls to the mistress.

But I'm scared of what I'll find. Of what he'll think. Scared he'll leave—now that the trail toward Vesper is heating up.

I don't want to ask. But I need to.

"What did the Noctis mean," I ask gently, "when he said you move like them?"

Kody stiffens. "Nothing. Just a scare tactic." He tries to shrug it off, but his eyes stay locked on the fire. "They like getting in your head. Doesn't mean it's true."

"But, it rattled you… I could see that much."

He exhales, slow. "I've trained hard. Lived on edge for a long time. Maybe it shows."

I don't press. But he doesn't believe his own excuse.

"And what they said about the Baileys. About… preserving bloodlines." I bite the inside of my cheek. "Kody…" I say, voice barely above the flames as I hesitate.

He looks at me, and his expression softens instantly—like he's been waiting for me to say it. "Do you want me to go with you?" he asks, before I can even form the words.

The gentleness in his voice undoes me. He knows.

I let out a shaky breath, looking away. "I hate to ask. I promised—"

"You didn't ask," he says firmly. "I offered."

It's the way he says it. Like it costs him nothing and everything all at once.

My heart skips. Maybe it's the firelight in his eyes, or the quiet way his hand finds mine across the mess of papers—fingers lacing slowly, like it's the most natural thing in the world.

"I'll go with you," he says, his voice low.

And then he leans in to kiss me. It's not rushed, or desperate—just real. Fierce and unguarded and slow enough that I feel every ounce of his resolve in it.

When he pulls back, his forehead rests against mine and he sighs like I'm the only thing keeping him from falling apart.

"Wherever it leads," he whispers.

And I know. Maybe it's the simple acceptance in his voice, or maybe just the way he's looking at me. But he'd follow me anywhere. Even if it breaks him.

48 - Cassia

Iron gates loom before us, their blackened bars stretching into ancient stone walls that disappear into the fog-drenched dusk. Beyond them, the Bailey estate rises from the earth like a memory dredged up from a nightmare—grander than I imagined, but wrong. Hollow… and watching.

My stomach twists. "How do we get in?"

"We could jump it." Kody's voice breaks the silence, low and dry. The joke doesn't land, and he knows it. Still, the corner of his mouth lifts like he's trying to make the moment easier.

He presses a tarnished brass button near the gate and a speaker crackles to life—its static cutting the quiet.

"Yes?" A voice. Flat, measured, genderless and unwelcoming.

Kody leans in, his voice calm and practiced. "My name is Mr. Akers. I was told I might find contact information for the Bailey family here. A key was left for them at the church in Emmen."

There's a pause, then the gates groan open—iron screaming against iron.

He glances back, brow lifting like he expected nothing less. I manage a nod and step beside him as we move forward. The gravel beneath our feet is too clean and precise. Not a leaf is out of place. It's as if nature here has been forced into submission.

Wrong, my instincts whisper. *Wrong. Wrong.*

Felix's words return, unbidden. *Family reunions. Desire. The Mistress.*

My chest tightens. Each step is harder than the last.

"Cass?" Kody's voice cuts through the static in my head.

My knees lock mid-step and I stop, heart lurching against my ribs. "I—I can't do this," I breathe, barely hearing myself over the pounding in my skull.

He's beside me in an instant, one hand at the small of my back—warm, steady… real. But it doesn't stop the way my chest tightens, or how the edges of my vision start to blur.

"This place…" My voice catches. I bend forward, bracing my palms against my knees like I can force the air back in— my lungs scraping for breath that doesn't come fast enough. "It like it's waiting to swallow me whole."

"What do you want to do?" His voice is soft, careful.

"I don't know." The words tumble out on a thin breath. "We could leave. Go after Vesper. There's still a trail. We don't have to stay here. This place—" My throat constricts. "It's not home. It's just more of my ghosts from the past… and maybe that's where they belong."

Kody doesn't answer right away. Just watches me, his eyes quiet and sharp, like he's listening to all the words I haven't said aloud. To the fear I'm trying not to drown in.

Then, calm and firm, "You've come this far. You're owed answers. Whether they're here or not… you deserve to look them in the eye. Or bury the past for good."

I slowly look toward the house.

The windows peer down like watching eyes—old and hollow, heavy with memory. The air is still, and quiet. Not peaceful… Suffocating. Like the land remembers what happened here and hasn't forgiven it.

I squeeze my eyes shut. Pull one long breath through my nose and let it burn like whiskey in my lungs.

"You're right," I whisper.

I didn't survive all this just to run now.

Then louder, steadier, "I deserve to know. One way or another."

A faint smile curves his lips. "Damn right you do."

I glance up at him, tension loosening just enough for the edge of a grin. "Still up for running away if it all goes to hell?"

He looks at me then—dark eyes steady and warm. "You say the word, and I'll set the place on fire myself."

A beat. A breath. And I smile.

We walk the final stretch in silence—every step crunching beneath us like a warning. The front door towers, carved wood and heavy, untouched by time.

Kody reaches for the iron knocker and lets it fall—the sound a verdict.

My hands twist together, heart thundering in my chest. *How is he so calm? Doesn't he feel it too? The house listening... waiting.*

The door swings open.

And the breath I'd been holding shatters in my throat.

A young woman stands framed in the doorway, and for one horrible moment, envy flares sharp in my chest.

Did she grow up here while I was thrown out like an afterthought?

But then I catch the details—formal service dress, hair pulled back, posture crisp. Staff, not family. I breathe through the heat curling behind my ribs.

Focus, Cass.

She inclines her head. "Mr. Akers, I presume?"

"Yes," Kody answers, his voice calm and measured, with just enough charm to ease the tension. "And this is my companion." His hand hovers near the small of my back—close, reassuring. Not touching, but grounding me all the same.

"I am instructed to guide you to the meeting room," she says. "Please, follow me."

The door closes behind us with the heavy thud of finality—like a vault sealing shut.

"Thank you, Miss...?" Kody's tone is effortless, polite without sounding deferential.

"Dren. Olivia Dren." She leads us through a sweeping foyer laced with silence too still to be natural. The hallway curves beneath an arched bridge and staircase, the walls polished stone that reflects too much of the lamplight. Shelves line our path—leather-bound volumes, gold lettering catching the light like glints of watchful eyes.

A dark-paneled door appears ahead. Olivia gestures to it. "Please, make yourselves comfortable. The estate masters shall be with you momentarily."

Before leaving, Olivia pauses beside a polished sideboard. "As is tradition within the estate, the masters offer you garlic bread and tea." She gestures delicately toward the platter and teapot set with small, mismatched porcelain cups. "It is an old custom, practiced throughout these regions. A gesture of peace and transparency. No guest is received without the offer."

Her eyes linger on mine, just long enough to make the weight of her words clear. "You are welcome to partake… or not."

"Thank you, Miss Dren." Kody nods once. His smile is brief, but it lands, and I catch the faint flush of color dust her cheeks before she bows out, the door closing behind her with a muted thud.

I drift toward the window, more out of habit than necessity. The weight of the place presses down like it's alive, coiled around old secrets and watching closely.

"She liked you," I murmur, half teasing.

Kody drops onto the sofa with the kind of ease that says 'nothing in here scares me.' He stretches one arm across the backrest and lifts an eyebrow. "She's doing her job."

"Or you're just blind."

He huffs a quiet laugh. "Wouldn't be the first time."

"So… you are admitting she fancied you."

"Cass." His voice is soft but firm—patient, affectionate, and with just enough edge to stop the spiral. "I don't care if she did. I'm not interested. You already know where I stand."

I exhale, tension bleeding from my shoulders. "Sorry. That was... petty. I don't even know why I said it."

"You're human. And you're walking into something huge." He leans forward slightly, eyeing the tray on the table. "You want to pick a fight with a stranger because it's easier than facing whatever's about to walk through that door. I get it."

I nod, slipping onto the opposite end of the sofa. "I thought I'd be sick earlier. And then seeing her… someone young and polished and here. I just got so angry. Like she lived the kind of life I should've had." I run a hand over my face. "That's messed up, right?"

"It's not logical," he says gently. "But it's not messed up. You were a kid who lost everything. Of course this stirs shit up."

I glance at him, and sigh. "You always know what to say."

"Don't always say it right." He shrugs. "But I'll call you out with the truth. Even when it stings."

A small smile pulls at my mouth. "Yeah. I count on that."

He leans in, voice low. "Then count on this: whatever happens next, I've got your back." His hand finds mine. Steady, warm, and there. And I clutch it like a lifeline. Then the door creaks open.

We both rise, his fingers slipping from mine just before we turn to face whatever waits on the other side.

49 - Cassia

A tall, thin man enters first, his white shirt and tweed vest immaculate despite the late hour. His hair glows copper in the lamplight—the same shade as mine. I don't recognize him, but there's a weight in the angle of his jaw, the set of his shoulders, that coils deep in my gut with déjà vu.

A woman follows—brown hair coiled high in a perfectly engineered updo. A peach-pink collar fastened tight around her throat, connecting to a gown that leaves her pale shoulders exposed. She's flawless. Everything about her, arranged. Posed. Her skin is the same soft pallor as mine, but it's the way she moves that sharpens the unease prickling beneath my ribs. Each step fluid and rehearsed.

Her eyes find mine—and widen. One hand flies out to grip the man's shoulder. "Eli… Cassia." Her voice cracks on my name, wonder threading through it. But beneath that wonder, a glint of hunger, or maybe obsession, flashes too fast to place.

Eli follows her gaze, his posture going rigid when his eyes settle on me. Then the silence takes hold—dense and suffocating. I don't dare breathe.

Kody shifts closer, the heat of him at my side, steadying me. When he speaks, it's with that calm, clipped authority I've come to recognize as a warning. "Lady and gentleman of the house—we're hoping to acquire information about Mr. and Mrs. Bailey." A pause, measured and controlled. "My name is Mr. Akers. I have something for them."

The man narrows his eyes. "What could be so important it warrants interrupting our peace at this hour?"

"That depends," Kody says, tone sharpening just enough to draw blood. "Are you Mr. and Mrs. Bailey?"

The woman steps forward. Her smile is slow, eyes locked on me with rapture. "We are."

The answer should feel like closure. Instead, it lands like a trap snapping shut.

I've imagined this moment a thousand different ways—aching reunions, bitter confrontations, hollow apologies. But this? The chill. The stillness. The way they look at me like I'm a long-lost heirloom returned for appraisal. It all feels… wrong.

"Jori, we don't know these people," Eli murmurs, his voice lower now. But his eyes never leave my face.

"Oh, hush." Jori presses her fingers to her lips as if to stop them from trembling. "Can't you see it? She's grown… but those eyes… oh, Eli. It's her. It's Cassia. Our daughter's finally come home."

She steps forward, arms wide. I flinch too late as her hands, colder than they should be, cup my face with reverent care when she pulls me in. Her perfume is sharp with hyacinth, undercut by something metallic. Blood or metal, I can't tell. My lungs seize as she whispers, "My baby," and draws me closer again, fingers tilting my chin as if to verify what she already knows.

My own arms lift—hesitant… trembling. Part of me wants to believe this. To fall into the rhythm of memory, to be a child again in the arms of someone who claimed to love me. But my instincts scream with every breath. Her skin is cold, her touch too precise. But tears burn down my cheeks anyway, and I can't even tell if they're born of grief or terror.

Eli steps in, folding me into a second embrace, eyes never leaving Kody. He smells like waterfront, moss, and memory, and still it doesn't sit right. Fake and calculated like a performance we're all pretending to believe.

I force myself to hold him back and put on a smile when they pull away.

"Hi," I whisper, voice raw.

"Come, come—sit!" Jori's tone brightens. She pulls me down beside her on the sofa. "You must tell us everything about your journey home. We've waited so long." She reaches for a silver bell and rings it with a practiced flick. The sound seems to echo through more than the room—like it vibrates somewhere deeper in the walls.

Eli sits across from us in a high-backed chair, posture ramrod straight.

Kody remains standing, arms crossed, tension wired through every muscle. "We won't stay long," he says, voice edged now, harder. "We're on a time-sensitive route."

"Oh, nonsense," Jori laughs, waving a dismissive hand. "We insist you stay for supper." Her smile sharpens a fraction.

My stomach knots and I look to Kody. His expression is unreadable, but his jaw flexes once.

After a long pause, he nods. "Alright," he says, voice neutral. "If you insist."

"Good!" Jori claps once, far too delighted. "You must be exhausted. Come, dear, tell us everything."

Kody sits at the far end of the couch, but his presence tethers to me. My eyes dart to the corners of the room where the lamplight falls just shy of the darkness. The way the shadows pulse, the way neither of my parents seem to breathe like they should... Everything looks perfect.

And nothing feels right.

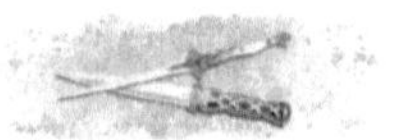

THE MAZE-LIKE corridors between my assigned changing room and the dining hall are more disorienting than they should be. Cold stone walls stretch in every direction, lit only by dim sconces that do little to push back the deepening shadows. I round another corner and nearly collide with Kody, who looks just as lost.

A breath of laughter escapes me at the surprise on his face. "You too, huh?"

His gaze sweeps down, lingering just a moment too long on the emerald silk gown Jori insisted I wear. "You look..." His voice lowers. "Flawless."

Heat creeps up my neck and I glance away. "I feel... exposed. Nowhere to hide a dagger in this thing."

Kody arches a brow, a faint smirk tugging at his mouth. "I could help you find a place. Not that you'll need one tonight." His tone is playful, but the way his eyes flick down the hall suggests he's scanning for threats beneath the charm.

I lower my voice. "Something seems off. And I don't just mean the dress."

He pauses, the smirk fading. "I know." That admission stills me. "But we'll get through dinner," he adds, offering his arm. "And you won't need your blades with me beside you."

I slip my hand through the crook of his elbow, grateful for the excuse to stay close. The whisper of silk against the stone floor keeps my focus on walking straight. Every step feels scripted, like I've wandered onto a stage I wasn't meant to see.

The dining hall is grand. Perfectly arranged with gleaming crystals and candles flickering low. My parents wait at the far end of the table, seated like royalty. Between them sits a young girl in a sky-blue dress that makes her look more porcelain than flesh. A lace choker hugs her throat and her blonde hair is neatly brushed, but her pale blue eyes catch on mine with a chilled knowing.

Did they have another child after sending me away?

Jealousy rises before I can stop it, followed swiftly by guilt.

"Easy," Kody murmurs at my side, reading my tension. Then, he says louder, "What's your name?"

The girl glances toward my parents. They nod in unison, their smiles pristine and practiced.

"I'm Calanthe. But everyone calls me Cali. You can too—if you want." Her voice is light and singsong, but it grates against the stillness in the room.

"It's a pleasure, Cali." Kody tips his head, drawing a delighted giggle from her.

"The pleasure is quite mine, good sir!" she chirps, sitting straighter, like she's playing a part she's been rehearsing.

Kody smiles. "And how old are you?"

"I'm seven. But I'll be eight on the fourteenth!"

He leans forward, voice dipping into mock secrecy. "That's a very important age. I bet you know all the best hiding spots around here."

Cali beams. "Would you play with me?"

My chest flutters, but my parents clear their throats in unison.

Cali stiffens under their gaze, her smile wilting as she straightens her posture. "I mean... maybe a game more proper for a lady. A tea party, perhaps."

Kody hides his mouth behind his hand, his stage-whisper

exaggerated. "You're in luck. Tea parties happen to be my specialty. But don't tell anyone, or I'll have a line out the door."

Cali giggles again, glancing shyly at my parents who now watch in silence, their smiles unchanged with eyes too still sending a shiver crawling beneath my skin.

I follow their lead during the meal, noting how little they eat despite the spread. Every gesture is smooth and rehearsed. A fork lifted here, a napkin dabbed there. No wasted movement, with no real appetite. Actors in a perfect scene.

After the dishes are cleared and they send Cali off to bed, I grip the edge of my seat and force the question out—the one that's festered for years. My voice is careful, but it still feels too loud.

"I don't know how to ask this politely, so… I'm sorry if it sounds wrong, but—" I meet their eyes. "Why didn't you come for me after I was sent away?"

Jori's hands fly to her mouth, her breath catching audibly.

Across from her, Eli's expression darkens with a wound deeper than anger. "You weren't sent away by us," he says. "You were taken."

The room stills.

"What?" I look between them.

"Holli," Jori chokes on the name. "She stole you from us. That night—"

"No. Holli saved me." The words come out fast and defensive. "She told me to follow the North Star. That someone would be waiting."

"Mr. Parker," Eli mutters, bitterness sharp in his tone. "We searched for months. No one had ever heard of him. The chapel was empty."

"I never made it there." I stare at my hands, ashamed of the truth. "I got scared. There were noises in the woods and I ran."

Jori's hands tremble against her lap. "And we thought… when we saw the blood—"

"We kept searching," Eli says. "But there was no body. No sign. Authorities couldn't—" He cuts himself off.

"I found people," I whisper. "A few homes. One was a retired hunter. He started training me on my twelfth birthday."

"Training you?" Intrigue flickers behind Jori's eyes.

"Combat. Self-defense." My voice hardens as I stare at the silver rimmed plates on the table. "He was… a perfectionist."

Eli's jaw tenses. "You were twelve?"

I nod, the chill in the air finally sinking into my skin when the silence after my last words stretches, heavy and unresolved.

Kody's hand brushes against mine under the table, steady and grounding. But before I can speak again, Eli clears his throat.

"Did either of you notice the state of the city?" he asks, his tone casual, but the pivot is abrupt enough that I blink. Kody and I exchange a glance, wary.

"Noticed what, exactly?" Kody says, guarded.

"There's quite the lack of gore within the streets." Eli's voice takes on a strange formality, like he's delivering a well-rehearsed speech.

My stomach knots.

"Indeed," Kody says carefully, his expression unreadable.

"Every ten years," Eli begins, "people are invited to what's called the gleaning."

I tense. "Gleaning?"

Jori folds her hands primly. "An arrangement, of sorts. A compromise."

Eli continues, matter-of-fact. "Each house selects a number of healthy civilians—le collé, they're called—to offer to Noctis. For feeding."

I glance at Kody. He doesn't move, but I can see the tension threading through his shoulders.

"So, Noctis take their pick," he says slowly, "and keep them like livestock until they're too sick to stand." His eyes darken.

Eli adjusts his sleeve. "The governor believed it better than the alternative. The region is trying to integrate with our neighbors to the south—Emmen, Lucerne… They sought peace."

"Peace," Kody scoffs. "Being shackled to your predator isn't peace. That kind of thinking is why hunters left this region. If not for that, the guild would've—"

"The guild abandoned us long before this," Eli interrupts, voice tight. "Zurich was caught between feuds that had nothing to do with us. We were left to fend for ourselves."

Kody's jaw flexes, but he holds his tongue.

"The city maintains stability through these… arrangements," Jori says, but even she sounds like she's quoting someone else. "Still, it's not safe for you to be seen—not with the next gleaning approaching."

I blink. "What do you mean?"

"You'd be safe here," Jori says gently, leaning forward. "On the estate. We can keep you hidden until after."

"After what?"

Eli meets my gaze. "There are those who might… take interest in you. Powerful people. Even we must be careful."

"Like the Mistress?" The name slips out before I can stop it.

They both go still and an icy silence creeps into the room.

"Where did you hear that name?" Jori's voice sharpens.

"Around the city," I say quickly. "People talk."

"Then you understand why you must stay hidden," Eli says. His voice leaving no room for debate. "At least until the gleaning passes."

Kody leans forward. "And what about Cali?"

Jori's tone turns instantly firm. "Cali will not be attending any gleanings. You can be certain of that. Everyone on our estate is protected."

"Cassia found her way back to you on her own," Kody says, his voice deceptively calm. "She's strong. Capable. But now you're saying unless she agrees to stay locked away, you'll send her off into danger?"

"Kody, it's okay." I touch his arm gently.

"You don't have to decide tonight," Jori cuts in smoothly. "Stay. Rest. Let us get to know the woman our daughter has become."

"Both of you are welcome," Eli adds, glancing at Kody. "You've clearly looked out for her."

"That's kind of you," Kody says, his voice respectful but cool. "But I can't accept your hospitality. I have business in town."

"I'm afraid we must insist," Jori says quickly. There's a flicker of hunger behind her eyes—smiling and sharp.

"I appreciate the offer," Kody replies. "But I'm needed elsewhere."

Their eyes turn to me.

"Cassia," Jori says, softer now. "Would you stay? Just a while longer? Let us be a family again."

I look to Kody, searching his face for direction. But his expression is unreadable. He's leaving this to me.

A war stirs in my chest. I don't trust this place. I don't trust the way they speak in polished sentences or how their eyes flicker when I mention things they shouldn't flinch at. But I also don't trust walking away from it—not yet. Not until I understand what this really is.

"I'll stay," I say finally. "For a little while."

Kody doesn't argue, but his silence says enough. I only hope he can read the unspoken reason behind my words.

"Wonderful!" Jori rises, her smile luminous. "Come, let's get you settled. There's so much to catch up on."

As we leave the dining room, I notice the way the staff press themselves against the walls as we pass, their eyes downcast, movements clipped and tense.

I don't know what exactly I've agreed to stay for.

But I intend to find out.

50 - Kody

Kody's hand stays near the hilt of his concealed blade throughout dinner, though he doubts silver would do much against Noctis this old. It might slow them—interfere with the enzyme their cells use to knit back together—but not for long. Not the old ones.

They're too careful.

Every movement is deliberate. Every blink, mechanical. Every breath lands exactly where it should. Most would miss it. He used to—before enough years on the trail taught him what control looks like.

But he hasn't missed a thing tonight.

He brushes the hilt beneath his coat—smooth, worn, warm against his hand. Blood-bound, like every blade the Guild forges. Quenched with his own blood the day he took the oath.

Most scoffed at the ritual. But the ones who lived long enough, stopped scoffing.

The old forge master's voice rises from the heat and oil, same as it always does when the blade hums.

"This was Hale's doing," the man had muttered, lowering *the glowing blade into the oil. "One of the first. Helped build the Guild after the war turned. Said blood remembers what steel forgets."*

"'A weapon forged in blood doesn't forget the hand that shaped it,'" he'd added, voice gravel-thick with ash and

reverence. "That's what he told the others. And whether you believe it or not..." He'd looked at Kody then, gaze steady. "...the Noctis do."

It hasn't left his side since, and tonight, it hums like a warning in his bones.

A sharp clatter snaps him back—porcelain on stone, the shatter too loud in the vaulted quiet.

The server stiffens mid-breath, eyes flicking to Jori before she drops into a bow so fast it's more instinct than choice. Shards scrape across the floor as she fumbles for them, hands shaking hard enough to cut.

Jori's gaze settles on the girl—cool, unblinking, like watching a bug squirm beneath glass.

The other servants shift tighter to the walls, heads bowed, necks angled just slightly away. Not out of respect, but out of instinct. Their pallor isn't just fear—it's drained. Controlled. Fed on.

The sound still lingers in the high ceiling. Cassia rises halfway, ready to help, but then sees the girl curled tight around the shards, trembling. Cassia freezes. Her hands clench in her lap and she watches. Silent.

Across the table, Cali straightens, neck craning to get a better view. Then Jori's eyes flick her way. The girl shrinks instantly—shoulders pulled in, lips pressed into a line so practiced it doesn't belong to a child at all. She knows better than to ask.

Cassia doesn't look away from her parents. Whether she notices Cali or not, she doesn't show it. Her eyes stay fixed on Jori and Eli, drinking in every word like she's afraid to miss anything. Or maybe afraid to stop believing it. That look, half guarded half yearning, twists the comfort in Kody in a way he can't quite name.

She's already halfway to forgiving them. Because she needs this to be real.

And they're good at it. Eli's voice cracks on cue. Jori's hands tremble just enough to look human. It's grief, staged to perfection.

Maybe some of it's real, and that makes it worse.

But Kody's seen better actors, and worse monsters. Even Cali knows her cues. She gives him wide eyes, all innocence and manners—rehearsed charm in a tiny frame. But it's Jori's gaze that twists his gut. She watches the girl not like a mother, but like a trainer.

He's seen it before—Noctis households that raise their meals with lullabies and warm blankets. Praise good posture. Insist on bedtime stories. Keep them fed just enough to keep them sweet. Just long enough to last.

"Noctis take their pick. Keep them until they're too sick to stand." The words come out sharp, but not untrue.

Eli flinches, shame flashing across his face like a crack in foundation stone. Kody's seen that look before too. But shame doesn't stop the feeding, it just follows it.

Then Cassia says the name, the Mistress, and the air shifts. Not fear of the name itself, not exactly. The fear lands around Cassia.

Jori leans forward too fast, her voice sweet and urgent as she insists Cassia stay hidden. It isn't protection—it's containment.

She looks at him before she speaks. But he already knows what she's about to say.

She's trying to be strong—trying to walk toward the fire without flinching instead of away from it with fear of regret. Trying to believe that what's behind these walls is worth saving.

Even knowing what's coming, it's still a gut punch when she nods. All he can do is nod back, slow and sure. The way you steady someone on a ledge and lie with your eyes.

Inside, every instinct claws to stop her. When they offer to let him stay, he declines with a smile that costs him more than he'll admit. Staying would tip the balance too soon. A hunter under their roof would only drive their secrets deeper. It's better to stay mobile. To keep watching even if it feels like ripping out a piece of himself to let her stay without him.

He watches her follow Jori out of the room and doesn't say a word.

He doesn't like turning his back on threats, but the game only works if they think he's playing by their rules.

After dinner, Kody follows a servant down a narrow corridor veined with old cracks and candle soot. The girl walks too fast, shoulders stiff, and when she gestures toward a worn wooden door, her hand trembles hard enough to rattle the cuff of her sleeve. Pale skin, two fresh puncture marks just visible beneath her collar.

"How often?" he asks, voice low and even.

She startles, eyes snapping up. The fear in them is immediate, raw. She doesn't answer—just darts a glance over her shoulder like someone might be listening. "Please, sir," she whispers. "I can't—"

"I know." He slips the vial into her palm before she can turn away. "Vervain extract. Three drops in water. Every day."

Her fingers close around it like she expects it to vanish. A heartbeat later, she disappears down the hallway without another word.

He waits until her footsteps fade, then continues walking—slow, deliberate, eyes scanning each door, each seam in the stone. There's a rhythm to it, like falling back into muscle memory: count paces, note exits, pressure hinges on the east window, loose floorboard by the servants' stairwell. It's all the kind of details you only learn on rescue missions—usually the ones that start too late.

Above, a floorboard groans and Cassia's voice follows, lilting with undercurrents of joy. She's asking a question. Jori answers, too soft to catch, but her cadence is sweet, and too warm. Rehearsed.

He doesn't stop walking, but the sound sinks under his ribs like a blade. She wants so badly to believe this is real.

A flicker in the corner of his vision pulls him to a halt. One of the hallway sconces wavers, though there's no breeze. Then a panel of wall shifts, almost imperceptibly, and Eli steps out.

He closes the hidden door with a deliberate motion, slow as ritual, then turns. Their eyes lock across the corridor and neither of them bothers to smile.

"She doesn't need to know yet." Eli's voice carries that resonant undertone Noctis can't quite hide once they stop pretending. "Let her have this time with us."

"Until the gleaning?" Kody makes it a challenge, not a question.

"We're trying to protect her."

"From the mistress? Or from what you are?"

Eli's expression hardens—an ancient shadow staring out

through borrowed eyes. "You know nothing about us. About her."

"I know enough."

"Then you know she'll never forgive you if you tell her and pull her away from getting to know us." He closes the distance, each step unnervingly precise, joints bending at angles a human body wouldn't trust. "There are changes already in motion. The chaos you see now will give way to order… elegance… and mercy."

"You speak as though servitude can be dressed in finer clothes. As though mercy makes it less of a cage."

Eli stops beside him, his voice dropping to a whisper meant to linger. "So let her choose. When the time comes. After she understands what's been set in motion."

"And if she chooses wrong?"

Eli smiles, lips pulling wide to reveal a sinister gleam. "Then perhaps you're not as great a teacher you thought you were." He drifts down the hall, movements weightless, until shadow swallows him.

Kody stands in the silence, carrying the weight of everything left unsaid. Everything he's letting her step into blind. But Eli was right about one thing—Cassia has to choose. And he can't be the one to reveal what they are involved in, not if he wants to keep her trust. He just prays she decides before choice becomes an illusion.

On the climb back upstairs, he passes servants readying the rooms for nightfall. They move with quiet efficiency, but their eyes betray them—hollow, resigned, careful not to linger on him. He's seen it before, households where obedience is cultivated like livestock. Where protection is only another word for possession.

Cassia's laugh drifts down from the upper floor—bright, unguarded, everything he's wanted for her. Everything he may have to tear away if the threat gets too loud.

But not tonight. Tonight she can have this fragile peace with the family she's fought to find, even if their warmth feels rehearsed.

His hand settles on the hilt of his silver blade. Sarah's words echo back—families of choice holding stronger than bloodlines, love sometimes demanding you let people walk headlong into truth.

He has time. Not much, but enough to learn what game the Baileys are running. Enough to be certain Cassia has a real choice when the mask finally slips.

Until then, he'll keep watch. He'll wait. He'll keep his distance while standing close enough to strike.

Because he refuses to lose another person he loves to Noctis games. Not this time.

51- Cassia

The estate settles into its evening hush, the air heavy as velvet. Servants drift along the walkways with lowered heads, lighting lanterns one by one, their pale glow spreading across the gardens. I wander the stone paths, restless, my thoughts circling the same knot they have for days.

Kody has been distant. Watching. Waiting. Always standing at the edge of shadow, as though he's half here and half already gone.

I pause near the study windows, ivy curling thick around the stone. A low voice cuts through the quiet—smooth and deliberate. Eli.

"Payment will be arranged, seeing as she was delivered unharmed."

My breath stalls.

Delivered. As if I were a parcel.

My stomach turns cold.

Kody answers, but his voice is muffled, too low for me to catch. I inch closer, pressing against the stone.

Eli again, sharper now, each word deliberate and sharp: "Though I wonder how the Guild will respond when learning you've been in her bed. Protectors are not meant to rut with their charges. You've broken more than laws, Akers. You've made her cheap by your weakness."

The words slice into me. My body goes rigid, hands on my stomach, throat closing. For a moment I can't breathe, can't think. *Payment. Delivered. Cheap.*

I don't wait to hear Kody's response. My legs carry me blindly down the path, away from the window, heart hammering in my ears—willing myself not to be sick.

I FIND HIM in the garden after walking, lantern light catching on the scar above his brow. He looks up the moment he senses me, but whatever he sees on my face stills him.

"How long were you planning to keep lying to me?" The words tear out raw.

His brow furrows. "What?"

"Did you think I wouldn't find out ?" My voice breaks on a laugh that isn't a laugh. "Unharmed delivery, arranged payment—was I just a mission to you? Cargo you get rewarded for dropping off?"

Color drains from his face. "Cassia. That's not—"

My hands curl into fists, heat flaring in my ears. "You knew you'd bail—so what was I? Just convenient?"

He flinches, jaw locking hard. For a long moment he says nothing—no denial, no excuse. The silence is worse than if he'd shouted.

"Is that your idea of honor? Or did you just think I was desperate enough not to see I was being used?" My heart pounds so hard it hurts to breathe. "You've been hiding things since Zurich. Don't mistake my silence for blindness. I'm not too stupid to see what's in front of me. You just don't trust me with it."

"You done?" He stands there, arms folded as though he expected it—his calm, infuriating.

"I already told you once not to lie to me, Kody."

"You didn't hear all of it," he says, voice low, strained.

"I heard enough." My chest burns.

He drags a hand over his face, the motion harsh, almost desperate. "I'm trying to protect you."

I cut him off, bitterness rising sharp as bile. "Always the hero. Did it ever occur to you that I don't need you to?"

His eyes flash, but his voice lowers, raw. "I'm trying to shoulder what I can so it doesn't bury you." He swallows hard. "If I'm wrong about this, what we have won't survive it. If I'm right... it tears down everything else."

The words strike like iron bars slamming shut. "So you'll decide what I get to know?"

"I'm deciding how much weight to drop on you at once."

His voice roughens, carrying that dangerous edge I've only heard in battle, but beneath it a fracture runs through. Tears sting my eyes. "This is standard risk assessment."

"This is my life, not just your job. I've known you for years, Kody…"—I turn from him, hugging my arms tight, refusing to let him see me splinter—"and right now you feel like a stranger." The estate looms over us, every window a dark eye watching, listening. And in its shadow, the heat in my chest calms—setting a silent prayer for him to reach for me. To be someone who won't walk away.

His hand finds my arm, heat burning through my sleeve. For a heartbeat neither of us moves. The garden holds its breath, shadows pooling at the edges of the lantern light.

"Cass…" His voice is ragged. "I don't want this fight."

"And yet here we are." I force myself to turn, meet his eyes. They've seen me through every step of training, wounds, and intense battles. They've seen me more clearly than my parents ever could. "It's been made clear—I can't have both. Them or you. And I don't know how to choose."

His hand rises, cupping my cheek, thumb brushing away tears I hadn't realized escaped. His voice shakes. "You don't have to."

He presses his lips to mine—fierce, desperate, and nothing careful in it. A silent tribute to us and a goodbye tangled into one. My fingers clutch at his shirt, unwilling to let go, as if I can anchor him here by force.

When we break apart, he rests his forehead against mine as I search his face. "Don't leave." I whisper, voice catching.

"I have to." His eyes close, jaw tight, muscles trembling beneath his skin. "Stay sharp, Cass. Trust your gut about this place, it's truth will keep you safe. If the answers don't add up, write them down. Question everything." His voice roughens. "You're stronger than you think. And if you need me—send word, and I'll come." He exhales, pain threading through every word. "But I can't stay. I need you to trust me—it's important."

"More important than us?" The question slips out, small, terrified.

He pulls back, hands shaking as he lets me go. "Nothing matters to me more than you. And that's why I have to go." His voice cracks on the last words, hollow with truth. "You'll never get your answers with me here."

A door opens across the courtyard spilling light over stone. My mother's silhouette stands framed in the glow, her smile poised and cold. "Come inside, dear," she calls. "The night air isn't safe."

Kody strides toward the gate, shoulders stiff with the effort of walking away. Each step pulls him further into shadow. The kiss still burns on my lips, a claim and devotion, while my mother's voice lingers in the dark behind me.

When I finally look back, the lanterns burn steady on their hooks, and my parents' silhouettes linger at the far end of the path. Waiting for me to choose.

And for the first time, I'm terrified of making the wrong choice.

52 - Kody

The archives carry a distinct smell of mildew mingled with the past. Kody's fingers trail the cracked spine of another brittle volume, shoulders tight from hours hunched over fading ink. Three days since their fight in the garden, since the kiss that felt like a confession and a goodbye, and sleep has not come once. Every time he shuts his eyes, he sees Cassia's face, the hurt in it, the way her voice shook when she asked if she'd been convenient.

A folded paper slips free as he opens a book. It flutters to the desk, edges worn soft with age. Sarah's handwriting. He hasn't seen that sharp, deliberate script since the day they sealed her effects.

His pulse falters, breath catching in his throat. Of all the ghosts buried on these shelves, he never expected hers to climb out and take his hand. His fingers tremble as he unfolds the ink-bitten fibers.

Found another reference to the Bailey line. Third this month. The name surfaces in Noctis records more than it should—never turned, but always marked significant.

Kody's jaw locks, eyes dragging over the words. He'd dismissed this once, filed it under Sarah's obsession. Now it reads like a wound splitting open.

The Mistress fixated on them, kept accounts of encounters. Always incomplete. Always unsatisfied.

His stomach knots. The pattern clicks too easily with Cassia's parents and their gilded halls.

Vesper appears in the margins—near Bailey line more often than chance allows. Never striking. Never pursuing. Entries redirected. Interference unexplainable.

Kody's grip tightens until the paper nearly tears. He had brushed off Sarah's theories back then, too disciplined to chase what the Guild dismissed as speculation. But now, Cassia's parents steering her toward the Mistress, servants walking pale and drained through their halls, he feels the truth pressing down piece by piece.

The Mistress's obsession wasn't random.

More documents follow—feeding logs, failed transformation trials, bloodline charts. Each arc of ink bends back to the Baileys. Each margin carries a smudge that looks like interference—entries cut off midline, redirected by a hand he can't see.

Halfway down a ledger page, Sarah's pen turns harder, the nib scoring the paper. Underlined twice:

Tenebris moves again.

Kody frowns. He's heard that name recently—hissed in an alley by a Noctis who recoiled as if it burned his tongue. Why would Sarah be tracking him?

He flips another page. A rushed scrawl, almost an afterthought:

Vesper = Tenebris

The air leaves his lungs. His vision narrows. Sarah knew. And now, so does he.

A shadow cuts across the desk. "Finding anything interesting?"

Kody tenses, hand tightening over Sarah's notes. But the guild's historian only watches him, her expression unreadable.

He starts to close the folder, but she waves him off. "She was right, you know. About all of it. The Mistress. The bloodlines. Vesper." Her voice drops lower, almost reverent. She glances over her shoulder before continuing, as if even the shelves might be listening. "The question is—are you ready to see what she saw? To understand what it cost her?"

Silence stretches. Books breathe dust.

"You won't find the answers in those volumes." The historian steps closer, gray hair slipping from its severe bun. "The Bailey records were… altered after the incident."

Kody's fingers still on the cracked leather binding. "Altered how?"

"Pages missing. Whole sections… burned." Her gaze sharpens. "Strange, isn't it? A family of that stature, and half their history disappears. As if someone wanted the ink trail broken—particularly where it touches arrangements."

Her eyes flicker, betraying unease, before she lowers her voice. "Others believe the records weren't destroyed. They were taken."

Kody exhales slowly. "By who?"

The historian traces the spine of an ancient ledger. "Not all knowledge is meant to be found, hunter. Some things are hidden—protected. Even from us."

His jaw tightens. "The Keepers."

A pause. The faintest tremor in her hands. "I've already told you more than I should."

The unease in Kody's gut sharpens. The same cold coil settles under his ribs—the one that tightened when he first saw Eli and Jori's names appear where they shouldn't, alive on ledgers dated years after their supposed deaths. It's the coil that tightened again in the Bailey halls, watching servants edge along walls as if staying clear of an unseen border.

"I need reports on disappearances near the Bailey estate. Last twenty years. And servant transfers between households." His voice comes out flat, professional—the way it always does when the personal cuts too close.

The historian studies him for a long moment. "That girl you brought to the Zurich library. She's a Bailey, isn't she? Like the others who vanished before the arrangements were formalized."

Kody says nothing, but his grip on the ledger tightens until the leather creaks. His mind fills unbidden: Cali, too young to see the fate being shaped for her. The servants, thinned by use, moving like prey through gilded halls. And Cassia—standing so close to her parents, convinced she'd found what she'd lost, never realizing the complexity of the cage she was already in.

A bile clenches his stomach—sick over having left her

there alone before he realized it went deeper than her parents being simple users of a Noctis feeding system.

"Reports won't help her." The old woman shakes her head. "What she needs is someone willing to face the truth. About the gleanings. About what happens to those chosen as le collé."

The word lingers. Kody knows it—Eli's voice still echoing from dinner when they first arrived, explaining how the invitees were bid upon, how the Noctis called themselves Keepers once they claimed a le collé. The memory churns his stomach now. Cassia was never being welcomed home. She was being positioned.

The truth lands hard, sharper than ink on the ledger. It's been circling him since the night he saw her eyes staring back at him from a portrait of Eden Bailey—the same eyes that haunt his nights. Proof of a bloodline the Mistress will never release. Proof Cassia's freedom was always an illusion.

The historian disappears into the labyrinth of shelves, reemerging with a thin folder. "Last known sighting of Eli and Jori Bailey. Three years after their recorded deaths." She holds it out. "Note the witness statement. Their tie to the Mistress with their new arrangement."

Kody takes the folder. His practiced calm cracks one line at a time as he reads. Fury threads through his muscles until his teeth ache with it. He had dreaded this, but seeing the names inked alongside the Mistress strips away every denial.

Her parents aren't victims. They chose their role. And Cassia is the currency they mean to trade.

He slams the folder shut, the crack echoing through the stacks. "I need transport back to the Zurich. Tonight."

"The roads—"

"I don't care." His voice is harsher than he intended, but he doesn't rein it in. "I need to get there before the Mistress takes her."

The historian nods slowly. As he turns to go, her hand catches his sleeve. "Whatever you find there… remember. Sometimes the kindest cuts are the quickest."

He wrenches free, unwilling to meet her gaze.

The folder drags at his hand, heavier than iron, confirmation pressing until his jaw aches. He'd suspected, but now the names inked beside the Mistress's trade connect the rest of the threads he hadn't pinned down before.

Duty and love tear at him in equal measure. Both demand the same thing: get back to her before it's too late.

He strides through the guild halls, steps ringing against stone. His mind won't let go of the memory of her mouth against his, the heat of her clinging to him even as she pushed him away. The tremor in her voice when she begged him not to leave. He has no right to think of any of it now, but the thoughts come like reflex.

He forces his mind to the present. Cassia, surrounded by smiling predators who share her blood—blind to the price they mean to collect.

Storming the estate would satisfy the part of him that wants to tear the doors down and drag her into daylight. It would also tip their hand before he understands the rules of the game. The Mistress has circled this bloodline for centuries. Sarah knew that—died for it.

He has to move. Has to reach her before the Baileys can deliver her to the Mistress. He shoulders through the archive door into the cold night. The city hums beyond the guild walls, indifferent. He will move fast—pull every thread Sarah left, pry at every door the Keepers closed, chase the rumor of Tenebris through the places that still speak his name in a whisper until he finds Vesper. Because if Kody wants to save her, he might have to find the one monster who knows why she's a target.

Cassia may not see the bars of her cage yet, but he does. And until he tears it down, he'll move heaven and earth to keep her alive.

53 - Cassia

My fingers trace the high wall surrounding the courtyard, stone cool beneath my touch. Three days since Kody left, and each one stretches longer than the last. The estate feels different without him—colder, though the afternoon sun warms my shoulders.

I stop when the masonry shifts shades where newer stone tries to mimic the old but doesn't quite hide the joint. My hand finds the faint seam of a door—my escape route all those years ago.

The pendant-turned-pin Holli gave me sits heavy at my collar as memories stir: her urgent voice telling me to run, the sting of smoke in my eyes, the metallic tang in the air as glass shattered behind us. My eight-year-old legs trembling, heart hammering. The world splitting in two before and after.

"Cass, Cass!" Cali's voice pulls me back as she dashes across the lawn, perfect blonde curls bouncing.

"Hi, Cali."

"Are you going to the party?" Her eyes gleam with excitement. "Mother picked the most beautiful gown—you'll look just like a princess."

"Party?" My stomach tightens. "What party?"

"The special one tonight!" She spins on her toes. "Though I can't go." A pout tugs at her lips. "Mother says it's only for grown-ups."

I kneel so we're eye to eye. Away from Jori's gaze, she relaxes—shoulders lowering, words tumbling freer.

"You're already a princess, Cali," I say softly. "Even without the party."

Her giggle is real, bright. For a heartbeat she looks like the child she should be, not the careful miniature adult Jori molds her into. But the moment fades as quickly as it came.

"Cali, dear." Jori's voice sweeps across the courtyard. The girl's posture stiffens instantly and she bows her head, perfect once more. "Time for your lessons."

Cali's hand slips from mine. I notice, as I have before, how she rubs her neck when she thinks no one's looking. She won't say why.

Jori glides closer as Cali walks past, silk whispering over stone. "Enjoying your walk?"

"The grounds look different," I say.

"Decades of change, Dove. You've changed, too."

"The lake entrance—" I glance at the bricked-over door.

"Beyond the wall is dangerous." Steel edges her voice beneath the sweetness. "That door was a weakness we can not afford."

"Because of the fire?" The words slip before I can stop them.

Her eyes sharpen. "What do you remember of that night?"

"Not much." I lie, my fingers lifting to the pin. "Only Holli."

Jori's body stiffens at the name. "Ah yes. Poor Holli."

"What happened to her?"

"She did not survive the fire." Each word sings flat, precise. "We searched for you for so long after she took you."

"I was eight." My throat aches with old questions. "I barely made it to the next town. How didn't you find me?"

Her eyes glint, but her smile doesn't waver. "We looked everywhere. Every orphanage, every foster home within a hundred miles."

"For how long?"

"As long as we could." The tone leaves no comfort.

I swallow.

As long as we could. Not as long as it took.

"And Cali's parents?" My voice is careful. "Did anyone search for them?"

Her smile doesn't falter, but the subject vanishes like smoke. "Enough of the past. Have you considered our offer?"

I hesitate. "This place is beautiful—"

"Wonderful!" she says, clapping lightly. "We'll make it official. A small gathering in two days to welcome you home."

Cali's words echo. *A party tonight. A gathering in two days.* The dissonance twists in my stomach. My skin prickles beneath Jori's hand as it lifts to my cheek—cold, firm, deliberate.

"Only a small gathering, Dove," she assures, her tone honey-sweet. "To present you properly."

The word 'present' scrapes through me like grit beneath silk. Not welcome. Not celebrate. Present. As though I'm an offering. A chill runs through me, and I can't ignore why anymore.

When Jori turns away, I take a deep breath to settle into the choice that was just made for me. I nibble my lip and look back to the masoned doorway—my cheek still tingling where her hand pressed cold against it. I keep walking, circling the garden paths until the stone corridors swallow me again.

Each hallway feels heavier, the air thick with polish and silence. By the time I reach my room, the sun has shifted, changing the shadows across the floor.

The air in my room is a different kind of quiet. Sitting at the vanity mirror, I slide out a folded scrap of paper. My pencil scratches a line:

1. Courtyard door sealed. Called a weakness.
2. "Protection" = command, not comfort.
3. Jori avoids questions about Holli, and Cali's parents. Changes subject quickly.

I fold the scrap tight and tuck it into the leather of my boot.

But the restless buzz in my gut won't fade. I glance to the window and then the door before leaving again, letting my steps guide me.

I drift through the quieter wing of the estate where the corridors are lined with shelves and the air carries a musty tang. My pulse quickens—the library. If I can't trust their words, I'll trust what the ink remembers.

The corridors in the maze to the library seem longer without Kody's shadow at my side. I walk slowly, counting sconces, memorizing cracks in the plaster—clinging to every detail I can turn into evidence. The silence presses heavier here than outside; even the air tastes stale, as if secrets rot between the walls.

The library smells of old paper and ink. Eli sits at the desk with Cali perched beside him, her small hands steady around a pen.

"Morning," he says, voice lined with that strange resonance he uses when he's relaxed. "You're just in time to see a prodigy."

"Look!" Cali beams, showing me the page. CASSIA is written in careful, perfect strokes.

"It's beautiful," I say, and mean it.

"She practices daily," Eli says, pride softening his face as he guides Cali's hand over the page. "Lineage requires discipline."

The word makes me bristle. "Lineage requires control, you mean."

His eyes lift to mine, calm and steady. "Families value order, Cassia. Without it, fear consumes everything."

"Order built on what?" I press. "Blood?"

His smile curves faintly, shadowed. He adjusts Cali's hand on the pen, guiding her fingers with careful precision. "Even mercy needs a system."

My brows knit. "Mercy?"

Eli dips the nib into ink, shakes off the excess, then sets it back in Cali's grip. His voice stays level, practiced. "Humanity didn't ask to be invaded by the Noctis. We tried to beat them—we failed. They're faster, stronger, and superior in every measure. So people are left with two choices: live in fear of an uncontrollable slaughter, or accept an organized compromise." He nods toward the word Cali traces. "That compromise is the gleaning."

The word rasps across my nerves.

He straightens Cali's posture with a gentle touch, his tone as smooth as the ink line she pulls across the page. "Those chosen are clothed and fed. Kept in comfort, not cages. When their strength is spent, they're released instead of discarded."

I can't stop the question before it slips. "And have you ever seen someone… released?" I growl.

The pen stutters in Cali's hand, blotting the page. Eli stills, just for a heartbeat, before covering it with calm instruction. "Steady, love. Smooth strokes."

Only then does he look at me, expression calm, the words

flowing with practiced ease. "It happens," he says. "When their time is complete—when strength declines or the allotted years are fulfilled. They are released, returned to their lives, provided for so they may continue in peace."

Cali glances up from her letters, lips moving as she echoes, almost soundless: returned to their lives for peace. Eli smooths her hand back to the page, guiding her pen as though nothing has passed.

A chill rakes my spine. A tidy lie wrapped in silk, meant to soften the truth that hangs above it all: servitude. Released back into the world like emptied vessels, marked forever by what was taken.

Eli closes the ledger with deliberate care, brushing Cali's curls as she leans into his arm. "That's enough for today," he murmurs. She beams at the praise, hugging him before darting off toward the corridor.

I rise, needing space, but his words stay with me—*mercy needs a system.* They echo like a draft through the halls as I climb the stairwell, searching for air.

He joins me on the mezzanine, steps measured, hands clasped behind his back as though nothing in our conversation had unsettled either of us. From here the south gardens spread in neat rows. Gardeners overturn the soil again and again, dark earth gleaming under their tools.

But nothing grows. No seedlings. No packets waiting to be planted. Just soil, tilled daily, as if the act itself mattered more than the result.

"Beautiful, isn't it?" Eli murmurs.

My pencil scratches in my mind:

4. South beds turned daily. Never planted. Ritual, not growth.

I glance sideways. "What's the point, if nothing grows?"

"Tradition," he answers after a beat. "Soil remembers. Renewal requires tending, even when you don't see it."

"Sounds like faith."

He exhales, almost a laugh but with no humor in it. "Faith, duty… they blur." His eyes soften when he looks toward the courtyard where Cali usually plays. "Some duties are chosen. Others—pressed upon you."

The weight in his voice draws me closer, but before I can press, his expression shutters. "Come. The afternoon grows late and there are preparations."

When we part, he lingers by the balustrade, gaze distant. I descend the stairs alone, thoughts turning over like the empty soil outside. The estate feels both vast and airless, every path funneling me back toward the same locked questions. By the time I reach my room again, my nerves are strung tight.

Strings weave through the puzzle pieces floating around the information I've gathered when a knock sounds.

"Cassia?" Cali stands there with a velvet box. She holds it up with a smile. "Mama says you forgot your brooch."

Inside lies a crescent-shaped pin, the Bailey crest. Severe. Heavy.

"To wear on your silks for special dinners," Cali whispers proudly. "It shows where you belong."

The words sink in my gut like stones—chest tightening as I pin it in place. *Where you belong.* As if belonging is a chain meant to be displayed.

I set the velvet box aside, but the brooch's weight seems to cling to me even after I pin it on. Servants glance as they walk by, then avert their eyes, as if the crest itself casts a shadow. I return to my desk and jot another note, though my hand shakes.

5. Brooch = Bailey crest. Servants react immediately. Not decoration—symbol.

The pencil barely stops when another knock comes, firmer this time, then Jori's voice announces the fitter. I tuck the scrap into my boot again and rise.

After an hour of standing on a pedestal, the fitter pins green silk against my shoulder with the final design while Jori inspects every detail.

"The hem needs two inches," she says. "And the sleeves tighter. We want to highlight her frame."

Her words brush over me like I'm fabric, not flesh. I stand still, heat prickling beneath my skin, while pins bite sharp against my ribs.

Eli appears in the doorway, gaze traveling over me in silent appraisal. His nod is curt, approving—not of me, but of the picture they've cut me into. Then he leaves without a word.

The brooch glints in the mirror, crescent sharp against the silk. My reflection looks less like a woman and more like a portrait: composed, curated, owned.

6. Jori and Eli frame me as prize to be presented, not a person.

I press against the folded scrap in my boot, steadying myself with its edges.

When they finally leave me, the room is still and the mirror holds only my reflection—stiff, draped in green, the brooch sharp against my collar. I strip the gown away, but the foreboding clings, prickling along my skin.

Eighteen days until the gleaning. The number presses down like a lid, sealing every exit. I press the scrap of notes in my boot and whisper the tally again like a ward: eighteen days to find the truth. Eighteen days before the cage door locks.

54 - Kody

The guild annex is bare stone and shadow. No polish, no vellum—just rough walls and the flicker of his lamp.

Hunting is the only thing that steadies him against the five days since he left her there. When the ground shakes, fall back on the pattern: mark the signs, follow the trail, close the distance.

Sarah's note lies open on the slate table, edges worn soft, ink pressed so hard the letters cut ridges into the page. He isn't here to brood. He needs leverage—answers he can carry back to the estate before the Baileys turn "family" into a transaction.

Vesper = Tenebris.

He tips the page toward the lamp, studying the grain. Sarah's hand always pressed too hard when she was working in a fury—he can almost see her sitting there, pen driving until the nib bit paper. He runs his nail along the strokes, feels the grooves, and angles the sheet again. There—faint, almost lost: a watermark of a broken ring crossed by a narrow key.

Keeper mark.

Sarah always left trails. This was no different.

He drags the annex catalog toward him, a thick ledger most hunters never touch. No confirmed kills here—only confiscated seals, failed experiments, scraps of history the Guild pretends not to keep. The kind of fragments Sarah always chased.

Flipping through the symbols, he finds the broken ring

paired with its key. Three separate entries. Each one ends the same way: Transferred. Restricted. Not destroyed. Not lost. Moved.

Beside the last notation, a location scrawled in cramped hand: *St. Paul's Cathedral annex, sub-cellar II.*

The trail doesn't just suggest a place—it narrows into a map.

Good. A direction.

His chest tightens. Sarah was reckless, but brilliant. She was like a sister to him. And she never stopped digging, even when the Guild told her to leave it buried. She'd bled for chasing trails like this. Following her notes now feels like trespassing in her shadow, walking the same knife's edge that cut her down.

But it also feels like carrying her with him, one step closer to the truth she died for.

So the Baileys' pages weren't just "lost." They were copied, relocated, and flagged for anyone who knew where to look.

He pockets Sarah's note, snuffs the lamp, and goes.

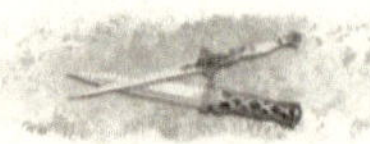

THE READING ROOM hums with polite scholars and the rustle of vellum. He bypasses them for the door marked Records Closed for Conservation. The latch gives under his pick.

Thirty steps down. Three turns left. He counts them the way he always does when laying out routes in his head— numbers sink deeper than names.

Air cools—draftless. He kneels at a knee high grate, fingers tracing iron until he tastes copper on his tongue. Two clicks under his pick, the bar eases, and he slips inside.

Shelves line the walls, shallow as coffins. Each holds a single ledger, wrapped in waxed linen and tagged with bone etched in glyphs. He works down the line until the broken ring and key repeat.

Inside, the script isn't inked. It's pressed—drypoint grooves over lemon-washed parchment. He tilts the lamp to catch the faint scratches.

Bailey line—evaluations attempted. Mistress notes: flavor variations persist; stability unsatisfactory.

Interference observed at each approach. Shadow on the periphery. Alias: Tenebris.

Tenebris sightings—Zurich, Lucerne, Rhine bend. Pattern circles sanctuaries and houses with Keeper seals. Orbiting radius consistent.

Later hand, pressed harder:

Tenebris favors old bells. Moves with the hour, not the sun. If you need him, make the hour ring.

Kody's grip tightens as he exhales until the ledger creaks. Dates would be better, but this is enough. He'd dismissed Sarah's theories then, called them obsession when he should have called them truth. She wasn't chasing ghosts—she was tracking interference. Tracking Vesper.

And he left her to do it alone.

He copies the lines he needs in block print, folds the strip twice, and tucks it under the leather at his wristband where no one would search him.

Footsteps pass outside. He kills the lamp and waits, blade loose—every nerve listening. A caretaker passes with a crate of candles. No pause. When the steps fade, Kody re-locks the grate, retraces each turn, and leaves the place looking untouched.

Outside, weather sits low. He heads to the runner's post for a short-range courier at the estate perimeter and a fresh set of Guild seals keyed to Zurich sigils. The clerk slides the packet across without questions.

He's almost out the door when a runner barrels in from the square, breath fogging.

"Akers," she pants. "Dispatch from House Bailey."

Every muscle locks. "How did it land here?"

"Shared loop for guild addresses. Their seal is on half the merchants." She sets a card on the counter.

Thick stock. Raised print.

Viewing advanced.

A date shifted forward. Days shaved clean off the clock.

The clerk swallows. "They're shifting schedules across

three houses. Reads like a cluster valuation."

A cluster means multiple Umbral Noctis in the room and a shortlist on the table.

Heat climbs Kody's throat—angry, sharp, and clarifying.

He palms the card, tucks it away, and turns to the clerk. "I need a rider stationed at the lower gate of the Bailey estate. No crest. No lamps. He waits outside the pine line until he sees a candle on the ground by the third fence pillar. If there's no candle by the hour, he leaves. If there is, he takes the passenger who walks to him. If a second body appears, he rides without questions."

The clerk blinks, then nods quickly, scribbling. "Yes, sir."

"Double his pay," Kody says. "Triple if he waits past the hour."

She stamps the order and slides it into the outbound tray.

He doesn't imagine Cassia finding that candle. She won't know it's for her, won't know to look. That's fine, this isn't for her. It's for him—for the chance, however slim, that he can drive her that far before the house closes its fist.

He steps back into the corridor, the scent of ink and wax fading behind him. The estate waits, and the clock is already moving faster than he can.

By the time he walks the square again, his mind is already mapping the approach. From Cassia's room to the side stair. From there to the service hall skirting the east wing. From the hall to the hedge line. Every step folds into muscle memory until he can run it blind.

Force breaks doors, leverage breaks systems, and he wants to do both.

Cassia waits inside those walls. And this time, he will not leave her behind.

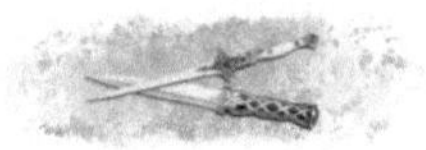

HE COULD WALK through the front door and break his way out with Cassia. He'd get her to the courtyard before the house closed around them. The Mistress doesn't rule by accident, and the Baileys didn't outlive their own death records by luck.

He splits his route. Vault for gear: silvered steel; a thin stiletto for tendons; chalk and wire; a spring snare flat as a coin; a smoke ampule to blind a small room for thirty counts. No charges. He isn't scorching earth.

Back by the clocksmith's, he lays a line under the lintel where Sarah used to leave her marks:

The hour is yours. Bells will ring. Come if you guard what I guard.

He signs it the way Tenebris will read: two notches on the edge, mirror to the coin. Then he turns for the stable yard.

The night smells like rain and horses as he swings into the saddle, breath steady. Sarah's page rides at his ribs while Cassia's voice sits under them, small and relentless.

The Baileys moved the viewing. There isn't time to draw Vesper into daylight first. Kody has to move without him.

If the bells pull a shadow to the estate's edge while Kody is cutting a way out, all the better.

He heels the horse, keeping the river on his left until the city thins, then turns for the hills and the house that sells safety by storybook pages.

At the ridge he reins in, scanning the windows blazing against the dark. On the mezzanine, a figure moves—Cassia, framed in lamplight, hair burning like copper in the glow. The sight cuts him raw.

For an instant his hand twitches on the reins, ready to drive straight through the gates and drag her clear. But the ache hardens into cold resolve and he forces himself still.

Not yet. Rushing her out now saves one life. But waiting, watching… confirming the Mistress's hand? That might topple more than this single house. Proof matters. And if he can trace how they mean to deliver her, he can end the chain instead of just snapping one link.

Cassia's silhouette disappears as the light shifts. He lowers his head, spurs the horse on, and swears the wait won't cost him her life.

55 - Cassia

The third time I notice Martha in a high collar despite the heat, I start keeping track. One week without Kody and the house carries a different temperature—polished on the surface, but cold underneath. Sunlight pours through the tall windows, yet shadows cling in the corners like mold.

I don't trust myself to leave a trail in plain sight. A note in a pocket can be found. So I keep the list in my head until I can slip away, then scrawl the details in the scrap of paper hidden in my boot.

11. Collars higher at dusk.
12. Staff vanish for "rest," return pale, unsteady. Martha, Anne, Thom—rotation?

I'm still turning the details over when I round a corner near the linen stores. Anne hurries past with folded sheets pressed to her ribs, the weight nearly spilling from her arms. Her hands tremble, and beneath the lace at her cuffs I glimpse bruises blooming like ink stains.

She glances at me once, quick and fearful, before leaning closer as if the walls themselves might listen. "You shouldn't walk after the tenth bell," she whispers. "The halls… change."

My breath snags. "Change how?"

Anne's eyes dart to the darkening windows, then back to the floor. Her voice thins, fraying to nothing. "Please, miss. Don't be there to see it." She clutches the linens tighter and scurries away, leaving only the faint rustle of cloth in her wake.

Anne's warning sticks in my skull long after she's gone. I find myself back at the courtyard wall, fingers tracing the seam where a door once stood. Not memory this time— evidence. Proof that escape was once possible, and was sealed away.

The pin at my collar drags heavy against my skin. Records said Jori and Eli died the night of the fire. I saw their names in guild ledgers, marked and buried. Yet here they stand—alive, pressing me into gowns, staging dinners, calling it protection while parading me before strangers.

If safety is what they mean, why so many eyes on me? Why keep whispering of danger and then ushering in guests?

13. Parents recorded dead since fire. Still alive. Untouched. Contradiction between secrecy and display.

The hours drag like weights. I drift the corridors with my scrap of paper burning in my boot, pretending to admire portraits, pausing in alcoves when servants pass. Every hallway feels the same—polished floors, heavy curtains—but I keep moving, mapping the rhythm of the house.

By late afternoon, the estate shifts again. Banisters already polished are rubbed until they shine. Vases don't just change flowers—their pale blooms vanish, replaced with deep red, as if the walls themselves are bleeding into dusk. Curtains are pulled straighter, shutting out the light inch by inch.

The servants keep their eyes down as they work, clearing corridors with the precision of stagehands, setting the house for a performance no one will name. Watching them, I feel less like a daughter returned home and more like an actress waiting to be cued.

14. Evenings: flowers swapped, curtains drawn tight.

I tap the pencil against the vanity surface when there's a knock. I slide it under the jewelry box just as the door opens. Jori doesn't wait for permission to enter—green silk draped over her arm.

"Early dinner," she says lightly. Jori's eyes flick over the worn leather, and her smile never falters. "A few patrons will view the library afterward." She crosses the room and lays the gown across the back of my chair, fingertips brushing the fabric as though it were holy.

"The library," I echo, my reflection tight-lipped. "A viewing."

"A small one. You don't need to attend." She shakes the gown loose, fabric whispering as she lays it across my shoulders. Her fingers fasten the hooks with a precision that makes it clear she doesn't trust anyone else to do it. "New faces can... overwhelm."

"I won't overwhelm." The words come sharper than I mean them, but my stomach twists with curiosity.

The library. More strangers. More chances to see what they don't want me to.

Her smile warms in practiced kindness. "Another night, then. Tonight you'll dine with us and retire early. Rest helps the body keep up with change."

"Change," I repeat, flat.

"Not these," she murmurs, tugging at my sleeve with a delicate pinch. "No hunter's garb tonight, Dove. Stand." Her hand curls around my arm, guiding me up, turning me toward the mirror. The silk gleams between us, a command disguised as kindness.

She smooths the silk at my sleeve and pins the crescent brooch to my shoulder. The weight drags at me. "Beautiful," she murmurs. "It suits you."

I shift beneath her touch, the gown already clinging too close.

Did she plan this? Dressing me herself?

My own hands haven't touched a single hook. "Where's Cali?" I ask.

"In the nursery." Jori's smile softens. "She's practicing introductions."

"For library books?"

"For guests. You know how she loves to please." She kisses my temple in a way that would look maternal in a painting, but the gesture chills more than it comforts. "Library tomorrow, after breakfast. Eli has a ledger you'll enjoy."

When she leaves, I sit long enough to let my breath even out. Then I fold the paper and slip it into my boot, pressing the sharp corner into my skin until my nerves steady.

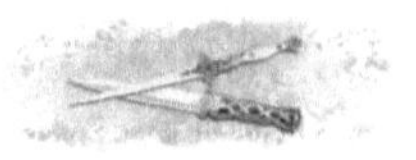

DINNER IS THEATER, not nourishment. The table gleams with polished silver, candles burning so low their smoke curls like script in the air. Eli asks about hunter training, his questions circling without landing, measuring me without showing the scale. Jori tells a story about summer lights strung through trees, her voice lilting, polished—like it's recited for patrons, not her own table. A maid hovers at my shoulder, refilling my glass after every sip until the wine feels more like a leash than a courtesy.

The food cools untouched, then vanishes between courses as if it never existed. I add the thought silently to my tally:

15. Meals staged, not eaten.

Two servants stand at the doors, another posted near the corridor toward the east wing. Their presence is too still, too deliberate. The house itself listens, the way a pond holds silence until a stone drops—rings spreading unseen beneath the surface.

I test the silence. "Your guests," I ask lightly, "do they dine like this too? Or is this only for me?"

Jori's laugh is soft, practiced. "Hospitality is a discipline, Dove. Guests deserve to see our house as it should be."

Eli sets down his fork with more care than the gesture requires. "Discipline isn't only for guests." His eyes rest on me longer than they should, as if weighing words he doesn't speak.

The silence stretches thin before Jori lifts her glass, smiling without warmth. "Tomorrow, Cassia, you'll see the gardens at their finest. The beds are turned for a reason."

When the last dish is cleared, Jori dabs her lips with a napkin. "Sleep now. Tomorrow will be a full day."

"I'll walk first," I say quickly.

"In the garden."

I meet her gaze, steady. "I'll see where my feet take me." The words taste like defiance, but I keep my voice level, almost casual, as if I'm only humoring myself. Reckless to say, controlled in the way I say it.

Her smile tightens, silk pulled taut over steel. "Don't tug old threads, Cassia. You'll pull the whole weave apart."

The words land heavier than the food. Eli doesn't look at me, but his hand stills over his wineglass, the tremor slight and quickly masked. Enough to remind me that not every performance is flawless.

I rise, bowing my head just enough to make them think I'm finished, and let the servants usher me from the table. But Jori's warning gnaws at me. *Don't tug old threads.* She's right about one thing—threads unravel if you pull them.

In my room, I strip the green silk and trade it for dark clothes that won't shine—hair braided loosely to the side, knife at my thigh.

The house shifts again, as it does every evening—flowers darkened, curtains drawn, corridors emptied. And Jori and Eli? They'll be in the library, entertaining their patrons. The perfect distraction.

I make one slow pass by the library, pausing just long enough to glimpse light spilling across the carpet and hear voices softened by distance. They're occupied, eyes turned elsewhere.

Good.

I count paces the way Kody taught me. Twenty-three to the side corridor. Ten past the arch. The air thins near the rise into the east wing. The step is as shallow as a book spine where a faint wheel rut stops short at the line. No wax polish here, despite what I was told earlier. Instead, a copper tang clings, sharp as blood on a bitten tongue.

I place my foot on the rise.

"Hold there." A man's voice drifts from around the bend, low.

I step back into shadow as two servants push a covered trolley into view.

Linen skirts the wheels, brushing stone. At the rise they stop, angle the cart sideways, and lift the load by hand across the threshold. The woman's collar rides high; a loose thread gapes at the seam, exposing pale skin. The man's sleeves slide up as he heaves; the inside of his elbow is dotted with pinpricks.

Neither looks toward the wing. Both keep their eyes on the floor, careful and reverent. And when they set the trolley down again, they shift their steps to follow faint chalk arcs along the wall, never straying outside the loops—guiding the trolley away once the load is clear.

16. Trolley stops at rise. Load passed by hand across. Cart avoids crossing. High collars. Pinpricks. Eyes down. Chalk marks = routes?

Church bells roll, six slow strikes. A maid at the far end pauses, counts softly under her breath, then moves again—her steps within the same marking along the floor.

I crouch. Thin chalk loops trace the baseboard, overlapping, broken, buffed nearly flat. Fresh, based on the shine. Not decoration—measurements? Or safety markers.

The air here sits different. Pressed thin, as if a vent pulls it sideways. A low hum prickles my ears, faint but steady, like machinery behind the wall. And beneath it all, the copper tang sharpens—blood, or the residue of whatever these marks are meant to conceal.

Footsteps echo, breaking my concentration. I rise before Eli's shadow lengthens across the wall.

"Can't sleep?" he asks mildly.

"Dinner was early." I step from the shadow.

"The south path is kind in moonlight." His hand gestures toward the garden. "The old wing keeps rules."

"Closed?"

"For now." His smile is gentle, but his eyes are not. "Ancestral places prefer respect."

"What happens if I don't respect them?"

"Best not to test limits you don't understand." His gaze flicks to the brooch. "That edge will catch if you let it hang out." He turns toward the garden, not waiting for me to follow. I don't.

When the corridor clears, I crouch again. Dust clings bone-white to my fingertip. The hum vibrates faintly through the stone, carrying into my bones like a warning.

Back in my room, I lock the door and sit on the rug.

17. Chalk loops at east wing threshold. Fresh. East Wing = containment? Hum behind walls. Copper strong at entrance. Staff sync movements to bells. Guests = library cover.

HUNTERS DON'T LEAVE doors locked when answers hide behind them.

I wait until the estate quiets, until the murmur of patrons in the library thins and the servants' steps fade into silence. Only then do I slip back into the East Wing corridor, keeping to the chalked edges the staff obey so religiously.

The house exhales softly as I walk its ribs. Down the hall, a door hushes open, voices glide, feet whisper. Guests, late. The air smells of clove laid sharp over metal.

The east wing rise accepts me without sound and the long hall beyond lies colder than the rest of the house. Moonlight cuts across dust that hangs unnaturally still.

Halfway down, I find a seam flush with the wall. No handle. A chalk loop traced across the baseboard and another over the hinge.

The pin behind my ear slides into the seam. The wood gives a fraction, then holds when I hear footsteps—sending me into shadow.

Two servants round the bend. One carries a ledger, a ribbon marking a page. The other balances a tray beneath linen. They stop at the seam.

The ledger-bearer whispers a number as he writes it down. A muted click follows, low in the wall, like gears shifting inside stone.

The seam splits open without a sound.

For a heartbeat, I glimpse the room beyond—machines rising like metal ribs, tubes pulsing with dark fluid, the steady thrum of power alive in the air. Heat rolls out, tinged with copper, before they step through and the panel seals again.

I press deeper into shadow. It's clear the door answers to more than the numbers.

When they return, the tray linen hangs heavy, stained dark, and the ribbon in the ledger marks a new page.

18. Hidden door mid-hall. Opens on ledger count + mechanical trigger. Machines inside. Dark fluid through tubing. Tray returns stained. Ledger ribbon moved.

I wait until their footsteps fade, then edge closer. My fingers trace the seam, searching. Smooth stone. Cold wood. Nothing obvious.

I press my ear to the panel. The hum inside vibrates faintly against my skin—steady, unnatural, a sound I've only ever heard from refrigerators in forgotten kitchens.

I slide my pin along the crack and for a breath it catches, answering with a soft click in the wall. My pulse jumps.

Not the numbers, then. Something hidden in the frame.

I lean in—a woman's voice drifts through, low and lilting, words curling like smoke. One cuts sharp enough to pierce the muffling wall: Anne.

A whimper follows, quick and stifled.

Every instinct snaps tight, a whipcord yanking in my chest. My pulse hammers, stomach hollowing, muscles ready to bolt though I force them still. The air grows thinner, sharper, every sound sharpened to a blade.

I retreat one step, then another, heel careful on each board. My breath comes shallow, ribs aching from the effort to keep quiet.

The hum presses against my spine until, at last, it softens on the locked side of my chamber door. Warm air creeps back, brushing my skin like a release.

Only then do I let myself exhale—slow, shaky, as though that voice might call *her* name again through the wall.

I write fast, hand unsteady.

19. Library "viewings" = cover. Guests watch me, not books.

20. Parents alive though records list dead since fire. Why cover survival?

21. Hidden door mid-hall. Opens with ledger count + mechanical trigger. Machines inside. Fluid warmed. Tray returns stained.

The latch stirs. "Cassia?" Jori's voice, low. "Awake, Dove?"

I slide the list under my boot lining and pull the coverlet close. "Yes."

She steps in with a candle cupped in her palm, her smile painted on. "I thought you might wander. New rooms invite new paths."

"I couldn't sleep."

"You and I are alike that way." She sets the candle on the table and smooths my hair with a touch that makes my skin crawl. "Tomorrow you'll spend the morning with me. No library. We'll write letters. Invitations to our allied houses. It's good to be seen."

"Seen by who?"

"Friends of the house," she says, smile fixed. "They adore promise."

Her hand lingers on my shoulder, cold through the fabric, then lifts. "Rest."

She leaves, candle still flickering on the bedside table. I pinch the flame dead between finger and thumb and slip the taper into my sleeve once the wax has cooled.

21. Jori expects wandering. Cancels library. Letters instead. "To be seen." Guests.

I should leave.

My mind spirals.

I could climb the servants' landing, drop to the path, and reach the pine line before anyone counted the bell.

But Martha's collars ride higher each day. Anne hides bruises she can't keep covered—and now, when I close my eyes, I hear the sound of her whimper echoing through that wall. Thom limps when he thinks no one watches.

And Cali rubs her neck after lessons, never asking questions out loud.

I'm not leaving them.

Hunters don't break a door down unless they're ready to carry everyone through.

Sleep doesn't come easy through the line of questioning and doubt in my mind. When it finally does, it tastes like iron.

56 - Cassia

Morning light spills through the tall windows, catching the mezzanine rail in pale gold. Jori has transformed the space into a desk: heavy paper laid out in neat stacks, each sheet faintly embossed with a crescent watermark that only the sun reveals. She places a pen before me, the nib sharpened to a point, and gestures to a list of names already inked in her hand.

"Friends of the house," she says. "Notes of regard."

"Regard for what?"

"For you, Dove." Her smile is warm. "It's time they know you're home."

She dictates while I write. Polite weather. The health of gardens. Harmless phrases—until the pattern sharpens: *We look forward to receiving you on the eighth… We'll be at ease for the sixth… If you prefer the tenth, the house can oblige.*

Not pleasantries at all, but coded hours, disguised in ink.

"Why hours?" I ask, lifting the pen.

"Tradition," she answers, smile fixed. "When to arrive matters more than how."

I bend back to the page. She corrects nothing, though I feel her gaze on my hand as if the weight of every letter matters.

Eli arrives with Cali mid-morning. He kisses Jori's cheek, then rests his palm on the chair behind me. His presence presses close, a shadow at my shoulder. "Fine hand," he murmurs, eyes on my script. "Legible. Restrained."

"Restraint isn't the same as compliance," I say.

He laughs softly, as though I've offered him a clever jest,

not a truth. "Language suits you. But so does the sword."

Cali slips into the seat beside me with a tray of sealing wax and matches. Her curls frame a face too young for such careful solemnity. "May I?" she asks, eyes bright but watchful.

"Of course," Jori says. "A crescent seal at the bottom edge."

Cali strikes a match with steady hands. The sulfur burns sharp, catching in my throat. She holds her breath until the flame takes the stick of wax, dripping perfect circles onto the parchment. Only when Jori nods does she press the seal down. She doesn't blink until the soft click marks the impression.

When the last letter is sealed, Jori stacks the envelopes with reverence, grouping them in neat bundles. "Courier loop at noon. Some will send replies by afternoon. We'll be ready."

"Ready for what?"

"Introductions," Eli says mildly. "Our friends value lineage."

"Value is one word for it."

His head tilts, studying me the way one might examine a specimen pinned beneath glass. "Have you worn the brooch long enough to notice? People look differently when they see it. Their posture changes first—and yours will, too, when you understand what it means to them."

I keep my expression still, but the words lodge deep. A piece of metal teaching me how to stand? No. It isn't the brooch shaping posture—it's the allegiance it signals. Another note for the list.

Jori rises, smoothing my hair as if she owns the right. "Library tomorrow," she promises, tone sweet. "Old ledgers with your father. The ones I mentioned before."

"You canceled that yesterday," I remind her.

"Today is for letters." Her words settle like a door shutting on velvet hinges.

I spend the rest of the morning under watchful eyes, hands cramped from ink and wax. By the time the table is cleared, the house feels restless—staff passing in pairs, glances traded like signals. Patterns I can't yet read.

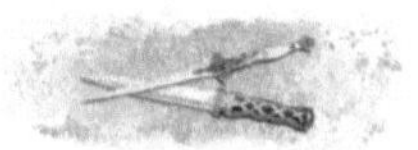

AFTER LUNCH, I drift until the courier gathers her satchel. She moves briskly down the servants' stair, leather strap hugged tight against her ribs. I trail far enough back not to draw notice. At the side entrance beneath the eaves, she pauses, counts under her breath, and waits for the bells to finish before stepping out.

I count with her. Twelve. The city answers in waves—bells echoing across roofs, carrying replies I can't hear.

By dusk the house shifts again: flowers, curtains, halls emptied. I slip toward the east corridor before anyone can redirect me.

The threshold sits where I left it—shallow rise, chalk loop buffed nearly flat. I touch the stone, the brooch at my collar dragging heavy against my throat. Voices filter from the bend ahead and I flatten into shadow.

"Eleven on the hour," a man whispers. "Then thirteen."

"And six if they send word," the woman answers. "If not, hold."

"Hold," he repeats.

The hidden door opens and closes without a sound. Linen flashes once between panel and frame, chased by a curl of clove and metal—the air warmed faintly with copper.

When the hallway empties, I kneel at the seam. Two nail marks still notch the wood where I left them. The chalk at the hinge has been renewed—faint but fresh enough to catch under my nail.

Footsteps behind me.

I rise slowly, turn, and find Eli at the arch. Hands in his pockets. Posture relaxed, reach calculated.

"You like this wing," he says.

"It's quiet."

"It prefers quiet. Protocol keeps its order. Numbers are part of that."

"Do the numbers count as manners?"

He smiles faintly. "One could say so."

His gaze lingers longer than courtesy allows, an aching sadness clinging to the corners of his eyes. "Join us for a small gathering at seven," he says. "We'll keep it gentle."

"Gentle for who?"

"Everyone." He leaves without waiting for me.

AT SEVEN THE house arranges itself into a smile. Lamps bloom one by one, their glow reflected in polished glass. From the mezzanine, music drifts soft and careful, as though the strings themselves have been trained not to falter.

Jori meets me at the stairs, her fingers light at my elbow, and guides me to the vantage above the south parlor. The mezzanine looks down into an atrium where vines climb the rails and plants coil through marble planters. Beyond the high windows, the south gardens stretch dark against the dusk. The whole scene feels staged, as though even the ivy has been told where to grow.

Guests filter in with collars high and hands bare. Names hissed at the threshold tell me nothing and everything. They drink from glasses that catch the light oddly—liquid darker, thicker than wine should be. Plates of sugared fruit pass untouched, their sweetness only for show. The talk that does ripple through the room drifts in circles: lineage, vintage, rarity.

Jori keeps me near the rail as if the view were a gift. "First faces," she murmurs near my ear. "Let those eyes fall in love and then withdraw. It builds desire."

"I'm not a painting," I say.

"No." Her voice is velvet edged with iron. "You're legacy."

Below, Eli moves through the room like water, never pausing long enough to anchor. A woman in pale silk presses a card into his palm. He glances once, folds it with a practiced motion, and slides it into his pocket.

"What is that?" I ask.

"Preferences," Jori says, as if naming pastries. "Old families are particular."

The music shifts. In the east hall a clock chimes the quarter, and the room seems to breathe with it. Heads turn in unison, subtle but certain, as though only they hear the cue.

"Will there be a second course?" I ask.

"Not for us," Jori replies smoothly.

"Because we're not guests."

"We're hosts." Her fingers pause against the brooch at my collar, adjusting it as though aligning a frame. "And hosts provide."

Across the room, a servant slips through the far door with a covered tray. Another joins him, and together they turn away from the east corridor, taking the long route instead.

I don't realize my hands have curled tight until Jori covers them with her gloved palm. "Relax," she whispers. "You'll bruise the silk."

"How many nights like this?" My voice stays level. "How many practices before the main event?"

Her smile doesn't falter. "Only enough to remind the world who you are." Her gaze stays fixed on the room. "We adapt to the calendar."

"Whose calendar?"

"Everyone's."

The music ends. Polite applause ripples through the atrium before a door opens. Another set of faces enters, eyes flat with appraisal, measuring, weighing. Jori's hand tightens fractionally on mine.

"We'll retire," she says, already steering me back from the rail. "Leave them wanting."

"I'm not a painting," I tell her again.

"No," she says, velvet over steel. "You're the frame."

She leads me to my door and brushes my cheek with a kiss that feels like possession. "Sleep," she whispers. "Tomorrow, letters again."

"What about the library? With Father?"

Her smile doesn't shift. "Tomorrow, after letters," she repeats, and the hall swallows her steps.

I lock the door, lean my forehead against the wood, and breathe until my pulse slows. The wax candle Jori left last night sits on the dressing table where I hid it after dousing the flame. I weigh it in my palm. Plain taper. Nothing special to anyone but me.

Kody used to make me walk the perimeter in darkness, count posts by touch, find blind angles without looking. Third from a corner is where most sentries fail, he'd say. They trust the start and the end, forgetting the middle.

I tuck the candle into my sleeve and pull on a dark coat. No silk. No shine.

The garden hums at night—the hush alive with sounds I missed by day. Gravel shifts under my boots. The south beds gleam as if turned again after sunset. I keep low by the hedges and count stone columns along the lower wall. First. Second. Third.

I set the candle at the base and crouch with my back to the wall. One match. One flame, cupped until it lengthens and steadies. I leave it there—a small, stubborn pool of light at ankle height, then melt into shadow and wait.

Minutes pass, measured by breath. A fox crosses the path, pauses at the flame, and slips on. Far along the wall, movement stirs at the treeline. Not a full shape—just a shadow adjusting, a shift of weight, the faint scrape of a boot. Watching. Recording. Then silence again.

Good. The house sees.

I pinch the flame out, pocket the stub of cooled wick, and ghost back along the hedge.

In my room I add to the list before memory can soften.

23. Letters = hours coded as arrival slots.
24. East wing door: ledger count + hidden trigger. Servants log numbers, schedule tracked.
25. Guests move on the quarter chime. Bells = signals.
26. Jori's language = host / legacy / provide.
27. Third stone column at lower wall observed from tree line. Candle noted, not removed.

I slide the paper back into my boot and stare at the ceiling until plaster turns to map lines again.

They want me visible. They want me polished—to learn the grammar of display and call it belonging.

Fine.

I'll learn the grammar. I'll change the meaning. And when the bells ring, I'll be where they don't expect me.

57 - Cassia

Cali's practice parlor looks built for a porcelain doll, not a child. Sunlight slants across white furniture, catching on the glass buttons of dresses lined neatly in her wardrobe. Dolls sit in a row along the table's edge, their stiff curls and frozen smiles angled toward her like an audience too intent. The brightness in the room clings unnatural, staged, and brittle as spun glass.

She sits at her little table with her back impossibly straight, pouring imaginary tea into empty cups. Every motion bears Jori's precision, rehearsed until it looks effortless.

"May I join you?" I ask from the doorway.

Her face lifts, the smile flickering across it sparkling and borrowed. "Of course! I've been practicing my hosting. Mother says it's important to learn proper manners."

I lower myself into the child-sized chair, knees awkwardly bent. The china clinks faintly as she serves, her tiny hands folding a napkin with exact symmetry.

"You're very good at this," I say.

"Mother says I must be." She pours another cup with a delicate tilt. "She says guests only love proper girls at the dinners."

The words bite. "Which dinners?"

Her voice dips to a whisper, eyes darting to the dolls as if they might overhear. "I'm not old enough yet. But when I watch from the stairs, I see the trays go by. It looks so fancy."

My hand slips to the knife at my thigh. "Fancy?"

"The way the guests lift their glasses, the way they smile. Mother says I'll learn when I'm older. That it will be beautiful." She smooths the tablecloth as though it were silk, her fingers careful and reverent.

A doll catches my eye—white dress, high collar, hair in stiff curls. It sits close to the edge, as if waiting to be chosen.

"Is that new?"

She beams. "Mother had it made for me. It matches my dress." She jumps up and tugs open the wardrobe. Inside hangs a gown—white with a high collar, stark against cedar. The faint scent of starch and cedarwood spills into the room, too sharp for something so small. "It's for when I'm old enough to help."

My mouth dries. "Help how?"

She shrugs, eyes fixed on the gown. "Mother says it will be my honor. One day I'll make the guests proud." Her voice brightens again. "Do you want to see my curtsy? Mother says it is nearly perfect."

A knock interrupts. Anne stands in the doorway, paler than usual, her hands trembling around a folded apron. "Time for your lessons, Miss Cali."

Cali's spine straightens even more. "Will we practice serving today? Mother says I must be ready for when my gown is needed."

Anne winces. "Perhaps table etiquette instead." Her eyes flick to me, pleading, then drop.

"But I want to do what Mother expects when I'm older." The words echo Jori's cadence so precisely my stomach knots.

"Not yet," Anne says quickly, too sharp for a servant's tone. "You're years from that. Come."

Cali claps her hands and skips ahead, curls bouncing, white shoes whispering across the rug. Anne follows with her collar tugged high, knuckles bloodless on the doorframe until she disappears.

I stay behind, staring at the doll in its white dress, at the wardrobe door still ajar, at the dustless space reserved for the gown's occasion. The smell of cedar lingers, as a sharp reminder.

Back in my room, I open the strip of notes and press the words in before memory can dull.

35. Cali trained for "dinners." Dolls, gown. Speaks of

honor. Anne afraid.

I close the paper, but the vow has already carved itself deeper than ink:
If I run, she stays.
And I can't leave her in this house.

58 - Cassia

The library air is different at night. Still, but not the stillness of day—deeper, heavier, as though the shelves are holding their breath. Moonlight spills through the tall windows, turning rows of books into pale cliffs and casting shadows deep enough to drown in. Dust drifts like ash. The silence presses so hard I hear my own pulse in my ears.

I tell myself I'm here to read, to keep hunting for answers—why my parents speak of safety with voices that sound like chains. But really, I'm stalling. Choosing books over sleep, lists over dreams.

A floorboard groans. I whirl, knife half-drawn.

Martha stands in the moon glow, a bundle clutched to her chest. Her face is carved with worry. "Take it." She thrusts it into my hands, voice breaking. "Please don't let them know I helped."

The weight is small but solid. I peel back the cloth and find a leather-bound journal, cracked at the spine, pages swollen from years of turning. The front cover bears a name, faded but unmistakable: *Holli.*

My chest seizes. "This was hers?"

"She wrote what she saw." Martha's eyes flick from door to shadows, never still. "Read fast. Burn it after."

Before I can ask more, she slips away, leaving only the faint smell of dust singed by candle flame.

I retreat into a window alcove, open the cover, and let the moonlight do the work.

THE HANDWRITING ISN'T neat. Holli's strokes lurch across the page, quick and cramped, blotches where the nib caught, smudges where she must have written in haste. Words pressed hard enough to fray the paper's edge, as though the act of writing had to carve warning into the page itself.

Another servant collapsed tonight. She drains them beyond use when her anger grows. No one satisfies her hunger. She remembers the night she tasted Bailey blood. Eden's blood.

My stomach twists.

She keeps the Baileys searching for kin, for fragments of the line. I hear names whispered in corridors I should not walk. I watch the house reset itself for guests who leave hungrier than they arrive.

The ink grows darker, strokes jagged, as if Holli's hand shook:

There is one who circles from the edges. He interferes when others close in. They call him "V." Whether he guards or stalks, I cannot tell. Both, perhaps. He frightens even them.

My hand trembles as I turn the page—an old, familiar memory closing in on me. The scrape of glass shattering the night Holli shoved me into the dark. The smell of smoke. My parents' voices, low and wrong, calling my name with tones that didn't belong to them. The sensation claws up my throat now, raw as if it were still that night.

The Bailey's speak of alliances with powers they do not control. They call it protection, but it is barter. If they find Cassia, they will dress it in duty. They will call it safety. It will be neither.

The last line trails into a smear, as if the pen were yanked from her hand.

I flip faster, desperate. Pages full of sketches of high collars, of servant rotations, tally marks cut off mid-column.

One page edges into the east wing—chalk loops by thresholds, trays carried in, doors that open on schedules she was not meant to witness. *Machines warm what should not be warmed.* The words blur before I can breathe past them.

A scrap slips loose into my lap. Fresher ink gleams in the moonlight:

The house is no refuge. She marks what she wants as hers. Leave, before she comes again.

No name. No seal. Only the words.

Footsteps in the hall and my chest seizes. I shove the journal behind atlases, heart slamming hard enough to rattle my ribs.

The door opens.

"Can't sleep, Dove?" Jori's voice, smooth as lacquer with candlelight outlining her shape—all grace and polish. "The library can be… enlightening at night."

"Just restless," I say, forcing calm.

"Understandable." She glides between tables, trailing a finger along bindings. "Nights stretch long when we await important arrivals." Her gaze lingers. "The house sharpens itself, knowing eyes will soon be watching." She sets the candle on the desk. The flame splits her smile, throwing it into a mask of light and shadow. Perfect. Lifeless.

"Rest," she says. "We begin preparations tomorrow." Then, lighter: "And if you see Martha… tell her I'd like a word."

The words freeze me. "I haven't seen her."

"No?" She huffs, almost amused. "Unfortunate. The house runs best when everyone remembers their place."

The candle's flame gutters in her wake as she leaves, stretching her shadow long across the wall.

When the latch clicks shut, I drag the journal back out. My hands shake so badly the leather slips. Not just fear of being caught. Fear of truth burning through paper into skin.

At the back waits one final entry, words angled sharper than the rest:

If you read this, it means I failed. They will not protect you. They will consume you. You are not their legacy—you are their feast.

Run, child. Better hunted in shadows than seated at their table.

IN MY ROOM, I add to my own list with ink that blots from the pressure of my hand:

36. Holli knew. Journal = record of draining + gatherings. Parents call it safety = cover for offering. "V" circles. Who is V?

The nib snaps under my grip. Ink splatters the margin like blood drops.

From the corridor below comes a muffled thud. Voices flare, sharp and quick, then hush as if pressed down by force. I hold my breath, straining for Martha's voice—but the silence that follows is absolute.

I slide the knife beneath my pillow, my hand refusing to let go. The hilt cuts into my palm until my fingers ache.

Holli shoved me into the dark to keep me free of this fate. And I walked straight back into it—willingly, desperate for answers, blind to the cage closing around me.

A fool's choice.

But not a victim's.

If the house thinks it can dress me for sacrifice, it will learn I came back with teeth.

59 - Cassia

Silk whispers against my skin as another gown is pinned. Jori circles me with the precision of a hawk, tugging seams, lifting fabric, appraising every line. "No. This shade is wrong. Deeper colors carry presence. Crimson, perhaps."

I meet her eyes in the mirror. "Presence for what?"

She smooths a wrinkle that isn't there. "The celebration. You'll be presented properly, as you deserve. Guests expect perfection."

Three more servants have vanished since I found Holli's journal. The ones left drift like shades through the corridors, necks covered, voices hushed. The house itself feels braced, like the calm before a storm.

"Everything must be in order," Jori continues, fussing with my hair until my scalp prickles. "Our circle watches carefully. And with certain… elements sniffing around, we cannot afford a misstep."

"Elements?"

Her smile holds, eyes flat. "Spies. Old rivals. They'd love to spoil this. Even now, eyes press at the edges of the city. So we must be careful who learns of your presentation."

A crash echoes from downstairs, sharp enough to make us both jump. Jori's lips flatten. "Continue the fitting," she tells the seamstress. "I'll see to it."

The door closes behind her. Pins still hang loose at my side when I slip free of the gown and the seamstress's protests, sliding into a robe when I enter the hall, following the sound.

The library glows with firelight. My father sits before it, shoulders drawn, drink in hand. Flames carve new lines into his face—age and strain where I remember certainty.

"Eli?"

Relief flickers across his features. "Cassia." He gestures to the chair beside him. "Escaping your mother's preparations?"

I sit as the fire pops, throwing heat that doesn't touch the room's chill. He watches the flames a long while before speaking.

"Do you remember," he says, voice low, "how you'd sit on my lap here while I read? Tales of knights and kingdoms."

"The chair seemed larger then."

A faint smile. "Everything did." He takes a sip, hand trembling slightly. "I missed so much. Your training. Your hunts. Years I can't reclaim."

"We have time now."

"Time," he echoes. The word dragging heavy out of his lips. He sets the glass down hard, liquid jumping the rim. "Perhaps not as much as we'd hope."

My chest tightens. "Because of the celebration?"

Pain flashes across his eyes. His fists clench and unclench at his knees. "Cassia, I—" He breaks off, rubbing his face. "You don't have to… we could find another path."

"Another path for what?"

"To keep you safe." His voice roughens. "Your mother has expectations. Arrangements. But you're my daughter. I should be able to protect you."

"Then tell me the truth. What's happening at the celebration?"

He paces before the fire, jaw taut. "It's a welcome presentation. That's all." His hands knot into fists. "Though perhaps you shouldn't—" He stops, dragging a hand over his chin. "There must be another way."

"Eli." Jori's voice slices the air as she glides into the room, steps weightless and even as candlelight sharpens her smile. "What are you doing?"

"Speaking with our daughter," he says, steel under his words.

"Is that what you call this weakness?" She closes the distance, resting a gloved hand on his arm. "Pathetic sentimentality?"

"She deserves to know."

"She deserves to take her place *with* us." Her voice drips honey, but her teeth flash in the light. "As we agreed. Unless you'd prefer our honored guest hear you've faltered. I'm sure understanding will come… at a cost."

His face goes ashen. His shoulders bow in defeat—like a man holding too much weight.

"Come, darling," Jori croons, threading her arm through his. "You need rest."

I watch them vanish into shadow, my chest tight with unease. The library feels colder despite the fire and its vast silence pressing around me.

In the corridor as I navigate back to my room, a figure detaches from the dark. A frail old man, skin parchment-thin, eyes clouded like milky water. He grips my wrist with surprising strength.

"Not all who watch mean harm," he whispers, breath warm and edged with metal. "Some still guard the bloodline."

"The bloodline?" I stiffen. "Who are you?"

His grip tightens once. "There are those from the beginning who remember. And I am loyal to him." Desperation burns in his dim eyes. Then, as quickly as he appeared, he's gone—swallowed by the dark hall without a sound.

I stand frozen, pulse hammering, until I force myself toward my room.

After dressing in a night gown, I sit on the edge of the bed when a soft knock sounds. My hand goes to the knife resting under my leg.

"Cass?"

Cali peeks in, hair tangled from sleep, white gown trailing like a mist "I had a bad dream. Can I stay?"

I pat the bed. "Of course."

She curls beside me, small and warm. Her voice is drowsy, muffled against my shoulder. "Mother says tomorrow's so important. That if the bad people find out, everything will be ruined."

"What would be ruined?"

"The party." Her words slur with sleep. "But you'll look so pretty…"

She drifts off as I stroke her hair—remembering the doll

dressed in white, collar high, glass eyes fixed. Watching.

Outside, I hear the shuffle of staff carrying roses with every thorn cut away. Linens pressed so crisp they could slice. The house is remaking itself, perfect and pure. Preparing for my presentation.

I open my strip of notes and press the nib hard enough to bite the paper:

Eli conflicted. Spies in the city. Celebration = more than social event.

Kody's voice rises from memory—dry, patient: *Trust your gut. It learns faster than your eyes.* I add one more line, ink heavy:

Trust gut. Prepare to move. With Cali.

I slide the list back under my boot lining and set the journal aside. Fingers close on the knife beneath my knee—its weight steadying.

Whatever this "presentation" is, I'll be ready.

60 - Cassia

The seamstress smooths the last fold of silk and steps back. "There, miss. Perfect."

The mirror shows a stranger. Blood-red silk clings and then flows, pooling at my feet in liquid ripples. The color turns my skin pale as bone, my copper hair darker, almost metallic. It looks like spilled wine—no, spilled blood.

"Beautiful." The word drifts from the doorway where Eli stands braced against the frame—his eyes locked on me with an expression that tightens my chest. He crosses the room, fingers grazing the edge of the train, then the strap at my shoulder. His hands tremble.

"The first time I held you," he murmurs, "I promised you'd never know fear in this house." His voice frays. "Some promises are harder to keep—"

"Eli—"

"Let me look at you." He steps back, blinking against tears. "My little girl. Grown. Ready for the welcome that should have come years ago."

The words sit heavy in the air. A welcome. The way he says it makes it sound like surrender, not celebration.

"Eli." Jori's voice cuts the moment in two. She glides into the room, posture precise, smile sharp. "What are you doing here?"

He stiffens. "Can't a father admire his daughter?"

"Not when there's work unfinished." Her tone sweetens, the edge hidden just beneath. "Our final guests arrive shortly. Do you want to explain to them why their chambers aren't ready?"

Eli flinches, but his gaze stays on me. For a heartbeat, he looks ready to defy her. Then he leans down, and presses a trembling kiss to my forehead.

"You are precious," he whispers. "Remember that. No matter what."

The anguish in his eyes hollows me out before he turns and leaves.

"Sentimental fool," Jori murmurs, lifting a velvet box. She opens it, and pins the Bailey crest at my collar—silver and jet black glinting against the blood-red silk. "Still, he was right about one thing. You are perfect."

I stare at the mirror—at the dress, the crest, the painted image of a girl I barely know. The silk gleams like fresh blood while the pin brands me as theirs.

And in that reflection, I don't see finery. I see a shroud, draped over a lamb dressed for slaughter.

61 - Kody

Kody keeps to the shadows as he threads Zurich's narrow streets. Cobblestones gleam wet though no rain has fallen—lamplight pooling in colors too red. Night falls early this close to the mountains, and the air tastes of iron, copper, and decay dressed in expensive perfume.

A bell tolls. Nine strikes. The hour when Noctis stir, when shutters close and the city learnt to breathe shallow. Doors slam, lanterns snuff, and only servants and feeders remain outside.

The Guild's cautions hum in his skull: Approach with extreme caution. Mistress's presence confirmed. But it isn't the Guild's orders that drive him. It's Sarah's notes. It's the way Cassia looked down from the mezzanine when he turned away days ago, light framing her hair like fire, her eyes searching the dark for him. The ache of leaving her then cuts sharper now.

He won't leave her again.

Mist curls from alleys despite the dry season, carrying that cloying scent of Noctis territory. Every breath coats his tongue with memory—hunts gone wrong, corpses found too late.

A figure peels out of shadow ahead. Graceful, wrong. Noctis—but trained. Shoulders squared, weight balanced, rich silk draped to hide the armor beneath. An Umbral.

"The estate is closed tonight," he says, voice resonant with an older timbre. "The Mistress's people fill the city. Even stone walls have ears."

"I need to get inside."

"Then you'll die. Like the one who carried Holli's pages."

Kody's grip tightens on his blade. That thin voice from the Guild reports echoes in his mind—another servant silenced because he'd chosen patience.

"The Mistress arrives soon," the guard continues. "The presentation begins tonight. Interfere, and you won't reach the first stair."

"I'm taking her out."

Moonlight catches the worn circular spiked insignia at his collar—half-hidden, not quite the Mistress's crest. The guard steps closer, eyes unreadable. "Some paths, once taken, can't be turned back. Her blood calls too loudly. Powers gather you aren't ready to see."

Steel whispers free. Kody's blade touches the guard's throat, silver edge gleaming. "Move aside."

"Strike me, and they'll hear the echo. Leave me, and you might last long enough to reach her." His voice lowers, almost human now. "When the tenth bell tolls, the ritual begins. Nothing stops it then."

Mist folds between them. By the time it clears, only the scent of old cloth and iron lingers.

THE BAILEY ESTATE rises ahead, windows lit in a sickly gold. No more "preparations." Tonight is the night. Servants hurry like ants, carrying thornless white roses and spotless linens, all of it a performance of purity. The scent rides the air heavy, suffocating.

Kody circles to his old route over the wall. His muscles remember the climb, but the grounds no longer feel the same. Shadows cling thicker, the very stones seeming to pulse with a hunger older than the house itself.

Sarah's voice echoes in memory—warnings about bloodlines, about bargains written in generations of suffering. He hadn't listened then, only thought of revenge. Now he sees the cost of his blindness in every bowed head and every bandaged throat.

Cassia's window glows above, a beacon. For an instant his chest seizes—he wants to call her name, to let her know he's close. But stealth is the only currency he has left. One wrong move and the Mistress's court will descend like locusts.

He sets his hands to the stone. The wall is slick though the night is dry. Above him, the blood moon hangs swollen, unblinking.

This time he doesn't think about waiting, or about proof. This time the only vow left is carved into his ribs:

He will not leave her behind again.

Not tonight. Not ever.

62 - Cassia

The dress drapes over me as I stare through the window into night. The moon hangs heavy and wrong above the estate, shadows writhing across paths lined with white flowers and spotless linens. Every detail made perfect for tomorrow.

Once, I thought I saw him. A shadow at the edge of the grounds, too steady to be a servant, too familiar to be anyone else. I told myself it was only hope, a trick of moonlight. But the memory lingers.

A sound at my window makes my hand fly to the knife hidden in my skirts. I whirl—

"Kody?"

He slips inside with the silence of a whisper. For a moment we only stare. His face is sharper, eyes darker, shoulders taut with strain. But it's the way he looks at me, like he's been starving for the sight of me, that steals my breath.

"I thought…" My throat closes. "When you left—"

"I'm sorry." His voice is rough, scraped raw. "I shouldn't have gone. Not like that. Not after—"

"You came back."

"I'll always come back for you."

He crosses the room. Night air and steel cling to him. His hand rises to my cheek, thumb brushing skin, and I lean into it, greedy for proof he's real.

"You can't stay here, Cass. You have to leave. Right now. You're not safe here. Not with the gathering tonight."

"Tonight?" My heart stutters. "They said it was a rehearsal tonight, gathering tomorrow."

His jaw tightens. "A lie. The presentation is tonight.

They've moved the hour up. They mean to offer you before dawn." His gaze drops to the silk dress, and the pain there nearly undoes me. "You're already dressed for it."

The floor seems to tilt beneath me. All the warnings I've pushed aside out of desperation crash together—the servants, the locked doors, Eli's haunted eyes. I knew. My gut knew, and now he's giving me the words I couldn't force myself to say.

"Eli…" My voice trembles. "He's been… I thought—"

"You thought right." His hands grip my shoulders, solid through the fabric. "He knows what's coming. That's why we can't waste time. We need to move before they close the walls."

"Not without Cali."

"Cassia—"

"I won't leave her here. Not after what I've seen. She's a child, Kody. They're grooming her."

He studies me, the battle clear in his eyes. Finally, he nods once. "I'll get her. But if anything happens—if we're separated, look for the candle at the lower wall. Third column from the corner. If it's lit, you go. No waiting, got it?"

The words slice through the fog of my fear. "Lit candle… third column."

"There's my girl." His forehead presses to mine, his breath ragged. "I won't let them take you, Cass. Not you."

I silence him with a kiss. It isn't careful. It's desperate—hungry and defiant. His arms lock me to him like he'll never let go.

When we break apart, I'm gasping. His fear isn't for himself. It's for me.

"I'll find Cali," he whispers. "Be ready to run."

"Kody." I clutch his hand, refusing to let it go. "I should've told you before you left. I—"

"Hey." His thumb strokes my cheek. "We'll have time. I swear it."

A whimpered scream cuts the night—high, female, strangled too fast. My stomach knots.

"Another servant," he says tightly. "They're feeding before the presentation." He turns to the window, already scanning shadows.

"Be careful," I whisper.

He looks back once, and the way he looks at me carves

itself into my bones. "Always." Then he's gone, swallowed by the dark that seems to reach for him like it already knows.

I press my fingers to my lips, still burning from his kiss, and whisper the words like a lifeline: third column, lit candle, run.

63 - Kody

Kody's instincts scream danger before he even reaches Cali's door. The air hangs unnaturally still, heavy with copper and salt. His skin prickles the way it always does before a strike, and he trusts that warning more than sight or sound.

The latch gives beneath his hand—moonlight spilling across the child's bed. Cali lies motionless, framed in curls, neck marred by punctures still wet. Not deep enough to kill—but deep enough to brand her.

Eli kneels beside her, shoulders shaking, hands trembling uselessly above the blankets. "What did they do?" His voice cracks. "My little girl…"

Kody steps closer, gaze fixed on the faint rise of her chest. Breathing steady. Whoever fed knew the exact amount to take. Cold. Surgical.

"She's alive," Kody says, voice drawn tight with rage. The scent hits him next—perfume steeped over blood. Not Cassia's or a staff member's… the Mistress's guard.

Eli lifts his face, eyes red and wet. "You have to help her. Please. I can't lose another daughter."

Kody is about to answer when the faintest disturbance whispers across the room. Instinct seizes him. He pivots—just as a chain whistles past his head, sparks spraying off stone.

Felix emerges from shadow, eyes hollow but lit with venom. "Did you think I wouldn't notice the way she looks at you?" His mouth pulls into a jagged grin. "The way you keep stopping me from getting what's mine?"

Kody steadies, blade loose in his hand. "Cassia's not

yours to claim."

Felix's grin twists. "You always had the advantage. Faster, stronger. You think that's just training?"

Three more figures slip from the corners, coils dragging behind them. The chains gleam faintly, wires threaded through metal, humming faintly, alive with stored current.

The first strike lashes across Kody's shoulder. Pain detonates in his nerves, his arm jerking against his will. He snarls, forcing his grip on his sword to hold.

Another chain catches his ribs. The jolt surges through his chest, buckling his knees. It's not just pain, it's disruption, his own body misfiring—betraying him.

He drags himself up, teeth gritted, breath tearing ragged. He's fought with broken bones, with lungs full of blood, but never with his own muscles turning against him.

A guard lunges. Kody fights the current and pivots, instinct in his blade as sharp as ever as it plunges through a shoulder. The man collapses screaming. Another chain coils his thigh, current ripping through him. His leg convulses, and he crashes into the wall.

Felix circles, chain sliding through his hands like a predator testing its leash. "See?" His voice drips venom. "You're not invincible. You never were."

"I don't need to be," Kody growls, driving his blade in a desperate arc. It tears across a guard's cheek, blood spraying. The victory lasts seconds before another chain lashes his back, current ripping down his spine. His vision fuzzes and his arms drag like anchors.

Why can't I shake this off?

He's always the one left standing. Always.

Jori's voice slides through the air like poisoned silk. "Did you never wonder, hunter?"

Kody wheels toward her, chest heaving. She glides into the lamplight, gown gleaming like oil, eyes sharpened to points of triumph.

"Wonder why you outran men twice your size?" She tilts her head, circling him with a predator's patience. "Why you healed faster than wounds should allow? Why nests that shredded others barely slowed you?"

His jaw tightens. "Years of training. Discipline."

Her laugh is soft, mocking. "Oh, sweet boy. Is that what they let you believe?"

Another chain cinches his arm, current biting deep. His muscles convulse until his blade slips free, ringing as it clatters against stone.

Jori leans in, smile carving cruelty across her face. "You were never just human. Your precious guild knew. They kept you close for a reason. Because your veins carry the ancient blood… of a Turig soldier."

The words detonate inside him.

No. Impossible. Turigs died out centuries ago.

But his pulse still pounds steady, even now. His body thrums with an alien hum. All the years of speed, endurance, the guild's distance—every unexplained edge crashing together in revelation too sharp to deny.

Felix's laugh slices through. "That's why you were always better. Not skill. Not will. Blood." He jerks the chain, yanking Kody to his knees. "You were never just human."

Kody fights to rise, but every link drags him down. Current claws through muscle, burning him from the inside. The harder he resists, the more his strength eats itself alive.

Then he hears it. Footsteps in the hall. Light and quick. Cassia.

No. Not now.

He surges, desperation breaking the paralysis. He has to warn her—

Jori's shadow cuts the wall, her hand driving into his chest. Flesh parts, wet around her fingers, sliding through muscle. Pressure clamps his ribs at the grotesque invasion. Pain surges white-hot, spilling red and black across his vision.

Her nails scrape against bone as she hooks her hand deeper, pressing dangerously close to the steady pound of his heart. He chokes on blood, lungs heaving against the intrusion.

Her lips graze his ear. Breath sweet, voice venom. "The thing about Turig blood… it sings when it breaks. It makes everything so much more satisfying."

He convulses, chains jerking his body upright as the guards hold him. A sickening crack echoes through the chamber—his shoulder dislocates with the force, body twisting violently in the restraints.

Cassia's footsteps. He knows them even through the roar in his collapsing world. He strains for her name, but blood floods his throat, bubbling out in a wet gasp.

Cass...

"Don't fret, hunter. Cassia will join you soon enough. After the Mistress has had her fill."

Kody's throat strains, but only blood answers. His vision tunnels, the world drowning in shadow. Footsteps rush closer. He knows the rhythm.

At least he kept one promise.

He came back for her.

Even if it killed him.

64 - Cassia

The gown laces bite into my fingers as I claw them loose—silk whispers, resists, clings. Every knot grips like a trap, every thread a tether to the role they chose for me. The presentation dress gleams in the lamplight—a perfect shade of blood-red, heavy and smooth, meant to dazzle the eyes of strangers and hide the chains beneath.

"Come off," I hiss, ripping through one stubborn tie. The silk finally gives with a sharp sound, the fabric tearing like a wound opening.

The dress loosens, sliding over my shoulders in waves. It feels alive—grasping, pulling at my skin as if reluctant to release me. For a sickening heartbeat I imagine it clinging tighter, swallowing me whole, until I vanish into its folds like all the others prepared for sacrifice.

I wrench it down, step free, and kick the puddle of scarlet away. It sprawls across the floor like spilled wine—no, like fresh blood. For a moment the sight roots me in place, dread rising thick in my throat. That dress was supposed to transform me from survivor into ornament. A lamb fattened and decorated for slaughter.

Not tonight.

I drag in a breath that tastes of river salt and dust. My hands tremble, but I force them steady as I reach for my old clothes. Leather worn soft with use—the vest Kody pressed back into my hands after training sessions. Boots scuffed from hunts that scarred my shins and calloused my heels. Fabric that smells faintly of oil and smoke, not perfume and performance.

I pull each piece on like armor. The familiar weight grounding me, reminding me who I am—not the daughter they claim, not the prize they intend to display. A hunter. A fighter. Someone forged by years of running, bleeding, and enduring.

The knife slides into its sheath at my hip with a clean sound. The feel of it steadies me more than anything. Cold steel. Honest. Not like their silk lies.

The mirror catches me as I tie the vest. For a moment I see both versions of myself at once: the woman swathed in blood-red finery, eyes hollow with fear, and the hunter standing tall in leather and scars, gaze burning with fury.

I rip the silk heap from the floor and hurl it into the wardrobe. Let them search for their perfect daughter tomorrow and find only air.

Family. The word tastes bitter. For years I carried the hope of them like a talisman. Dreamed of a father's steady hand, a mother's warm embrace. That hope is burnt now. Monsters wear those faces, smile those smiles. The truth is colder, sharper: the family I wanted is gone. What remains would rather deliver me bound and dressed to their mistress than keep me safe.

And still—still—some small part of me aches. For the memory of being brushed into braids at dawn, for bedtime stories read in a low voice. For what could have been. That ache… is the cruelest wound of all.

I press a hand to my chest, where Kody's warmth once lingered after his kiss. He'd held me like he was afraid I might disappear, like the night itself would steal me if he let go. The memory makes the silence in these halls unbearable. He promised he'd return, and he should have been back by now.

Shadows slip under my door, then retreat. Staff, moving like ghosts, their eyes fixed anywhere but mine. They creep through the house as though hunted, though the monsters are the ones they serve.

The silence is heavy. Like the estate itself is holding its breath, waiting.

I check the window. Outside, the moon hangs swollen and wrong, casting light that turns the gardens into bone. Linens draped across tables glow pale as shrouds, red thornless roses gleam. The perfection of it all makes my skin crawl.

A sound pierces the quiet. A bird, its cry too sharp, and

human, before the silence hits again—thicker than before.

Every instinct in me screams: move.

I slip the list from my boot and mark another line:

—Silk gone. Hunter's skin on. Knife steady.

The words scratch across the page like a vow.

Kody taught me this—always write, always mark, always make memories into record. Because when panic blurs, paper doesn't.

He also taught me to listen to my gut. And my gut says this house is already closing its jaws.

The corridor beyond my door yawns long and dark. I slide into it, leather silent against stone. Every flicker of lamplight blinking like it's watching me. Every hush of movement from servants scurrying away reminds me: they know. They always knew.

"Be ready to run," he said.

I grip the knife at my hip and my pulse steadies.

I am ready.

The knife is steady in my hand as I move down the corridor, boots whispering against the runner. Every instinct hums sharp, tuned to the silence pressing against the walls. Shadows cling thicker than they should, carrying the copper tang I've learned to fear.

The house doesn't feel like a home anymore. It feels like a trap sprung tight, every window an eye, every door a mouth waiting to swallow me whole.

I pass servants shrinking into alcoves, skin covered, eyes fixed on the floor. They flinch from me the way prey flinches from predators. As if they already know the night has teeth.

Another sound cuts through the stillness—soft, choked, almost a sob. My grip on the knife tightens as I follow it, the air colder with every step.

Cali's door hangs ajar, moonlight spilling across the threshold, pooling in pale streaks along the floor. My stomach twists as I step closer.

65 - Cassia

Beyond the doorframe, Eli kneels at her bedside, shoulders bowed, his hand clutching Cali's limp one. Her chest rises shallowly, faint punctures marking the hollow of her throat.

"Eli?" My voice cracks.

He lifts his head, eyes rimmed red. For a heartbeat he looks like the man who once read me stories in this very room. "I tried—" His voice splinters. "I couldn't stop them. I couldn't…" his voice drops quieter. "save her."

Movement to my right snaps my gaze across the room. *Kody.*

He's half-slumped against the wall, chains biting deep into his arms, blood slicking his shirt in heavy sheets. Felix holds him pinned, glee pasted across his face, while two guards hover nearby, iron glinting in their hands.

Kody's body jerks, staggering as he tries to stay upright. His eyes find mine, desperate and burning. "Go," he rasps, voice raw and broken. "Cass… run."

I take another step, heart pounding. "Let him go." The paralysis shatters and I surge forward, breath ragged, heat flooding my ears. Out of the shadow she slides—Jori, eyes gleaming, her hand sunk wrist-deep into his chest. Kody's breath rasps around it, wet and broken, the sound twisting my stomach into ice.

"Kody!" The cry rips from me as I lunge forward.

The sound as she withdraws is wet, and final—like fabric ripping, only it's flesh… it's him. His body slumps lower, held up only by the chains around his arms and she looks down her nose at him, disgust and disapproval radiating from her.

The chains clank loudly against the floor as they fall, along with his body.

"No!" I drop to him, catching his hand in both of mine before he slides down the wall to the floor. His skin is clammy, his grip trembling with his last scraps of strength.

Jori watches, crimson dripping from her fingers, her smile sharpened into mock affection. "Dove, you're early. Did I not stress the importance of arrival time?" She lifts one finger, letting it rest on her tongue like a delicacy, then sighs. "The presentation isn't for hours."

Kody's breath rattles, blood slicking his lips, but his eyes track mine. "Cass…" His voice is shredded, barely air. "Vesp—"

"I know," I whisper, though I don't. I press my forehead to his, desperate to keep him here. "Hold on. Just—hold on."

Jori's shadow looms, silk whispering across the floor. "He doesn't have long, Dove. But you don't have to lose him. We can make him one of us. He'd be stronger. Eternal."

Kody's hand jerks weakly, fingers clawing at mine. His eyes widen—pleading, furious. "No…" A cough tears through him, crimson spraying. "Let me… die."

Behind shadows, Felix laughs. "And here I thought he'd last longer." The sound rips me apart.

My panicked breath burns away into silence—a silence so heavy it hardens inside my chest. I rise, knife flashing in my hand before I can think, the grief boiling into rage. "You did this."

Felix spreads his hands, mock-innocence. "You think he ever really wanted you? He was always halfway gone. I—"

The knife drives into his arm before he can finish. He howls, stumbling back, clutching the wound as dark blood pulses between his fingers.

Jori's hand snaps out, catching my wrist before I can strike again. "Enough," she hisses, eyes blazing. "This behavior is unbecoming."

But it's not enough. Not nearly.

Felix snarls through gritted teeth, staggering toward the wall. "You've made your point."

"Get out," Jori barks at him without looking, her grip like a vice on my arm. "You're finished here."

Felix hesitates just long enough for me to see the war in his eyes—rage, humiliation, and darkness flickering beneath—and then he vanishes into the shadows with a clank of chains on blood.

One of the guards still holding the chains takes a wary step back. "Mistress said she was to be presented," he protests.

"Then go fetch her yourself," Jori spits. "Before I decide your blood will do in her place."

That's all it takes.

The two remaining guards glance at each other, uncertainty giving way to survival. They drop the chains and flee, boots scraping across the stone as they vanish into the hall.

Cassia stumbles back, breath heaving. Her gaze locks on Kody—still bound, still bleeding. His head hangs, barely conscious, chains wrapped taut against trembling arms.

Jori follows her line of sight, expression softening into something almost reverent.

"Why cling to him?" she croons. "Hunters always end the same way—bleeding on the floor, forgotten." She steps closer, eyes gleaming as she drinks in the sight of him.

"But this one… his blood hums differently. As if it remembers." Her gaze shifts slowly back to Cassia. A knowing smile blooms—slow, cruel, triumphant.

"Which makes sense. After all… he found you." Jori tilts her head, voice dropping to a purr.

"You're the reason he bleeds. The reason he burns. You were always meant to lead him here." She spreads her hands, fingers still slick with Kody's blood. "You're ours. You always have been."

My father groans by the bed, voice breaking. "Jori, stop. Not here. Please."

For a moment her mask slips—cold fury twisting her face. "You weak, pathetic man. You'd risk everything for sentiment? For a daughter you lost years ago?"

Her distraction is all I need. I drive the blade upward, burying it beneath her ribs. Her eyes widen, shock flashing where superiority once lived. Crimson spreads over her gown as she grips my arms.

I step closer, looking her right in the eyes. "You took *everything* from me."

Jori tilts her head, almost pitying. "You'll understand one day." She drags a bloody hand across my cheek. "Family is sacrifice."

"And you call yourself a mother." My voice trembles—low and jagged, breaking beneath the weight of it. "All you fed me was lies."

She makes a sound—small, startled… almost human.

I rip the steel free and, in one clean arc, sever her head.

Blood spurts hot across my face, painting my cheek, my mouth. Her body jerks once and collapses, lifeless.

I spin toward Eli.

He stands frozen at Cali's bedside, hands raised in surrender, lips moving around a name he doesn't dare say.

For a heartbeat, I see the shadow of a man who once read me stories in this room. But that man wouldn't stand silent while Kody bled out. That man wouldn't watch a child be raised for slaughter.

"You let it happen," I breathe.

His eyes glisten. "Cassia, I tried—"

I don't let him finish.

My blade plunges into his chest, sliding between ribs. He gasps, like it surprises him, and slumps forward against me.

I step back, letting his weight fall.

Then I kneel, grab his hair, and bring the blade down.

The room goes still.

Two bodies. Two heads. A house full of ghosts.

I stagger toward Kody, knees buckling as I sink beside him. His eyes are open, searching mine—not clouded yet, but fading.

He saw it. The whole thing.

"I'm here," I choke, pulling him into my lap. His blood soaks into my clothes, seeping hot through my knees, my thighs, my arms. It clings to me—his life. "It's done. They can't hurt us anymore."

His lips twitch, a ghost of a smile. "Knew… you'd fight." A pause, breath rattling. "Love… you."

The words rip me apart and I clutch his hand to my chest. "I love you. Always."

His eyes soften with relief, pride… love—then the light gutters out. His body slackens in my arms, and for the first time I understand what it means to break beyond repair.

I bow over him, my cheek pressed to his blood-soaked shirt, clinging to the fading warmth of the man who was everything—teacher, protector, love—and now, loss carved into flesh. Sobs shudder through me as the knife slips from my fingers, forgotten. For a long moment, there is nothing but my breathing and the crackle of the fire in the grate.

When I can move again, I brush his hair back, kiss his forehead, and whisper, "The Guild will honor you. I'll make sure of it."

Cali lies still in the center of the bed, chest rising in shallow pulls. She's alive. Pale and quiet… but alive. Her nightdress is streaked with red where Eli fell, his blood soaking the sheets, spattered across her skin.

I sink beside her, shaking as I brush curls from her damp face. Kody's blood stains my hands, sticky and dark. His warmth clinging to me as she wears Eli's. Monsters and man—both of them marking us.

"You're not staying here," I whisper, though she can't hear me, and gather her carefully into my arms. She's light— her head falling against my shoulder. The stains on us mingle as I lift her, there's no separating it now.

I force myself to stand, swaying. Blood pools across the floor, his, theirs, all mingled, and the weight of it grounds me. The house is hollow now, emptied of its deceit.

Stepping over Jori's body, my blade drips shadows in the moonlight. I look at the three bodies. Jori, Eli, Kody. Mother, father, lover. Monsters and man. All gone in one night.

And I understand, in that moment, that the uncertain, scared girl who came here searching for family is gone too.

All that remains is a hunter.

Epilogue

The night air reeks of ruin. The city died years ago, but the bones remain—broken walls, hollow windows, streets where even the rats move quietly. I press my back against the crumbling brick of an alley, fingers tight on the dagger's hilt. The hunt has stretched for just as many years, each lead thinner than the last, until finally it ends here.

Every night since the estate I've dreamed of this moment. Of finding the one who betrayed me. Who stood smirking while Jori tore Kody's chest apart.

Felix steps into the open.

For a heartbeat, my body refuses to believe it's him. The tilt of his head, the familiar smirk—it's the same boy who once shared stolen apples with me, who showed me how to scale the compound wall without tearing my palms. But his movements are wrong, his stance is too still, his breathing, undetectable. And when he lifts his head, the moon catches silver in his eyes.

Noctis.

My grip on the dagger tightens, my pulse pounding like war drums, my legs rooted in place.

"Cass." The sound of my name from his lips unravels me for a moment. He says it the way he used to, like we're still kids sneaking out of dormitories. Like he didn't help murder the man I loved.

He shoves his hands into his pockets, casual, as though nothing's changed. "Took you long enough to track me down."

I don't answer. Rage hammers through me, sharp and steady, but beneath it another current stirs—a grief I thought I'd buried.

Felix steps closer, slow as if coaxing a frightened animal. "You look different. Stronger." His eyes flick over me. "Not the girl who woke up screaming at night. Not the girl who believed her parents would come back."

"And you," I say, voice like ice, "are still a coward."

He chuckles softly. "It's not cowardice. It's survival. You think I died back then, Cass, but I didn't. I became more." His eyes glint, bright with fanatic hunger. "You still could too. We could… together."

The words churn my stomach. He was the last person who knew me before, and now he speaks as if Kody never existed. As if the memory of him, his blood, his voice, his final breath, aren't the only things keeping me alive.

"You disgust me." I lunge.

The blade flashes toward his throat, clean and precise. He twists aside, faster than I remember him ever moving, and my strike cuts only air.

I attack again, a second strike, then a third. He dodges, laughing. The sound is wrong in this dead city, too alive, echoing off the stones like mockery.

"Still so angry," he says, stepping back as I drive him toward the wall. "I thought maybe, once you saw the truth, you'd stop fighting it."

My blade grazes his ribs. He gasps, face twisting, but instead of falling he surges faster, a blur. In the next instant I'm slammed against the wall, wrists pinned above my head.

"What will you do when I'm gone?" he whispers, breath hot against my cheek, the weight of his chest falling against mine. "When your revenge is over? What purpose will you have then?"

His grip is iron, but the weight of his words hits harder. He's right—Kody is gone, Jori and Eli are ash, Holli's long dead. I have no one left. Only this purpose.

"The mistress is still out there," I growl. "I owe her a blade for what she planned. And Vesper..." Dark recognition crosses Felix's face at the name. "His name was one of the last out of Kody's mouth. I promised to deal with him. For Sarah. For everyone he's destroyed." I drive my knee into his groin.

He stumbles, grip loosening enough for me to twist free and strike.

The dagger sinks into his side, just beneath the ribs. His eyes widen, lips parting in a pained laugh. "That's the Cassia I knew. Always hitting harder than anyone expected."

"Don't you dare say my name like you know me."

His voice lowers, almost tender. "I was the last one who did know you. Before all this. Before him."

The words shake me in ways I don't want to admit. For a moment I see the boy he was—the boy who made me believe I wasn't entirely alone. And I hate him more for it.

"Then you're a ghost," I whisper. "And I'm here to bury you."

This time I don't hesitate. I draw my second dagger and drive it into his chest, angled true toward the heart.

Felix chokes, eyes widening. Blood bubbles at his lips, but even dying he manages a broken smile. "All I ever wanted... was to be near you..."

I kick him back, ripping the blade free, and take it across his neck. His body hits the ground with a dull thud, limbs splayed as his head topples down beside it.

The silence afterward is heavy. My breath comes ragged, my dagger slick. I stand above him, staring down at the last tie to the girl I used to be.

I crouch beside his severed head, almost without thinking, and brush my fingers across his cooling cheek. He looks younger like this, human. The Felix who once whispered jokes under his breath during lessons, who once swore he'd never leave me behind.

But that boy died long before tonight.

"You were the last person who knew me before," I murmur. "Now no one does."

I wipe my dagger clean on his shirt and stand. My chest is hollow, but inside that emptiness, sharp resolve takes root.

There is no going back.

The gleaning is a year away. Time enough to make them remember me—to make them fear me.

The alley smells of blood and smoke, though no fire burns yet. I gather wood from the ruined buildings—dry splinters, broken chairs, anything that will catch. I stack it around him with methodical care. The familiar ritual feels like a consummation. As I work, the moon climbs higher, casting long shadows that seem to reach for his corpse like hungry fingers.

The match flares bright in my hand, sulfur biting my nose, and I drop it.

Flames take quickly, crawling over cloth and hair, licking up his body until he is nothing but light and shadow. For a moment the fire paints him alive again—the boy who shared food, who grinned at me like I mattered. I let myself watch, let myself grieve that ghost.

But I don't cry.

The fire roars, sparks, spiraling upward like lost stars. Somewhere in the distance, a bell tolls midnight. The hunting hour. Soon the streets will crawl with Noctis and their hunger spilling into the night.

But for months they've been learning to fear the dark too. Learning to whisper warnings about the hunter who leaves only ashes behind.

The scarlet death, they call me. A ghost in the shadows with steel blades and merciless hands.

But it's not nearly enough to stand among the chosen at the gleaning. That place is reserved for lineage, for beauty, for bloodlines too tempting to overlook.

I have time. Time to sharpen myself into legend. Time to make the Mistress's gaze fall where she least expects it. She likes to collect what fascinates her—so I'll make myself unforgettable.

The flames eat through Felix's body until he is nothing but ember and ash.

I think of Kody, Sarah, and Holli. Of every servant drained in silence, every child "prepared" for sacrifice—the weight of Kody's knife still warm at my hip.

I stand over the pyre, letting the smoke wash me in heat and memory, until the girl who once loved and lost feels burned away too.

"I'll keep my promise," I whisper to the flames, to his memory, to whatever's left of the girl I used to be. "I'll stop them all. Vesper. The mistress. Anyone who feeds on innocent blood." The smoke carries my words into the dark.

Behind me, the city breathes with ancient hunger. But I'm

not afraid anymore, for I am the hunger now. I am the thing that hunts the hunters.

And when the gleaning comes, they won't just remember me—they'll fear me.

They'll call me the Scarlet Death.

Acknowledgments

Thank you for reading this story. I'd love to hear your thoughts. You can scan the QR code below to visit my link-tree, which will have a direct link to leave a review for this book.

If you can spare a moment to leave details, that is appreciated. If you prefer to leave it at a star rating, I understand, but just know your feedback is valuable. Think of how many books you would purchase that have little to no reviews.

Regardless of how you felt about this book, leaving a rating is the best way to help any independent author.

Respectfully,

Melody Kepler

Turn the page for a sneak peek of book three, Vesper's Grasp ⟶

Scan me to leave
a review!

Chapter 1 - Cassia

They spared no expense convincing the public that The
Gleaning was a grand affair—gold-laced invitations,
orchestras, candlelit balconies. If the more people knew what
really waited behind the chandeliers, they'd never get away
with calling it an honor.

Gold trim matches the dress code I suppose. The thought
twists in my stomach. Every ten years, the city's invited step
into a gilded cage, smiling for monsters who will keep them
as trophies until the next selection. Most never make it home.

A draft from the cracked window sends gooseflesh racing
up my arms. In the candlelit mirror, my reflection looks more
like a stranger dressed for slaughter than a trained fighter. The
up-do was a choice—easier to fight when my hair isn't
strangling me. But it bares my throat, leaving my pulse
exposed to the predators like an invitation.

Peppermint glaze tingles on my lips. A hunter's trick: it
sharpens the breath, masks adrenaline. I reach for the slim
glass bottle on the dresser—frosted surface etched with two
raised letters: EB. A relic from another life. The glass stopper
clicks when removed before dabbing it against my wrist and
rub the perfume along each side of my neck. The scent
blooms sharp and sweet. Jasmine mixed with black current
and the mask of vervain I've grown so familiar with. Works
like a charm.

I smooth the emerald-green fabric over my hips and lift
the draping tulle to free my legs. From the top drawer, I draw
the dagger with the CB engraving on its exposed blade. It
slides into the thigh holster with a familiar whisper. The

second blade follows—EB engraving, mother-of-pearl handle, emeralds set like eyes. Too ornate for practicality, but its weight steadies me. The dress leaves few options; concealment is half the game.

A coil of twenty-gauge wire joins the silk pouch at my wrist. Fingerless leather gloves first, cracked but reliable, then dark silk gloves drawn over them—elegant camouflage for calloused hands. If the night goes well, I'll take one trophy. Maybe two. The Gleaning isn't about numbers; it's about making a difference where it hurts them the most.

I fasten the last emerald earring, adjust the shawl across my bare shoulders, and take in the rooms smell of candle smoke, mint, and jasmine. Outside, carriage wheels grind over cobblestones, too slow to be casual. Somewhere in the distance, a violin warms up—one high note slipping out of tune like a rusty hinge.

In the mirror, the bodice beadwork catches the flame and scatters it across the walls. Beautiful, but lethal. I test each hidden seam and sheath one final time before lifting the candle holder from the dresser. The wick's glow trembles as if it senses what's coming.

I glance once toward the window. Beyond the frost, the skyline flickers with lanternlight—festive from afar, hungry up close. Tonight's hunt should be easy; gatherings like this always are. Plenty of shadows to hide in. Plenty of things pretending to be human.

I loop a string over the door handle, balance a copper coin atop the jamb, my silent alarm, and blow out the candle. Smoke curls toward the ceiling, thin and reluctant.

The door clicks shut behind me, sealing the scent of peppermint and steel. Off in the distance, the bells begin to toll.

The Gleaning awaits.

Chapter 2 - Vesper

I pin a golden leaf to my brown tie and smooth it beneath the buttons of my tweed vest. Pomade slicks stray hairs into place, but the mirror still makes my stomach turn. After all these years, I can't look at my reflection without a flicker of disgust. The face staring back wears civility like a mask.

A flash of fang catches the light when I test my tongue against the sharpened cuspids, a faint metallic taste blooming on the air. The urge rises—brief, electric—and I press it down, breathing through the ache until it fades.

From the mahogany armoire, I draw my leather suspenders and settle them across my shoulders. The familiar weight grounds me. A dagger slides into the pocket stitched between the crossed straps at my back—habit, not vanity. I roll my olive sleeves to the wrist, covering the black-inked tree roots and compass etched into my forearm. Symbols of direction. Of everything I've lost.

The Gleaning comes every decade, though the collé grow more restless each time. They want it sooner now, their hunger gnawing at reason. I can't blame them. Stress weakens their bodies; fear rots the mind. The more they starve, the more they hunt. A cycle that feeds on itself.

This will be my fourth attendance. I've avoided the others when I could. The smells alone—perfume, sweat, blood beneath—make the air thick enough to choke on. A celebration for the enslaved; an atrocity dressed in lace. Guests pretending to enjoy themselves while waiting for le choix—the choosing.

This year's attendance was mandatory. Even for me.

I shrug into a black wool jacket, adjust the collar, and step into the hall. The red-carpeted staircase yawns downward toward polished stone. I pause beside the bronze urn on the mantle, its surface dulled with dust and age.

My palm rests against the cool metal. "I'm sorry, Cal," I whisper. "Too many years. Too many failures."

The silence that answers feels heavier than the coat on my shoulders. I raise two fingers in salute—a habit from a life that's gone—and turn away before the memory can tighten its grip.

Outside, the bells begin to toll. The gleaning awaits.

Chapter 3 - Vesper

The old Capitol's ballroom still smells of rot beneath its perfume. Mildew clings to the red velvet drapes like memory, softening the gold light that spills across marble pillars stretching into the dark above. I take my place behind one of them, the folds of velvet brushing my sleeve. It's always better to watch from the outskirts—close enough to scent the room, far enough to stay unseen.

Guests drift in by twos and threes. le collé move in cautious clusters, their heartbeats thudding in sync, while we, the seigneurs, prefer solitude. Keeping our distance from most unlike us, save for those taken when the insatiable hunger strikes. The sensation that takes over when you have a good connection with your food is… intoxicating. But that's the whole point of this gathering, to stop that behavior.

The air thickens as the room fills. Perfume and candle wax can't hide the undercurrent of blood and fear. I draw a slow breath, letting the scent map the crowd—cheap brandy, starch, sweat. Then, something else. A note so clean and unexpected that it stills me mid-breath.

Currant and jasmine.

The memory hits like a pulse behind the eyes. My mouth waters before I can stop it. A tremor runs through my jaw as the tip of a fang catches my tongue. I pocket one hand, feigning composure, and follow the thread of scent between the pillars.

An hour passes in that haze—faces, laughter, meaningless chatter—but the scent doesn't fade. It lures me down a side corridor lined with portraits of long-dead founders. Dust thickens the air; the candle sconces flicker like breathing. I reach up to wipe a plaque with my handkerchief and a knife kisses the side of my throat.

"Tisk-tisk, dear one." I keep calm as the back of my collar tightens in the other hand of the knife wielder. "What makes you think you can get away with such a bold move?"

"Shut up." she snaps. "It's not bold, it's just cleaning up scum."

"In the middle of a party?" I murmur. "Dangerous place for righteous work."

Her scent coils through the air again—black currant first, ripe and tart; jasmine unfolding beneath it, soft as memory; and, faintest of all, the cool sting of peppermint. The combination shouldn't exist. It drags a long-buried image from the dust—sunlight through hazed windows, laughter caught between breaths, the taste of something… someone, once human.

The knife presses deeper and warmth beads along my neck. "Removing even one of you is worth my life."

"You'll start a panic," I tell her. "And you'll die before your second swing."

"My life is worth sacrificing to get yours."

I let a slow breath slip past my teeth, the hunger of memory stirring like an echo. "Ah-ah-ah," I whisper, raising one hand in mock surrender. "Careful. Blood never calls softly, and there's always someone willing to answer."

She shoves me harder—the portrait pressed against my cheek rattling in its frame.

"How would a founder feel about your take on this?" I ask.

"I don't follow the rules of the founder," she says. "I follow the rules of humanity."

"I see." I turn just enough to catch a flash of her reflection in the gilt frame—fire-red hair, skin like winter—and the glint of letters carved near the hilt of her blade: CB.

"Don't move."

For a heartbeat, the world narrows to those two initials. Shock flares, sharp and private, but I swallow it down and let a smile ghost across my lips.

"Or what?" I ask calmly. "You'll kill me?"

"I will kill you regardless." The blade bites again, and she gasps, almost imperceptibly, as the point grazes deeper.

"Then get on with it." Music swells from the ballroom beyond, signaling the start of le choix. "They'll sweep this hall soon. If you want to be useful to your cause, finish your deed and vanish before they catch you."

"What?" Her voice shakes, just enough to give away her hesitation.

"You have no idea how long your scent lingers after you're gone. I do." I inhale deliberately, letting the nostalgia break through restraint.

A small wooden home in a clearing. Currant and jasmine churning with the scent of her blood under the setting sun. A tight grip, falling away from mine with a whisper on her lips.

"Black currant. Jasmine. And peppermint. Unmistakable." I close my eyes, willing the moment that haunts me to revive an image I seem to have forgotten.

A flicker of uncertainty ripples through her grip. "Why won't you fight back?" she demands.

I laugh once, low. "I've heard of you, Mort Écarlate. The Scarlet Death."

"Then you know I'm ruthless."

"Oh, I do. I also know that if you don't leave now, every human in this building will pay for the mess you make."

"You monsters are disgusting."

"Which is why you're about to murder one in front of dozens of your own kind… while they're surrounded by their predators?" I tilt my head just enough that her blade slips from the wound. "Sound logic."

"Shut up." she hisses as the pressure vanishes.

"You do well staying hidden." I smile as her scent recedes down the corridor, fading like a ghost through cold air. "I won't even be able to discern who you are when we meet in the hall after this little chat." I murmur to myself and turn to look up and down the empty hallway.

I touch my neck; the blood smears bright against my fingers. She's gone.

Theron's footsteps echo down the marble corridor. I pull my handkerchief free, dabbing the cut as his brisk voice carries down the hall. "Vesper, please take your seat. The others are eager to begin."

I turn, expression composed. "I'm sure they are. Nobody likes to be hungry."

He falls into step beside me as we move toward the hall. His olive skin has lightened over the years, enough to mark his change, but his hair remains a deep black, a reminder of youth frozen in time.

"What were you doing out here?"

"Oh, Theron." I twist the handkerchief between my fingers. "When you've lived as long as I have, you may find yourself wandering back to remember what made you this way."

He frowns. "Why would I want to do that?"

"Because forgetting is worse. Remembering is the only thing that separates us from the monsters."

We cross the stone archway into the grand hall—a ripple of movement spreading across the upper landing. As I take my seat beside Whitmoore, I nod to him with a habitual apology for tardiness before glancing out over the sea of tables below. No empty chairs, just circled tables of anxious faces.

The air hums with fear and perfume. le collé, the human donors, sit stiffly. Some whisper prayers, others stare blankly ahead.

Whitmoore rises, his voice carrying easily, polished by centuries of practice and repetition. "Welcome to the seventh Gleaning ceremony. We are pleased with everyone's attendance this evening. It is important for both le collé and ourselves to remember, upon each le choix, why we gather."

He gestures toward the crowd as if offering them comfort. I study their faces instead. Fear. Anger. Resignation. A few hollow enough to seem almost tranquil. Those are the ones who'll survive longest; the body learns not to waste energy on panic. Then there's those with the hopeful gleam in their eye—the ones who wish to be selected like it's the honor it's claimed to be.

Whitmoore continues, "As tradition would have it, two humans are selected for each of the three covens to resource for nutritional supply."

Murmurs stir below. I sense tension sharpening, the air thickening with the musk of dread.

"Many of you know," he goes on, "there has been a recent outbreak of Noctis slayings in retaliation to the wild pod that passed through this region to feed."

A heavy woman near the center table—red-haired, trembling—bursts into sobs. I watch her, idly wondering how long she's been avoiding full meals to taste less appealing.

Whitmoore lifts a hand to calm the noise. "This is not how things are run here. Local covens maintain order through arrangement: two humans every five years, no more, no less. We have worked tirelessly to bring the wild pods into compliance. Unfortunately, our numbers have grown too many."

He glances toward Dr. Bravo. "A change must be made."

She stands, crisp and deliberate. "Extensive studies have determined the optimal frequency to sustain equilibrium. The Gleaning will henceforth occur every ten years."

Gasps ripple through the room, faces turning upward in relief. Hope smells like ozone—sharp and fleeting.

"The unfortunate component," Dr. Bravo adds, her tone faltering, "is that the number of selections will increase from two people per coven… to one person per estate."

Silence. Then the noise hits—shouts, protests, sobs echoing off the vaulted ceiling. Whitmoore's hammering voice cuts through it.

"Each household is required to provide an environment in which its collé can remain healthy and productive. Weekly rations will be maintained, and yearly inspections will ensure their well-being. After the first five years, evaluations will determine adjustments before the next selection at the following Gleaning."

I lean back, scanning the crowd. So many redheads tonight. Too many coincidences. My gaze snags on the trembling woman I'd noticed earlier—face buried in her hands.

My eyes drift, searching for anything to anchor me—and then she looks up.

The sight rips through centuries.

Fair skin. Eyes like glacial light. Red hair gleaming and an emerald gown that shimmers under the chandeliers.

For a moment, the ballroom fades. I'm back in that small house—debris around us, the smell of sunset curling through the air, the sweet trace of blood in the warmth of her breath against my skin. The memory hits so hard my lungs seize and familiar ache blooms in the hollow where no heartbeat should reach. In an instant, she's in my arms again—warm and real.

Black currant. Jasmine. Peppermint. It's her scent—her ghost staring up at me.

And yet she's not a ghost. She's here, among the terrified and the damned, offered up to the same hunger that once ended her life.

The shock fractures, giving way to anger sharp enough to taste.

A ghost shouldn't have to die twice.

www.ingramcontent.com/pod-product-compliance
Lightning Source LLC
Chambersburg PA
CBHW030439120726
47903CB00003B/1038